ALEX MILLER

Alex Miller grew up in London but at seventeen left alone for Australia. His four previous novels include *The Ancestor Game* which won the Commonwealth Writers Prize and the Miles Franklin Literary Award. He lives in Melbourne with his wife and two children.

Also by Alex Miller

The Sitters
The Ancestor Game
The Tivington Nott
Watching the Climbers on the Mountain

CONDITIONS of FAITH

'Deceptively "easy" to read, but within the boundaries of this narrative he's brought up notions of whether it's better to fail than succeed, what so called "science" can bring to this world, the efficacy of religion in everyday life, the influence of history on all of us (and whether we should believe any versions of history) the effects of personal ambition on both male and female humans, the savage origins of Christianity and how we've prettied it up, the globalization of family, what it means to discover and live in your own "home" and, most movingly and profoundly, the terrible demands of biology on all of us, particularly women, particularly as they become mothers, especially if they're not emotionally set up for that biological project . . . It's astonishing' Carolyn See in the *Washington Post*

'Subtle, beautiful language, a substratum of thoughts, impulses and obsessions: a story barely separating the conscious act from the unconscious desire . . . thoughtful, introspective and achingly affecting. Superb' *australian style*

'Whether describing the sleet-shrouded streets of Paris or Chartres, the sun-drenched North African landscape, an interior or the myriad little gestures that define an individual, Miller reveals outstanding gifts of observation, and the ability to convey those observations in lucid prose . . . admirable' Andrew Riemer in the *Australian Book Review*

'The narrative has an absorbing quality, so that the reader is eager to discover what happens next. It is evocative in style and richly detailed in a diversity of scenes' Helen Daniel in the *Melbourne Age*

'It is a portrait of a lady, but Emily does not become opaque to us as Henry James's Isabel Archer does. Her condition is viewed more with the unrelenting scrutiny of Thomas Hardy. Ultimately, the debt to either writer is not great; Emily's pregnancy, the moral problems surrounding it and the astonishing sequence in which its eventual dramatic outcome is narrated are all handled with an explicitness that an earlier realism could not have approached . . . it's a truly significant addition to our literature' David Matthews in the *Australian*

'A beautiful novel about learning to stay true to your inner self . . . a moving and absorbing read' *Shine*

'A bold book where the narrative drive is powerful and unapologetic for being so . . . this book should establish Miller as one of the most seriously rewarding of modern Australian novelists' Peter Pierce in the *Sydney Morning Herald*

CONDITIONS
of FAITH

ALEX MILLER

SCEPTRE

Extract from *Jacques the Fatalist* by Denis Diderot. Translated by Michael Henry (Penguin Books, 1986) © Michael Henry, 1986. Reproduced on pages 43 and 47 by permission of Penguin Books Ltd. Extract from *Mont-Saint-Michel and Chartres* by Henry Adams © 1933 by Charles Francis Adams. Reproduced on pages 86–87 by permission of Princeton University Press. Extracts on pages 174 and 179 from *Acts of Christian Martyrs* edited and translated by H. Musmillo (Oxford: Clarendon Press, 1972). Extracts on pages 221, 222 and 245 are all taken from *The Aunte-Nicene Christian Library* (Edinburgh: T & T Clarke, 1970). Bradfield's letter on page 352 is extracted from *Sydney Harbour Bridge: report on tenders* by John Bradfield (Sydney, 1924). Georges' quotation on page 370 is taken from the Conclusion of *Studies in the History of the Renaissance* by Walter Pater (London, 1873)

First published in 2000 by Hodder and Stoughton
A division of Hodder Headline
A Sceptre Paperback

10 9 8 7 6 5 4 3 2 1

A CIP catalogue record for this title is available from the British Library.

ISBN 0 340 76667 0

Printed and bound in Great Britain by
Mackays of Chatham PLC, Chatham, Kent
Hodder and Stoughton
A division of Hodder Headline
338 Euston Road
London NW1 3BH

For Stephanie

ONE

—◠—

When Emily reached the warm shallows she stood up and waded to the edge of the sand where she had left her towel. As she came to the shore through the soft lapping of the water she reached and pulled off her bathing cap and shook out her long brown hair. At the sand she bent and picked up her towel then turned and stood looking back out to sea, her hand raised shielding her eyes from the glare off the water. Two hundred yards offshore her father was stroking a steady overarm toward the partly submerged wreck, his solitary advance breaking the silvery membrane of the sea. The air was still and hot, the bay luminous and flat in the afternoon sunlight. Farther down the beach toward the yacht club with its thicket of bare masts, isolated bathers stood about listlessly in the shallows gazing out to sea or toward the beach. Far out a white-hulled passenger liner was steaming slowly toward the port past anchored cargo vessels; the grey smoke from its twin funnels was pencilled against the white of the sky and stretched behind it over the horizon. The sharp cries of children at play carried to Emily and somewhere behind her in the tea-trees that grew thickly along the slope below the road a dog barked repeatedly. Already the cooling effect of her swim was wearing off and the heat beginning to press down on her. She watched until her father reached the wreck, waiting until he turned and began the return swim, then she started up the beach toward the tea-trees and the line of gaily painted bathing boxes.

Outside her family's blue bathing box Emily's mother was still sitting in her deck chair beneath the shade of the red-and-white-striped umbrella. She was no longer reading her book, however, but was gazing off into the distance, or perhaps had fallen asleep. Beside her mother, their visitor's deck chair was empty. Georges Elder had moved across onto the sand, where he was sitting cross-legged on a towel in the sun. Emily saw that while she had been swimming he had changed into his bathing costume. He was bent forward, drawing again in the blue notebook he carried about with him. The sunlight blazed on his coppery hair and his white shoulders. She had failed earlier to coax him into the water. As she approached him she examined his body. His shoulders were broad and well muscled, his arms long and pale, the veins of his forearms and biceps standing out in the hard sunlight. Fine coppery hairs glinted on his arms and chest as he moved. He looked up and saw her approaching and raised his hand and waved. She and her mother had wondered about his age and had supposed him to be in his middle thirties.

She drew level with him and stood looking down at his drawing, the hot sand beginning to burn the soles of her feet. He held the notebook at arm's length for her to see, his head on one side and his lips pursed. 'The future of your city,' he said lightly.

The drawing was not an artist's impression but was a rendering of the major elements of the landscape as simplified structures: the long curve of the bay framed by the yacht club on the left and far over to the right the huddle of city buildings, the You Yang hills on the western horizon. There was no attempt at texture. The bay was indicated merely by a single line. In the drawing there was a roadway that was not in the actual landscape. The fanciful road of the future escaped into the air from the crosshatched mass of the city and swung out over the distant hills, disdaining the congested structures of the city and the natural contours of the landscape and sweeping on its tall supporting columns in an elegant arc over the horizon westwards toward Geelong.

'Is that a road or a bridge?' she asked.

He considered his drawing. 'The road will have to *become* a bridge.' He turned and looked up at her, squinting with the sun in his eyes, trying to see her. 'To bridge the city,' he explained and smiled.

She touched the reddening skin of his shoulder with the tips of her fingers. 'You're burning,' she warned and she moved into the shade of the bathing box. He closed the blue notebook and put it aside, watching her spread her towel and arrange herself on the sand, her back against the painted weatherboards. She took a packet of cigarettes from her bag and leaned and held it out to him. He took a cigarette and waited, watching her and holding the cigarette close to his mouth, while she struck the match. Her mother's deck chair creaked and she asked sleepily, 'Is that you, darling?'

'Not asleep, Mother?'

'I *was* asleep. I thought I heard you talking.'

'Mr Elder has done a drawing.'

'How nice.'

Georges got up on his knees and crawled forward, bringing his towel and his notebook into the shade at Emily's feet. He lay on his back, smoking and staring up at the pointed overhang of the bathing box.

The smoke from their cigarettes drifted in the still air between the bathing boxes and into the tea-trees. The dog barked persistently.

Emily looked down at him. The sea might have washed him up at her feet.

'That dog's treed something,' he said.

'A possum,' she suggested.

He rolled over and raised himself on his elbow. 'Let's go and look.'

She smiled and shook her head. He lay down again. He had been with them at Richmond Hill for almost a week after spending a month in Sydney. He was in Australia to report to a Belgian construction firm on the feasibility of tendering for the design of the great bridge over Sydney Harbour. It was Emily's father, Richard Stanton, the professor of civil engineering at Melbourne University and Australia's leading authority on the new steel alloys, whom Georges had come to Melbourne to consult. Emily was remembering their initial meeting among the cool shadows in the hallway of her parents' house on Richmond Hill. Coming out of the sun he had looked tall and a little stooped, as if he inclined himself toward her, modestly, to place himself in her trust. The sunlight through the lead lighted windows of the front door an amber radiance through the tangle of his hair. His gray eyes had searched quickly for her thought, as if he had been cautioned by her father to expect a difficulty or a challenge. His manner restrained, even grave. She had expected a French accent. But he spoke with a lowland Scottish burr. A certain formality. 'How do you do, Miss Stanton.' She welcomed him and put him at his ease.

Before dinner that first evening she took his arm and led him to the mantelpiece in the dining room and handed him the photograph of herself and her parents taken in Paris when she was five. The framed image of a little girl in a pale dress standing between her unsmiling parents and clutching a hired model sailboat against her ribbons and flounces. Her mother's enormous black hat, like an untidy vulture in the act of alighting. The rank of marble statues of famous French women behind them and the avenue of dark trees, limes or perhaps lindens. Georges examined the photograph closely before pronouncing his confident verdict, 'It's the terrace overlooking the octagonal pond in the Luxembourg Gardens.'

She stood beside him, her arm brushing his sleeve. 'My father returned to Cambridge for two years. On the way home we visited Paris.' Georges turned to her, seeking a likeness in the features of the young woman at his side to the stubborn, rebellious child in the photograph. 'I've imagined,' she confided to him, 'that I'll go back one day and claim Paris for myself. It's been a kind of promise.' She looked at him, unsure if he would understand. 'You know, not a real ambition, but one of those things you tell yourself . . .' She didn't finish, however, for his expression of faint puzzlement had not encouraged her to persist. She reached to take the photograph from him. 'I still remember that sailboat.'

'She clings to her little ship of liberty,' he said with a smile, returning the photograph to her.

She replaced it on the mantelpiece. 'I'd been told I had to give the boat back. But I was determined to keep it. Children can't believe in the idea of hiring something. To be given a coveted object for half an hour and then to be told to give it back. I'd set off on my perfect adventure in that little boat.' She reached and straightened the frame with her fingers. 'I'm still convinced it belongs to me.'

He teased her lightly, 'Then why not come back to Paris with me and claim your property?'

'My ship of liberty,' she said and had laughed with him; but all the same it had been a secret pleasure to imagine a mysterious destiny in their meeting; something arcane and concealed from everyone but herself, for which his heroic design for the Sydney Harbour Bridge was to provide them merely with a resemblance of purpose. His teasing invitation, *Come back to Paris with me and claim your property*, sounded uncannily right to her. She put her arm through his, 'Excellent, Monsieur Elder, ainsi sera fait.' His pleased surprise at the readiness of her French.

Lying on the sand now in the shade of the painted bathing box she closed her eyes. She was enjoying the steady heat of the summer afternoon, the taste of tobacco smoke on her palate, aware of Georges Elder just below her and behind her mother's deck chair, attentive and undecided. He was lying on his stomach looking up at her. She could feel his gaze on her body. In his silence she sensed his preoccupation, his uncertainty; the skin of her bare thighs tight and tingling not only with the sea salt. She was sure that if he did not speak within the minute, he would touch her. She was waiting for his first caress, the question of his desire in her mind.

'I've been dreaming of coming to Australia all my life.' He spoke softly, for her benefit only and so that her mother would not hear. 'I was twelve when I first read about the Sydney Harbour Bridge competition. It's been with me all my life.' He fell silent and she opened her eyes, conscious of his appeal to something serious. He was examining the arch of her foot. 'I was in boarding school in Glasgow.' He touched her foot lightly with his forefinger, then looked up at her. She did not withdraw. With his finger he followed the curve of her instep, delicately brushing away the grains of sand that clung to her skin. She curled her toes, encouraging his caress. 'You here dreaming of Paris,' he said, his voice a little unsteady. 'While I was over there dreaming of Australia. Now here we are on this beach together. Your beach. It's extraordinary.' His fingers remained touching her foot.

Behind him Emily saw her father wade out of the sea and start up the sand toward them; a large, broad-girthed man of sixty, but still strong and without any hesitation in his step.

Catherine Stanton, who faced the sea and could not see them, said lazily from her deck chair, 'Oh, not so extraordinary, Mr Elder. Here we all spend our lives dreaming of Paris.'

There was a soft drift of air, the first sign that the heat of the day was to give way soon to the cool of evening, and for a moment the honey perfume of the tea-tree blossoms invaded the shade where they lay.

Richard Stanton came up and stood looking down at them, his small eyes bright and intensely focused, shifting from the young engineer to his daughter.

Georges had removed his hand from Emily's foot. He sat up.

'How about drinks for everyone then Em?' her father said.

Emily drew up her legs and hugged her knees. She looked up at her father but made no move to get up. 'If you like,' she said.

Richard Stanton was over six feet tall with a thick powerful body and heavy facial features. The moment he stopped speaking his mouth drooped at the corners, making him look sulky, disgruntled and on the point of anger. His hair, which was thick and long and completely grey, was plastered to the dome of his skull and lay in wet licks against the loose skin of his neck.

Catherine Stanton twisted around in her deck chair and examined the three of them.

Seeing that Emily was not about to get up, her father laughed shortly. 'A glass of something, then, Georges? Catherine, for you?'

Catherine Stanton reached and touched her husband's hand, accepting his offer of a drink. 'I've been thinking about the You Yangs,' she said, determined to share her private contemplation with their visitor. 'That bluish smudge on the horizon, Mr Elder. There! Do you see?' She was pointing, a tremor in her long pale finger.

'Georges has already put them in his drawing,' Emily said softly and she looked at Georges, who was dutifully attending to the You Yangs.

'Those modest little hills were there before we human beings were put upon this earth. And there they are today and we may sit here and drink our lemon squash – when Richard has been kind enough to bring it to us – and admire them as if they had been put there just for us. Doesn't it make you a little breathless to think of that, Mr Elder? How long, I wonder, before we arrived had the You Yangs risen out of the plain? Three hundred million years? A hundred million? Sitting there waiting for us to notice them.' She sounded astonished, awed and unbelieving at the thought of the silent vigil of the hills. 'The Paleozoic, isn't it? The *most* ancient? My ignorance of these things appals me, but I am curious nevertheless.' She reached and took the tumbler of lemon squash from her husband's hand. 'When *did* human beings evolve, Richard? I know you've told me before, but I've forgotten.'

Richard Stanton stood by his wife's deck chair looking out toward the bluish smudge of hills on the far side of the bay. The fingers of his large hand absently kneaded her shoulder. Slowly he drained his glass, then he turned and looked down at Georges and Emily. 'Yes, the You Yangs,' he said and he breathed and turned and went into the bathing box. A moment later he called to them, 'Another drink, anyone?' They heard him shifting things about in the bathing box.

Catherine Stanton's attempt at conversation had failed. The three of them sipped their lemon squashes and gazed steadfastly across the bay in silence. They might have been pilgrims assembled at this sacred shore to witness a revelation at an appointed hour, patient, silent, certain their faith was to be rewarded. The dog barked and the heat of the summer afternoon was sweetly perfumed by the tea-tree blossoms.

Emily placed her empty glass on the sand against the wall of the bathing box and stood up.

Her mother and Georges Elder turned and watched her tuck her long hair into her bathing cap. Then she ran down the beach and into the shallows. She waded out and when the water reached her waist she dived and began to swim.

Catherine Stanton said in a measured voice, 'I do believe, Mr Elder, Emily is expecting you to swim after her.'

Georges shielded his eyes. 'I'm afraid I'm not a swimmer, Mrs Stanton,' he said regretfully.

'Oh dear! That *is* a pity, Mr Elder.' There was a silence between them then. Catherine Stanton eventually turned and looked at the young man who sat on the sand gazing out to sea after her daughter. 'I'm afraid my husband has a . . . well, a rather unorthodox approach to Emily's prospects, Mr Elder. He would like you to think she is a bluestocking and is destined for an academic career. It is because she did so well at the university. But you mustn't take Richard too seriously. Emily is sure to see to things in her own way when the time comes for her to decide.'

Georges Elder looked at her then looked away and said nothing.

Together they watched Emily swimming through the dazzle of sun on the water.

Richard Stanton came out of the bathing box and stood and looked with them. 'There's no telling how far she'll go,' he said.

A couta boat passed slowly between the shore and Emily, its dark red sail slack against its thick mast, the boatman leaning and pulling at the oars, dragging his heavy vessel through the viscous sea. When the boat had passed, Richard Stanton said, 'She's going out to the wreck. She's just as likely to stay there till dark and make us all wait for her.' He was impatient with something and sat heavily in the deck chair beside his wife. The feet of the chair sank abruptly as his weight struck the canvas and the professor's bottom rested heavily on the sand.

Georges stood up.

Richard Stanton turned and looked at him, examining him critically, his thick fleshy lips pushed out, frowning from under his bushy eyebrows at the younger man, his eyes glittery and alert with sudden malice. 'Ye-es,' he said eventually, as if he resolved a question of great weight. 'We all want big bridges, Georges. But big bridges often destroy the men who build them.' He settled himself resolutely in the inadequate deck chair and folded his arms across his stomach.

Catherine Stanton turned to him. 'Goodness, Richard! What a dreadful thing to say to Mr Elder. My husband is jealous, Mr Elder,' she explained. 'He wishes he had made the harbour bridge his own life's work and not left it to his old friend John Bradfield. They have been rivals, you see, since their time together at the university in Sydney.'

Richard Stanton thrust his broad feet into the sand, as if to anchor himself against the approaching squall. 'What bloody nonsense you do talk, Catherine!'

'My husband had his chance at your great bridge, Mr Elder. That is what he regrets. His ambition is compromised. That is why he is so ambitious now for Emily.' She laughed, a short, nervous bark, fearful that she had gone too far.

Richard said tightly, warning her, his voice thick with anger, 'That will do my dear, I think.'

'Well, I don't know why you will say these things! It is such a provocation.'

They were silent, staring out to sea.

Georges leaned down and picked up his blue notebook from the towel and brushed at it. Its boards had curled in the heat. He opened the book at his drawing and stood examining it: Port Phillip Bay, the city of Melbourne, the modest outcrop of hills to the west, and the elegant sweep of his reinforced-concrete skyroad sheering away into the future – offering its new promise of the freedom the city had failed to provide men with. He closed the book. 'I might go and see what that dog's found,' he said and he didn't wait but set off across the sand, his notebook clasped to his side.

In their green canvas deck chairs beneath the red-and-white-striped umbrella that was no longer shielding them from the sun, which had progressed to the last quarter of the sky and now hung redly over the You Yangs, Richard and Catherine Stanton watched the tall, slightly stooped figure of their guest as he walked away from their little family encampment toward the belt of tea-trees where the dog was barking.

Catherine Stanton said, 'I believe our Mr Elder has grown quite fond of Emily.'

Richard Stanton grunted.

'I shall organize a dance at Richmond Hill before he leaves us.'

'I don't think Mr Elder will be with us for very much longer. Our young engineer is determined to have his big bridge before he's forty, and I doubt if there's much room in his mind for anything else.'

They fell silent once again, disagreeing.

Catherine Stanton felt compelled at last, however, to hazard the question that had been maturing in her mind ever since Georges Elder's arrival in the household. 'Do you think Emily likes him enough?'

'Enough?' Richard Stanton shifted impatiently. 'It's not marriage that's Em's answer.'

She turned and looked at him, and she laid her hand gently on his arm. 'I know you're disappointed, my dear, but she won't have you direct her life forever. No matter what you care to believe about Emily, it is every woman's secret longing to have a home and a family of her own. Emily's no different from other women in this and I believe it's time you accepted that fact with good grace.'

Richard Stanton glared at the embalmed sea. He did not wish to be convinced. At school Emily had excelled at French and Latin. After two or three worrying changes of direction at the university – her wasted years, he called them – she had at last graduated the previous year with a first in the history of classical civilizations. But instead of applying for a scholarship to one of the women's colleges at Cambridge, as he and her university tutors had advised her to, Emily postponed a decision. 'I'm not ready to decide anything yet,' she told him. Almost a year had gone by since then and still she had not resolved her situation. She had stayed in bed until lunchtime and read novels and taken long walks and gone to stay with friends. 'You're becoming intellectually lazy,' he accused her. 'You're wasting the best opportunity life is ever to offer you.' He was angry and disappointed with her. 'If you were my son, I'd compel you!' he said bitterly to her one day. She had laughed at him. 'But I'm not your son and you can't compel me.' He lost his temper and said something to her then that he had wished every day since that he could unsay. 'You're weak!' he had accused her venomously. He shifted uneasily now in his deck chair at the memory of it. 'What is it that you want?' he demanded. And she had told him calmly, 'I want you to allow me to not know what I want. That's all. To take my own risks and not to do as you've done.' She had accused him quietly, 'You've never risked anything. I thought you'd be satisfied when I got a first, but you're not.' Since that day she had not confided in him and he feared he had forfeited her respect. He regretted bitterly the loss of the effortless trust that had existed between them ever since she was a little girl. Unhappy, regretful, but unable to bring himself to apologize to her, he had asked her gloomily if she were looking for a husband. She had not replied.

The dog suddenly ran out of the tea-trees to their left. It looked back, barking and prancing excitedly, eager to play with its new companion. Georges Elder came out of the trees and threw a stick for it.

'He's not bringing that bloody dog over here with him is he?' Richard Stanton's voice was filled with contempt. 'For the love of God, Catherine, don't tell me that's the man who's going to design our bridge for us!'

She laid her hand on his. 'Please, Richard, don't get upset.'

'She's worth two of him!'

She reached and took his hand in hers and would have held it on her lap, and perhaps have stroked it, but he withdrew his hand and hauled himself out of his deck chair. Without a word he strode across the warm sand to the edge of the water and stood gazing at the rusting hulk of the iron ship that lay scuttled on the rocks two hundred yards offshore. Emily stood on the high side of the sloping deck, a gilded figure silhouetted against the red sun, poised to dive into the deep green water below her. The iron wreck glowed, as if it had been heated in a furnace. He waited until she dived, then Richard Stanton waded out and began to swim to meet her, his arms rising and falling, the broken water sparkling around him, showers of gold in the summer air.

By the blue bathing box, under the umbrella, Catherine Stanton read her book. A little way along the beach, Georges Elder played with the stray dog. He had been joined by some children. When Georges paused in the play to stand and gaze toward the wreck, his arm lifted to his eyes, the children stood and gazed with him, frowning at the sinking sun, certain the stranger witnessed some wonderful unfolding of events.

— —

The saxophones and trumpets competed with each other, high and thin and reedy, urged to their squeaking limits by the speeding trip-hammer of the drums. He danced her across the lawn, his arm around her waist, spinning her in and out between the abandoned tables, the white cloths waving in the wind and snapping at the flying tails of his coat. The coloured lanterns, strung above the lawn from the eaves of the house to a branch of the peppermint gum, swung about in the strengthening southerly, red and green and blue and yellow shadows dancing across the lawn with them. She had kicked off her shoes and was dancing barefoot, trusting her weight to his arm, her head thrown back, the lanterns whirling above her. When the record came to an end, he held her against him, breathless and laughing. Then he leaned and kissed her on the lips.

They were alone in the garden. There was no one now at the tables on the lawn. It was three in the morning and the last guests had left. Georges and Emily stood together in the thin light by the glowing trunk of the peppermint gum, his arm around her waist, and looked toward the lighted house. Richard and Catherine Stanton were dancing without music in the silence of the dining room, which had been emptied of furniture, its French doors thrown open to the summer night, the light streaming out onto the black-and-white marble flagstones of the gallery.

Emily was transformed. On an impulse she had had her long hair cut short for the dance. Her hair was without ornament; a tight cloche that closely followed the contours of her skull and feathered across her forehead. Her features had emerged from the dark frame of glossy hair, her brown eyes large and oval. She appeared younger than her twenty-four years and might, in the enchanted lantern light of the garden, have been a girl of eighteen. She had not calculated the effect, but without the long hair that she had worn ever since she was a little girl, Emily seemed to have been liberated from her past; and from the weight of Cambridge, *that* future abandoned with her old plumage.

Georges pressed her to his side. 'I'm not going back to Paris without you.' He looked down at her. 'I think you already know that.'

She looked up at him. 'What if I say I shan't come with you?' She reached into the inside pocket of his jacket, her hand brushing his chest, and she drew out his gold cigarette case. 'What about your bridge? You must go back. You can't stay here. What if I decide to go to Cambridge after all?'

'You're not going to say no to me.'

'You can't be sure of that.'

'Yes I can.'

She laughed. Her heart was still racing from the exertion of the dance.

The strings of coloured lanterns dipped and jumped about in the rising wind, the unsteady illumination playing across Emily's features and over the glossy folds of her deep blue gown. He held his lighter for her, his hand cupping the flame against the wind. She drew on the two cigarettes, then took one from her lips and passed it to him.

On the tables on the lawn there was a litter of dirty plates, half-eaten sandwiches, the scattered remains of cakes, cigarette butts in saucers, and empty glasses stained with the purple dregs of claret cup. He felt for her hand and held it. A gust of wind drove a paper doily across the lawn toward them and Emily tensed, seeing the flapping doily for an instant as an injured gull struggling for flight. She tightened her hand in his and blew the smoke into the wind. 'You're a traveller,' she said softly. 'Travellers fall in love, then they go home and forget.' From a branch of the gum tree above them a frayed end of rope swung back and forth emptily in the air. It was all that remained of the swing her father had put up for her nearly twenty years earlier.

In three days Georges was to join the Blue Funnel Line's *Demeter* at Port Melbourne on its way to Le Havre via the Cape of Good Hope. From Le Havre he would make his way home to his bachelor apartment in Paris and resume his life as consulting design engineer for the Belgian firm of Baume Marpent. By the time he got back to Paris he would have been away for more than five months.

Emily watched her parents revolving slowly in each other's arms. 'They are still lovers,' she said.

They smoked their cigarettes and watched her parents pass and repass the open doors. French chalk had been spread on the boards for the dance and, gathering it as she danced, Catherine Stanton's black velvet gown now seemed to be hemmed with white lace. Her dark abundant hair was coiled on top of her head in a glowing chignon and was ornamented with loops of pearls. She was dancing with her eyes closed. Richard Stanton, patrician and elegant in his evening dress, held his wife in a tender, formal embrace.

'Don't you think my parents are sad and magnificent tonight?' she said. 'Poor Father. I've so disappointed him.' She was seeing herself in Paris, in the modest bachelor apartment in rue Saint-Dominique that Georges had described for her, five minutes' walk from the Invalides and the Champ-de-Mars, the Eiffel Tower and the Seine. She was seeing Paris, foreign, longed for, exotic; her decision already made – almost made *for* her – foreshadowed that first moment in the entrance hall when he had searched in her eyes for something familiar and expected, the tall stranger of her imagination. The photograph of herself in the Luxembourg Gardens waiting on the mantelpiece for him for almost twenty years. He had joked its truth into the open: *She clings to her little ship of liberty*. What had made him say it?

Richard Stanton was putting another record on the gramophone and Catherine had come to stand at the French doors. Catherine Stanton was looking out into the garden, her hands raised to her hair, adjusting a loop of pearls, her bare shoulders and her white arms above the sable gown, her long black gloves, her full figure sculptural in the soft light.

'It is quite definite, then?' Georges said, just a little breathless, a little less steady, now that it seemed she was to yield to him.

Emily laughed and turned to him. 'You know it is.' His need for reassurance surprised her, the sudden tension in his voice taking her off her guard. She experienced a moment of clarity then, a moment almost out-of-time, as if she stood on her own in the night wind, some way above this scene. She searched in his grey eyes. This man and I are strangers, she told herself calmly. She might have asked him for time to reflect on his proposal, to be permitted to *not* know her own mind on this matter, as she had asked her father for time to reflect on Cambridge and the career he wished her to have. She might have lit another cigarette and have walked away from Georges at this moment, across the lawn to the hydrangea bushes, and have taken a moment to imagine her future with him – to visualize the daily realities of a life in Paris . . .

He said, 'You have to be sure, Emily.' He was unsmiling now, and she saw in him a quality of reserve and judgment that she had not seen in him before, an earnestness that might prove humourless. He turned and looked down at her, waiting for her reassurance.

It was her opportunity to gather her resolve, to steady herself and tell him it was not love after all but was the night and the dancing and the thought of Paris and a new life that had made her foolish. But perhaps she had had enough of indecision. She tucked her arm in his and lifted her face to him and kissed him on the mouth. 'Mother's been longing to claim you for her son-in-law since the minute you arrived.'

'Your father hasn't. He's not going to be pleased.'

'Do you care?' she said. Her voice was gay and light in the rising wind. It was not the assurance of certainty he had asked her for.

As they walked together arm in arm toward the house, Georges and Emily were struck by the first heavy drops of rain from the approaching storm. Emily stopped to pick up her shoes where she had kicked them off. She steadied herself with a hand to the table's edge to slip her shoes on. Then she straightened and lifted her face to the raindrops and closed her eyes, breathing the eucalyptus smell of the peppermint gum, which was suddenly strong in the wash of air.

Catherine Stanton watched them approach, waiting for them at the open doors, one hand in its long black glove held to her white throat in a gesture of riveted anticipation. Richard Stanton stood up from the gramophone and swept his long hair back from his forehead with his hand and danced a few short steps to the four/four time of the fox-trot he had put on. Then he heard his wife call to him, and when he looked around he saw that an important moment had matured while his back had been turned.

The following afternoon, when the members of the Stanton household had roused themselves, Georges telephoned the offices of the Blue Funnel Line and canceled his passage on the *Demeter*. Then he and Emily took the tram to the central post office in Bourke Street, and while Emily went off to do some shopping he composed the difficult cable to his mother in Chartres. *Am to marry Emily Louise Stanton, the only daughter of Professor and Mrs Richard Stanton of Richmond Hill, Victoria, on 17th February.* He stood at the counter considering whether he could include an apology to his mother for the abruptness of his important news without making it sound as if he were sorry to be getting married after all these years of bachelorhood. In the end he simply asked his mother for her blessing and left it at that. As he made his way through the busy arcade to the teashop where he was to meet Emily, he imagined a postcard from his future. It was a picture of the great arch of the Sydney Harbour Bridge, more or less as John Bradfield envisaged it, with Emily and himself and their happy brood of children standing proudly in front of it. It was a postcard to himself, but it seemed to Georges that this image must satisfy not only his own ambitions but must satisfy also the hopes of the young woman who was soon to become his wife.

Georges was anxious to get home to Paris. The wedding was arranged with so much haste that Catherine Stanton feared people might talk.

'I'm already weeks late with my report to the directors,' he objected when she wondered if they couldn't be just a little more leisurely with their plans.

'No one will be able to give enough notice to their dressmaker or milliner,' she explained to him, but not with any asperity or firmness; and in case he thought she was going to resist him she put her arm through his and added encouragingly, 'You're a man with a vision, Georges. And we must all bend a little before it.' She liked him and was content that the question of Emily's future was resolved.

As she watched Emily and Georges laughing together in the garden, she realized, with a hollow feeling in her stomach, that her only child would soon be gone from home. Emily, always, in a slightly troubling way, more a stranger the older she grew. When she had seen Emily with her hair cut as short as a boy's the other day, Catherine Stanton had been thoroughly startled and had thought she really was a stranger. 'What have you done to yourself?' she asked, as if Emily had had herself tattooed.

'Oh, don't carry on, Mother. It'll grow again.'

'After the golden years of childhood, when they've stopped believing everything we tell them,' she said suddenly to Richard when they were sitting together on the terrace having a cup of tea, 'can we ever know who our children really are?'

'I've no influence with her anymore,' the professor said, and he shook his newspaper and went on reading the cricket results. A moment later Emily's shout of laughter carried to them across the lawn and he lowered the newspaper and looked over the top of his glasses to where she and Georges were lying on the grass in the shade of the peppermint gum.

In case there should be any doubt, Catherine Stanton said, 'She's happy, Richard. You have to see that.'

Richard frowned and raised his newspaper. 'For how long?'

At eleven o'clock on the morning of the 17th of February 1923 Georges and Emily and Richard Stanton and Georges's best man stood side by side before the altar in the massive bluestone parish church of Saint Ignatius Loyola on Richmond Hill. The Stantons were not regular churchgoers but haphazard and occasional in the practice of their Catholicism. This was the first time since Christmas Eve Mass that they had all been in church together. The nave on Emily's side of the aisle was crowded with her old school and university friends, and her aunts and uncles and their families, and the numerous friends and associates of her parents. The blues and greens and pastels of the women's hats and dresses a nervously shifting field of blossoms. On Georges's side of the aisle, except for the solitary figure of an inquisitive bystander, the long nave of the great church was empty. Even Georges's best man was a colleague of Richard Stanton's and had been introduced to Georges only that morning.

Georges had received no reply from his mother to his cable, and as he waited for the solemn order of the service to begin he was thinking of her. He was regretting her absence from this moment in his life. His mother was a devout woman and for twenty years had walked from the lower town to the cathedral every day to render thanks to the Mother of God, to kneel before the niche of *Notre-Dame-du-Pilier*, the Black Virgin of Chartres, who was said to reward the loyal devotions of women with the blessing of children and grandchildren. As he stood waiting for the service to begin, Georges could feel his mother's resentment of the occasion. A resentment that drew deeply on their pasts, on the years of her struggle after his father's early death, and on their unspoken promise never to abandon each other. While he had a moment to spare he sent up a small, fervently conceived prayer that his mother would make Emily welcome. He added, And if Mother doesn't make her welcome, please, God, give Emily the grace to understand!

The priest had begun to address them.

Emily tightened her arm in her father's. She didn't register what the priest was saying but was remembering his words to her two days earlier. '*Matris Munia,*' Father Kane had said portentously, the phrase sticking in her mind as if the Latin contained a solemn admonition to her – a surprising secret in the priest's keeping to be disclosed to the betrothed woman at the last moment. 'The holy sacrament of matrimony, my dear, is so called because the female who contracts it undertakes to fulfil the office and duties of motherhood.' She had said nothing, but his words had left in her a feeling that the priest suspected her of some forbidden desire. She had wanted to tell him, 'I stopped believing when I was a child of eleven, Father.'

At a little before midday, after Richard Stanton had consented to give his only child away and Georges and Emily had made their solemn vows to each other before God, Father Kane pronounced them to be husband and wife.

Under a white-hot summer sky, Georges and Emily sailed from North Wharf on the *Kairos* for Adelaide and ports beyond. The *Kairos* was a merchant ship and Monsieur and Madame Georges Elder were her only passengers. It was the first available ship from Melbourne bound for Le Havre and was the best Georges had been able to manage at such short notice. The holds of the *Kairos* were filled with bales of merino wool for the European spinning mills and there was a smell of sheep in the air. They might have been out in the dry paddocks of the inland instead of on board ship at the edge of the ocean.

It was not a festive occasion. There was no bunting or streamers or bands or crowds of cheering well-wishers to farewell them from the wharf on their journey to Europe, as there would have been if they had been sailing on one of the great passenger ships of the White Star Line. Richard and Catherine Stanton stood beside each other on the wharf among the cranes and gantries and the lorries and the dockside workers and waved their handkerchiefs as the *Kairos* drew away and steamed under her pilot down river toward the open water of Port Phillip Bay and a first sight of the You Yangs. At the last minute Richard Stanton called, 'Good luck, darling!' and he put his arm around his wife's shoulders and drew her against him.

Georges and Emily stood together at the rail in the fierce sunlight until they could no longer make out the figures of her parents on the wharf. Georges offered her his handkerchief. 'It's not forever,' he consoled her. 'You'll be seeing them again soon enough.' He was relieved to be on his way. 'If Baume Marpent wins the tender, we'll be back in Sydney in a year.'

'I'm not crying because I'm leaving my parents,' Emily protested. She wiped her eyes with his handkerchief and handed it back to him. She didn't know why she was crying. As the *Kairos* slipped down the channel and the skyline of Melbourne dwindled behind them, the emotion had welled up in her chest and she had begun to weep. That was all. It didn't matter why. Not bitterly or with sorrow. Her tears may even have been from a sense of relief at having made good her escape; or from a momentary sadness of her spirit that was not to be explained.

They made their way below together into the cool of their cabin. It was the owner's stateroom and there was much gleaming brass and bevelled glass and glossy French-polished timber. An enormous double bunk, taking up nearly half the cabin space, was built against the iron bulkhead. Around the bed hung blue velvet curtains, to be drawn together for privacy. Georges closed the cabin door and took her in his arms. They undressed and made love and afterward lay beside each other. They were silent and thoughtful, listening to the ship's engines, uncertain with their nakedness and with what they shared.

At last he asked her, 'Are you happy?'

She did not hesitate. 'Yes,' she said, which seemed a practical reply and no less than the truth.

When the note of the ship's engines suddenly deepened and the *Kairos* groaned and lifted its bow into the long swell of Bass Strait, Emily got onto her knees and looked out through the porthole.

'We've gone through the Heads,' she said with sudden emotion. She stayed kneeling at the porthole, watching the sunlit headland fall away behind them, the white tower of the Point Lonsdale lighthouse a beacon of the past.

Georges reached up and drew her down beside him and lay with his leg over her, pinning her beneath him and studying her.

'What is it?' she asked him, uneasy with the intensity of his scrutiny, in which there was perhaps a mixture of admiration and impatience.

'You're like a beautiful child sometimes,' he said.

She laughed and pushed him away. She got up and went over to the stack of luggage piled by the door and lifted one of her suitcases onto the end of the bed. She opened the case and took out her green housecoat. She put the housecoat on and tied the belt at her waist and turned to him.

'Which drawers do you want? The top ones or the bottom ones?'

He didn't answer but lay propped on his elbow watching her.

She took her dresses from the suitcase and hung them in the wardrobe, then folded her underclothes and placed them neatly one on top of the other in the top drawers of the chest.

Georges watched her from the bed for a while, then he got up and fetched his toilet articles from a bag and went into the bathroom and closed the door. The ship trembled and heaved, lifting over the long swells and settling in the troughs. As she put her clothes away and unpacked her books and writing things and set them about the cabin, making a little home of it, Emily sang softly to herself, 'My Bonnie lies over the ocean, my Bonnie lies over the sea, my Bonnie lies over the ocean, oh bring back my Bonnie to me.'

They soon grew accustomed to the thudding of the propellers driving the *Kairos* through the water and ceased to notice the continuous tremor that made the ship a living thing. The smell of engine oil and coalsmoke and sheep were no longer novel but passed for normality. Their daily negotiations of the iron gangways and narrow steps – the hazards of the track between their cabin, the dining saloon, and the deck – were soon familiar to them. John Anderson, a Glaswegian like Georges himself and the captain of their floating world, made available to Georges a small chart room adjoining his own cabin, where Georges spread his papers and began to work on his report to the directors of Baume Marpent on the feasibility of tendering for the design of the Sydney Harbour Bridge.

At dinner Captain Anderson said to Emily, 'Imagine it if you can, Madame Elder! Fifty thousand tons of steel poised in the air above the water of the greatest natural harbour in the world!' The Captain's astonished gaze remained fixed on her, as if he spied the finished contours of the bridge deep in her eyes and expected her to chant with him, Hurrah for the Scots and the biggest bridge in the world!

She smiled. 'Oh, I do imagine it, Captain Anderson. Frequently.'

Between mouthfuls of roasted mutton Georges was more cautious. '*If* I convince Baume Marpent to tender, and then only if our tender is successful.' He caught Emily's look, seeing her amusement at the Captain's visionary depths. 'There are a great many uncertainties yet between us and this bridge, Captain Anderson.'

Emily said gaily, 'Oh, the bridge, the bridge. It is a certainty. Isn't it why we're here together?' And she laughed. The two men looked at her, unsure of her meaning. Captain Anderson's heavy brows were drawn together. 'Yes, Madame Elder, the bridge.' He reached for the decanter and filled their wineglasses with claret. Then, solemnly, as if he poured a libation to his gods, he slowly filled his own glass until the red wine trembled at the rim and revealed to him a message concerning the state of the ocean and his ship. His intention, it had seemed for a moment, was to propose them a toast. Emily and Georges waited for him, their fingers ready on the stems of their wineglasses. But Captain Anderson drank steadily from his glass and said nothing, gazing before him as if they were no longer with him. Then he set his glass on the white linen and took up his utensils and resumed his meal in silence.

When they had returned to their cabin after dinner, Emily said, 'Captain Anderson no longer thinks of reaching land as we do. He is at home in the oceans.' When Georges did not respond, she looked up at his reflection in the glass of the dresser before her. Georges stood gazing out the porthole into the blackness. 'I shan't mind if you want to go and do some more work,' she offered.

He turned and came over and leaned and kissed her. 'I'll only be an hour,' he said gratefully.

He left her and returned to the stuffy chart room next to the captain's cabin. He had already spent ten hours there since that morning, searching assiduously among his figures for the anomalies that he knew would be detected at once by the sceptical old men in Belgium if he did not detect them first himself. Once Georges was seated at the chart table with his calculations in front of him he soon became so engrossed that he ceased to notice the passage of time. It was after midnight when Captain Anderson opened the door to the chart room and looked in on him.

'You'll have a dram before you turn in, then, Georges?'

Georges consulted his watch. 'I'll have to be getting back, John. I'd no idea it was so late.'

'Aye, you'll not be wanting to leave that wee wifey of yours on her own any longer than necessary. We'll make it a quick one, then, lad.'

Sitting in the Captain's cosy cabin, the two men drank whisky and smoked cigars and talked of their birthplace and of ships and great engineering projects, as if they knew but one language between them. It was three in the morning and the whisky bottle was empty when Georges got up to leave.

Emily woke early each morning and left Georges to sleep on. She drew the blue curtains around their bed to shield him from the daylight and she took a book for company and ate her breakfast alone in the saloon. And after breakfast she stood at the rail and looked at the sea.

'I've abandoned you,' Georges said, coming up on her and putting his arm around her.

She turned to him and reached and touched his cheek. 'You look tired. Don't think of me. I'm happy. Prepare your report. There's plenty for me to do.'

She found a place out of the wind in the sun on deck and she read Flaubert's pitiless narrative of *Madame Bovary* in French and watched the sea for hours. And when she was not reading or watching the sea, she sat at the mahogany desk in the cabin and opened the expensive green morocco writing case, with her initials embossed in gold on the cover, that her father had given her as his farewell gift, and she wrote letters home. 'Keep a journal of your travels,' her father had directed her solemnly when he gave her the writing case, as if this was the purpose of his gift. 'One day your children will read it. If we do not write it down, we forget everything. We lose it all. Your mother has always regretted not keeping a journal of our travels when you were a child.'

But Emily's attempts at journal writing dried up and came to nothing. *I feel a kind of vertigo in it*, she wrote to him, attempting to explain so that he would not see her failure as a proof of her desire to go against him in everything. *If you were to attempt it yourself, you would see at once what a terrible inhibition it is to be writing something that is to have no end. I bring my letters safely to an end after a few pages, when I have faithfully recorded my impression of the past few days. But a journal, if it is to serve its purpose, must go on for years or for decades. It must go on, in fact, until I have lived the life the journal is to record! It makes me dizzy to think of it, and while I'm writing I find it impossible not to imagine myself looking back from the journal's future, an old woman already and at the end of the life I am recording. The present loses its meaning for me the instant I begin to record it with the cold abstracted gaze of the future.* To keep a record of her life for her children, she discovered, was to see herself already dead. She tore out the few pages she had managed to write and threw them over the stern into the southern ocean. She watched the white pages tossed by the wind like exhausted birds, falling farther and farther behind in the seething wake of the *Kairos* until they were lost to her sight.

A week out from Adelaide, while they were crossing the Great Australian Bight, the fine weather they had been enjoying changed abruptly. Purple-and-ochre banks of cloud came up from the south and covered the sky, the wind grew bitterly cold, and the ship was lashed by driving rain and seaspray. Before they joined Captain Anderson for dinner that evening the *Kairos* had entered a storm depression and was standing on her stern one minute, shuddering for a timeless second, then swooping bow first toward the base of a dark hill of water, as if she was going to the bottom. Emily was entranced and on the way to dinner with Georges she left the shelter of the companionway and hung over the rail to watch the sea explode over the black bow of the ship in a geyser of green-and-white spume. The broken sea coursed along the deck toward her and Georges reached and snatched her arm and drew her into the shelter of the companionway.

'For God's sake, Emily!' he shouted at her above the roar of the wind and the sea.

She turned to him, her cheeks wet and flushed and her eyes bright with excitement. 'Will we all drown?'

'You're not afraid,' he said, as if he accused her of some dangerous impropriety.

At dinner Captain Anderson steadied his plate and looked at them and observed with exaggerated gloom in his heavy Glasgow accent, 'Ships go down without a trace in weather like this.' He gazed at Emily. 'Not a signal, Madame Elder. Nothing.' And as he spoke his ship staggered and seemed to stop in her tracks as a giant sea struck her. A moment of silence followed. Anderson's gaze was steady on Emily. The propellers raced and the lights dimmed then brightened, and the long, slow stomach-churning dive into the abyss. When the ship began to climb again, Anderson nodded at the raging torrent outside the porthole, his bushy eyebrows bunched together. 'There she goes,' he said, as if each wave were bent upon some mysterious destination. He resumed his meal. 'That's one that's no for us.'

On the fifth day they sailed out of the storm into sunshine and a long rolling swell. Emily heard the seamen laughing and calling to each other again, and she realized the storm had brought out a silence in them. That evening she went up onto the bridge and stood and gazed into the darkness. Captain Anderson pointed. 'There! It's the Cape Leeuwin light.' A bold white star swept the sea briefly in the darkness to their north. 'D'you see it there, lass?' The Captain was a freer man on his bridge. 'That's to mark the southwesternmost limits of your country. We'll be around the corner by the morning.'

When they cleared Fremantle two days later, Emily and Georges stood at the stern rail under a red evening sky and watched the flat western coastline of Australia sink behind them over the horizon.

'My next letters will have a foreign stamp on them,' she said. She turned to Georges and he smiled quickly and murmured something that she did not catch. She saw the preoccupation in his tired eyes, how he struggled with his fatigue now, the endless conversation he was conducting with himself about the bridge. 'I'll be a foreigner for the first time,' she said.

'Ceylon,' he corrected her mildly. 'It's British.'

'Well, foreignish, then.' She laughed, but he didn't respond. They stood and watched the sky turn from crimson to purple, the mild night wind tugging at their clothes. She tucked her arm firmly in his and pressed herself against him. When she didn't speak, he looked at her.

'In some ways,' she said, 'don't you sometimes feel we almost know each other less well now than we did that very first day when we met in the hallway at Richmond Hill?'

He studied her in silence. 'What a strange thing to say. We didn't know each other at all then.'

'Yes,' she said, persisting despite his difficulty. 'That is what I mean. But we imagined each other that day, as if we believed we had met before. I know it will be different once we're living together in Paris in your dear little apartment. The ship is such a disconnected world, it seems to have disconnected us.'

'I'm afraid I'm neglecting you,' he said.

'I can just see the sitting room as you've described it, overlooking the courtyard and the view of the Dôme of the Invalides from the bedroom window.'

'It's a very modest bachelor flat, I'm afraid. I hope you're not going to be disappointed.'

'We'll be in Paris! How could I be disappointed?'

A few minutes later they turned from the rail to go below. She paused at the top of the companionway and looked back. Australia was gone. There was no hint of the vast continent that lay just over their horizon.

Georges came out of Anderson's cabin and took a few steps in the darkness along the deck. He swayed and clutched the rail to steady himself. The *Kairos* was three weeks out and approaching the Gulf of Aden. Anderson had been in an insistent mood this night and they had broached a second bottle of whisky together. As he looked over the side at the rushing sea below him, the velvet touch of nausea caressed Georges's palate. He leaned and vomited. The tropical night wind touched his skin. He was clammy with fatigue. He raised his eyes to the silvery horizon. The ocean stirred and glittered under the stars. He was dismayed by the desolation. A landscape on which human intervention had left no trace. A world alién to the civil engineer. He was impatient to be on land again, to be liberated from the endless hours alone in the confinement of the iron chart room, to be home in Paris and at work once again in his office in the rue des Petits Champs, welcomed by his colleagues, his report accepted and the decision to tender for the Sydney bridge confirmed by the directors, the great design work underway at last.

The roll of the ship pressed him against the rail and he gazed down at the shattered fragments of marine phosphorescence, glowing like cold fire along the iron side of the ship, as if the sea mocked the passing trace of the ship, mocking light itself with its superior power of darkness. Georges felt the shuddering of the ship through his belly and his heart shuddered in his chest. His fatigue hung on him like age. He remembered Richard Stanton's words on the beach that day, *We all want big bridges, Georges. But big bridges often destroy the men who build them.* He pushed himself away from the rail and made his way unsteadily along the deserted deck to the cabin.

He did not put on the light but went quietly into the bathroom and washed his face and cleaned his teeth. In the cabin afterward he undressed in the dark and climbed into the bunk and lay naked beside her. Gratefully he pressed himself against her, breathing the sleepy warmth of her.

She woke from her dream and turned to him, catching the strong smell of whisky and cigars and the smell of his maleness. 'What time is it?' she murmured, as if she feared they might be overheard.

He reached for her and drew her against his body, bringing his hands up under her nightdress and following the soft contours of her nakedness with his fingers, as if he searched for an impossible reassurance. He moaned softly and pressed his lips to the fragrant skin of her shoulder.

She put her arms around him and stroked his hair, which was cold and damp from the seanight air, and she caressed him and confessed to him in breathless whispers under the cover of darkness the intimacies of her dreams, to work, to love, to create, to be.

After they had made love, he fell asleep almost at once, his breathing constricted and his mouth open, an anxious frown furrowing his glistening forehead in the purple starlight. She lay awake, aroused and unsatisfied beside him, studying his features. His handsome face might have been the face of a dead man, transfigured in the moment of bewilderment. She felt a sadness for him and for herself. This puzzling bond of intimacy. A bond almost of strangers who find themselves the victims of a common disaster. Not intimacy as it is imagined, but their humanity laid open to each other like a wound, aching for something that is not to be discovered: what they are and what they will never be. She touched his unshaven cheek, his skin coarse and feverish under her fingers. He groaned and moved his hand, reaching through sleep for her. His manly nakedness was uncompromised by his struggle against the effects of the whisky now and she moved her hand down across his chest and his belly and with her other hand caressed herself. The tension of her pleasure was fraught with the uncertainty that he might wake . . . The first strong pulsation of her orgasm drew a gasp from her and she shivered and smiled; the bevelled mirrorglass glinting and the polished brass of the rail behind the door and the mahogany desk, gleams of light in the trembling darkness.

T W O

The *Kairos* steamed past the mouth of the Seine and into the port of Le Havre on a chill overcast April morning. The great timbers and steam winches of the locks and the rearing bulk of the merchant ships berthed along the quays glistened black and metallic through the smoke and the soft drizzle of rain. On the bridge Captain Anderson stood with his hands behind his back watching the French pilot ease his ship through the locks and past the towering transatlantic liners tied up in the Bassin de l'Eure, and bring her at last through to the Quai Frissard, where she was made fast to the dock in front of the commercial warehouses. Captain Anderson unclasped his hands and stepped across to the pilot and he thanked him and resumed the command of his ship. He leaned and looked down to where Emily and Georges already waited on the deck for the seamen and dockside workers to secure the gangway. Their baggage was piled near the rail beside them, ready for the porters. Georges was wearing a black overcoat and brown kid gloves and a brown trilby hat. In his right hand he held his briefcase. The collar of his overcoat was turned up against the damp and his left hand was pushed deep into his pocket. Emily held his arm. They stood together, waiting, observing the busy scene on the dock below them. She was wearing her dark green coat open over a pleated skirt and a gray felt hat without a brim that came low over her forehead. The sudden boom of iron striking timber made them both turn. Behind them the crew were opening the holds to begin the unloading of the wool.

Emily glanced up and saw the Captain watching them. She raised her hand and waved and he lifted his hand in salute. French stevedores ran up the gangway, laughing and calling to each other and to the members of the crew. As they came onto the deck each man looked appreciatively at Emily. The scene below her was little different from the scene at Port Melbourne which they had left seven weeks earlier. The steam engines and the wagons and the lorries and dock workers with their steel hooks and wooden barrows, the smell of coalsmoke and sheep and the rearing arms of the gantries and the featureless brick walls of the warehouses. These were no different here. But the chill drizzling rain drifting from the low grey clouds transformed the scene and made it foreign and exquisite, requiring from her a special acuteness of attention, as if the situation called upon her to be experienced flawlessly, as nothing had ever been experienced before.

She turned to Georges. 'We must speak only French from now on.'

He smiled at her enthusiasm.

'How long will it take us to get to Paris? Will we be there today? Does anyone know we're coming?'

'We'll be home before dark. I'll telephone Madame Barbier from the railway station. She'll have everything in order for us in the flat.'

Two porters came up the gangway and they touched their caps and spoke to Georges and started carrying the luggage down to the dock. Georges and Emily turned and looked up at the bridge and waved to Captain Anderson, then followed the porters down the gangway and onto the dockside. The taxi took them past the long lines of warehouses to the railway station, which was a half-mile distant from the *Kairos*'s berth. Five and a half hours later they arrived in Paris, at the Gare Saint-Lazare. The sun came out as the taxi sped across the boulevard Haussmann and past the Madeleine, and on across the enormous open space of the place de la Concorde, past the fountains and the obelisk and the shaded porticos of the crowded galleries. Emily sat on the edge of her seat gazing out the window, trying to see everything. Then suddenly they were crossing the Seine.

Georges touched her shoulder and pointed. 'The Invalides. We're nearly home.' Two minutes later they entered a narrow crowded street and at a word from Georges the driver slowed and turned in through a covered way. Above the timber door Emily had time to read an old sign from which the gold lettering was flaking. She made out the words, LINGERIE MERCERIE BONNETERIE. They came through the covered way into a sunlit courtyard. There was a robinia tree growing crookedly in the centre of the courtyard. The old tree was surrounded by iron railings that leaned with it. The branches of the tree were in new spring leaf, pale and golden and translucent in the sunshine, still glittering with the morning rain. A woman was sitting on a folding chair in the thin shade of the tree. There was a basket of linen at her feet. She held her sewing on her lap and paused to watch them get out of the taxi and unload their luggage. On the four sides of the courtyard tiers of shuttered windows fronted by little iron balconies rose to a height of five stories before meeting the slope of the mansard. A stout woman came out of a door in the covered way and hurried across to them, wiping her hands on her apron and calling to two old men who were sitting on a bench to come at once and help with the luggage.

The woman came up and she tucked a loose strand of hair into her scarf and clasped Georges's hand. 'Welcome home, Monsieur Elder! So you had a good journey then? You're glad to be home, I can see that. I've got a heap of post half a mile high in there for you. You're going to be a busy man. But first things first. Let's get you settled.' She relinquished his hand and turned to examine Emily.

Georges took Emily's arm, 'This is Madame Barbier, darling, our concierge. Madame Barbier, may I present my wife.'

Madame Barbier took Emily's hand in her own. 'Welcome to Paris,

Madame Elder. We haven't seen the sun for six weeks and now here it is shining all of a sudden just to let you know it's spring. I daresay you're exhausted after all your travelling? Everything's ready for you.' She let go Emily's hand and turned and shouted to the old men to get a move on and to bring the luggage. She went ahead of them through a doorway. 'This way, madame. Now mind, the steps are still wet.'

Emily and Georges followed the concierge up the stairs. On the first landing Madame Barbier paused and looked back at them, blowing out her cheeks and taking a breather. 'I hope you like climbing stairs, Madame Elder. There's another five floors to go.' The curl of white hair had escaped from under her headscarf again. She absently reached and tucked it in, but it sprang out again at once, bouncing like a broken spring against her ear. She lifted her skirts and went on, the heels of her brown socks, heavily darned and pulled on over lisle stockings, came out of her black shoes at each step. The treads of the stairs were bare wood. They had been freshly scrubbed and shone luminous and green in the dim light. There was a stale smell of cooking and of disinfectant.

They gathered on the landing of the sixth floor, waiting while Madame Barbier recovered her wind and found the key. There were two doors facing each other across the bare wooden landing. The door to Georges's apartment was nearest the top of the stairs. Beside the other door a short passage ended in a steep flight of narrow stairs. No windows let onto the landing and practically no light penetrated the dirty skylight high in the ceiling. A single electric bulb in a coolie hat shade hung from the centre of the ceiling, bathing the landing in a soft light. Below them the old men cursed and struggled with one of the cabin trunks. Georges stepped forward and offered to open the door of his apartment for Madame Barbier with his own key, but the concierge waved him away. 'Don't trouble yourself, monsieur! I've got it right here.'

Georges stood back and waited for her. Emily took his hand and they looked at each other. 'We're here!' Emily mouthed at him in English. He squeezed her hand.

The concierge opened the door and stood aside. 'Here you are, then! You'll want to make sure everything's in good order. There's not a lot you can do with these old places, but you'll find it's clean, madame.'

Emily stepped into the long, narrow room. The ceiling sloped from the entrance toward a row of three dormer windows spaced along the wall opposite. The shutters were open and the room was bright and cheerful with the afternoon sunshine. In front of the centre window was a plain deal table with a telephone and a bundle of rolled plans and some blueprints. Two straight-backed chairs were pushed in against the table's edge. A large draughting board mounted on a heavy timber stand leaned against the wall nearest the door. Behind it a bookshelf was untidily crammed with books piled on their sides, and with bundles of plans and papers and periodicals. There were more journals and books on the floor. In front of the farthest window a black cast-iron gas fire was attached to the wall by a short length of flue. The fire was squat and round-shouldered, with lions' feet and a small oval window. In the centre of the room a frayed brown-and-grey-striped rug partly covered the dark-stained floorboards. Across the rug two worn leather armchairs faced each other squarely. Between these chairs was a low circular table with a tall brass reading lamp. A pewter ashtray in the shape of a swan with its wings spread was the only object on the table.

Emily crossed the room to the middle window, trailing her fingers over the back of the nearest armchair and then the table as she went past, and she stood in the sunlight at the window and looked down into the courtyard. The woman was still at her sewing under the robinia tree. Emily turned back into the room. Georges and Madame Barbier were standing by the door watching her. Madame Barbier's arms were folded across her ample bosom and she was sucking her cheeks and murmuring to herself. The top of her head scarcely reached Georges's shoulder. Without taking his eyes from Emily Georges leaned and set his briefcase on the floor beside the door.

'It's just as I imagined it,' Emily said. 'I can't believe we're really here.'

Madame Barbier went, 'Hmm, well there you are then,' and she glanced up at Georges. 'Some people are easily pleased.' Then, 'You'd better come and have a look at the bed linen, Madame Elder. You'll see everything's been fresh-laundered.'

The door to the bedroom was opposite the end window. Beside the door a framed engraving hung on the wall. It was the only picture in the room. Emily paused to examine it. A heavily crosshatched rendering of a massive antique stone bridge under construction, the tiny figures of the workers perched precariously on rearing scaffolding among massive pulleys and wheels and gantries from which huge blocks of stone hung in the air.

Georges looked at the engraving. 'It belonged to my father.'

Emily followed Madame Barbier into the bedroom. There was scarcely any space to move about in the small room, which was furnished with a large oak chest of drawers, a tall mahogany cheval mirror, and a wardrobe that touched the low ceiling. A middle-sized iron bed with one brass knob missing was pushed hard up against the far wall under the single narrow window. Beside the bed on the twin of the rug in the living room was a low wooden cupboard with a black-lacquered reading lamp fashioned to resemble bamboo. The lamp had a bulb but was without a shade. Through the window there was a view of the nearby roofs, and beyond the roofs the gilded Dôme of the Invalides glowed in the spring sunshine under a blue sky from which the last rainclouds were fast disappearing.

Madame Barbier drew back the bedclothes and bent and sniffed at the sheets. 'You won't get fresher than this, Madame Elder.' She plumped the bolster and pillows. After inspecting the linen, they went out into the sitting room again. Georges opened a door in the end wall. 'Come and look at this!'

Emily went over and looked in through the door past his shoulder. A narrow iron bed with a bare ticking mattress was the only thing in the tiny room, which was lit from a small, dirty skylight set in the sloping ceiling. 'We can store the cabin trunks and suitcases in here,' she said.

Georges put his arm around her waist and drew her against him and whispered in English. 'It will do for a nursery, don't you think?'

The men with Emily's cabin trunk between them bumped in through the front door. The older of the two shouted, as if they were miles away, 'Where do you want this, then, monsieur?' He turned to Madame Barbier and said flatly, 'It's full of bricks.'

'My books are in it,' Emily said and laughed. 'You can leave it there for now.'

'We can leave it here for now,' the older man said to his mate, catching the tone of Emily's French. They laughed and coughed and eased their shoulders and went out.

Madame Barbier showed Emily the small kitchen area to the right of the door. Along one wall was a single gas ring and beside it a cracked and discoloured porcelain sink with a brass tap. A white enamel gas water heater hung over the sink. On the wall behind the gas ring, and in the triangular space of the corner beside it the small surface area of bench was tiled with delicately patterned blue and-white tiles. A collection of blackened pots and pans and colanders and various items of china were stacked on the tiles and on shelves next to the water heater and were hung from various hooks attached to the wall. A box of cutlery was screwed to the wall and a grey tin bath hung from a hook beside the doorway.

'Don't worry,' Georges said. 'You won't have to do much cooking.' He stood looking around at his kitchen. 'In the evening we'll eat at Madame Curel's. It's only a step away.'

They went back into the sitting room.

'I want to cook,' Emily said. 'I'm not going to be just a tourist. I'll go to the markets while you're at work and I'll buy fresh vegetables and chickens and veal and herbs and spices and all sorts of lovely things. I'll make us soups and pies and delicious stews.'

He laughed. 'On that gas ring?'

'I'll make do. You'll see. Australians are good at making do.'

Madame Barbier observed them. She had propped herself on an arm of one of the leather chairs and was leaning forward with her hands clasping her fat knees. She heaved herself up off the chair with a sigh. 'I'll send one of the lads up with your post a bit later, Monsieur Elder. Those stairs have skittled me.' She drew an enormous blue-checked handkerchief from her apron pocket and shook it out as if it were a duster and blew her nose into it noisily.

When the concierge had gone and the men had finished bringing up the luggage and Georges had thanked them and given them a generous tip, he closed the door and went over and stood with Emily by the window in the sun. He put his arm on her shoulder and offered her a cigarette. They stood together smoking, looking out at the spring day.

'It's strange being here with you.'

She covered his hand with hers. 'This place is just like you. I can see you here at this table on your own with your calculations and your reports working till midnight without giving a thought to anything.'

'You don't mind it?' He looked around. 'It's very plain. I could look for somewhere a bit bigger if you like.'

'I love it. And anyway you'd hate having to do that. I'm going to be happy here. It's just what I hoped it would be like. Even the smell.'

They fell silent. The woman in the courtyard picked up her basket and folded her chair and went out under the covered way. The bell of Saint-Pierre-du-Gros-Caillou was tolling. Georges said, 'I'll take my report into the office in the morning and give Jean-Pierre a chance to read it before getting it typed. He's sure to have some good suggestions. I'll only be gone for an hour or two. I'll be back by midday. We can have lunch and do some sight-seeing.'

'I'd enjoy that.' She turned to him. 'But I don't need to be entertained. You're not going to have to change your life to fit it around me.' She reached and touched his cheek. 'Promise not to worry about me. You have your work.'

'I'll be home by midday,' he said firmly. 'We'll go out together.' He went over and fetched the pewter swan ashtray from the low table and held it out for her. She stubbed out her cigarette. She waited for him, seeing that he wished to speak of something.

'I didn't telephone Mother from Le Havre this morning.'

She watched him grind his cigarette between the spread wings of the swan and waited for him to go on.

He put the ashtray on the windowsill and looked at her. 'I need a chance to feel I'm actually back in Paris before facing my mother. I'm not just putting it off. The deck still seems to be heaving about, doesn't it?'

'It's not all going to be as easy as today has been, is it?'

He frowned. 'Mother's going to be all right. I'm sure of it.' He sounded just a little defensive. 'I need to feel I'm steady on my feet before I speak to her. That's all.'

'Chartres,' Emily said, considering the word.

'It's just a country town.'

'No. I know it's more than that. You can't say Chartres like you can say Mansfield or Wollongong. It's not the same thing at all.'

'Well,' he said. 'We'll see.' He gestured at the pieces of their luggage that lay about the floor. 'Let's leave this till tomorrow and go out and have a drink and get something to eat. I'm starving. Come on, Paris is waiting for you. Forget Chartres. We'll have more than enough of Chartres before we're finished.'

Emily tugged the catch and the window stuck, then let go and sprang open, scattering a silvery shower of droplets onto the skirt of her dressing gown and letting in the rushing sound of the morning traffic. She leaned and looked down into the courtyard. Spring rain had crept over Paris during the night and transformed the dark cobbles and the roof slates into leaden dragon scales. The courtyard was empty, then Georges came out of the doorway. He walked to the railings by the robinia tree and turned and looked up at the window and he lifted his hat and saluted her. In his other hand he held his black briefcase. Emily leaned from the window and blew him a kiss. She watched until he had gone through the covered way, then she withdrew into the room. The morning was mild and she left the window open.

She sat in one of the straight-backed chairs at the table. The table was covered with the remains of their breakfast and their empty coffee cups. Beside the breakfast things were piles of her unpacked books. She lit a cigarette and sat smoking and listening to the sounds of this first Paris morning. Next to the table her cabin trunk stood with its lid thrown back. Their other suitcases were spread about the room, some open and half unpacked. Someone was practising the piano in the apartment across the landing. It stopped then started again. She heard a woman's voice raised, alternately scolding, then encouraging, the playing faltering, repeating a few bars, then going on. Emily smiled to hear a familiar Bach minuet she had struggled with herself years ago.

She stubbed out the cigarette and got up and collected the breakfast things and carried them into the kitchen and put them in the sink. Then she went on with the job of sorting through the contents of her cabin trunk. She piled some things on the floor beside her to be put away later and stacked others on the low table between the armchairs. While she worked she sang a song that was running in her mind, 'Ole man Johnson's jazzin' aroun'. Don't push him, don't shove him, or he'll fall to de groun'.'

At eleven she gave up unpacking and went into the kitchen and took the tin bath down from its hook and filled it with jugs of hot water from the gas heater. She fetched two white bath towels from the bedroom, then stood in the kitchen and undressed. She knelt in the bath and sang the song and soaped herself, then washed her hair. After she'd finished her bath, she looked out the window to see what the weather was doing. The clouds were breaking up and a watery sun was touching the roofs here and there. She went into the bedroom and put on fresh underwear and a blue cotton dress and a white knitted jacket with blue forget-me-nots embroidered around the cuffs and the collar. She was ready by a quarter to twelve.

She sat by the window and waited for Georges. The building was quiet. Children came out and started playing chasey round the robinia tree in the courtyard. At midday a clock in a neighbouring apartment solemnly struck the hour. She watched the children playing and waited for Georges to come through the entrance to the covered way. At half past twelve she reached and took Diderot's *Jacques le Fataliste* from the pile of books on the table in front of her and began to read. *How did they meet? she read. By chance like everyone else. What were their names? What's that got to do with you? Where were they coming from? From the nearest place. Where were they going to? Does anyone ever really know where they are going to?* There were hurried footsteps of someone running up the stairs. She closed the book and put it aside and waited. Voices on the landing and the sounds of someone being admitted to the apartment across the way. A door slammed and a moment later another faltering interrupted performance of the Bach minuet.

By two o'clock Georges had still not returned. She was hungry and her throat was dry from smoking. She sat staring at the book, reading over the same line for the third time without registering its meaning: MASTER: *Ah! You villain! You rogue! You traitor! I can see what's coming.* She looked up, wondering if perhaps Madame Barbier knew the telephone number of Georges's office. She was reluctant to put herself so completely in the concierge's power on her very first day, however, and didn't have the courage to go and ask the woman for her own husband's telephone number.

Wondering what she was to do, she stood looking out the window. The sudden shrilling of the electric doorbell made her jump. She had not heard him come up the stairs or seen him cross the courtyard. She went over and opened the door. A short balding man stood in the ivory gloom of the landing. Straggles of faded blond hair mixed with strands of grey fell untidily over the collar of his jacket at the back and sides of his neck. He was dressed in a loose-fitting pale brown suit of a tweed material. A yellow-and-blue silk cravat was tied at his throat and tucked into the front of his waistcoat and a large handkerchief, matching the cravat, flowed from his breast pocket, its drooping folds like the petals of a wilting lily flower. He withdrew a thin cigarette from between his lips and exhaled a cloud of smoke pungent with the spicy aroma of cloves. In the crook of his arm, as if he carried an infant, he cradled a large bunch of pink-and-blue snapdragons.

'No?' he ventured after he had given her an opportunity to examine him. 'I see you're definitely not expecting me, Madame Elder. Georges didn't telephone you? Of course not. Forgive me. I'm Antoine Carpeaux. I have the good fortune to be an old friend of your husband's.'

She stood holding the door. 'I see.'

Antoine Carpeaux lifted his narrow shoulders expressively. 'Georges has been delayed at the office. That's the way it goes. He begs me to convey his regrets to you and to assure you that such a thing will never happen again.' His manner was exaggerated and a little theatrical, inviting her to be amused by the situation. He stepped forward and presented her with the flowers. 'Madame! A bouquet of spring blooms to welcome you to Paris.'

She took the heavy bunch of snapdragons from him and looked at them. 'They're lovely. Thank you.'

He gazed momentarily beyond her into the room. 'Georges's apartment always lacks flowers.' He watched her, preparing his invitation, curious and alert for her reaction. 'Will you join me for lunch? Georges has suggested I might show you some of the amusing sights of Paris.'

'My husband has mentioned your name to me, Monsieur Carpeaux. But that's all. I wasn't expecting you. It's true.'

'Well, my name. It's something. With Georges we never know what will be mentioned and what will be quite forgotten.'

'I'm sorry you've been put to this trouble. It's kind of you, but really I . . .'

'Scarcely a trouble, madame. Unlike your husband, I am not occupied with any pressing business just at present. But I do understand you.' He stood considering her. 'If I may venture an opinion. To someone who has known your husband for a long time this situation is not so . . . well, so utterly unexpected, let me say, as it might seem to someone who has known him for, perhaps not so long.'

'You don't have to excuse him. I'm sure Georges has a reason for not ringing and telling me these things himself.'

Antoine Carpeaux looked about the landing quickly, his movement nervous and inquisitive, as if a fleeting and puzzling shadow caught his attention, then he returned his gaze to her face. 'Well, it is his work, Madame Elder. Bridges! We can only envy him and forgive him. Once Georges sees his work before him he ceases to be with us and is drawn into that other world by the incomparable charm of its exquisite detail. And can anything draw him out again, except his own exhaustion?' He hesitated, perhaps wondering at his chances of being understood. 'For Georges, Madame Elder, the problem of a reason for living can scarcely ever have occurred.' He smiled, his dark eyes alight with interest, with a challenge even, and just possibly with the enjoyment of some faintly mischievous intention.

She was wary but intrigued. 'The problem of a reason for living, Monsieur Carpeaux? You speak as if such ideas are a commonplace of daily life for the rest of us.'

He examined his meagre hand-rolled cigarette, which had burned down to a small damp stub. He held the smouldering stub delicately between his stained forefinger and thumb – it might have been an insect he had snatched from the air in flight and was eager to release.

'Please!' she offered and stood to one side. 'There's an ashtray on the table.'

'The welcoming swan,' he said. 'Thank you.' And he stepped past her, his movements youthful and eager. He crossed the room and went over to the table by the window and placed his cigarette stub in the ashtray.

She stood waiting at the door, watching him.

He lingered by the table, touching her books lightly with the tips of his fingers and making little exclamations of surprise and enchantment, reading their titles aloud, his small, perfect features animated. He turned and smiled at her and held out his arms as if he wished to encompass something large. 'So, you are reading Diderot? Our great *immoraliste*.'

When he returned to the door, she asked him, 'Do you have the telephone number of Georges's office?'

He fished around in the numerous pockets of his jacket and his waistcoat. He brought out in turn a white linen handkerchief, a slim silver cigarette case, a brass lighter, a small worked-silver casket, and a leather wallet. He looked from the articles in his hands to her. 'I'm afraid my little book is not with me.'

'It's all right. It doesn't matter. Really. Let's forget it.' She held the door ready, a little disappointed now.

He held a hand out in front of him and examined his long fingers.

He turned his hand toward his face, as if he read his lines from his palm. 'There's a post office five minutes from here in the rue de Grenelle. Why don't we walk there and look up his number in the directory?'

She considered him.

Like a cat that is being stared at steadily, Antoine Carpeaux seemed to fold a little into himself.

'All right, then,' she said at last. 'Do you think I'll need a coat?'

He clapped his hands. 'Yes! A coat will be a good idea.' He followed her into the sitting room. While she searched in the kitchen for a vase for the snapdragons he picked up Diderot's novel and rested against the window in the sunlight and opened the book at the last page and read aloud. *'If it is written up above that you will be cuckolded, no matter what you do you will be. If, however, it is written up above that you will not be cuckolded, no matter what they do you won't be. So sleep, my friend.'* He closed the book and replaced it on the table. He might have just finished it in its entirety. He looked up at her as she came out of the kitchen.

'There isn't a vase,' she said. She had put the snapdragons in a large jug. She pushed aside the books and set the stoneware jug in the sun at the centre of the table. They admired the flowers together. He reached and playfully pressed together the cheeks of a bloom so that it opened its little pink mouth to them. 'The sinister jaws of the dragon,' he said. 'We have transformed Georges's apartment with poetry and flowers.'

They went out and down the stairs and walked together along the crowded pavement of rue Saint-Dominique. She gazed into the windows of the baker's and the butcher's and examined the fruit and vegetables at the greengrocer's and they paused together to look in the window of the wineshop. She observed the housewives with their big black shopping bags. It might have been an exotic pageant that she was soon to be called upon to play her part in.

When they reached the narrow rue Amelie, he touched her arm. 'Here, we'll go this way.'

There was a florist's shop on the corner. On the footpath outside the shop tall green buckets were filled with fresh blooms and stacked in tiers on wooden racks. The air was heavy with the sweet perfume of spring flowers. They stopped to admire the spectacle. 'So, Madame Elder,' he said, 'you arrive for the very first time in Paris during our old Republican month of Germinal.' His manner was teasing and she looked at him, uncertain of his intention. 'It is the month, madame,' he explained, 'when trees unfold and the womb of nature opens! Is this another commonplace of existence or are we to see in it a portent? April is from the Latin *aperire*, is it not? To unfold and to disclose that which has remained hidden.'

'You're mistaken,' she said, teasing him in her turn. 'This is not my first time in Paris. I've been here before. When I was five.' She turned and looked at him. 'Does that count, do you think? Or is five too young to count?'

'Oh, *everything* must count!' he said with certainty. 'If everything doesn't count, then nothing will count. That is the rule.'

'The rule of what game, monsieur?'

'There is only one game, madame.' He took her arm and stepped into the narrow roadway and they walked together to the rue de Grenelle.

On their way back from the post office they stopped at a café opposite the Métro entrance in the avenue Bosquet. They sat outside at a table in the cold sun. The tables along the busy street were crowded and noisy with conversation, the shouts and laughter of the other patrons and the shuffling and coughing of the pedestrians who hurried up the steps from the Métro.

He lit one of his pungent cigarettes and leaned back and examined her. He might have been a collector who had found an interesting vase and was wondering if it were genuine or were only a rather well made fake.

She returned his gaze levelly. 'How did you meet Georges?'

'I was on the point of asking you the same question.'

She smiled. 'But I asked you first. And in my game the rule is that the first to ask is the first to be answered.'

He drew on his cigarette, narrowing his eyes and letting the smoke drift from his lips and gazing into the distance. 'Georges?' he said. 'It wasn't really a meeting. Let's say Georges gently infiltrated our lives. Modestly, generously, and with a certain Scottish grace that was not at first obvious to us.'

'I think that is how my mother feels about him.'

'It was before the war. He was working for the same consulting firm he works for now. He was strengthening bridges then in Tunisia and Morocco to take the heavy locomotives from the phosphate mines. He worked for many months on two bridges over the Medjerda River near my father's farm. My father drove over to his camp and invited him to billet at our house. But Georges declined. He wasn't like the French engineers. Georges lived in the camp with his Arab workers, which was very unusual. This offended my father, who with the rest of his kind believed the Arabs to be a race of beings without souls. But in the end my father came to admire Georges. As we all did. I was living in Paris, of course, and only met Georges when my father fell ill and I went home. Georges was interested to see the country and we rode together on horses into the Atlas Mountains and I showed him the Roman sites where the shepherds and the Berbers had taken up residence. While we rode we talked and soon we knew each other's lives. Later, after my father died, Georges came to visit me in my house at Sidi bou-Saïd.'

Antoine fell silent and waited, but she offered nothing. While talking of Georges his manner had lost its teasing playfulness.

'It puzzles you, I see. But your husband and I don't have a friendship of like minds, Madame Elder. It isn't that at all. There is no good reason for our friendship, but we are friends all the same. Georges respects everyone and there's an end of it, as far as he's concerned. He builds the world for us and doesn't ask us what we intend to do with the world he builds. That is our business, what use we shall put it to, and involves a kind of moral uncertainty, I believe, for which Georges possesses no curiosity. Even in those days, when I scarcely knew him, sitting our horses in the ruined theatre of Dougga watching the sun set over the valley, I saw that Georges's mind was elsewhere, with his calculations, and when I ventured to ask him what he was thinking – which is a question he has never once put to me in all the years I've known him – he told me about his dream of building the biggest bridge in the world in Australia. He spoke of his heroic ambition so modestly and in such a matter-of-fact way that I knew it was not some kind of youthful bravado with him but was the truth. Perhaps his only truth. His most precious truth. And that is when my admiration for him began. It was a kind of stealthy envy of him at first. I thought I disliked him. That someone so young should live by such certainties offended my sense of reality. My own life was a sea of emotion without point or purpose.' He laughed softly and fell silent again, smoking and looking faintly regretful or amused. 'It's only when I look back now that I see my envy then was the beginning of my desire for him to succeed.' He looked at her. 'We're reassured, don't you think, to know there are such people as Georges in this world. It is their orthodoxy that holds it together. So while we envy their certainties we long to see their dreams become realities.' He brightened. 'But now he has astonished me. It is not like him to go after a bridge and return with a bride.'

'Do you think he has astonished himself?' she asked.

Antoine reached and sipped his coffee then set the cup in its saucer. 'What do you think?'

She looked around restlessly at the other tables. 'I'm hungry. Can we get something to eat here?'

'If you promise to tell me the story of how you bewitched Georges and took his mind off bridges long enough for him to think of marriage, I'll take you to my favorite brasserie. I lunch at the Brasserie Équivoque every day to remind myself why I live in Paris. Casimir's fried eels are exquisite.'

'Everything is just as I expected it to be. It really is an enchanted city.'

'No!' he said firmly, as if he admonished a child for touching something it had been forbidden to touch. 'Paris is just another city. Paris is a place to lose yourself in. Here we can forget and be forgotten. If you want to see beauty, you must visit me at my house in Sidi bou-Saïd.'

'We're always critical of our own homes.'

'Tunisia's my home. It is the most beautiful and the saddest country in the world. You see, Madame Elder, like you I'm a colonial.'

She laughed. 'Nonsense. You're a Parisian.'

'We're all Parisians here. It only takes a year to become a Parisian. I've been here twenty years.'

'But you are French, nevertheless.'

'A little more French than Georges, perhaps, but not French enough to be a Frenchman among those who are truly French. I was born in the valley of the Medjerda River and grew up there. With the smell of peaches and grapes and apricots ripening in the sunlight of the open fields, not espaliered against garden walls as they are here. Secretly, and absolutely against my father's prohibition, my nanny, the grave and beautiful Mounir the blessed, taught me to speak the local Arabic. When my father overheard me speaking Arabic one day, he sent me away to boarding school in Montpellier, where he thought I would be safe from the dangers of Africa and the soulless barbarians. The day I left Tunisia I cursed my father and wept for Mounir. On that day I knew myself cast out of Eden, Madame Elder.'

They took a taxi. The brasserie was crowded. It was noisy with conversation, laughter, and the shouts of the patrons for the attention of the harried waiters, the air swirling with a dense cloud of cigarette smoke and a strong smell of garlic. Waiters in long white aprons ducked about between the closely packed tables and the gesticulating patrons delivering the plates of food. Antoine ordered fried eels and a bottle of wine and when the wine came he lifted his glass to her. 'To your beauty, Emily. I shall call you Emily.' He swallowed a mouthful of wine. 'And to French cooking.' He emptied the glass in one go, then reached for the bottle and refilled it and drank again.

Men at other tables hailed him and he waved a hand carelessly to them.

The chilled wine filled her mouth with the flavour of peaches. While they ate she told him about Australia and her family and how she and Georges had met. When they had finished their meal, they smoked cigarettes and Antoine ordered another bottle of wine. He drank, his cigarette held before his lips, the soft radiance of the lights through the wispy straggles of his hair, as insubstantial as the smoke that drifted about his head, his eyes glittery and unsteady.

'You're a woman who's accustomed to her freedom,' he said, and when she would have objected he waved his hand to silence her. 'You are afraid of nothing. And . . . you are prepared to defy us all.'

She laughed, uneasy with the direction of his mood. 'You'll never earn your living as a fortune-teller. I'm afraid of all kinds of things. To think of the future terrifies me. Why do men always think they know us better than we know ourselves?'

'What men? Now you're speaking of your father again.' He reached across the small table and took her hand in his and looked at her. 'Enjoy the liberties of the foreigner, Emily. One year! That's all you've got. After a year, when our world is no longer strange to you, when you've understood everything there is to understand about us—' He broke off, indicating the other patrons of the restaurant with a sweep of his arm. 'Look at us! We've had our chance. We've understood everything.' He gripped her fingers and said, 'Live a passionate fairy story for us! That's what we want you to do. In a year the enchantment of being a stranger will lift from your heart and you'll be condemned to suffer for your sins just like the rest of us. Another *Parisienne*, Emily! That's what you'll be.' He withdrew his hand from hers and delved into a side pocket of his jacket. 'Here! Let us put your knowledge of classical history to the test.' He was half playful and half serious. With a ceremonious gesture he laid on the tablecloth in front of her the little silver casket she had seen in his hand on the landing outside the apartment when he had been hunting for his notebook. He stared at the silver box. 'Does your study of classical civilizations tell you the origins of this? Open it.'

She reached and picked up the little silver casket and examined it. 'It's beautiful.'

'Open it!' he urged her.

The pattern on the casket was worn smooth with age and use, the design almost obliterated. She removed the lid. Nestling in a blue velvet bed inside the box was a yellowed shard of ivory set in a silver frame.

'Where does it come from? Take it out. Hold it to the light,' he urged her, watching her.

She took the brooch out of the box and held it up.

He reached and traced a line across the face of the dark ivory with his fingernail. 'There! See him?' There were the faint remains of an intaglio figure, robed and holding something under its arm, half turned away, as if on the point of departure.

'Well?' he said, 'I'm waiting to hear your opinion.'

'You don't understand,' she said. 'This is the first time I've ever seen anything as old as this. The history I studied was . . . It wasn't something *real*, Antoine.' She looked at him and laughed. 'We didn't have any primary sources,' she explained. 'We studied George Grote's *History of Greece* and tried to imagine the capture of Troy and we read Gibbon and looked at pictures of the Roman Forum, and it was all utterly remote from us and was just ideas and never touched our lives in the slightest way. It was just names and places. The past was not mysterious to us, only difficult.'

He frowned, 'Then why did you persevere with it?'

'Please don't test me,' she begged him. 'I abandoned it, remember? I persevered for my father's sake.' She cupped the medallion in the palm of her hand and explored its surface with her fingers. 'It's beautiful.' She looked at him.

'It's yours,' he said softly.

'No!' she objected.

He put his hand on hers, preventing her from handing the medallion back to him. 'It's our welcome. A Tunisian custom, Emily. From me and Mounir. Please don't refuse it. It's something from my home.'

'Why do you give it to me? I can't possibly accept it.'

'Don't refuse it, Emily. The Arabs say that all gifts are from God and to refuse a gift is to refuse God.'

They looked at it together.

'It may be a fragment of an early Christian pyxus,' he said. 'Fourth or fifth century. We're not sure. One of my father's workmen found it more than twenty years ago. My father had a Berber silversmith make the frame and the box for it. There's a pin on the back. See? It can be worn as a brooch.' His gaze lingered on the piece as she turned it in her hand. 'It lay in the ruins of the Roman arena at Carthage for more than fifteen hundred years. Now you're holding it in your hand, Emily.' He smiled at her. 'Its journey's not over yet.'

'I shall treasure it, Antoine.'

'I've carried it with me for years. Now you two will travel together for a while.' He sat back and waved his hand at it. 'Put it away!' He drained his glass and leaned forward heavily and set the empty wineglass carefully on the cloth before him and sat gazing at it. He looked up and gestured at the glass. 'I drink too quickly.' He shrugged. 'Then I get excited.' He laughed and fumbled for his cigarette case. 'What is it about the future that terrifies you?'

She reached for her glass and drank the wine and looked at him. 'Only that I may find no purpose in it for myself.'

'Or that you *may*,' he said and smiled, considering her, admiring her – the collector who has found the mark that convinces him the vase is genuine. 'And the danger that you will find something you truly desire one day, that is what makes you so restless and afraid.'

'I didn't say desire, I said purpose.'

He shrugged. 'Purpose? Ambition? Desire? What's the difference? All passions are the same passion. Our passions always require from us a betrayal of our former state.'

She glanced at him, hesitating as if she considered asking him something, then changed her mind and looked down at the brooch in her hand. 'When you took it out of your pocket just now, you didn't mean to give it to me,' she said. 'Then on the spur of the moment you decided. It was an impulse, Antoine. You'll regret it. You'll miss it. You'll want it back.'

'Never! It's yours for a while now. Your talisman.' He laughed. 'One day it will belong to someone else. When we reach a certain age, we understand that ownership is temporary.'

When they left the brasserie and were on the street, he put his arm through hers. 'I've talked too much,' he said, as if he wished to introduce a more sober note into their meeting, to caution her and himself – to reassure himself, perhaps, that he had not unsettled her with his speculations. 'You're right, I'd never make my living telling fortunes.'

A week after their arrival in Paris, the concierge, Madame Barbier, looked around the door and called to the young girl who was waiting on the landing outside the apartment, 'Come in and let Madame Elder have a look at you.' When the girl stepped into the room, the concierge took her by the hand and pulled her to her side. She began impatiently unbuttoning the girl's grey gabardine coat. 'You can take this thing off. Madame Elder doesn't want to see your old raincoat.'

Under the coat the girl wore a long black dress with the severe cut of an old-fashioned convent tunic. The hem reached almost to her ankles. The concierge tugged at the shoulders and pulled at the sides of this garment. 'There!' She turned to Emily, 'My niece, Madame Elder, Sophie Lemaire. She's a good Catholic girl from the convent at Chantilly.' She plucked a thread of lint from Sophie's dress. 'She made the dress herself.'

Sophie waited modestly while Emily and the concierge admired her plain black dress.

Emily said, 'It's very good, Sophie. I'm afraid I'm quite useless with a needle.'

'Thank you, madame.' Sophie's voice was soft and clear, her hazel eyes steady on Emily's face. She neither smiled nor frowned but stood waiting to be approved of, her old raincoat folded neatly over her arm.

Madame Barbier said, 'If there's any sewing or darning you need besides the cleaning, Sophie can turn her hand to it. And my sister tells me the nuns have taught her a bit of cooking.' She gestured toward the ceiling. 'The chambres de bonne are all taken, so she'll be staying with my other sister in Belleville until one of the girls here gives notice.' She turned to Emily. 'Unless you and Monsieur will have her in the little room till then?'

Emily came forward and offered her hand to Sophie. 'Welcome to Paris, Sophie.'

Sophie hesitated, then she took Emily's hand delicately by the tips of the fingers and gave a little curtsy. 'Thank you, Madame Elder.'

'Is this your first time in Paris?'

'Yes, madame.'

Emily smiled. 'Then we're both new.' She turned to the concierge. 'We've stored our trunks and Monsieur's drawing board and a few other things we shan't be needing in the little room for the time being.' She turned back to Sophie, 'But you might care to stay here and look after things while Monsieur and I are visiting Chartres?'

'We'll see about all that,' Madame Barbier said. 'I can always find space downstairs, you know, for your unwanted pieces if you're looking for a bit of extra room. If Sophie's to stay in Belleville, Monsieur will need to give her a couple of extra francs for the Métro. She'll be here by ten prompt each morning except Sunday. Unless you especially want her on a Sunday and then you'll need to give her notice. And Sundays will be extra, of course.' While she talked Madame Barbier repeatedly wet her thumb and forefinger with the tip of her tongue and nipped at Sophie's dress, making a surprised clucking sound with her tongue each time, as if it astonished her to find scraps of lint or hair or loose cotton on her niece's clothing.

Sophie ignored her aunt's fussing and watched Emily, her features grave and expectant.

When the concierge had finished detailing the conditions of Sophie's employment, she gave the skirt a last sweeping brush with the flat of her hand and stood back. 'Well, what do you say, Sophie? Madame Elder's offering you the position until she sees how you manage.'

Sophie said, 'Thank you, Madame Elder.'

'There's plenty to do,' Emily said. 'You can help me make curtains. And we'll have to do something about these chairs, won't we?' She turned to the two sagging leather armchairs that faced each other squarely across the rug in the middle of the room. 'They look as if they're about to pounce on each other, don't they?'

Sophie's features relaxed and she smiled for the first time. 'Yes, madame.'

'Like a couple of old pugilists.'

'Well, which one's our Georges, then?' Madame Barbier said, and she stepped up and gave the back of the nearest chair a thump with her clenched fist.

Surprised, Emily turned to her.

'Georges Carpentier, Madame Elder. France's hero. He's fighting Jack Dempsey in New York next month.'

They all laughed.

'I'll make a cup of tea,' Emily said. 'You'll stay and have a cup of tea with us, Madame Barbier?'

Madame Barbier gave Sophie a little push. 'Go on, then, girl. Get yourself started. Sophie'll make the tea, madame.'

Sophie laid her raincoat on the back of one the chairs and went into the kitchen.

'She's only seventeen, and if you do want her to stay back a bit some days for these curtains and whatever else you've got in mind, you'll make certain she gets away well before dark, won't you? Belleville's not the Seventh, you know.'

Later, when Madame Barbier and Sophie had gone, Emily got out her writing case and sat at the table by the window. She lit a cigarette and sat smoking and looking out at the spring day. She picked up her fountain pen and began a letter to her father.

I have met one of Georges's friends. He is an interesting and unexpected man and I doubt if you would feel at once drawn to him, but I feel he and I are to become firm friends. His name is Antoine Carpeaux and he is from Tunisia. I could not imagine meeting such a man in Melbourne. Already, after scarcely more than a week, I feel that I am writing to you from a place where I am to be more at home than I ever was at Richmond Hill. What an odd thing this is to say, and even to feel, but it is true nevertheless. I am confident you will not misunderstand me. The vast intricacy of Paris convinces me that almost anything is possible here. In Melbourne I carried my little map of the city about with me in my head and everything was familiar. Tomorrow we leave for Chartres to meet Georges's mother and his aunt. I believe Georges is just a little afraid of his mother and expects to have to make amends to her for having married an Australian. Don't worry, dearest Parent, I shall know how to stand up for myself . . .

The letter went on for two pages. She sealed it and put on her coat and hat and went out to the post office in the rue de Grenelle. The spring day was clear and fine and the streets were busy. At the corner of rue Amelie she bought a bunch of violets at the florist's. As she walked along with the crowds, Emily felt that her life was just beginning.

THREE

From a distance of two or three miles the town was not visible from the window of the train and the cathedral seemed to Emily to rise abruptly from the broad green expanse of the spring wheatfields, a solitary greystone monolith, as if it were a dramatic feature of the natural landscape, its towers and spires and finials hidden in low cloud.

'It looks so silent and so permanent,' she said. 'You have to wonder why it's here, of all the places it might be.'

Georges leaned against her and looked, his shoulder pressing hers with the rocking of the carriage. He gazed out the window, then turned aside and began to gather his notes, which were spread on the seats opposite and beside him.

By the time Georges and Emily got off the Paris–Rennes train at Chartres it was raining heavily and a cold wind was blowing across the forecourt of the railway station. The taxi drove beside the river for some way, then turned and crossed a stone bridge before entering an exceedingly narrow street enclosed by tall houses whose upper storeys seemed to lean in over the road.

'This is it,' Georges said, and he reached and gripped her hand and smiled at her. 'I used to dream this street into my nights in Glasgow.'

She returned the pressure of his hand.

'Are you nervous?' he asked her.

'Of course. Very.' She looked at him. 'But you are too. Just a little.'

He grimaced. 'It will be all right. I'm sure of it. It's just that this moment always reminds me of when I was a boy coming home from Glasgow for the school holidays. It's been almost a year this time. I never know quite what to expect.'

'And now there's me.'

'Us,' he said.

'You must promise not to abandon me,' she said, a little awed by the grey town and the rain and the prospect of his mother. 'I can manage on my own in Paris, but this is different.'

'Don't be so silly, I'm not going to abandon you.'

He reached and tapped the glass and motioned to the driver to pull over. They got out of the taxi. There was no one about in the street. The rain swept down from the roofs like seaspray over the bows of a ship. Georges helped the driver with their luggage and paid him. The driver got back into his cab and drove away.

They stood in the empty street holding their suitcases. The door of the house in front of them gave directly onto the footpath, which was barely wide enough for one person. There was no knocker or bell. Georges reached and hammered on the door with his knuckles. He looked at her.

'What shall I call your mother?' she whispered urgently.

'Call her *belle Maman*. That will please her.'

The door was opened by a thin, stooped woman in a grey-striped dress with a long black apron tied firmly around her waist and a scarf over her hair. She exclaimed when she saw them, 'You're drowned, the pair of you!' She took the suitcase from Emily and stood aside and ushered them in out of the rain. The passageway was narrow and dark and smelled of the river and of liniment and old women.

Georges hugged his aunt, then drew Emily close. 'This is my Aunt Juliette, darling. Aunt Juliette, this is my dearest wife, Emily.'

The old woman clasped Emily's hands and kissed her on both cheeks, then she held her off and examined her from head to foot, giving the flesh of her upper arms an approving squeeze. Aunt Juliette's gaze was shrewd, intelligent, and amused. 'Welcome to Chartres, my dear,' she said with feeling, and she drew Emily to her and kissed her warmly again. 'Come!' she said briskly. There was a nervous, energetic haste in her manner, as if she were eager to get on and to have this moment done with. She waited while they took off their coats and hats and hung them beside the door, then she went ahead of them along the passage and stood at the first door on the left.

Inside the room Madame Elder was seated in an old mahogany armchair on the far side of the fireplace. The chair's tapestry had come away from the frame on one side at the bottom and hung down untidily. The curtains were drawn across the single window and the only light was from the yellow globe of a murmuring gas bracket to one side of the mantelpiece. The large figure of Madame Elder was set among shadows of bric-a-brac and old photographs and the heavy Scottish oak furniture she had salvaged from a more promising age. There was no fire in the hearth and the room was cold.

Aunt Juliette said from the door, 'Here they are, Heloise,' and she stood aside and allowed Georges and Emily to enter the room.

Madame Elder put her weight on her cane, and she gave a gasp and got up from her chair. Georges went over to her and they clasped each other and stood in a silent embrace for a long while. When Georges's mother at last released him, she reached and took his face between her hands and gazed at him searchingly. It was a peculiarly ambiguous gesture. She might almost have been holding up her son's severed head before her and offering it as an object of veneration or disdain, intending either to give thanks for his safe return or to deliver a curse on his house.

But whatever the compressed emotion that passed between mother and son at that moment it was private and excluded the two women who watched. An oak-cased clock on the mantelpiece went tock-tock-tock and the yellow radiance of the gas flame shone on Georges's damp and faintly troubled features.

Aunt Juliette made an impatient noise with her tongue against the roof of her mouth such as carters make when urging a reluctant horse into motion. Madame Elder and Georges turned together and faced Emily. Madame Elder held Georges's arm firmly against her ribs, keeping him at her side or perhaps needing his support.

'This is Emily, Mother.' He was unable to step forward without relinquishing his mother's arm, and he held out his hand, encouraging Emily to approach and join them.

Emily thought she might curtsy as Sophie had done, but she instinctively rebelled at the last moment and offered her hand instead. Madame Elder was almost as tall as Georges. She had the same long features, her straight nose and high forehead suggesting the possibility of aristocratic breeding, or a reserved and disdainful intelligence. She was considerably younger than her sister Juliette but was heavier and slower and clearly without her sister's spry energy and impatience.

Emily wondered if she should address her as *belle Maman* at once or wait until an intimacy had been established. 'How do you do, Madame Elder,' she said.

Madame Elder's embrace was formal and brief and seemed ingeniously designed to establish a distance between them rather than to extend a welcome. She smiled and murmured something and gestured at a faded maroon velvet couch that stood square-on to the empty grate at the extremity of the hearthrug. 'Aunt Juliette will bring us some tea.'

Georges helped his mother settle herself again in the armchair.

He drew up a straight-backed chair for himself and sat beside her.

She put out a hand and placed it over his and sat looking at Emily, who was sitting alone in the middle of the velvet couch.

Emily smiled.

'So your father is a professor, Emily?'

'Yes.'

The clock ticked and the gas bracket hissed faintly. There was the sound of Aunt Juliette singing in the kitchen at the end of the passage.

Emily cleared her throat. 'Were your own family engineers, Madame Elder?'

'Georges's father was an engineer. Our father was a corn broker. And his father before him. But the Hervieus were once tanners and have lived in Chartres for centuries.' Madame Elder paused to scan the room briefly with her gaze, as if there might have been an audience for her remarks beyond that of her son and his wife. 'The Hervieus are mentioned in the cartulary of the cathedral, Emily,' she explained. 'They assisted with the rebuilding after the great fire of 1194.'

They fell silent once again, perhaps out of respect for the memory of the Hervieus.

Georges got up and opened the door for Juliette. She came in and set her tray down by Emily on an octagonal sewing table in front of the couch and stood looking at them. 'Well,' Juliette said after a moment, 'you're here at last.' She put her hand on Emily's hair.

Emily looked up at her.

'Look in to the kitchen on your way up.'

When Juliette had gone, Georges suggested Emily pour the tea.

Madame Elder turned to him. 'You've sent your report to Haine Saint-Paul, then? That's the important thing. When do you expect them to decide?'

After they had finished their tea, Madame Elder excused herself. She explained that she tired easily these days. 'If I don't rest in the afternoons, I find I can't manage the evenings.'

Georges helped her to her feet and she asked him to escort her to her room.

After they had gone, Emily heard a door close along the passage. She sat and waited. Several minutes passed. A lorry went by along the road outside the window, its gears whining as it climbed the hill. The house was silent. The room was cold. She looked about at the darkly polished surfaces of the furniture, its shapes receding into the shadows and merging with the heavy red-and-purple stripes of the embossed wallpaper. She could see herself sitting in the gaslight, like a dark painting, reflected in the windows of a glass-fronted bookcase that stood in the corner beside the window. She got up and went over and looked through the glass, reading the spines of the books. They were English. The three volumes of Ruskin's *The Stones of Venice*, with gold Venetian lions on their brown embossed spines. Beside these the two volumes of Richard Burton's *Personal Narrative of a Pilgrimage to Al-Madinah & Meccah*. Then a small green volume of *Marcus Aurelius*. She opened the door of the bookcase and took out the *Marcus Aurelius* and opened it. It was an English translation. The pages were uncut. It had never been read. She put it back and took out the first of three green clothbound volumes, *The Lives of the Engineers*, by Samuel Smiles. Pasted on the front endpaper was a presentation bookplate, *Glasgow University, Via Veritas Vita, session 1877–78. Presented to Ross Andrew Elder. The D. S. Nairn Prize, In recognition of outstanding achievement*. Behind her the door to the passage opened and Georges came in. She pushed the book back into its place on the shelf and closed the cabinet.

Georges came up to her and put his arm around her waist and kissed her on the cheek. 'Father's books.' He peered in at the shelves. 'We'd better take our things upstairs and get settled.'

She looked at him.

'Mother made a suggestion for tomorrow.'

Emily waited.

He shifted uneasily and brushed at the polished desktop of the bookcase with his fingers. He looked at her. 'She wants me to go to Mass with her in the morning.'

Emily said, 'You mean, just the two of you? Without me?'

'We always went to Mass together the first morning I was home from school for the summer holidays. We've kept it up over the years whenever I come down to Chartres. It's become a sort of tradition with us. She expects it.' He shrugged, uncomfortable with his petition, and moved away from her, searching in his pockets for his cigarettes. He stood looking down at the cold hearth. 'Every day while I'm away she walks up to the cathedral on her own. When I come home, we walk up there together. We meet the neighbours and the shopkeepers along the way and they find out how well her son is getting on in life. There isn't anything else for her. It's what makes sense of this.' He turned and gestured at the room. 'Living here with her unmarried sister. Waiting. Not having a real life.' He found his cigarettes and lit one.

'And her son getting married?' Emily failed to keep the hostility from her voice. 'That's not going to interest the neighbours and the shopkeepers? Won't they be curious to have a look at his new Australian wife?'

'While we're at Mass Mother thought you might like to join one of the tour groups and see something of the cathedral. You can walk up with us and meet us again afterward. The neighbours will see you then.'

Emily stood looking at him. 'You promised you wouldn't abandon me.'

'Well, do you want to go to Mass with us?' he asked reasonably. 'You don't usually go. I was sure you wouldn't mind not going.'

'That's hardly the point, is it? Whether I *want* to go.' She wondered if she were being unreasonable but couldn't control her resentment. 'Your mother doesn't want me to go. She wants to pretend it's still just you and her.'

'You're making far too much of this.' His tone was mild but firm, as if he wished to instruct her. He stood with his back to the hearth looking at her. 'Why don't we go up and unpack now? You must be tired. We can decide about this later.'

Emily stood her ground by the bookcase.

'When my father died, I was ten and my mother suddenly discovered she was poor,' he said, endeavouring to explain. 'He left her his debts, that's all. To keep me at school she had to sell her house in Glasgow and move back here with Juliette. This is Juliette's house, not my mother's. My mother doesn't have a house. What you see here in this room is everything she salvaged from her marriage to my father.'

'And you,' Emily said pointedly.

'Yes, and me.' He turned and dabbed the ash from his cigarette into the hearth. 'I do what I can for her, but she refuses to let me give her money. I was only able to convince her to let me have the telephone installed because I need it whenever I'm down here. Since my father died Mother and I have had this unspoken understanding between us that one day I'd . . . well, not exactly take my father's place, but make it up to her. Restore the family, if you like. Something like that. Restore *her*. I don't know. Make sense of it for her.' He was silent, then he said quietly, 'Attending Mass at the cathedral with me is important to her.'

Emily moved away from the cabinet toward the door. 'Juliette asked us to look in on her before we go up.'

'You don't have to be so hostile. I shan't ask you to do this sort of thing again. I promise.'

'You're promising again. Which is silly. Antoine said I'd learn to expect this from you.'

'Antoine said that?' Georges looked hurt. 'D'you think that's fair?'

'You keep disappearing back into your old life without taking me with you. Then promising you won't do it again. Then doing it again.'

He stared at her. 'I'm sorry. I hadn't realized. I suppose it must seem like that to you.'

'Yes, that is how it seems.'

⸺⸺

She woke to the bleating of penned sheep. She had been back in Australia with them in her dreams. The closed room was airless and musty. She lay in the bed beside Georges, remembering the interminable evening with Madame Elder in her chilly sitting room. She sat up. 'I can hear sheep?'

'It's the sheep market,' he murmured. He rolled over and reached for her. 'Lie down. Tomorrow you'll hear horses. We eat horses here, you know.'

She removed his hand from her thigh and got out of bed. Aunt Juliette had left water in the jug. She poured some of the water into the basin and dabbed at her eyes. When she pressed the towel to her face, it gave off an earthy smell, as if vegetables had been wrapped in it. 'Everything's mouldy.'

'It's the river.'

She reached and pulled at a corner of the wallpaper. It peeled away softly. The broad blue-and-yellow bars of the heavily embossed paper, which covered the low sloping walls of the bedroom from floor to ceiling, were mottled with stains. She went over to the narrow window and opened it, letting in a gust of cold air.

Georges sat up and looked at her. She was standing against the morning light, the silhouette of her nakedness through the material of her nightdress. 'Come back to bed,' he said.

She remained by the window looking out at the morning. Soft grey clouds drifted through the tall green poplars and across the glistening roofs of the houses on the opposite bank of the river. There was the road they had come along in the taxi the previous afternoon, and fifty yards or so downriver, the elegant arches of the stone bridge. A hooded baker's van with a donkey between the shafts was the only vehicle on the road. A black-and-white dog trotted along underneath the van, keeping out of the rain. The driver's whip lifted and fell against the donkey's steaming back. The penned sheep bleated into the deep rural silence of the morning.

'It's probably not a good idea to wear this while we're down here.'

She turned from the window. Georges was examining Antoine's silver casket. She had put it on the table beside the bed with a few of her things when she unpacked. 'I'm afraid my mother doesn't understand Antoine.'

'You mean she doesn't like him either.'

'Well, he must have liked you. I've never known him to be without this.'

Emily turned back to the window and watched the donkey and the van turn onto the bridge. The dog stopped to piss against the cornerstone of the bridge. She heard a clink as Georges replaced Antoine's casket on the side table.

'Mother's aged.' He was silent for a while. 'She's not well.'

Emily turned and looked at him. A spike of pale hair was sticking up at the back of his head and his jaw twinkled with a russet growth of beard, in which there was already a peppering of grey. 'The bleating of those sheep waiting to be slaughtered,' Emily said. She reached and pulled the window closed.

Georges suggested he telephone the station for a taxi.

'When you've gone back to Paris, I shall have to walk to the cathedral just as I always do,' Madame Elder said. 'So we'll walk today.' She took his arm. Her progress was slow and she rested her weight on her cane and on Georges and stopped frequently to speak to the shopkeepers and acquaintances they met on the street. The rain had ceased and they did not need to open their umbrellas.

When they emerged from the narrow street onto the open square before the west front of the cathedral, Madame Elder stopped. The clouds were lifting and patches of sunlight were beginning to break through. Tourists and pilgrims were assembling in groups with their guides. They stood about gazing up at the towers topped by their tall spires, their expressions rapt, intent, and expectant. Worshippers hurried into the great church, entering by the right door, which stood open to the square.

'It's France's finest,' Georges said.

'Europe's finest,' Madame Elder corrected him.

Georges turned to Emily. 'Well? What do you think of our great cathedral?'

Emily said, 'I expected it to be bigger.'

Madame Elder snorted.

Georges said, 'That's what Americans always say. It's its reputation. No church can be as large as the reputation of Chartres.'

'Mr Henry Adams was an American,' Madame Elder said. 'That isn't what he said.'

'What did Mr Henry Adams say?' Emily asked, a touch of studied innocence in her tone.

Madame Elder looked at her quickly. 'There's a copy of his volume in the bookcase. Georges has told me you are a reader. You may borrow Mr Adams's book and take it back to Paris with you, if you wish.' Madame Elder urged Georges forward. 'Let us see if Emily is more impressed with the interior of our cathedral.'

'It looked bigger from the train. From a distance,' Emily said, explaining, but they had moved off and were not paying attention to her. She followed, a step or two behind them, through the railings and up the steps and out of the watery spring sunlight into the vast luminous interior of the church, the lofty windows glowing red and blue above them, and before them deep shadows filled with the wavering light of candles and oil lamps, figures moving, and muted voices. It had been agreed that while Madame Elder and Georges attended Mass Emily would read up on the medieval stone sculptures and stained glass in her *Baedecker*, then join one of the hourly guided tours.

She parted from them in the north aisle and stood and watched mother and son walk slowly away together arm in arm toward the small apsidal chapel where the Mass was to be celebrated, withdrawing into their old life without her. She waited but Georges did not turn around.

When they had gone, Emily went out onto the north porch and stood and looked at the tall stone figures that flanked the doorway. She was too angry with Georges and his mother to consider the idea of studying their cathedral. She turned away from the stone carvings, repelled by their pious, Byzantine expressions, the faces of conspirators. She unbuttoned her overcoat and examined the scene below her. She felt that she had been left to aimlessly fill in her time once again. 'It's my own fault,' she said aloud to herself. She was longing for a cigarette. She determined to ask someone where she could find a café. She put her hand in her coat pocket and fingered Antoine's silver casket. *Live a fairy story for us*, he had said. But how was she to do that? How *did* one rebel against the pointlessness? How was it done? She felt a wave of frustration and panic rising in her chest and was gripped by a sudden intense regret that she had not obeyed her father and gone to Cambridge. Her marriage seemed to hang over her, as irrefutable and as incomprehensible as the grey stone church at her back. 'Do I love him?' she asked herself and was dismayed by the question. 'I don't know what I want. I don't know anything.'

Emily stood alone and motionless in the shadows of the deep north porch, her red *Baedecker* bright against the dark green of her overcoat, her other hand thrust into her pocket, her fingers gripping the silver casket. Below her on the broad steps a group of pilgrims had begun to assemble. Two young women in the group ran up the steps and stood in the porch beside her. They helped each other unpin their hats and fix their hair. Both young women had short brown hair done in the modern style very like Emily's. When they had fixed their hair, one of them turned to her and smiled and touched her arm and pointed to the stone figures and said something in German.

Emily replied in French, 'I suppose they are conspirators.' She wondered if the young woman had seen her tears.

Just then the guide, who was accompanied by a priest, began calling to the assembled pilgrims from the roadway below the steps. As the group moved off behind the guide, the young woman who had spoken to her took Emily by the hand and urged her to join them. Emily shook her head and smiled. At that moment the guide, a slight figure in pale tweed knickerbockers, turned around and walked backward a few paces, holding his cane above his head and checking that his charges were obediently assembled behind him. Seeing Emily and the young women still on the steps, he called to them, motioning imperiously with his cane for them to hurry and catch up. The two young women tucked their arms in Emily's and, one either side of her, they went off with her, speaking to her animatedly in German and following the earnest group of pilgrims.

Emily did not resist.

The priest unlocked a pair of iron gates and exchanged a few words of instruction with the guide before leaving them. The guide led them out of the sunlight through the gates and down a broad flight of stone steps into the crypt. The pilgrims stood together, silent in the pale lamplight at the bottom of the steps, the air cold and the atmosphere heavy with the smell of damp and the earth, the mysterious subterranean fust of centuries. Emily buttoned her coat and turned her collar up.

A moment later they moved off behind the guide, his voice echoing among the vaults and leading them forward into the glimmering darkness, 'Es ist nicht genau fest tzu legen wann diese Stadt zuerst von Christen bekert vurde, doch . . .' After they had gone some way, they paused in a side chapel, their eyes raised to the courses of the vault, the point of the guide's cane tapping at the stone above his head, punctuating his lecture and directing their gaze.

Emily looked around but could not see the young women. She pulled off one of her gloves and reached and touched the glossy stone of the wall beside her. The stone was cold and smooth and as sensuous as ivory under her fingers. A moment later she looked up and realized the group had moved on, the voice of the guide growing distant and less distinct in the complicated spaces of the cathedral's antique foundations, his foreign words rendered mysterious and archaic. She held her breath and listened. When they were gone, she took her cigarettes from her bag. The flare of the match lit her face, the tears glistening on her cheeks. She rested her back against the wall and inhaled the smoke hungrily and she closed her eyes, the cigarette held to her lips, her other arm across her breasts. Small lamps glowed in recesses at intervals along the vaults. The guide's voice came and went, distinct and close one moment, then mysteriously distant. A few minutes later the booming echo of a heavy door closing passed along the vaults and died away. Emily opened her eyes and shifted her weight against the wall, lifting her heel and pressing her foot to the stone. She stood smoking the cigarette, leaning against the wall and gazing straight ahead as if she waited for someone.

When she had finished the cigarette, she dropped the butt and crushed it on the flagstones with the heel of her shoe. She turned and walked back along the vault the way they had come. After she had been walking for a while, she realized she was lost. She went back and tried to find the place where she had smoked the cigarette, but she couldn't find it. Cautiously now, and a little afraid, she ventured into the low vaulted gallery that stretched ahead of her, the velvety blackness relieved at intervals by the soft yellow glow of a lamp here and there in its niche. She paused to examine alcoves and heavy doors barred with rusty bolts that seemed as if they had not been opened for centuries. At one place she stopped to look down a flight of narrow steps that ended against a solid wall of massive stones, as if the builder had been called away in the middle of his excavations and had never returned.

Eventually she came to where a hurdle had been placed as a barrier across the vault and she knew for certain now that she had not been to this spot before. She stood with her hands on the worn timber rail of the hurdle, wondering what to do and looking into the darkness ahead. She had no idea where she was. Somewhere above her Georges and Madame Elder were offering their earnest responses to the priest. A solitary glimmer of light far down the vault ahead of her showed where there was a recess or a side chapel. She looked back the way she had come, then she lifted the skirts of her coat and her dress and climbed over the hurdle. On the other side she stood listening, as if she expected to be challenged. Then she hurried toward the light, the heels of her shoes rapping loudly on the flagstones.

When she got there, she found that the light she had seen from the hurdle was coming from a low barrel-vaulted chamber. The vault ended about five feet in at a heavy timber door. A smoky lamp burned in a niche in the rear wall beside the door, as if someone were expected. A narrow wooden bench was set against the wall. On the bench was a wicker basket lined with straw. The walls of the vault had been plastered long ago and bore traces of a decorative mural, a cursive pattern repeated in broken lines of chalky blue and russet. The place was deathly silent. The air colder than the air in the main vault, and there was a distinct and puzzling smell of fruit. Emily went into this vestibule and stood looking at the door. Then she turned aside and sat on the bench. She sat for some moments, her elbows on her knees and her chin in her hands, gazing at the deeply scored flagstones. After a few minutes she straightened and opened her overcoat. She pulled her grey skirt up around her thighs and tightened her suspenders, extending her toes and turning her foot first one way then the other, stretching her slim legs. When she had done, she kicked off her shoes and rested against the back of the bench and closed her eyes, her stockinged legs thrust out in front of her, her heels resting on her shoes.

She had been sitting there for some minutes, the cold creeping into her, when she had the feeling she was being observed. She opened her eyes and sat up and pulled her skirt down. There was a small scraping sound and the door opened.

A man stood in the doorway. His features were hidden in the deep shadow cast by the hood he wore. He had canvas gloves on his hands and a soiled apron over what appeared to be a priest's soutane. The sleeves of his soutane were pushed up above his elbows and held in place with coarse twine.

Emily slowly reached for her shoes and stood up.

The man put up a hand and swept back the hood, revealing his face in the lamplight. 'I'm sorry. I didn't mean to startle you,' he said. 'What are you doing here?'

She put a hand to the wall to steady herself and, without taking her eyes from him, she reached and slipped her shoes on. 'I lost my way,' she said, guardedly.

They stared at each other. He was her own age, or younger, with the powerful shoulders and arms of a working man. His gaze flickered down the length of her legs then returned to her face. 'No one ever comes here.'

She was blushing. 'I was just resting for a minute before finding my way back to the entrance.'

He stepped through the door and leaned and picked up the basket from the bench. 'There are many entrances to the crypt,' he said and laughed, as if he had suddenly begun to find the situation amusing. His gaze met hers steadily and he waited for her to respond to his amusement. He was shorter than Emily, his black hair clipped close to his skull like a boxer's. His voice, in contrast to his appearance, was soft, his French careful, correct, and educated. He seemed to wish to reassure her.

She examined him. 'Are you a priest or a gardener?' she asked. The smell of ripe fruit was intense now.

He looked down at his soiled apron. 'A gardener today,' he said and looked up at her. 'No, really, I'm a priest.' He shrugged. 'I don't know. Both probably, or neither. A gardener one day, a priest the next. Who knows? Are you always the same thing every day?'

She said, 'I've got to be getting back. There are people waiting for me.' She did not move to go, however, but stood her ground.

'You'll only get lost again without a guide. The crypt's a confusing place. I'll take you back. There's a quick way. I'll show it to you.' He looked at her steadily. 'I know the crypt.' He gestured at the room beyond the door and stood aside for her. 'The way's through here.' He pulled off his gloves and dropped them into the basket. He urged her, 'Come through.'

She stepped past him through the doorway and looked around. She was in a wide, deep vault lit by small lamps placed at intervals along the walls. The vault was lined to the height of a man with tiers of timber racks. Narrow gangways separated the racks from each other.

He placed the basket on the floor and closed the door. 'I'll show you,' he said. 'Come. The conditions here are ideal for the conservation of fruit.'

They stood beside each other looking at the racks. She could smell him. A tangy mixture of the soil and straw and the ripening fruit. And something of a contact with timber and physical work. It was a man's smell. The white vapour of their breaths mingled in the lamplight.

'There's coolness and a steady uniform temperature throughout the year down here.' He turned to her and smiled, his dark eyes bright in the lamplight, his deep voice hollowed by the cave of the vault. 'Combined with darkness and moderate but not excessive dryness. A dry cool cellar well away from the river. It makes an ideal fruit store. It was the bishop's own idea. He likes things to be practical and useful.'

'So you're the keeper of the bishop's fruit,' she said and laughed. 'I didn't think priests did that kind of thing. What about your sacred duties?'

'Priests are men too. We must eat. We have appetites like other men.' He turned to her. 'All duties are sacred to a priest. If everything isn't sacred, then surely nothing is.' He smiled slowly. 'Are you English?'

'No. I'm Australian,' she said.

'What's the difference?'

'I don't know. But there is one.'

He offered her his hand. 'I've never met an Australian. You seem English. I'm Bertrand Étinceler. I'm from a village near Fruges in Artois.'

She hesitated, then took his hand. 'Emily Stanton.' She used her maiden name without thinking. Through the soft kid of her glove his hand was hard. Her own hand small and enclosed by his steady grip. 'And I've never met anyone from Fruges.'

'So we're equals!' He narrowed his eyes, then looked down at their clasped hands. 'I'm sorry I startled you just now.'

She drew her hand away from his.

He said, 'I thought you were waiting for someone. And they were late. I wondered who the companion you waited for might be.'

'So you *were* watching me?'

'I was resting when I heard your voice and the clatter of your shoes. I looked through the lock. I was astonished to see you there. I thought you must have arranged a . . . well, a romantic tryst.'

She laughed shortly.

'Don't be offended.' He hesitated, then drew a breath. 'When no one came to meet you, I decided you must be waiting for me. Why else would you come here? No one ever comes here.'

'You're absurd. We've never met before. Why would I come to meet you?'

He shrugged. 'In the matter of friendships we can never know how we are to be used.'

'Now you are beginning to sound like a priest, not a gardener.' She laughed and looked at him. 'And you kept your hood on just to impress me, I suppose.'

He ran his hand through his hair. 'I forgot I had it on. I've been turning the fruit all morning. You forget what you're doing in a job like this. Hours can seem like days down here. Like months! Honestly.' He looked at her. 'This is a job for a solitary dreamer.' With a careless and casual gesture, as if they were children or intimates, he took her hand and led her into the deep shadows of the narrow way between the nearest racks.

There was a scattering of straw underfoot and a layer of straw was spread over the timber battens of the racks. Pears and apples were laid out singly on the straw, their polished skins a faint sheen of gold in the lamplight.

She did not resist but let him lead her deep into the vault until they reached a small open space at the far end of the racks. A pile of loose wheaten straw and a pitchfork rested against the wall. It was a kind of encampment. There was a three-legged stool and a small haversack. A priest's square biretta rested on the haversack. Beside it was a black stove. The window of the stove glowed red and there was a smell of kerosene. A smoky hurricane lantern hung from an iron hook in the wall, shedding a poor light over the scene.

They stood together in this small open space, their hands clasped, their shoulders touching lightly. She could hear his breathing. He reached and felt about in the straw on the rack in front of them and drew out a large pink-and-yellow peach.

'You must close your eyes,' he told her, and he held the peach behind his back.

'Why?'

'It's the rule. Just close your eyes. It won't work if your eyes are open. Close them!' he insisted.

She closed her eyes.

He held the peach under her nose. As she breathed, he breathed. 'There!' he said, exhaling his breath and gazing at her.

She opened her eyes. 'I saw an orchard in the sunlight.'

They looked at each other.

She swallowed nervously and would have taken her hand from his but he tightened his grip. He touched the peach to her other hand. 'It's for you. It is yours.'

She accepted the peach from him. Something gracious and solemn in the exchange surprising them, impressing them, and rendering them mute. In the surrounding darkness, the deeper shadows of his eyes, the sharp gleam of reflected light within his pupils.

He asked softly, 'Do you know how we ripen the fruit as it is needed?'

'How?' she asked, the firm globe of the fragrant peach enclosed in the palm of her hand between them. 'Tell me.'

'To ripen, their skins must touch. We lay each piece of fruit on the straw singly or they would all ripen together.' He reached into the straw on the rack and removed another peach and he took the peach from her hand and set the two peaches together, their rosy skins touching. 'Now they will ripen each other.'

'Is this really true?' she asked, a little breathless, a little childlike, gazing at the two peaches as if she expected them to ripen magically before her eyes.

'It's true. Fruit kept singly for too long rots before it ripens.'

'I must get back,' she said, but she did not withdraw her hand from his.

'Who is waiting for you?' He looked into her eyes.

She hesitated. 'I'm with a party of tourists. They must think by now that I'm lost. They'll be looking for me.'

'But you *are* lost. You said, I lost my way.' He waited. 'You came here as if you knew the lamp had been lit for you.'

She withdrew her hand from his. 'I must get back to my group.' Her voice was unsteady.

'You're not with a group,' he said, a touch of fierceness in his voice.

'Yes, I am.' His smell was close and warm in the chill air.

'You're alone. I can tell.'

'I came with a party of Germans. That's the truth,' she whispered helplessly.

'You came in search of something. You persisted until you reached this place. You must have climbed the barrier. Why?'

'I don't know.'

'*I* know!'

'It's no good,' she said hopelessly. 'I must get back!' He was looking up into her face, his neck thick and powerfully muscled. She reached and with the tips of her fingers she touched the vein in his neck and felt his heartbeat surge beneath her fingers.

The German guide and the priest were standing together in conversation at the top of the steps when Bertrand and Emily came up. The guide and the priest stopped talking and turned and watched the two young people emerge into the sunlight from the darkness of the crypt. Bertrand was no longer wearing his apron and the sleeves of his soutane were rolled down and buttoned at his wrists. His biretta sat squarely on his head.

On his left arm he held the wicker basket. The basket was filled with apples and pears. On top of the apples and pears were two large pink peaches.

Bertrand nodded to his brother cleric and greeted him and Emily gazed straight ahead. At the top of the steps they turned left and walked along the street beside the cathedral together toward the square, passing the north porch with its silent stone conspirators. At the corner Emily touched Bertrand's arm. He stopped and turned to her.

'You must come no farther,' she said. 'I'll find them on my own now.'

'I'm coming with you,' he said, and he would have gone on but she clutched his sleeve.

'No!'

He paused, half turned toward her.

The German guide and the priest watched them from the entrance to the crypt.

She let go of Bertrand's sleeve. 'It's my husband who's waiting for me,' she said. 'He's waiting with his mother.' She looked at him. 'I'm married.'

He stared at her. 'Then we are both married,' he said gravely, something uncompromising in his tone. His gaze went past her then and he lifted his chin. 'Is this your husband?'

Emily turned quickly.

Georges was hurrying across the square toward them through the throng of pilgrims and tourists. He lifted his hat and waved. Behind him, sitting on one of the wooden benches in the sun, his mother was in conversation with a companion. As Emily looked, they leaned toward each other and laughed.

Bertrand touched her arm. 'Come!' he urged her firmly. 'Let's go and meet him. You were lost. I've escorted you. That's all.'

Georges came up to them and looked at her keenly. 'Where on

earth have you been?' He turned to Bertrand and smiled. 'We were worried. It's my wife's first day in Chartres, Father.' He looked at Emily. 'I shouldn't have let you go off on your own.'

Emily said, 'This is Father Étinceler. My husband, Monsieur Georges Elder.'

The two men shook hands.

Bertrand was a head shorter than Georges. 'Your wife became separated from her guide in the crypt, Monsieur Elder.' He glanced at Emily. 'The crypt can be a deceiving place for pilgrims.'

'Thank you for bringing her back to us, Father,' Georges said, and he put an arm protectively around Emily's shoulders. 'Come and meet my mother. She'll want to thank you.' They walked across the open square together to the seat where Madame Elder was waiting. Georges leaned and asked Emily softly, 'Are you all right?'

'Yes,' she said tightly. 'Of course I'm all right.'

He frowned and looked at her closely, then suddenly reached toward her. She flinched, and he laughed and plucked free a length of wheat straw that was lodged between the collar of her coat and her blouse. He held it up between his thumb and forefinger. 'Straw,' he said wonderingly, then let it fall to the cobbles.

As they came up to them, Madame Elder and her companion broke off their conversation and the man stood and removed his hat.

Georges said, 'May I present my wife, Otto. This is our good friend Dr Otto Hopman, dearest. My mother's physician.'

The doctor bowed and took Emily's hand. He was a small, elderly man with exceedingly narrow shoulders and a trim hennaed mustache. 'Welcome to Chartres, my dear.' The sun was reflected in the lenses of his rimless spectacles as he inspected Emily.

'Mother,' Georges said, 'this is Father Étinceler. Father Étinceler, my mother, Madame Ross Elder. Emily got lost in the crypt,' Georges explained. 'Father Étinceler has brought her back to us.'

'And I've brought you some fruit too,' Bertrand said, and he stepped forward and set the basket of fruit on the bench beside Madame Elder.

'This is much too generous, Father,' Madame Elder exclaimed, delighted with the gift. They watched her select one of the peaches and hold it to her nose. She closed her eyes and breathed. 'Ah!' She reached and set the peach down again, placing it with care alongside its companion. 'My sister will want to thank you, Father. You must call on us.' She looked at Emily. 'And do you often come across pilgrims lost and wandering in the crypt, Father?'

'People lose their way, Madame Elder.'

They turned to Emily, waiting for her to speak.

'And have you rescued these other lost pilgrims, Father?' she asked him, her voice unsteady.

He gazed at her levelly. After a considerable pause, he said, 'Most people stay with their guide.'

Emily made a small exclamation and looked away.

Georges looked concerned. 'You'd better sit down, dearest.' He picked up the basket of fruit and made room for her beside his mother. Emily sat on the bench.

Madame Elder said, 'Will you call on us on Wednesday at four, Father, if your sacred duties permit it. We are in the lower town. Ask for the Hervieus, in the rue des Oiseaux.'

He thanked her and said he would call. He nodded to Otto Hopman and Georges and took his leave of them. With a glance at Emily he turned and they watched him walk away from them across the square toward the doors of the west front, the skirts of his soutane kicking out at each stride. He went up the steps and disappeared from their view through the central door of the royal portal. Madame Elder said admiringly, 'He has a presence.'

Otto Hopman looked at Georges. 'Your mother's kindly invited me to lunch, Georges. If you two youngsters want to step out briskly ahead of us, your mother and I will follow at our own pace.

Georges and Emily set off together, walking arm in arm down the hill away from the cathedral toward the lower town and the river. Georges hefted the weighty basket of fruit on his arm. 'Where's your *Baedecker*?'

She stopped. 'I must have put it in my bag.' She opened the small bag she carried. The *Baedecker* wasn't there.

They walked on.

'What happened?' Georges asked.

'Nothing happened.' Her voice was tight and unnatural.

'You were trembling when I touched you. You were agitated. Tell me what happened?'

'Please, Georges! Nothing *happened!*'

He thought she might be going to cry. He said no more and they walked on in silence until they had crossed the place de la Poissonnerie and were going down the steps. 'Whatever it was, I shan't be angry,' he said. 'But something upset you. I want to know what it was.'

She didn't look at him. 'It wasn't anything . . . Not really.'

'Not really? But what?'

'I was following the group. They were ahead of me. My heel went over on the steps and I fell. I was shaken. That's all. It was dark and I couldn't find my way.'

She held his gaze steadily and they stood looking at each other.

'I thought something quite awful must have happened.' He waited but she said no more. 'Did you hurt yourself?'

'No.'

They continued on and a few minutes later turned into the rue des Oiseaux.

'You're not telling me everything,' he said.

She spoke quickly. 'It was dark and unfamiliar. I felt dizzy suddenly and I slipped and fell against the stones. I could have hurt myself but I didn't. When I looked up, the others had gone on. Can we please forget about it now?'

'Your *heel* turned on the steps? Or you slipped and fell against the stones?'

'What's the difference?'

'There's no need to get angry. There's very little difference, I agree. But there *is* a difference. So which was it?'

'Are you interrogating me!'

'I just want to understand. And that is when the priest came to your assistance? But you were gone for such a long time.'

'No. The priest didn't come straightaway. I was alone for quite a while.'

'Where was the guide all this time?'

'They'd gone on. They didn't realize I wasn't still with them.'

'I just can't picture it,' he said. 'There was straw in your blouse. How did that get there?'

She ceased to answer him and they soon arrived at Aunt Juliette's house. Emily reached and knocked. A moment later Aunt Juliette opened the door and let them in.

In the passage Emily took off her coat and hat and hung them on a peg. She didn't look at Georges or Aunt Juliette. 'I'm going to lie down,' she said. She left them standing there.

Aunt Juliette and Georges watched her go up the stairs. There was the sound of a door closing.

'Our cathedral not to Emily's liking, then?' Juliette looked at the basket of fruit on his arm. Where did you get that?'

Georges gazed thoughtfully at the stairs. 'She had a dizzy spell, apparently, or something, in the crypt. She's upset. It's nothing.' He bent down and set the basket on the linoleum.

'A dizzy spell?' Juliette said with interest. 'I imagine you're hoping for a few dizzy spells, aren't you?'

He looked puzzled.

'You're such a bachelor, Georges.' She laughed.

'What does that mean?'

'It means you haven't got used to having a woman around you. Don't fret about Emily. She's all right. She's lovely, Georges.' She waited for him.

'What is it?' he asked.

'Don't you smell something! Boiled tongue and spinach! Your favorite. You didn't get boiled tongue and spinach like this in Australia.'

He kissed her on the cheek. 'You're wonderful, Aunt Juliette. Otto's joining us.'

'There's plenty for everyone. Where did you get the fruit? I haven't seen peaches like these for years.'

After lunch, Aunt Juliette set a fire in the sitting room. It filled the room with a warm smoky smell and the coals hissed and creaked companionably in the hearth. Madame Elder sat forward in her armchair, her left hand gripping its arm, Henry Adams's volume held open in front of her in her right hand. She angled the book to gain the maximum illumination on the page from the gaslight above her head and looked downward through the strong lenses of her spectacles.

Sitting opposite her, Emily gazed into the fire, her knees together and her hands folded in her lap. She was no longer wearing the blouse and skirt she had worn to the cathedral that morning but had changed into a grey wool dress and green cardigan. The buttons of the cardigan caught the firelight as she eased her buttocks on the chair.

The two women were alone.

Madame Elder's reading voice was measured and stately, her French accent ornamenting the English text with an exotic significance. *The Rose of France,'* she read, her head tilted obliquely at the page, *'shows in its centre the Virgin in her majesty, seated, crowned, holding the sceptre with her right hand, while her left supports the infant Christ-King on her knees: which shows that she, too, is acting as regent for her Son.'* On the word 'Son' she drew breath and paused.

Emily looked up from the fire. Their eyes met.

A blue lance of flame roared in the grate. There was a stillness in the house.

Madame Elder bent to the book. *'Around her, in a circle, are twelve medallions; four containing doves; four six-winged angels on Thrones; four angels of a lower order, but all symbolizing the gifts and endowments of the Queen of Heaven.'* She ceased reading, closed the book and took off her spectacles. She reached and handed the book to Emily. She did not relinquish her grip on it at once and Emily, who had reached to grasp it, was required to hold her position awkwardly.

Madame Elder's gaze was steady. 'No guide will reveal our cathedral to you as Mr Adams reveals it.' She relinquished the book and turned aside to a small round table that stood beside her chair. On the table were several framed photographs that she had taken down earlier from the mantelpiece. Madame Elder took up the first photograph and looked at it. 'Read Henry Adams. You will understand us better. Although my son has never lived here, Chartres is his spiritual home as it is mine.'

Emily held the book in her lap.

Madame Elder turned her attention once again to the framed photograph in her hand. Her gray eyes glistened moistly behind the lenses of her spectacles and her jaw worked with some determined thought, a nerve plucking at the skin of her neck. She offered the photograph and Emily reached and took it from her.

'Georges at his father's old school, the Academy in Glasgow.' Madame Elder's gaze remained on the photograph while Emily studied it. 'He was eleven.'

When Emily looked up, Madame Elder said, 'We had received news of his father's death in Panama less than a month before that was taken.' There was a determined matter-of-factness in the manner in which she revealed this crushing fact to Emily.

Emily said emptily, 'That must have been terrible.'

Madame Elder smiled and reached for the photograph.

Emily looked at it again. A sepia image of a lanky boy in school uniform standing to attention in front of a windowless brick wall. His shoulders narrow, the body of a child still, his spine curved as if against the cold. His heels together, his arms held to his sides, his expression older than his years. Even then he had possessed the bowed, preoccupied, earnest appearance of a man considering an intractable problem. She handed the photograph back to Madame Elder. 'He was tall for his age,' she said helplessly. Then added, 'And so sad.'

'Oh, you're quite mistaken,' Madame Elder was quick to contradict her. 'Georges took the news of his father's death bravely.'

'I didn't mean he wasn't brave.'

Madame Elder held the photograph in both her hands. 'This was taken in 1900, the year your Dr Bradfield announced his bridge competition to the world. The biggest bridge in the world for the newest country in the world. Glasgow was full of the news. We were certain it would be Glasgow engineers and a Glasgow firm that would build the Australian bridge. We knew that if Georges's father had been alive it was just the kind of massive project he would have been certain to have become involved in. But none of us could have imagined it would be Georges who would eventually build it. When Georges graduated, he went to work in North Africa. Then the war came and we forgot about Australia and bridges and everything else except defeating the Germans and getting them out of France.' She was silent, gazing at the photograph. 'Australia and its bridge,' she said, and she frowned at the photograph, a narrowly concentrated examination of the image of her troubling son.

She leaned and replaced the photograph on the table beside her and she looked at Emily. 'When he told me last year that he was to go to Sydney, I knew then that he must never have stopped thinking about Australia and the bridge all those years. I said to him, Is it still not built, then? That bridge? It seemed like something from another time to me. As if he was bringing the past back, the death of his father.' She sat waiting for Emily to speak, staring at her across the space of the hearthrug, her eyes bright and challenging.

The clock ticked steadily and the coals creaked and settled with small shifting sounds. Voices of people talking went past in the street outside the window. Emily turned away and looked into the fire.

'These things are never what we imagine them to be,' Madame Elder said. She grimaced and massaged her chest with the flat of her hand. 'There's always something we've not thought of.'

Emily closed her eyes.

'I believed he had forgotten all about Australia.' Madame Elder waited and when Emily said nothing she reached and picked up a large photograph in an ornate green-and-black frame from the table beside her and held it out to Emily. 'Here! His father.'

Emily opened her eyes and turned and took the photograph from Madame Elder's outstretched hand and she rested it on Henry Adams's book and looked at it. Three men stood side by side on the sloping batter of a huge earthworks. Two of the men were young and tall and faced the camera directly, one with his hands on his hips, the other with his arms folded across his chest. The third man stood between them. He was short, heavily built, and older than they. He had a bushy mustache, thick black eyebrows, and a wild mane of silvery hair. He was holding his hat in his hand and looking away from the camera toward a vast embankment. To the horizon the embankment was crowded with the figures of thousands of men at work among a forest of steam shovels. Emily looked up from the photograph directly into Madame Elder's watchful gaze.

'The excavations for the Panama Canal,' Madame Elder explained. Her delivery was flat and unemotional, as if she were reading a caption. She puckered her lips, her chin resting on her chest, and considered Emily over the top of her spectacles. 'The elderly gentleman in the middle is the great French engineer Ferdinand de Lesseps. The man on his left is his youngest son, Charles. And the man on his right is Ross Andrew Elder, the work's supervising engineer for Couvreux and Hersent, the excavation contractors. My late husband and Georges's father.'

Emily looked down at the photograph. Georges's father was the one with his hands on his hips. He had broad, heavy features, his lips thick and his nose like a boxer's. His expression, like his stance, was aggressive and faintly contemptuous. His square bowler was tipped a little over one eye. He appeared to be ready to challenge anyone who might consider taking him on.

Emily said, 'Georges looks more like you.'

'Georges is a Hervieu. He's his grandfather all over again. The year after that photograph was taken Monsieur de Lesseps and his son were bankrupt and in disgrace. My husband borrowed a great deal of money and formed his own company and in 1900 he returned to Panama and subcontracted the excavations for the Americans. That is where he died. Like thousands of others. From malaria.' She reached for the photograph. 'Georges's father left us little more than his debts.' She took off her spectacles and rubbed her eyes with her fingers. She put her hand over her eyes and rested her head against the yellowed antimacassar.

Emily watched her.

A minute went by.

Madame Elder murmured, 'It's the fire. It makes me breathless.' She sat up and searched around her chair. She located her cane and she gripped it and leaned on it and drew a heavy breath. 'Forgive me.' She got up and gestured at the other photographs that lay on the side table. 'Georges will tell you all about us. He'll be back soon.'

Emily stood and watched her leave the room, and when Madame Elder had gone she covered her face with her hands and bent forward, digging her elbows into her stomach until it hurt. 'Oh God!' she whispered, 'What have I done?'

The door opened behind her. Emily straightened and turned. Aunt Juliette came in carrying a blue ceramic bowl filled with several pieces of fruit. She set the bowl down on the round table in the centre of the room. 'There!' she said, and she stepped back to admire the effect. 'Imagine, peaches in April!' She turned to Emily. 'Unlike my sister I don't have a lot of time for the priests, my dear, but if this one's going to be giving us baskets of fruit then I say he can visit as often as he likes.'

Emily stood staring at the bowl of fruit in the center of the table, the two peaches glowing pink and golden in the gaslight.

'Father Étinceler!' Aunt Juliette said gaily, and she turned and went out and closed the door.

He lay in the bed watching her. She had opened the window and stood looking out into the night. Reflected in the river was the row of gaslights along the street opposite. In the windows of two of the houses lamps still burned. The others were dark. Through the swaying branches of the tall poplars a white half-moon rode in the sky, crossed by drifting tails of cloud. She turned from the window and took off her cardigan and she went across and hung the cardigan in the wardrobe.

He watched her undressing. When she was naked, she turned and bent and took her nightdress from the eiderdown and she raised her arms and slipped it over her head.

'Turn around,' he ordered her.

Obediently she turned her back to him. He reached from the bed and lifted her nightdress and he passed his hand over her buttocks. 'You've got bruises.'

She turned and looked down, holding the lifted nightdress and trying to see herself.

'That's it is it? From your fall?'

She stepped away and let the hem of her nightdress fall and looked at him.

'You fell on your buttocks?'

'I bruise very easily.' She reached and turned off the gas and got into bed.

They lay side by side, the moonlight bright on the floor and reflected in the wardrobe mirror. The sound of a car's engine faded into the distance, then grew louder and faded again until it was lost. The house around them was silent. They seemed to wait beside each other for a signal.

She raised herself on her elbow and leaned across him and kissed him hard on the mouth, almost as if she struck him.

They made love fiercely in the silence and afterward lay recovering, abashed by their intensity.

He reached for her hand.

A few minutes later his breathing deepened and she eased her fingers free of his. She waited another minute, then carefully got out of the bed. She went over to the washstand and poured water from the jug into the bowl and she wet the flannel and washed herself. When she had dried herself, she took her cigarettes from her bag on the dressing table and went over to the window. She lit a cigarette and stood smoking and looking out at the night, her arms folded across her breasts. The silvery moonlight ghosted across the tops of the poplars, the trees swaying back and forth in the wind like the masts of anchored ships. From a field at the edge of the town a nightbird called repeatedly, taw-*wit* . . . taw-*wit* . . . taw-*wit*.

When Emily came down in the morning, Georges had already had his breakfast. He was standing in the light by the window in the dining room reading a newspaper. Two places were set at the table and there was a smell of fresh coffee and fried bacon. He looked up at her as she came in and watched her. Neither spoke. She sat at the table and poured a cup of coffee from the jug. She stirred in sugar and cupped the cup in her hands and sipped the strong, sweet coffee. She took a piece of toast from the rack and spread it with butter and plum jam.

Georges folded his newspaper and came over and pulled out a chair and sat opposite her. 'I didn't wait for you,' he said. 'I have to go out.' He sat watching her. 'You've got grey shadows under your eyes,' he said tenderly. 'Couldn't you sleep afterward?'

She chewed the toast and looked at him and smiled.

'You're lucky. Looking tired suits you.' He watched her for a while. 'Mother's let her affairs get into a muddle. I saw her solicitor yesterday. I'll need to spend some time with him again this morning. There mightn't be another chance before we have to go back to Paris. I'm hoping for a telegram from Haine Saint-Paul at any hour now.'

'Do you think the directors will decide to tender?'

He shrugged. 'The old men of Haine Saint-Paul,' he said wonderingly. 'God knows. I hardly dare think what I'll do if they don't.' He reached across the table and took her hand. 'I'm abandoning you again.'

'I'll go for a walk,' she said. 'I enjoy walking on my own.'

'The cat who walked by herself.' He laughed.

'What do you mean?' she said quickly.

'It's a saying, isn't it? I don't know where it comes from. You'll be without your *Baedecker*. You could send your parents a postcard of the cathedral. Your mother would like that.'

'I'll follow the river. And I noticed there's a museum.'

'Yes, it's new. The Société Archéologique. It's supposed to be very good and will interest you. But I believe it's not open in the mornings. We can go together after lunch.'

She took her hand from his and reached for another piece of toast. She buttered the toast. 'Do you think Juliette would make me scrambled eggs?'

'You're hungry? That's good. Of course she will. She'd love to.'

'I'm afraid I might have offended her. I didn't eat her boiled tongue at lunch yesterday.'

'Then scrambled eggs today will make up for it.' He turned the folded newspaper, glanced at it, then put it aside on the table. He pushed back his chair and stood up.

She looked at him and waited.

'Well,' he said, 'I'd better get on, I suppose. I'll be back for lunch. We can do some sight-seeing together this afternoon. Just the two of us.'

'That would be nice.'

He leaned and kissed her and she reached and touched his hand and smiled.

After he had gone and she had finished her breakfast, Emily collected the breakfast dishes and carried them down the passage to the kitchen. She told Aunt Juliette she was going out for a walk. Aunt Juliette asked her to wait. 'I'll come with you. I've got a bit of shopping to do for tonight's dinner and we can walk as far as the bridge together.'

Aunt Juliette walked briskly, as if there were no time to lose, her long old-fashioned skirts kicking out and her shopping basket clutched to her side. Emily left her on the other side of the river and set off alone up the hill toward the cathedral.

There was a cold wind and the day was grey and threatening rain. The iron gates at the entrance to the crypt were padlocked. There was no one about. She stood looking through the bars down the steps into the darkness. It began to rain. She turned away and went in to the cathedral through the north porch. She stood looking across the nave, the vertical stone columns pale and insubstantial against the deep shadowed spaces in which lamps and candles glimmered and shadowy figures of worshippers at prayer were still, then shifted uncertainly. Above her the ghostly windows, soft and luminous in the grey gloom. There was the murmur of a guide's voice and the click and scrape of shoes on the flagstones. She turned and walked along the north aisle past the apsidal chapels and then continued on along the south aisle. She read the names of the priests above the confessionals as she passed them. His name was not among them. Two priests stood in the nave in conversation. The tight bodices of their soutanes pinched at their small waists, their skirts full and generous, flowed in black folds to sweep the flagstones as they shifted. She paused to look at them and might have asked them if they knew the whereabouts of their brother, Bertrand Étinceler, the conserver of the bishop's fruit, but they were like mysterious women from some alien and distant time before the light of day and she feared to speak his name to them in case they should know her secret at once by some uncanny means.

She went out the west front and stood beside the tall stone figures flanking the porch, and she looked into the drizzling rain that swept the deserted square. It seemed that nothing had changed for eight hundred years. The blue-and-red pennants on their poles beside the benches hung heavy and unmoving. She looked up at the porch above her. On the half-moon of the tympanum Mr Henry Adams's crowned Virgin Mother sat on her throne, sightless and serene, the Christ child between her knees featureless, defaced by the erosion of weather and the blows of unbelievers. The door behind Emily opened and a man came out. He stood holding the door for the woman who was following him and who was preoccupied with pulling on her gloves. Emily looked back into the dark interior of the cathedral. The man glanced at her and held the door, as if he thought she might wish to reenter.

'Excuse me, monsieur, can you please tell me where the priests live?' She had spoken without thinking.

The man and woman looked at each other. The man said, 'There is a seminary, mademoiselle. But if it's the cathedral priests you are referring to, then I believe they reside with the bishop in the Episcopal Palace.'

'Where is that?'

He pointed with his umbrella. 'If you turn right at the corner and go to the end of the north side of the cathedral, you will see the palace. It is the building within the iron gates.'

She thanked him and stepped out of the porch into the rain.

The man called. 'The Episcopal Palace, mademoiselle, is not open to the public.'

She stood looking in through the tall, ornate wrought-iron gates. An austere building – its architecture resembling the municipal offices of a country shire hall in Yea or Mansfield – faced empty lawns. Tall, white-painted windows divided into dozens of small panes, sectioned the stone façade symmetrically. A guard in a dark blue uniform, a sword at his belt and a cockade in his hat, observed her from his box inside the gates – the keeper of a secret world of vows and prayers and duties. There was no one else about. She turned and walked away. She had reached the lower town when a woman bumped her as she passed on the narrow footpath. Emily had stopped walking and was standing in the rain gazing before her.

Aunt Juliette came out of the baker's across the road and stood looking at Emily, then she hurried across the road and took Emily by the arm. 'Why, Emily, you're miles away, my dear!' Shall we walk home together? It'll be cosy and warm in the kitchen. You're feeling homesick, I daresay. I've never been away from Chartres for more than a few days my entire life. I can't imagine what it must be like to be on the other side of the world from your home.' She pressed Emily's arm to her side at the thought of it. 'You're young and full of curiosity, but all the same it can't be easy for you, my dear.'

That evening in the old house of the Hervieus in the rue des Oiseaux, just as the four of them were sitting down to Juliette's steaming chicken casserole, the telephone rang. When Georges came back from answering the telephone, he stood behind Emily with his hands on her shoulders and looked across at his mother.

'Well?' Madame Elder asked. 'Are you to make this bridge at last or not?'

'That was Jean-Pierre from the office,' he said. 'The directors have accepted my recommendation. They're going to tender for the bridge. We're to begin assembling the team tomorrow.'

'Tomorrow?' Emily said.

Madame Elder struggled to her feet and came around the table. Georges moved to meet her and they embraced. Her eyes shone. She put her hand to his cheek and gazed at him. 'You'll do what your father only ever dreamed of doing, my darling.'

He held his mother's hand and turned to Emily. 'We'll have to pack tonight. We'll leave for Paris first thing in the morning.'

Madame Elder was watching Emily.

'Congratulations,' Emily said, and she stood up and kissed Georges on the cheek. 'It's wonderful news.'

'If our tender's successful, you'll be home within a year, my dearest,' he said.

'I don't think I want to go home,' she said and sat down again.

'And you're going to miss your priest,' Aunt Juliette said. 'He's coming for tea tomorrow.' She ladled a large helping of chicken and gravy onto Emily's plate. 'The Australians have waited twenty-five years for their bridge, haven't they, my dear? So I'm sure they can wait a bit longer while we have our dinner. Pass Georges's plate, will you. He loves chicken casserole. I'll show you how to cook it the proper way next time you're down.'

After seeing Emily safely home to the apartment in rue Saint-Dominique the next morning, Georges left for his office. He promised he would not be late home. She stood at the window and watched him come out into the courtyard. He paused at the robinia tree and turned and looked up at the window and raised his hat to her. She blew him a kiss and withdrew and closed the window.

F O U R

After lunch, when Sophie had finished clearing up and had gone for the day, Emily got out her green morocco writing case. She opened the case and sat with it in front of her at the table by the window. She lit a cigarette and sat smoking, gazing at the yellow-and-white daisies which Sophie had arranged in a jug and left on the table. After a minute, she picked up her fountain pen and bent over the paper and began to write. She wrote in French for half a page but found she was unable to translate the flood of thoughts and emotions freely enough, so she abandoned the letter and began again in English. She would translate it into French for him when she had finished it.

The expensive paper her father had included with the writing case was stiff. It creaked as she rested the heel of her palm against it. In the apartment next door a student was haltingly playing an exercise, first the right hand, then the left hand, then both hands together. The spring sunshine shone onto the table and the sound of voices floated up from the courtyard. Emily wrote with care, the downstrokes of her elegant forward-slanting hand firm and confident. She made no smudges and she did not cross anything out, but from time to time she paused to sit and gaze out of the window. Antoine's brooch was pinned at the V of her blouse. As she wrote, her fingers strayed to the brooch and she pressed it against her breasts.

Paris, 27 April 1923

Bertrand!

It astonishes me to see your name, even though I write it myself. I returned alone to the cathedral the next day and searched for you. But it was as if you had never existed, except in the turbulence of my imagination. I stood at the gates of the Bishop's Palace in the rain and could not believe you lived and breathed behind those empty walls. I understood your answer to my question in the square in front of my husband and his mother and I believe, therefore, that I am not the first woman you have known. But you need not fear me. I shall not ask you to abandon your life for me. I must know only that I am not to be forgotten by you and that we shall see each other again. These things, however, I must know! I shall never forget you or your beautiful secret world beneath the cathedral. I will conceal nothing from you. It was revealing ourselves to each other that made lovers of us. That is how we have begun and that is how we must go on. When we touched, I thought my heart would burst. I have not known such ecstasy before, such happiness. Now I understand why the word passion serves both for the torments of sexual desire and for the sufferings of the martyrs.

Is ours not a conspiracy of truth? Without the inspiration of our truth are we not caught in this other life, this tapestry of lies? My life as a married woman. Your life as a priest. Must not such lives always be a deception? The family and the Church? How can their calm and reasoned certainties be anything but a perpetual mask of deceit? Do not imagine it is easy for me to write these things. I write with anguish, with fear, and with the horrible guilt that I have betrayed my husband. I can never again be the woman I was before I met you. That is not possible. And yet, although I am suffering from guilt and remorse, I do not care! I feel as if I have been liberated from a silence that has lasted all my life. Now at last I can speak because there is someone who will hear me. There is an astonishing satisfaction in writing this. Without you I could not speak these thoughts even to myself! I would not think them. Is there not a madness in a passion such as ours against which our reason is defenceless? Surely the truth makes outcasts of us? There is no one else in the world to whom I could write this and for whom it would make sense. We were together only for an hour and yet I feel certain I know you better than I know anyone else. Can what exists between you and me ever be denied? I will not attempt to say exactly and precisely what it is that exists between us, but I know that it cannot, and must never be, denied by us. I need to hear from you that you understand this as I do. If you do not, then I must be the loneliest person in the world. To have found my voice only to lose it again would be too cruel.

She stopped writing and lit a fresh cigarette. She had not foreseen that the act of writing to him would arouse her desire. She pushed back her chair and stood up. She started back as the pigeons flew up suddenly from the guttering below the window, their wings clapping like a spontaneous burst of applause. She leaned on the sill and watched them circle the courtyard, then alight on the cobbles in a flurry at the feet of the concierge. Madame Barbier threw handfuls of grain or breadcrumbs, which she took from her apron as if she were sowing seed in a field. When Madame Barbier had finished, she shook her apron and stood in the sunlight by the robinia tree watching the pigeons feeding and talking to them as if she were a farmer's wife talking to her poultry, her dun-colored apron swelling over her ample bosom and stomach. She looked up then at the window and her gaze met Emily's.

Emily drew back guiltily into the room.

She sat at the table and took up her fountain pen and read over what she had written. She was dismayed by her clumsy attempt to conceal herself from Madame Barbier.

> As you said to me in the street, you are as much a married man as I am a married woman. Or will you perhaps claim now that the vows of a priest are more solemn and more binding than the vows of matrimony? The unfortunate *Matris Munia* of my motherly estate, for which I can tell you I have no heart at this moment. For a priest, must not all vows made before God be equally binding? How will you reconcile yourself to me? To us, and to what we have done? But now I am writing only of my fears. How shall we continue our friendship and yet preserve the continuity of both our worlds, those ordered worlds to which we belong and which, through the circumstances of birth and the accidents of history, have made us their own? I ask myself how you and I can ever be happy again with each other, even for an hour, Bertrand, and keep our little truth safe? I can say no more. I shall wait for a letter from you.

She carefully translated the letter into French. When she had finished, she folded the two sheets and put them into an envelope. She licked the flap of the envelope and sealed it, then she bent and addressed it neatly, *Fr. Bertrand Étinceler, The Episcopal Palace, Chartres.* Before she could have any doubts about what she was doing she put on her coat and hat and walked around to the post office in the rue de Grenelle, where she had gone with Antoine to find Georges's telephone number on her first day in Paris.

She came out of the post office and returned to rue Saint-Dominique and went into the poulterer's and stood in the queue with the maids and the housewives with their big black shopping bags and creaking wicker baskets. While she waited her turn to be served she made her choice of what to cook for Georges's dinner. She bought two fillets of turkey breast, then she went to the greengrocer's and bought a bunch of vivid green spinach and a handful of new potatoes, which Juliette had told her he was particularly fond of. 'It's the last of the winter spinach, madame,' the greengrocer said, holding the bunch of spinach to his nose and sniffing. 'It's that fresh you can smell the dew on it. Here!' He would have held it to her nose but she recoiled and stepped away from him.

With her shopping bag on her arm Emily turned in under the sign and went through the covered way. In the courtyard Madame Barbier was sweeping the cobbles. She paused in her sweeping and greeted Emily. At the sight of Madame Barbier Emily realized with a shock that she had made a public fact of her secret. She stopped abruptly and stood staring at the concierge. She was seeing his name on the envelope, *Fr. Bertrand Étinceler*, in her elegant, womanly handwriting. For the young priest from Artois the arrival of a letter from a woman in Paris must surely arouse the curiosity and astonishment of everyone in the Bishop's Palace who saw it. She felt sick in her stomach at the thought of Bertrand's outraged superiors intercepting her letter and at once informing Madame Elder of its scandalous contents. Without responding to Madame Barbier's greeting, Emily turned and walked quickly out into the street again. She hurried back the way she had come.

She had only reached the florist's on the corner of rue Amelie, however, when she realized the hopelessness of her errand. The clerk at the post office behind his grille with his official blue cap and his gold braid had brought his stamp down with a bang on her letter. There would be no chance of this brisk official of the French State searching through piles of letters to find hers and meekly returning it to her. She walked slowly back along rue Saint-Dominique toward the apartment, imagining at every step Madame Elder's disgust and fury, and the dismay and humiliation of her own parents. She could not bear to think what Georges would do. She turned in at the covered way and stood staring at Madame Barbier. She felt herself to be a condemned person.

The concierge laid her broom aside against the wall and came up and put her arm around Emily's waist and took her by the hand. 'There, there, my dear. You'd better come in and sit down with old Françoise and have a cup of tea. There's never been a case so hopeless Françoise Barbier couldn't find a bit of comfort in it somewhere to ease the spirits of a fellow sufferer.'

'Thank you but I'm all right, Madame Barbier,' Emily protested shortly. She freed herself from the concierge and hurried across the courtyard and ran up the stairs. She let herself into the apartment and put her shopping on the table next to her writing case and she went into the bedroom and kicked off her shoes and lay down on the bed. She pulled a blanket over her and stared at the grey light of the late afternoon that was falling softly across the sloping ceiling. She felt ill with fear. She clutched the blanket to her throat and closed her eyes.

The sound of the telephone snatched her from sleep. The room was in darkness and for a moment she thought she was in the bedroom in Chartres. The telephone rang again. She got off the bed and groped her way into the sitting room and picked up the receiver. The shopping was still on the table by the telephone. 'Yes?' she said. 'Who is it?' Her heart was pounding sickeningly and her scalp was damp with sweat.

'It's just me, my dearest,' Georges said cheerfully. 'We're meeting Antoine and a friend for dinner. Get a pen and I'll give you the address. Ask Madame Barbier to call you a taxi. Or you can walk around to the Métro at École Militaire, if you like. There are always taxis outside the café.'

'I bought us some turkey for dinner,' she said, her left hand touching the shopping bag.

'Don't worry about that,' he said impatiently. 'Leave it on the windowsill in the kitchen. Sophie will know what to do with it.'

She asked him to wait. She set the receiver down and went over and switched on the light. Her fountain pen was lying on the English version of her letter on her open writing case. When she picked up the pen, her eye caught the words *I have not known such ecstasy before.* She put the receiver to her ear. 'I'm ready,' she said. As she was writing the address of the restaurant, she was imagining him returning while she slept and reading the letter.

'What shall I wear?' she asked him.

'Whatever you're wearing now will do,' he told her. 'We're only going to Madame Irena's. It's just a little family place.'

She hung up the telephone and stood with the English version of her letter in her hand wondering what she could do with it. She could see no obvious way of destroying it, however, so she folded it and pushed it into a side pocket of the writing case. She closed the case and fastened both its buckles firmly.

—— ·⊶ ——

The restaurant was a single gaslit room at the end of a narrow impasse off the rue de Sèvres opposite the Hôpital des Enfants Malades. Emily walked in and stood by the door and looked around. It was noisy with conversation, the atmosphere smoky and warm, rich with the smell of roasting game. There were fewer than a dozen tables. They were all occupied.

Antoine waved to her and reached across the table and touched Georges on the arm and said something to him. Georges broke off his conversation with the other man at their table and got up and came over to the door. He took her overcoat and handed it to the waiter and held her hands in his and kissed her on the lips. 'Come and meet Léon and have a glass of champagne. This is Léon's regular haunt. He's a specialist at the children's hospital across the road. Did you find something interesting to do today? You can tell me all about it later.'

Emily held Georges's hand and followed him between the tables.

'Léon Chaussegros, darling. Léon, this is my wife, Emily.'

Léon Chaussegros was a large, heavy man, his waistcoat stretched tight across his paunch. He had a full beard, dark and gingery and grey in patches. His wiry hair, which was abundant and completely grey, was combed upward into a dramatic shock above the glistening dome of his forehead. He rose from his chair with a delicate ease that was unexpected and reached across the table and clasped Emily's fingers and he bent over her hand and kissed it.

'You are astonishingly beautiful, Emily.' His voice was a throaty bass. His small black eyes glittered eagerly in the gaslight. 'I see now why my friend Antoine was lost for words to describe you.'

Emily caught Antoine's amused glance. His eyes went to the brooch at her throat. 'Thank you, Monsieur Chaussegros.' The waiter held her chair and she sat and the waiter pushed the chair in and stood and waited.

'Oh, do please call me Léon, Emily. It's enough to have to put up with being older than these two, without having to bear with ceremony.' He beckoned the waiter to his side. 'We're all having the venison stew, David.'

Georges asked the waiter to bring a bottle of champagne. 'Emily needs cheering up,' he said to the others. 'We've just been down to Chartres to see my mother.'

'Oh-h mothers-in-law!' Léon hugged himself. 'Shudder!' He took a long drink from his glass. He pressed his napkin to his moustache. 'But God bless your mother, Georges. I am deeply sad to hear she's not well. She's old, I know that. We all get old. Can she still get about? Is she cheerful?' He turned to Emily. 'Did you find your mother-in-law to be in good spirits? Does she trust in the everlasting mercy of Almighty God?' He lifted his glass to his mouth and emptied it. 'I remember the day my mother died. Who's her physician, Georges?'

'I didn't say she was dying,' Georges objected, mildly and he smiled at Emily.

'The heart can't go on beating forever, Georges.'

'Otto Hopman has looked after her for more than twenty years. He's half retired. I think he merely reassures her.'

'Merely reassures her, Georges. That's good. That's very good. The man must be a genius to reassure the aged and infirm. That is a beautiful gift and is granted to few physicians. I shall have to go and consult this half-retired Otto Hopman myself and get a little of his reassurance.'

The waiter came back almost straightaway and placed in front of each of them a deep china bowl brimming with a steaming brown stew thick with lumps of dark meat. Léon tucked his napkin into his waistcoat and began to eat hungrily at once, his fork in one hand and a large piece of bread in the other. He dipped the bread in the gravy. 'It's the reserved blood that makes this,' he said enthusiastically, his mouth full of bread and venison stew. 'You won't get blood in your gravy in those smart restaurants on the Champs-Élysées, Emily.' He leaned toward her and confided, 'Madame Irena's is the only restaurant in Paris where the game's worth eating.' He stuffed the sodden lump of bread into his mouth and washed it down with wine and he wiped his fleshy lips and his beard with his napkin.

Emily sipped her champagne. She had no appetite. She watched Georges and he turned and smiled at her and put his hand on hers. Would he understand and forgive her? she wondered. Antoine was watching her.

'You're wearing it,' he said, evidently pleased.

She touched the brooch.

'So Chartres was a great adventure? I'll call on you in a few days. Perhaps early next week?' he said. 'We'll go and do some more sight-seeing. You can tell me your Chartres story then.'

Georges said, '"Lost in the Crypt." That's the title of it.' He turned and looked at her. 'Yes, why don't you? You'll never see Paris if you wait for me. I have to recruit a team of twenty engineers and fifty draughtsmen before next week.'

'And when is this heroic project of yours to be completed, Georges?' Léon asked.

'Tenders will probably close in Australia next January.'

Léon calculated. 'Nine months!' he said. 'An appropriate period of gestation.' He pushed his empty bowl away and looked at Emily. 'So your husband is to be a great man? Your children will know their father as the man who built the biggest bridge in the world. What do you and I have to say to that, Antoine? What did our fathers do? Mine was a country doctor who drank himself peacefully to death without bothering anybody. And yours was a colonial farmer. And look at us! Not an offspring or a hope of greatness between us.' He laughed throatily and coughed into his napkin, signaling to the waiter to bring them another bottle of wine.

'Oh, there's no greatness left in steel, Léon,' Georges said a little defensively, bringing the conversation back to himself. 'Steel's been with us too long for greatness.' He was watching the older man. 'Eugène Freysinnet's reinforced concrete bridge over the Seine at Saint-Pierre-du-Vauvray. That's where you must look for greatness in the future of my profession. With Freysinnet's new material it will be engineers not architects who design our cities in the future. It was the city that once promised men freedom from their medieval masters, but for our children it will be Eugène Freysinnet's prestressed concrete roads that will offer them an escape from our cities.'

'Well, you know all about these things, Georges. But what do the rest of us know about them?' Léon airily waved his napkin at Georges. 'The biggest bridge in the world, Emily. That's all we know, isn't it? You can't argue with that. No one will be able to ignore it, will they? It'll change someone's skyline completely. You'll be a hero, Georges. There will be monuments in bronze,' he said lazily, and he reached into his pocket and took out a cigar case and held it up for her. 'May I, Emily?'

'I'll have a cigarette,' she said, and she reached for her bag.

Léon chose a cigar, trimmed it, and puffed it into life. 'And what do you believe in, Emily? Is yours to be a reinforced-concrete future too?'

The three men waited for her, watching her.

'I think I believed in everything when I was a child.'

Léon said, 'Reinforced concrete might be a bit narrow, but *everything*'s too easy. Santa Claus and God. But what about now? That's what we want to hear. Santa Claus has gone, we can be sure of that. What's left? If we're to understand our newspapers, yours is a generation of unbelievers.'

'I think I always knew secretly that the fat man with the beard coming around the moon behind his reindeer wasn't true.'

'Oh dear!' Léon laughed.

'My parents are Catholics and God was more difficult to dispose of. He didn't go all at once but sort of faded over a period of years. Until I eventually realized my prayers weren't getting through and stopped bothering about him.'

'You never look up, then, Emily, some dark nights and hope to catch just a glimpse in the firmament of the old chap?'

She laughed and drew on her cigarette. 'And what is it you believe in, Léon?'

'Oh, I believe in God, Emily. And the Devil too. They don't let me forget them. I see their work every day over the road there in the hospital with the little ones.' He looked at Georges. 'I'm afraid reinforced concrete wouldn't be much of a consolation in my line of work, Georges.' He narrowed his eyes and blew out a dense cloud of blue smoke. 'To observe a child who knows he is dying is to observe God. Courage! That is what surprises one. Confidence. One cannot believe a child will know how to die well, but he does and he confounds us and our melancholy. Every time I witness the death of a child I say a prayer. It is a kind of thanksgiving. But to whom or to what?' He smiled. 'The children know. Children possess wisdom. If they survive, of course, they soon lose their wisdom and become just like us. But you cannot be with them every day and watch them suffering and doubt their wisdom.' His cigar had gone out. He struck a match and touched it to the cigar and drew on it fiercely, glaring at the flame.

They looked at Antoine.

As if it were a game they had decided upon and it was his turn now, Antoine said, 'If God and the Devil really do exist, then religion is surely the Devil's invention.'

Léon said, 'You must tell us why, Antoine. Does your Devil have his reasons or is he senselessly malign?'

'To keep us separated from our gods. And, of course, from the unbearable wisdom of your dying children, Léon. Those are his reasons.'

'And it's not for you, is it.'

'Religion? Only the greatest souls among us are capable of surrender. The rest of us don't have the stomach for it. Surrender is for the pure and the strong. The rest of us must cling to the pathetic delusion we call freedom.'

'You see, Emily, a glass or two of Madame Irena's good Médoc and we think we're the three wise men of Greece.'

'Seven,' Antoine said. 'There were seven wise men of Greece, Léon.'

'Well, we think we're three of them,' Léon said, and he smiled at her. 'Georges has told us you achieved a brilliant first in history.' He waited for her, inviting her response. 'I think you didn't do that without the spur of ambition. Where does this ambition direct you today?'

She reached and ground the stub of her cigarette in the ashtray and looked at Georges. 'I wish you hadn't,' she said, her tone hard and accusing. 'Not a brilliant first, Léon.'

'Aren't all firsts brilliant?'

'I struggled. I'd ceased to care for what I was doing long before I read for my finals. I managed it. That's all. Nothing extraordinary was required of us. I was glad to be done with it when it was over. I haven't read a book since. Not a history book, anyway.'

Georges said. 'Emily's just being modest as usual. Her father assured me she was one . . .'

Emily turned to him and interrupted him, her tone sharp with fatigue and sudden emotion. 'What is it you are trying to insist on, Georges?'

He was startled and abashed. 'Forgive me. I was merely talking.'

'No. I'm sorry. It's me,' she said. 'I'm tired.' There were tears in her eyes.

Georges put his hand on hers and looked at the others. 'We must go. We've been travelling.' He shrugged, apologizing to his friends. 'Since January Emily and I have scarcely paused to catch our breath. I should have waited a day or two.'

They stood up and took their leave and Léon and Antoine stood with them and watched them leave.

'Till next week,' Antoine called. 'I'll telephone.'

Léon said, 'I never thought we'd see Georges married.' He resumed his seat and reached for the bottle and refilled their glasses and took a drink. He sat fondling the stem of his wineglass and smoking. He looked at Antoine.

'What are you thinking now?' Antoine asked.

'Come on, suggest something! Let's go to Le Perroquet. I need cheering up.'

'You shouldn't talk about dying children if you want to stay cheerful.'

'It's not the children. It's marriage. Marriage always makes me feel gloomy and old. Come on! Let's go and get dressed. I'll meet you there at nine.'

'What did you think of her?' Antoine asked.

'She's perfectly lovely.'

'She is. But what did you think of her?'

'That is what I thought of her. I don't possess your intensity. Emily is a lovely young woman filled with the soaring emotions and hopes that all young people are filled with. Aren't they? Were we? What more is there to say? I don't make a hobby of people. You know that. Who's going to pay for this?'

FIVE

Each morning Emily looked through the letters that Sophie brought up with her from the concierge. She dreaded to see among them a letter from the Episcopal Palace, and hoped for a reply from Bertrand. But the days went by and nothing came from Chartres. As the month of May wore on and the weather grew warmer, a silence seemed to grow around her, isolating her from the world. She longed for a woman friend with whom she could walk arm in arm under the elms along the paths of the Invalides and to whom she could confide the intimate details of her secret and her dilemma. 'There! You see, so what am I to do? I don't love him. That is not what this is. But what is it? And how am I to live with him or without him? Our mothers don't prepare us to expect such things as this in our lives. Everything else seems such a shallow pretence.' She heard herself confiding these things to her imaginary friend. And her friend was a little older than she and was very sophisticated and experienced and knew exactly what to do. She considered the whole thing, indeed, to be a great adventure and made light of it and reassured Emily that she was not unique in the possession of such an experience. They hugged each other and laughed together to think how dangerous and exciting, how filled with exquisite possibilities, their lives were.

Then she remembered that she had no such friend and was really quite alone. There were moments when she thought she would tell Sophie. She watched Sophie working at the sink and imagined herself saying, 'I can't bear it another minute!' And Sophie turning to her and staring at her, her hands covered with suds – waiting, expectant, then shocked and unbelieving to discover she was working for a woman who had betrayed her husband with a priest. Emily considered Sophie – happy, innocent, intact, perfect. Everything she appeared to be. No secret life to torment her. Loving the nuns and going to Mass every Sunday. Her life an unbroken spell of childhood. And she saw the impossibility of confessing her secret to this girl.

So Emily kept her remorse and her guilt and her confusion to herself. Georges seemed to notice nothing of her moods, her anxiety and nervousness, her sudden unaccountable and fierce anger. He might look puzzled for a moment, then continued thinking of his bridge. She observed his obsession with the bridge grow weightier and more compelling in him day by day, his gaze deeper, more inward and more preoccupied each time he returned late in the evening from a long day at the office. Antoine called for her from time to time and they went out and explored Paris together in the spring sunshine. They took the steam ferry up the river one day and sat together in the restaurant of the Jardin des Plantes and listened to the military band, watching the throng of people going by. She turned to him, resolute suddenly with a need to speak, and she said, 'I'm not happy, Antoine.' She waited for him, dreading he would ask her why she was not happy, prepared to confess and to face the awful consequences rather than go on in silence another day. But he lifted his shoulders and drew on his cigarette and smiled and did not ask her. She was glad and relieved and grateful to him for not asking. 'The longer I'm in Paris, the more a foreigner I know myself to be here,' she said, as if this might be the cause of her unhappiness. He was kind and made it plain to her that he knew something was amiss in her life. But he did not press her for an explanation and she did not feel called upon to provide him with one. His own private life remained a kind of mystery to her and he never invited her to his apartment. She loved him for his unassuming friendship, for his gentle permission to be unhappy and to keep her secret, and she wondered what he must think of her when he learned at last that she had betrayed his old friend. One day she touched his brooch and asked him, 'Why did you give it to me, Antoine?' And he looked at the brooch and replied, 'Sometimes I forget I no longer have it and out of long habit I slip my hand into my coat pocket and discover it is not there. At once I think of you and I remember you your first day in Paris. I see a young woman sitting opposite me in the Brasserie Équivoque, intimidated by her future and in need of a precious talisman to give her courage. Then I remember the impulse that made me give it to you and in my mind I give it to you again.'

Sometimes she hated Bertrand and bitterly resented her memory of him. But he persisted in her thoughts – as if he kept a secret for her that she could not take possession of without him. And when she made love to Georges in the dark of their bedroom late at night, it was not Georges she saw in her mind but Bertrand in the shadowy crypt beneath the cathedral of Chartres, strong and passionate and filled with desire for her. And when she moaned in Georges's arms it was not with ecstasy but was with anguish. After such a night, Georges looked at her uncertainly in the morning, as if he saw in her a stranger. He inquired with care, 'Are you happy, my dearest?' She laughed at his timidity. 'Of course I'm happy. What a silly question. Why wouldn't I be happy? I have everything any woman could possibly want. Do I seem unhappy to you?' He was quick to accept her empty reassurance. 'No, of course you don't. But I worry sometimes that I'm neglecting you.' She kissed him on the cheek and handed him his briefcase and saw him to the door. 'Well, and so you are, my darling.' As if this were the effortless banter of a bored young wife. If Georges was not entirely convinced by this performance, he was either too preoccupied or too afraid to challenge it. It soon became a habit between them to reassure each other that all was well in their garden of love. I love you, one said to the other, and the other replied,

And I love you. And between them the silence grew very deep, until it was so established in the pattern of their days and nights that only news of some great and momentous event could hope to breach it.

Georges had usually left for work long before Sophie arrived with the post at ten. This morning, however, he was late getting away. He had returned home from the office after midnight and had slept in. When Sophie arrived, he was still sitting at the table by the window in the sunshine finishing the breakfast of eggs and bacon that Emily had cooked for him.

Emily was sitting opposite him nursing a cup of coffee and smoking a cigarette. She was watching him eat. She was wearing her belted dressing gown over her nightdress. She jumped at the sound of the doorbell.

He looked at her. 'Time would pass more quickly for you if you had something to do,' he said. 'Are you going to let her in?'

She stubbed her cigarette. 'I don't want time to pass quickly,' she said, and she got up from the table and went across and opened the door.

'Good morning, madame.' Sophie greeted her cheerfully and came in. She was carrying a shopping bag. She went across to the table and reached into the bag and took out a bundle of letters and placed them beside Georges's plate. 'Good morning, Monsieur Elder. Here's your post.' She took her bag into the kitchen.

Emily closed the door and stood with her back to it, anxiously watching him go through the letters.

He glanced at each in turn then passed it across to the other side of his plate, as if he were dealing cards. He paused in his dealing and held one up. 'For you,' he said.

Emily stepped across quickly and took the letter from his hand. She looked at it. It was from her mother.

'And another.'

She reached and took the second letter from him, her fingers touching his. The envelope was identical. It was from her father.

Georges turned his attention to a brown official envelope. The envelope bore a crest. 'Something from Chartres at last,' he said and wiped his knife on his napkin and slipped the point into the fold of the envelope and slit it.

She stood beside him staring down at the sheet of crested stationery in his hand. In black ornate lettering beneath the crest she read the words, **Episcopal Palace**. The first student for the day next door began at that moment to play scales at a furious speed, then stopped abruptly, as if the piano teacher had lifted her bodily away from the keyboard. There was a small intense silence . . .

Georges flourished the letter. 'From Mother's lawyer.'

She snatched it from his hand and stared at it. The words Episcopal Palace were not on it. She handed it back to him.

Georges stared at her. 'What was that for?'

Sophie was standing at the kitchen door, watching them, waiting to speak.

Emily turned and crossed the room and went into the bedroom and closed the door.

Sophie approached the table and asked in a subdued voice, 'Would you like more coffee, monsieur?'

He put his hand on his cup. 'No thanks, Sophie.' He sat staring at the bedroom door, then he turned to the letter from his mother's lawyer.

Sophie collected the breakfast dishes from the table and carried them into the kitchen. She put the dishes on the blue-and-white tiles by the sink and took her apron from the hook behind the door, tying it round her waist. She pushed up the sleeves of her dress and filled the tin basin with hot water from the gas heater. As she worked she sang, her voice clear and childish and content. The sun shone through the narrow window and glistened on the soap bubbles on the backs of her hands as she lifted the plates and bowls from the steaming water and set them to drain on the wet tiles.

Georges finished looking through his mail, then got up and put on his brown trilby hat and overcoat and picked up his briefcase. He looked at the closed bedroom door, set the briefcase on the floor, and went over and knocked, opening the door without waiting for an invitation to enter. Emily was standing at the window. The gilded Dôme of the Invalides shone in the blue sky behind the roofs of the buildings. She turned and looked at him. She held the unopened letters from her parents in her hand.

He went up to her and put his arms around her and held her against him. 'You've been crying. What is it?'

'It's nothing.'

He held her away and looked at her and he reached and wiped a tear from her cheek. 'Tell me what's troubling you,' he said tenderly.

She smiled and took his hand and kissed it. 'It's just a mood.'

He looked at the letters in her hand. 'You're homesick, I know. I used to get terribly homesick at school. There's nothing to be done. It will pass and then you'll wonder you ever felt it.'

'You'll be late,' she said.

He hugged her. 'I love you, darling.'

'And I love you,' she said.

They went together to the front door and she kissed him and watched him go down the stairs. He turned and blew her a kiss.

She went back into the bedroom and closed the door and sat on the edge of the bed. She took her diary from her writing case and counted the days. Leaning over the diary, she carefully counted the days again, ticking each day with her fountain pen until she was certain she had not miscounted. She sat staring at her reflection in the cheval glass. She was four days overdue. It was as if a little gate had been stealthily sealed inside her without her knowledge. Her bleeding had never been late before. The pigeons on the roof outside the bedroom window cooed confidingly to each other.

'I'm having a baby,' she said aloud to her reflection. She unbuttoned her nightdress and slipped her hand inside and felt her breasts. A shiver passed through her at the touch of her cold fingers and goose bumps rose on her breasts. For the past week her breasts had been feeling tender and bruised. If she really thought about it, without panic but steadily, even now it was possible to convince herself that this tenderness was normal. Or that it was, at least, no more than a slight exaggeration of normal. But she could not reason away the four lapsed days. She looked down at the open page of her diary, her finger on the last day of May. The lateness of her bleeding was a fact. Her last bleeding had ended the week they went down to Chartres. Slowly she got off the bed, the chilling certainty of her condition a stillness deep inside her, unarguable, the steady centre of her dismay.

She took off her dressing gown and her nightdress and put on her underclothes. She carefully rolled on her stockings and went to the wardrobe and took out the blue summer dress. She could hear the clattering in the courtyard of the milkman with his cans. She frowned. It did not seem possible that life was to go on normally. When she had finished dressing, she went into the kitchen and told Sophie she could do the bedroom now. She made a fresh pot of coffee. Sophie had washed the window and scoured the pots and scrubbed the walls and the tiles and everything shone bright and coppery and clean in the morning light.

Emily took her coffee into the sitting room and put it down on the table by the window. She fetched her writing case and her parents' letters from the bedroom and sat reading them. She read right through her mother's letter without registering a word of it. She closed her eyes. She could see her mother so clearly – she could smell her mother – it was as if she were in the room with her. She opened her eyes and leaned and looked down into the courtyard. The woman was sitting under the robinia tree, her basket of sewing at her feet. The concierge was talking to her. Their voices and sudden laughter floated up through the open window.

She read the letter from her father. It ended, 'Your mother, God bless her, forbids me write to you of such things, but I cannot abandon the hope, dear girl, that the artistic and intellectual society you will enjoy with Georges and his people in Paris will stir in you, in some form that is consistent with your new status, a desire, which I firmly believe you once cherished, for an intellectual dimension to your life. Forgive my persistence and I am heartily sorry if I anger you. But I believe you were once ambitious, and I cannot imagine that anyone who has once been subject to such a hope for themselves can ever quite relinquish it. If ambition is not simply the empty desire for preferment possessed by every fool, then is it not at its truest and most private an eagerness and an energy for life? Doesn't such a vision haunt you still, just a little? Tell me I am wrong if you can honestly do so and I shall never speak to you of it again. I want only your happiness. I confess, my darling, that I have always feared I would fail as a father to you, and by some means that was beyond me. Tell me this is not so. I have reached an age when I need to be reassured. Don't refer to this in your letter to your mother. It will only upset her.'

She sat looking at her father's letter. She could see him at his desk writing it, the blue hydrangeas outside his study window wilting in the heat. She lifted a hand and wiped away the tears that ran down her cheeks. It was true. Once upon a time, years ago, when she was a child, she had believed herself to be accompanied by her father on a grand adventure. The university had then seemed the pinnacle of their hopes. When she did well in her first year, they rejoiced together, celebrating her success as if it must endure for them, a decisive monument in their lives forever. Then she lost interest in her studies. It must have been suddenly, overnight almost, that the exotic words lost their magic and the temple of Belus and Zaleukus the Lokrian ceased to be tantalizing and mysterious and became merely difficult, their understanding a futile exercise in pedantry, the stories of the Greek wars endless, detailed, and wearying. She saw suddenly there was no familiar landscape she could attach to the objects of her study, no experience or emotion to render it compelling. The remote past mysteriously ceased to belong to her, and on that day it lost its power to beguile . . .

She folded her parents' letters and put them back into the envelopes. She was afraid now that through the presence of the child in her body her own past would find a power to reclaim her before she had a chance to set herself upon a direction of her own. She tried to push the letters into the side pocket of her writing case, then realized it was the pages of the English version of her letter to Bertrand that were obstructing them. She pulled out her letter to Bertrand and opened it and began to read. 'I returned alone to the cathedral the next day and searched for you,' she read. 'But it was as if you had never existed, except in the turbulence of my own imagination.' Her emotions of that day came flooding back to her and she felt herself to be in Chartres again, vulnerable and betrayed by her passion. 'I shall never forget you or your beautiful secret world beneath the cathedral. I will conceal nothing from you . . . When we touched, I thought my heart would burst.' She could endure no more of it. She looked up from the letter. Sophie was standing with her bag in her hand and her coat on looking at her. 'What is it, Sophie?' she asked sharply. 'What do you want? Why have you put your coat on?'

'I said I've finished, madame. If there's nothing else,' Sophie repeated herself quietly, and she hesitated. 'I was wondering, would you mind if I leave early? I'll make it up, I promise.' Her dark eyes were shining with some expectation, her lips soft and pink against the pallor of her cheeks. 'The carnival's setting up on the Invalides.'

'Yes, I saw them there yesterday.' Emily stared at her. 'You are beautiful, Sophie,' she said, surprised. 'Are you meeting a friend?'

Sophie looked down at her hands clasping the handles of her black shopping bag. 'He spoke to me on the Métro, madame.' She looked up quickly. 'You won't say anything to Madame Barbier, will you?'

'Of course not. Your secret is safe with me, Sophie. Off you go. It's a beautiful day for the carnival.'

Sophie thanked her and left.

Emily called a warning, 'Be careful, Sophie!' She sat listening to the clatter of Sophie's hurrying heels on the stairs. She unscrewed the cap of her fountain pen and smoothed a fresh sheet of paper on the blotter in front of her and began to write. This time she wrote in French. 'Father Bertrand Étinceler, After the brief joy we knew together, your silence is terrible. It is a punishment I do not deserve. I can hear in your silence only weakness and betrayal. You deny the truth with it.' She sat staring at the paper for a moment, then continued. It was her intention to tell him she was having a baby. But she could not bring herself to write it. She could not, she decided, extort a reply from him. When she had filled almost two pages, she realized she was writing to herself and was never going to send this angry letter to him. She folded it and put it away with the other letter and fastened the buckles of the writing case.

She sat smoking and gazing out the window. She could not imagine ever again feeling for him the hot stream of lust that had brought them together in the strange, compelling silence of the crypt that day. And yet . . . to recollect that lust now made her cheeks grow warm and her heart beat a little faster. 'Damn you!' she said, and she crushed her cigarette between the outspread wings of the swan. 'Damn you! Damn you! Damn you!' She pressed the palm of her hand to her belly. 'It's not fair! I'm not going to be me anymore!'

— PART TWO —

PERPETUA'S MEDALLION

ONE

It was early on a fine summer morning toward the end of July and Emily was standing in the kitchen by the gas ring putting rashers of streaky bacon into the frying pan for Georges's breakfast when she fainted. Georges was in the bedroom dressing. He heard the thud of her head striking the edge of the porcelain sink and felt the tiny tremor in the floor beneath his feet. He stood gazing at his reflection in the cheval glass, his hands paused in the delicate action of inserting the smooth gold nugget of his front collar stud into the starched collar. When no further sound came from the kitchen, he stepped to the door, his collar still unfastened. 'What was that?' he called. 'Are you all right?' He went across the sitting room and into the kitchen.

Emily was lying on the floor. Her eyes were half open, her amber pupils sightless. Her cheeks were gray and drained of blood and the hollow of her throat glistened with a fine patina of sweat.

There was not enough space between the sink and the wall for Georges to pick her up. He bent and gripped her under the arms and dragged her to the door. She groaned and stirred as he lifted her into his arms and carried her into the bedroom. He laid her gently on the bed.

She opened her eyes and looked at him. 'I fainted,' she said, apologetic, her voice small and held inside her. 'I've never fainted before.' She closed her eyes and put a hand to her forehead. A swelling with a large blue bruise was forming above her eye on the left side of her forehead.

He sat on the side of the bed and leaned over her and stroked her cheek. Her skin was cold and clammy to his touch and her breath was sour. 'When I saw you lying on the kitchen floor I thought you were dead.' His voice was shocked and filled with concern.

She smiled weakly and reached for his hand. 'It's nothing. I'll be all right in a minute.'

'I'm calling Léon.' He went to get off the bed.

She reached for his hand, restraining him. 'I'm all right.'

He freed his hand from her grip. 'Lie still. I'm going to call Léon.' He got off the bed and went into the sitting room and asked the exchange to connect him. While he waited he leaned and looked into the bedroom. Emily had her eyes closed. One hand rested on her stomach and the other covered her forehead. Blue smoke drifted past Georges's head and was sucked out the window. He turned. Smoke was pouring from the kitchen door. He put down the telephone and hurried into the kitchen and turned off the gas. He put the blackened, smoking pan with the shrivelled pieces of bacon into the sink and turned on the tap. The boiling fat hissed and spat and sent up a cloud of steam. He turned off the tap and went back into the sitting room and picked up the telephone.

After he had spoken to Léon, Georges went in and sat with Emily. 'He'll be here soon.' He held her hand and watched her, his gaze troubled and anxious. His collar was sticking out sideways from his neck like a white bone. It waved back and forth every time he moved. He reached round with his free hand and undid the back stud. He put the collar on the table beside the bed.

Emily murmured, 'I'm sorry.' She groaned and sat up, clutching at the bedclothes, her other hand clamped over her mouth. 'Quick!' she gasped. 'Get something!'

Georges scrambled up and dashed out and fetched the tin basin from the kitchen. She snatched it from him and leaned over it. Her thin shoulders hunched under her dressing gown. She groaned and vomited a stream of thin green bile. 'Oh God!' she said several times. She panted, then retched again, gagging helplessly over the bowl. 'Nothing's coming up!' she wailed.

He held her and rubbed her back and tried to reassure her.

When Léon arrived, he asked Georges to wait in the sitting room. Léon went into the bedroom and closed the door. He put his bag on the bed and stood looking at Emily. There was a smell of vomit. He blew out his cheeks and pressed the flat of his hand to his chest. 'God!' he said. He was out of breath from climbing the stairs. 'Georges tells me you did this once before?'

She shook her head. Tears glistened in the corners of her eyes. 'No,' she said. 'I've never fainted.'

'A dizzy spell, Georges said. When you were visiting Chartres. Is that right or not?'

'Oh, that,' she said.

He sat on the bed beside her and examined the bruise on her forehead. He took a bottle of iodine from his bag and opened it and took a pinch of cotton wool from a roll. He dabbed the iodine on the bruise. 'This isn't going to look pretty tomorrow.' He put the iodine away and took his watch from his waistcoat pocket. He opened the face of the watch and held her wrist, counting her pulse. When he had finished he laid her hand on the covers. 'Your periods have been regular, I daresay.'

'I haven't had my period since April.' She closed her eyes and turned her head aside. Her hands on the blanket were closed into fists.

He searched in his bag. 'In my experience it's not so very unusual for a young woman such as yourself to feel a certain initial . . . well, reluctance at the idea of motherhood.' He straightened and looked at her. 'I gather you've not mentioned this to Georges, then?'

She shook her head.

'If you'll forgive me, that does seem a little strange. Georges is, I believe, eager to have a family. Is that not so?'

She watched him, her lips pressed together. 'I suppose I am definitely pregnant, then?'

'Three months? It seems very likely, wouldn't you say?'

'Can there be no other explanation?'

He stood considering her, his big belly pushing against his black waistcoat. 'Would you like me to find another explanation, my dear? Most other explanations aren't preferable to being pregnant, unfortunately, I can assure you.' He caressed his beard thoughtfully. 'No, I think you're having a baby. And I think you know you're having a baby and have known it for some time. Why you've chosen not to share this joyful news with your husband is your own affair. Unless, of course, there is a medical reason for keeping it to yourself. Have you been having alarming symptoms of another kind? If you have, I think you'd better tell me at once. I shall need to examine you anyway to be certain you are pregnant.'

'There's nothing else,' she said miserably.

He asked her to move aside and he covered her with the blanket. 'Please lift your knees and place your feet apart.' He went to the end of the bed and raised the blanket and examined her. 'Have you noticed any change in your breasts?

'They've been feeling bruised and tender for some time.'

He stood up. 'You can lower your knees, Emily.' He stood looking at her. 'You're going to be a mother. Your baby is due some time in January. I'm not sure from your manner, however, whether you wish to be congratulated on this event or not.'

She covered her face with her hands. 'I don't know what I feel.'

He stood looking at her. 'You'd better get into bed now. You've probably got a mild concussion. I suggest you stay in bed for a few days. I don't wish to add to your distress at this moment, but I have to tell you that everything is not quite as it should be. More of that, however, another time.'

'What do you mean?'

He picked up his bag and stood with his hand on the doorknob. 'Georges will speak to you about it. I'll call in and see you again tomorrow. I'll bring you an iron tonic.' He hesitated. 'I'm going to tell Georges that you are three months pregnant, Emily. Can I assume that this news will not displease him?'

She looked at him. 'Why should it displease him?'

'Very well, then. I'll see you tomorrow.' He went out and closed the door, murmuring to himself, 'Oh the merriment of marriage.'

Georges turned from the window.

Léon went up to him and offered his hand. 'Congratulations, Georges. You're going to be a father. Emily's three months pregnant. Your child is due in January.'

Georges took his hand and held it and looked into his eyes. 'Thank God! I hoped it would be this. She's all right, then?'

'It'll be a race, won't it, to see who's to astonish the world first, you with your bridge or your wife with your child. You did tell us your design must be finished by January, didn't you?' He held onto Georges's hand when Georges would have let go. 'A brief word, Georges, before you rush in and see her.' He drew Georges over to the window. He pulled out a chair from the table and sat down.

Georges stood waiting to hear him.

'My opinion is Emily's suffering from a mild form of anaemia. Chlorosis is the name we give it, to distinguish it from pernicious anaemia, which, as you may know, is almost always fatal. But in this case there's no need to be alarmed. I assure you, Emily's anaemia is not of the pernicious variety. But all the same we shall need to reverse it at once or the course of her pregnancy may be affected.'

Georges stared at him. 'You can cure this type of anaemia all right, then? How did she get it?'

'We don't know its causes. It only occurs in young women, either soon after they begin menstruating or when they first fall pregnant.' He looked up at Georges. 'Its onset is frequently associated with extreme nervous fatigue.'

Georges stared at him. 'Nervous fatigue? But Emily can't be fatigued. She's had nothing to do for months except read and write letters and enjoy Paris.'

Léon lifted his shoulders. 'Boredom may induce fatigue, Georges. Not the fatigue of the manual labourer, to be sure, but a kind of exhaustion of the spirit. Emily's had a lot to adjust to these last few months. Her life has changed completely. She has left everything familiar behind her. Friends and family and the happy places of her childhood. She's a sensitive young woman. You've been busy. You are a preoccupied man, Georges. Who would deny that? Your wife needs calm and rest. She needs the reassurance of a certain affinity if her system is to reverse this anaemic condition. Care, a good diet, and peace of mind . . . That's the essence, I believe, in her case, if this pregnancy is to run its course smoothly for you both. Could she go and stay with your mother in Chartres, perhaps? Your Aunt Juliette sounds to be just the person to care for her.'

'Somehow I don't think that would do,' Georges said.

Léon lit a cigarette and examined the glowing end. 'When she's recovered from the effects of her fall, let's say in a week or two, I strongly recommend a holiday somewhere. Somewhere quiet and completely out of the way. For a month.' He looked up at Georges. 'Think of something. Can you manage a month away from this business of yours?'

'If I don't have the tender ready by November, I won't get the Australian bridge.'

Léon watched him. 'It's as definite as that, is it?'

'I can't take a month off, Léon. It's not possible. I might as well resign and hand the tender over to someone else as take a month off.'

Léon lifted his shoulders in a gesture of resignation and blew smoke at the ceiling. 'Well, then, your problem is one I can't help you with, Georges. I'm sorry. You'd better go in and see your wife, before you do anything else. She may be feeling just a little lonely and afraid at this moment.'

Georges looked at him quickly. 'That's an odd thing to say.'

'It may surprise you to know how many young women weep when they hear they are to become a mother for the first time. You are a layman, Georges. You see nothing of this. But motherhood, believe me, is more of a dangerous mystery than we care to admit. Many women who survive the birth are defeated by it subsequently. Emily needs a woman at her side just now. Someone to whom she can confide her fears and with whom she can find the reassurance she needs. Is there no one? Your own mother won't do, you tell me. And her mother is on the other side of the world. So that's that. Think, Georges! It is important, I assure you. Can you not find a friend for your wife?'

Georges said, 'Antoine's going out to Sidi bou-Saïd in a week or two with people from the American Museum of Natural History who he's hoping to get some money out of.' He put his hand on the bedroom door and stood looking at his feet. 'Sidi bou-Saïd would be perfect for her.' He looked at Léon. 'Sonia would take care of her wonderfully.'

'And Sophie could look after you here. Are you sure there's no one closer than Tunisia? A desperate remedy, it seems to me. But it might be your answer, I suppose.' Léon stood up. 'I have to get back to the hospital.' He stubbed out his cigarette and picked up his bag. 'I'll call in again in the morning. If there's any change in her condition, give me a call at the hospital. I'll be there until late. If she develops a slight fever as the evening comes on, don't be alarmed. Wrap her up well and keep her warm. It's best to sweat these things out.' He held up his hand, palm toward Georges, like a traffic policeman stopping oncoming traffic. 'I'll let myself out.' He coughed heavily and breathed and murmured, 'Oh for a month or two in Sidi bou!' He opened the door and went out.

Georges went in to the bedroom. Emily opened her eyes and they looked at each other. He knelt beside the bed and took her gently in his arms. 'My darling,' he said. He cradled her head against his chest. 'My precious darling!'

The following morning Madame Barbier came up with the two old men. The old men lugged the trunks and suitcases and Georges's drawing board out of the little room and carried them downstairs to be stored. They laughed and cracked jokes and shouted at each other. Sophie brought her bag from Belleville and Madame Barbier provided her with bedding. By lunchtime Sophie had settled herself and her few belongings comfortably into the little room. Antoine came in the afternoon. He brought an enormous bunch of rose pink Aster daisies.

Emily was sitting up with a pile of pillows behind her. She was wearing a crocheted shawl around her shoulders and had done her hair and put on her makeup. She held out both her hands to him, 'Oh Antoine, how lovely to see you.'

He made a face at the purple bruise that covered half her forehead. He set the bunch of daisies on the covers. 'From our florist's on the corner of rue Amelie.' He took both her hands in his and leaned and lightly touched his cool lips to the bruise. 'So you're to come to Paradise with me sooner than we thought?'

'I'm so excited. I can't wait. I know it will be wonderful. The thought of it has cured me. I'm longing to get away from Paris.'

He sat on the bed. 'It's very hot there at this time of the year. It can be stiflingly humid.'

'I love the heat.' She laughed. 'Don't worry. Melbourne's fiercely hot in summer. It couldn't possibly be hotter than Melbourne in January.'

'The house remains cool . . . except when there's a southerly.' He reached into his pocket and took out a snapshot. 'I brought a photograph.'

They leaned together and looked. A sullen, ill-tempered-looking man with a heavy black moustache and shaved head leaned on a large American motor car in the foreground of the photograph, his well-muscled arms folded across his chest. The car was parked in a narrow gravelled square surrounded by high walls. A tall, heavily timbered door stood open behind the car. A full-figured woman of about thirty stood in the doorway. She was barefoot and was wearing a flowered dress. She smiled and held a child in her arms so that it faced the camera. An old man dressed in a long robe looked on at the scene from the steps behind the woman − as if he did not expect his own image to be included in the photograph. Antoine put his finger on the woman with the child. 'Sonia. This was taken a few years ago. Her daughter is a little girl now. Sonia will take care of you.' He shifted his finger to the old man. 'Mounir, Sonia's father. Mounir was my nanny. He will tell you our stories. His people were once farmers and he still grows his vegetables and his herbs among the ruins. He is proud of his garden and will wish to show it to you.' He touched the sullen man with the large mustache. 'Nabil. Sonia's husband. He is very proud of the car. He bullies us all. But he thinks I'll leave him the house one day, so he looks after it while I'm away as if it were his own.' He turned to her. 'Nabil will pretend to resent you. That is his way. But you will have very little to do with him. They are like my family, these people. We have our disagreements.' He turned to her and smiled. 'It will give me great pleasure, Emily, to welcome you to my home. Georges visited me there often in the past. So it will be a kind of homecoming for you. You will not feel yourself to be a stranger there. You will see.'

She held the photograph and looked into it. 'I feel already that I know them.'

TWO

❦

Together with the American archaeologists, Drs Olive and Kenneth Kallen, and their young protégé, Merrill Miles, Antoine and Emily left Marseilles on the *Gibel Sarsar* on the morning of the 16th of August. The seventeen-hundred-ton mail-and-passenger steamer of the C.G.T. French Line was on her regular weekly run to the port of Tunis. The ship was fully equipped with all the latest luxuries for the lucrative North African tourist trade; but the last Magic of Islam motor tour, so tantalizingly advertized in the brochures of Thomas Cook and Son, had gone out at the end of May and the North African season was closed. It was now high summer and the Maghrib was considered too hot for the comfort of Europeans. There were less than a dozen passengers on the *Gibel Sarsar* besides Antoine and Emily and the three archaeologists.

It was after one in the morning the first day out when the Americans at last retired to their cabins. They had all talked a lot and drunk a good deal of wine with dinner and Emily was too excited to sleep. She suggested to Antoine that they take a turn around the deck before going to their separate cabins.

They went up together and leaned on the rail and smoked a last cigarette. A fragrant night wind blew softly into their faces. They watched the dark, lazy swell slide past the hull of the ship below them.

Antoine pointed into the night with his cigarette. 'Sardinia,' he said.

Emily looked where he pointed but could see only the hollow sky, pale and gilded by an enormous yellow summer moon. Then she made out the luminous crests of a mountain range. 'I see it!' she exclaimed.

'The island of giants,' Antoine said.

They were silent, gazing across the sea toward the far-off island, mysterious and unreachable in the moonlight, as if it really were the enchanted home of an antique tribe of giants. 'You almost expect to hear them bellowing at us,' she said.

Antoine eased his weight off the rail and turned to her. There were dark shadows under his eyes and his cheeks were hollow and gaunt in the deck lights. 'It's been a very long day.' He smiled. 'It's been delightful. I'm sorry. I'm quite exhausted. I shall have to turn in.'

She took his arm and walked him along the rail toward the stern. 'Let's stay just another minute,' she said. She was restless and agitated. She had been in a nervous mood all evening, her emotions boiling just beneath the surface. She had heard herself bray with laughter over dinner and had seen Antoine look at her with concern. When they reached the stern rail, she looked down into the churning wake, white and foaming in the moonlight. She was reminded of when she had torn the pages out of her journal and thrown them into the southern ocean behind the *Kairos*. Had watched with relief as they fell away into the sea and disappeared from sight. She had felt then as if she were ridding herself of the last onerous duty of childhood, unable to keep a journal for her father. Now she was to be bound to the duties of motherhood. She drew a sharp breath and turned to Antoine.

He looked at her quickly, uneasy with her mood.

'Give me a cigarette!' She held out her hand.

He took out his slim silver cigarette case and held it for her. 'They're very strong,' he said, cautioning her. 'And . . . perfumed. Be careful. This is not just tobacco, you know. I mix a little something with it.'

'How exciting,' she said, and she took one of the cigarettes and placed it between her lips. 'I need something strong.'

He held the match for her but it blew out. They went into the lee of the deck housing and bent down beside the hatch cover. The flare of the match lit their features. She stood and drew on the cigarette, inhaling the perfumed smoke, the end glowing fiercely in the wind.

He watched her smoking, his dark eyes glinting in the deck lights. 'Not so fast! You must smoke slowly, Emily. You must savour it.'

She looked at him and laughed. 'You're not going to turn into my nanny, are you, Antoine?'

He shrugged and looked pained. He turned away and leaned on the rail.

There was only the rushing of the wind in the rigging and the steady thump-thump of the propeller. Where Emily's back touched the rail a tremor was transmitted into her side, as if it were some vital organ inside *her* that trembled, communicating its nervous, febrile message of uncertainty. 'You're so infuriatingly tentative sometimes,' she said, hearing herself saying these words and wishing she were not saying them but unable to halt the bolting images in her mind. 'When I told you on the train, you said nothing. You just looked out the window as if I'd said it was a fine day. But don't you think it strange, Antoine? That I feel nothing for this child?' Her tone was aggressive, demanding a response from him.

His expression was closed, carefully neutral, pained. 'Feelings take time,' he said.

'No! Georges felt something at once.' She waited for him to look at her. 'Georges didn't say anything, but he wept.'

Antoine examined his cigarette, then flicked it over the side and watched it arc into the wake. 'Georges has always wanted to be a father.' He looked at her. 'I'm going to bed.'

'There's no one I can speak to about this! I'm so . . .' She was caught by a sudden rush of emotion, her throat tightening and her eyes filling with tears. 'I don't know what to do!'

He put his hand on her arm. 'It's late,' he said, concerned, gentle. 'You drank too much at dinner.' He took the cigarette from between her fingers and threw it over the side. 'I was watching you. You were excited. You drank far too quickly. We can talk about these things in the morning. You're tired. You are overwrought. I've been charged with caring for you . . . not with . . .'

She pulled away. She was breathing hard, as if she had been running. 'I met a priest in Chartres, Antoine . . . when we were visiting Georges's mother.'

'I don't wish to hear this. I'm going below. You can stay if you want to.'

'Live a fairy tale for us!' she shouted. 'That's what you said!'

'I shall never forget saying it.'

'Live a passionate fairy story for us . . .' Her voice broke and she turned and faced the sea. The mountains of Sardinia were dropping behind, disappearing into the night. She looked at the mountains. 'This child may not be Georges's.' She didn't turn to face him. Suddenly she was sober. An intense calm followed her confession. Relief and regret. A kind of sorrow. 'I shouldn't be telling you this. I'm sorry. It is unfair of me. The priest may be the father of my child.' She turned around. 'I don't know! I just don't know. It's impossible for me to say.'

He said nothing.

'You'll abandon me now. I can see you will. I deserve it. It was a kind of madness, Antoine.' Then with sudden frustration at his silence, 'Don't men like you feel these things?'

He looked at her. 'Men like me? What do you know of men like me?'

'I'm sorry.' She reached for his hand but he avoided her. 'I'd no right to say that.'

'If you valued our friendship, you wouldn't burden it with this sad little confession of your commonplace dalliance with a priest. There's nothing astonishing in what you're telling me, Emily. Except that you are telling it to me.'

'It wasn't a dalliance,' she objected.

'There are women who recognize the value of reticence. If you think everything can be true and honest and open between friends, you're a fool.' He walked off a couple of paces into the lee of the deck housing and sat on the bench and lifted the collar of his coat and tried to light another cigarette. He cursed viciously when a third match blew out.

She went over and stood looking down at him, the wind swirling around the stern of the ship and whipping the light material of her dress. 'Don't abandon me, Antoine.'

'Before you decide to jump over the side and drown yourself, as you most certainly should do,' he said, sarcastic, angry, 'perhaps you'd light this cigarette for me. I don't seem able to manage it.' He held out the matches and his cigarette case to her.

She took them from him and sat beside him. 'I've been a fool,' she said miserably.

'Yes,' he said. 'You have. Please light the cigarette!' He watched as she sat on the bench against the hatchway and bent out of the wind.

When she had lit the cigarette, she handed it to him.

'Thank you.' He took the cigarette from her and sat smoking. 'You are cruel, Emily. Immoral. Foolish. And naïve. So this is your secret? You have surprised me, hurt me. Yes, and you have disappointed me.' He drew on the cigarette and examined her, his head on one side, one hand holding back the drift of hair that would have swept across his face.

'Can you forgive me?' she said miserably.

'No!' he said. 'Oh no. Forgiveness is the hardest thing. Forgiveness is harder even than celibacy. So I believe. You can be sure that whenever you and I have a little disagreement in the future, I shall revive this moment of my enmity and will dwell upon it. You really must try not to give in to the temptation to suffer for your sins, Emily. It is such a burden for your friends.'

She rested her head against his shoulder. 'I deserve your contempt. I feel a kind of contempt for myself . . . I no longer know what I believe or what I think. I wrote him a letter. I've had no reply. No message from him. Nothing! I don't love him. It isn't that. But I can't get him out of my thoughts. I'm haunted by him and by what happened that day.' She was silent for a moment. 'I know I shall have to go back and see him again before I will be able to forget him. I feel so angry and betrayed. I've been longing to tell someone. I've almost confessed to Georges several times.'

'That would have been even more foolish than this is.'

'But Georges's preoccupation has prevented me. When I look into his eyes, that is what I see . . . The bridge. As if he's having this endless conversation with himself. Reviewing the details of his design. It's always there, passing in front of him. He's like a man staring into the sea counting the waves as they go by, as if everything will be lost if he looks away even for a second and misses one. There's never a moment when he's free of it. I don't believe he sees *me* anymore. Only when he came into the bedroom after Léon told him I was pregnant. Then . . . When he wept. His gaze cleared for a moment and he saw me.'

'Georges sees you, Emily, have no doubt of that. He faces life openly. For Georges life is a problem which he believes he will solve through diligence, perseverence, and attention to detail. That is how he will succeed. Life will yield its little store of treasure to him if he works hard enough. That is Georges's belief. That is his vision. He is an honest man. A constant man. I know him. If I may say so, I know him better than you do. When he rebuilt our bridges in Tunisia, he shared his life with the men who worked for him. He was one of the very few Europeans who were truly respected by the Arabs. They recognized his stoicism in the face of God's implacable will, and they understood him and gave him their respect. Georges loves you and sees you. But he will not say anything about his feelings. He would not know how to do that. Instead he wept for you. And for the child. And for himself.' He turned to her. 'He revealed everything of himself to you. Georges has not wept for anyone else.'

The ship rose and fell, sliding over the Mediterranean swell.

'You mustn't hate me, Antoine. I couldn't bear it.'

'Oh, I don't hate you. Don't ask me why but I feel almost responsible for you.' He didn't look at her. 'The fairy tale has ended, then. Sooner than we expected.'

'In time I'll recover and be myself again.'

'Oh no!' he said quickly. 'We don't recover. Now you're deceiving *yourself*. We get over the loss we've suffered. We learn to live with it. But we never recover our innocence. Our betrayal remains a sweet wound with us for the rest of our days. We did not know what we were doing. But the betrayal makes hypocrites of us all the same. We never believe again . . . not with that pure clarity of belief. After our first passion has failed us, there remains a shadow at the edge of all our desires . . . And our search becomes in part a search for revenge. In the arms of our new lovers we remember our innocence with a regret that is exquisite and inconsolable and we cry out in anguish for our loss. That is what we fall in love with, time and again. There's something tragic in all our loves after the first. We tell ourselves it is merely our lust that we seek to assuage. But after the first, it's the delicious poignancy of regret that we can't resist.' He fell silent.

'It isn't like that for me. I shall never fall in love again. Not in that way.'

He laughed, delighted. 'Oh, how lovely to hear you say it, my dear! *I shall never fall in love again!* And with what conviction! When we're no longer in the first derangement of our passion, we no longer understand the person passion made of us and we judge that person harshly and see them as a weak and foolish stranger whose actions we wish to forget and to deny. We are ashamed of ourselves . . . ashamed to have abandoned so easily the autonomy of our mind . . . and we no longer believe in the emotion that made us do it.' He laughed, enjoying himself now. 'But before too long we're astonished by the beauty of someone else . . . and we abandon our sanity once again without giving it a second thought. Who cares for sanity at such a moment?' He turned to her and said cheerily, 'By the way, you're not thinking of martyring yourself for the sake of this priest, I trust?'

'What do you mean?'

'I mean the sensible and necessary thing now is to guard your secret. You mustn't give in to the need to talk about your infidelities every time you have a glass or two of wine. It would destroy Georges utterly if he should ever come to hear of this. And if you speak of it, then sooner or later he *will* hear of it. If Madame Elder were to hear so much as a whisper, she would be remorseless in the defense of her family's honor. She would make certain you and your priest were ruined. France isn't Australia. In France the law is the partner of the family, not of friends. We are alone, Emily.' He seemed cheered by this thought. 'It's friendship, and only friendship, that acknowledges our aloneness. All our other relationships deny it. Religion, the law, and the family, they are the three giants in league against friendship's liberties. They all offer us the same consolation. You are not alone, they say. And if we fail to conceal our secret life from them, they destroy us. To survive against them we must learn to play the hypocrite. Georges's mother fears me and dislikes me. When I used to stay with them in Chartres, she expected a scandal every minute I was there. She was convinced I was seducing half the young men at the seminary.' He laughed and said blithely, 'And, of course, she was right. I was. You and I have more in common than you think. Our friendship will not fail so easily.' He stood up and offered her his arm. 'I envy you your brilliant success in Chartres, my dear. My own efforts never met with anything like it.'

'That isn't how it was for me,' she said. She stood up and took his arm and they walked to the companionway.

'Oh, we all imagine our passions are unique.'

'You misunderstand me.'

He squeezed her arm. 'You and I will have to be careful, shan't we, not to fall out of friendship. Secrets of this kind are a dangerous currency to deal in.' When they reached the head of the companionway, he paused and looked toward the bow of the ship. 'Smell the air, Emily! Take your first breath of freedom! North Africa!' He pointed forward. 'It's off there in the dark up ahead. We've left the giants behind us for the time being.'

'I meant I'm not alone, Antoine, not that my passions are unique.'

He looked at her quickly.

She shrugged. 'I'm sorry. But it can't be that simple for me. You seem to forget, I'm having a baby.'

A touch on her shoulder woke her from a deep and dreamless sleep. Emily opened her eyes. She heard the clink of a china cup against its saucer. She turned over and sat up. Her mouth was dry and there was a pain behind her eyes. The stewardess placed the tray on the table beside her. 'Your tea, Madame Elder,' the woman said softly. 'We docked an hour ago, madame. Monsieur Carpeaux thought you might wish to be woken. He is waiting for you in the saloon.' The woman went out and quietly closed the door.

The *Gibel Sarsar*'s engines were silent. The ship was motionless. The air coming through the louvres smelled of dry land, coalsmoke, and the exhaust fumes of lorries. Emily pulled back the covers and knelt on the bunk. She looked out through the porthole. Sunlight was reflected off white harborside buildings. In the distance waves of heat rose from the city. The wharf was busy, crowded with men and lorries and piles of luggage and goods.

She washed and put on a white cotton dress with a shirt front and an open neck and she packed her things and left her bags ready for the porter. Antoine was waiting for her at their table in the dining saloon. He was alone. He was reading a newspaper. He looked up when she came in and folded the paper and put it aside.

He stood and pulled out a chair for her and held it while she sat. 'I had to send someone to rouse you.'

'Yes,' she said nervously, glancing at him quickly. 'I feel as if I've been asleep for a week.'

They were silent while the waiter set a china bowl of boiled eggs and a rack of toast on the table.

When the waiter had gone, Antoine said, 'Who's to say you weren't asleep for a year?' He offered her the bowl of eggs. 'Let's say, at any rate, that you've woken this morning to a new beginning.'

'If only that were true.'

'Make it true. Let it be your story. It's as true as anything else.'

'I don't know what came over me last night,' she said. She tapped the eggshell with the side of her spoon.

'A new beginning, my dear,' he said. He sounded just a little impatient. 'France is behind us. Everything here will enchant you.' He took her spoon from her hand and topped her egg neatly. He handed the spoon back to her. 'The Kallens left with Merrill an hour ago for their hotel in La Marsa. They were on deck to watch the dawn.' He chuckled. 'They asked me to pass on their apologies to you for not staying to say good-bye. You'll see them in a day or two.' He looked at her. 'That's if you feel up to a little excursion.'

'I'm not ill, Antoine.'

'Léon gave me my instructions.'

'Easier to take than the foul-tasting tonic he gave me.'

When she had finished her breakfast, they left the ship together. The day was hot. The air was still and humid and there was a strong smell of gasoline and exhaust fumes.

As they were going down the gangway, Emily turned to Antoine, 'It's just like a summer day in Melbourne.'

'Good! Good! The first thing Europeans do the instant they get off the boat here in summer is to complain bitterly about the heat and to ask when it will get cooler. I tell them nothing is going to change for them and that it is certain to get hotter.'

She pointed. 'There's Nabil!' She had recognized the hard, fit-looking man in his early thirties leaning against a black American motor car and surveying the scene in exactly the attitude of the man in the photograph Antoine had shown her.

On the dock Nabil greeted Antoine casually in Arabic, as if they had last seen each other that morning instead of nearly six months earlier. His manner was relaxed and faintly insolent, as if he wished them to understand that their arrival had interrupted his routine. Antoine introduced him to Emily. Nabil glanced at her and murmured something, then continued supervising the men who were loading the luggage onto a rack on the roof of the car. She watched him. He was without a hat. His thick black hair was shorn close to his scalp and he had the brooding, preoccupied look of a fighter. He repeatedly touched his hand to his exquisitely groomed mustache, stroking it with his thumb and forefinger in a gesture that was delicate and private. He was dressed in a white shirt and baggy fawn slacks. The cuffs of his slacks had frayed where they swept the dust. On his feet he wore leather sandals. And under the sandals bright green woollen socks.

Once he was behind the wheel of the car Nabil became animated. He drove at high speed through the morning traffic, leaving the streets behind them filled with a swirl of dust, sounding the horn continuously and gesticulating and shouting threats through the window at the other traffic and pedestrians who were slow to get out of his way.

They soon left the city behind. They drove along a straight dusty road across a plain which sloped gently on their left toward some low hills. The harvest was underway and men and women in bright clothes moved slowly across the fields of wheat and barley. Between the fields were patches of grey-green cactus. Slim Australian gum trees lined the road and there was the smell of eucalyptus in the air. Clusters of stuccoed buildings, surrounded by orchards and the thin dun shadows of olive groves, were scattered among the open fields. Small children, their clothes the color of the dust, herded goats on the grassy verges of the road. Over to the right of the road the still waters of a lake shimmered under the blue sky. Merchant steamers in the distance made their way in slow convoy toward Tunis and the port, the smoke from their funnels forming trails to the horizon.

Emily turned to Antoine. 'You were right,' she said. 'It is as if I was here long ago and must remember it.'

After a quarter of an hour's drive they entered a narrow street at the base of a steep hill. Nabil slowed down and changed into low gear. There was no other motor traffic and no pedestrians. Three boys minding a solitary goat that cropped the meagre weeds and desiccated tufts of grass sprouting from the base of the walls squatted in the shade. They watched the car pass without interest.

Nabil was silent, intent on his driving.

Antoine leaned across the seat and touched Emily's arm. 'Sidi bou-Saïd,' he said, as if the name of the village must hold a secret magic for her too.

The car ground slowly up the hill along narrow cobbled streets that twisted and turned between high stone-and-stuccoed walls. The walls of the houses were deeply weather stained and in disrepair, the loose pebbles of their interior fill exposed and dangerously undermined in places, like the banks of a gully that is periodically washed by sudden floods. The ground-floor windows were covered by unpainted timber shutters and the windows of the upper floors protected by elaborate iron grilles or fretted wooden balconies projecting over the silent streets. It was as if the population had fled, or had turned their backs on the world to conceal themselves within the fortified walls of their decaying houses. Dense clusters of purple bougainvillea and heavy tangles of creamy pink jasmine hung over the walls above the street, forming flowering verandahs that threw patches of deep shade onto the streets.

Close to the summit of the hill Nabil stopped the car then reversed it, manoeuvring carefully around a tight corner. Once around the corner he pulled up before a tall timber door set in the end wall of a small piazza. Emily realized it was the place of the photograph. The door had once been painted yellow. Its timbers were studded with hundreds of iron nails whose square heads formed elaborate arabesques. A cascade of flowering jasmine drooped heavily over the wall beside the door on the left. On the right of the piazza, a feature not included in Antoine's snapshot, there grew a stately redgum. The tree's pale roots melted over the ancient stones of the roadway, its clusters of grey leaves hanging down like veils of mourning lace.

Emily turned to him. 'Oh, Antoine!' she exclaimed. 'You didn't tell me about the tree.'

He took her hand and helped her from the car. 'I didn't think to mention it,' he said. 'There have been gum trees here ever since I can remember.'

When Emily stepped from the car the heat struck her and the ground heaved beneath her feet. She clutched Antoine's sleeve to steady herself.

He held her, a look of concern in his eyes.

'It's the motion of the ship,' she said. 'It's still with me. I felt it when we were on the wharf. Don't you feel it?' But it was the blazing sunlight in the small enclosed square, the heat and the sickly sweet perfume of the jasmine, thick and cloying on her palate. Her stomach lurched and a wave of dizziness passed over her. 'I hope my body's not going to let me down,' she murmured.

The timber door opened and a woman in a sleeveless flowered dress stepped out into the square. The woman's hair was bound up in a loose bandeau made of the same flowered material as her dress. She came across to the car and embraced Antoine, hugging him to her strongly, then kissing him on both cheeks and speaking to him rapidly in French. She held him off, her hands gripping his arms, and examined him. The skin of her bare arms was brown and velvety. She laughed and kissed Antoine again and turned to Emily. She embraced Emily without waiting for Antoine to introduce her.

In Sonia's embrace Emily caught the smell of cinnamon.

A girl of seven or eight stood by the open door looking out shyly at the scene in the square.

'I'm Sonia,' the woman said. She spoke in French with a strong accent. She stood and faced Antoine, holding Emily's hand with the easy familiarity of a schoolgirl holding the hand of a new friend. 'I'll take Emily to her room.'

'Welcome to my home, Emily,' Antoine said. He raised his hand and gave a little wave and turned to assist Nabil with the luggage.

Sonia led Emily through the timber door and up a broad flight of shallow stone steps. The steps were shaded on either side by scarlet hibiscus and pink oleanders and the deep green of old lime trees. The little girl ran up the steps ahead of them and disappeared through a tall arched entryway surrounded by blue-and-orange tiles. Sonia paused on the terrace and turned to the view. A light breeze blew steadily into their faces. Far below them across the white roofs of the village the Gulf of Tunis was a silvery expanse under the sunlight, the red-and-black hulls of the steamers small and remote. From a garden nearby a rooster crowed.

Sonia turned and drew Emily into the house. 'Come!' she said.

They entered a spacious hall. The light was blue, subdued and cool, the unfurnished spaces filled with glowing shadows. An old man sat on a wooden bench set against the wall beneath a shuttered window. He was drinking tea from a glass. When he saw them come in, he rested the glass on the flat arm of the bench beside him and stood and waited for them. He was wearing the traditional men's flowing jibbah and on his head a red woollen toque with a tassel. Sonia spoke to him in Arabic and he offered his hand to Emily and murmured a greeting. His drooping moustache and thin beard were white against his darkly wrinkled skin. His gaze was curious and kindly. He smiled and nodded and said something in Arabic.

'This is my father, Mounir Ziadeh,' Sonia said. 'He bids you welcome. He is reluctant to speak French to you. He thinks you are highly educated and will despise him for his poor pronunciation.' She laughed and touched her father's hand and led Emily across the hall. 'Don't worry, he will speak to you later. He is shy.' There was no sign of the girl. Tall timber doors painted blue and elaborately tiled archways led off the hallway into other regions of the house. They went through a low arch in the right-hand wall and ascended a short flight of stone steps. At the top of the steps they emerged into a courtyard. The courtyard was overlooked on all sides by blue-painted shuttered windows and doors and was open to the sky. At its centre there was a fountain fashioned from shallow fluted copper disks. Water trickled from a bronze spout at the top of the fountain and fell from one disk to the next, filling the courtyard with a musical tinkling, as if someone idled upon a xylophone. Four slim columns, one at each corner of the courtyard, supported a timber structure, which held aloft the python limbs of an ancient wisteria vine, its leaves casting the courtyard into a dappled shade. At the foot of each column clay amphoras filled with scarlet-and-green geraniums were set in iron casques. Fallen wisteria leaves lay about on the gray marble flagstones.

They crossed the courtyard and Sonia opened the last door on the right. She stood aside to let Emily go in.

Emily went into the room. It was a large, airy, barrel-vaulted chamber. The upper portions of the whitewashed walls, and the curving arch of the vault itself, were intricately patterned with plaster arabesque work, so that the effect was of a white lace canopy. An antique wooden bed stood against the left wall. The bed was canopied with a crimson-and-gold baldachin. On the floor beside the bed was a vine-green-and-indigo Persian rug, its colours rich, dark, and heavy against the lustreless gray of the marble floor. A carved and gilded French armoire of the previous century stood against the wall opposite the bed. Between the bed and the window at the far end of the room were two painted wooden armchairs, with red-and-green cushions, and between them a low circular table on a rug. On the table was a vase filled with scarlet hibiscus blooms. Next to the deep recess of the window there was a blue-painted table and a hard-back chair. On the table were three books and an electric lamp with a glass shade in the shape of a bell.

'It's beautiful,' Emily said.

Sonia took her hand and led her across the room and through a deep archway in the wall opposite the bed. 'This is your bathroom,' she said. A thin ray of sunlight from a circular aperture high up in the side of the pointed roof penetrated the gloom and formed a bright ellipse on the curved hollow of an enormous marble bath. From the side of the bath a bronze tap in the shape of a lion's head drooled a skein of vivid green down the pale marble. A scrubbed wooden bench and a long table stood against the wall. 'I'll prepare you a bath when you've settled in,' Sonia said.

They went back into the bedroom. 'I'll come back in an hour and prepare your bath.' Sonia kissed Emily's cheek and left her.

Emily went to the far end of the room and looked out of the window. The window was wide and deep, with a stone recess large enough to climb into comfortably. It was guarded by heavy shutters and an iron grille. The iron grille swelled out at the bottom like the belly of a pregnant woman, announcing to the world that this was a woman's room. A jasmine vine grew between the bars of the grille, its fluted blooms perfuming the air with their cloying sweetness. Below the window there was a wild garden, the gravel paths bordered by hedges of rosemary. A dry area of grass in the centre of the garden was flanked on one side by enormous oleander and hibiscus bushes. Beyond the garden a stone parapet overlooked the flat roofs of the village. Dogs lay stretched out in patches of shade on the roofs. In the distance the waters of the gulf shimmered, metallic, flat, and still in the sunlight. On the far side of the gulf the smoky blue shapes of hills rose softly into the canopy of heat.

Emily turned back into the room and picked up one of the books from the blue-painted table. It was an old French/Arabic dictionary. The other two books were volumes one and three of a French history of the Abbasid caliphate of the ninth century.

There was a heavy knock on the door. She went over and opened it. Nabil carried her suitcases and hatbox into the room and put them down just inside the door. She thanked him but he left without a word or a glance, as if he were a conspirator sworn to silence. Emily watched him cross the courtyard, then closed the door. She was unpacking a few minutes later when there was a gentle tap-tap at the door. It was the little girl. The girl held out a letter and said in halting French, as if she had memorized the phrase only a moment before, 'A letter for you, Madame Elder.' Before Emily could thank her she ran off across the courtyard and disappeared through the archway at the far end.

Emily opened the envelope. It was a note of welcome from Dr Raymond Domela of the Hôpital Civil in Tunis. He wrote that he had received a cable from his esteemed colleague, Dr Léon Chaussegros, of the Hôpital des Enfants Malades in Paris, and looked forward to the pleasure of calling on her in a day or two. After she had unpacked and put her clothes away in the enormous wardrobe, Emily lay on the bed. From beyond the door, in the courtyard, the fountain tinkled, and from the village street below the garden parapet the voices of children at play drifted into the room.

Sonia woke her, her hand on Emily's arm, her voice close, on her warm breath the sweet smell of nutmeg. 'I've prepared your bath,' she said, and she took Emily's hand and waited for her to get up. Sonia was barefoot. She led Emily across the room and into the cool shadows of the bathroom and she tucked her skirt up around her thighs and began to unbutton Emily's dress. Steam rose through the thin beam of sunlight from buckets of hot water set beside the marble bath.

Emily pushed Sonia's hands away and laughed. 'It's all right,' she protested. 'I'll undress myself.'

But Sonia only smiled and persisted, their fingers and their bodies brushing against each other as together they unfastened her clothes. Emily laughed with the strangeness of it, then ceased to resist. When she was naked, she sat on the scrubbed bench while Sonia leaned over her and ladled warm water, bending and lathering her body with fragrant black soap, her strong fingers delicately exploring. Emily sat with her eyes closed, submitting to the intimate pleasure of the other woman's touch. After the bath, she lay on her side on the bench while Sonia massaged her. Sonia's strong fingers worked along her body from her neck to her ankles, beads of sweat standing on Sonia's forehead as she laboured, her bare arms and thighs glistening in the bronze light as she moved in and out of the solitary beam of sunlight, her expression preoccupied – as if she performed upon the newcomer a secret purifying ritual of initiation.

After dinner that first evening, Antoine and Emily walked in the wild garden beneath her window. He pointed to the shadow of the bellying grille. 'Now you see where you are.'

She sat on the stone parapet and Antoine stood beside her, the endless sky purple over the gulf, the murmuring voices of the village men gathered for the evening at little tables outside the café in the street below them. Antoine leaned over the parapet and looked. 'Nabil is there. That is where he holds his court every evening and becomes the proud man of his own world.' The night was warm and still, the air fragrant with cinnamon and the spicy smells of cooking and the sweet perfume of jasmine and rosemary. In a courtyard somewhere nearby a woman was singing.

Antoine held the match to Emily's cigarette and she inhaled. 'How can you bear to leave this place and go back to Paris?' she asked him.

'If I lived here all the time, I'd be afraid I might begin to see this world as Nabil sees it.'

'Is he so unhappy, then? How can a man be unhappy in this house with Sonia for his wife?'

'It's not unhappiness that troubles Nabil. Nabil is like all rich men. He is discontent. As life has given him so much, including Mounir's beautiful and talented daughter, he believes he should have more. My presence in this house puts an end to his illusion that he is the real master here.' He laughed. 'Nabil and I understand each other. In Paris I'm as discontented as he is when I'm here. And when I'm here I'm as content as he is when I'm in Paris. Without my visits, Nabil would soon find a reason to be discontented all the time. So my existence provides him with a cause both for his discontent and for his happiness. But really his discontent is in his soul and he was born with it. You'll see how he glowers at me and treats me with a faint insolence, as if I am his older brother and not the employer who pays his wages.' He fell silent, gazing down into the street, where the light from the café spread a soft radiance across the cobbles and the tables and the dark figures of the men. 'Nabil is my captive lion. We understand the dangers of our arrangement.'

When Antoine laughed, she looked at him and saw his eyes glitter in the faint light reflected from the street, as if he enjoyed the prospect of the danger he spoke of.

'Nabil wishes to destroy everything that is not familiar to him. To rid his world of strangers, that is what Nabil would like to do. But he is inarticulate and cannot voice his complaint to the world. So he broods on it and awaits his time.' Antoine reached for her hand. 'Come, I'll show you Mounir's garden.' They went along a gravel path until they came to an enclosed ruin. There were the remains of low walls and the broken arch of a doorway. The roof and all else were gone. 'It's supposed to have been the home of a Spanish pirate in the sixteenth century. It was destroyed by the Turks.' They went through the broken arch and stood looking at neat rows of vegetables, dark shapes on the paler ground between the stones of the foundations. Antoine said, 'Nabil finds in my presence an affront to his pride. But really he would be just as discontented no matter what his fortune was and whether I existed or not.' He looked at her. 'Mounir's nature is otherwise. Mounir has never possessed Nabil's riches. He has seen his youth and his birthright taken from him. Yet Mounir is content. And if I were to propose this paradox to him, he would smile and ask me, Well, then, what is to be done? And I would have no answer for him.'

She took his arm and they left the garden among the ruin and walked back to the house. Before she left him in the hallway to go to her room Antoine said, 'Do you think you'll feel up to an excursion in the morning? Nabil will bring the car and we'll meet the Kallens and Merrill at the Roman amphitheatre in Carthage. It's not far. Just at the base of the hill. If you'd prefer, you can stay here and rest during the heat of the day and we can go sight-seeing together later, when it's cool.'

'No,' she said. 'I want to come with you.'

He considered her. 'You may find it interesting. You'll meet Père Delattre. He's a legend here. He's the head of the White Fathers. The order has been excavating the remains of Carthage for fifty years. They're always short of funds. It's taken me two years to set up this meeting for him with the Kallens. He has grand plans. If the Kallens can be convinced to speak on his behalf with the trustees of the American Museum of Natural History, it could mean an end to his dependence on the uncertain results of my fund-raising in Paris.'

She watched him, half-listening to his lengthy explanation. When he had finished, she said, 'I've never seen you look so serious. It alters you.'

He appeared uncomfortable with her remark, as if he feared he might have exposed to her an aspect of himself he would rather have kept concealed. 'In what way?' he asked shortly, his concern still with the meeting in the amphitheatre in the morning.

While speaking of Père Delattre's plans and the difficulty of raising funds he had lost for a moment his youthful manner and had become old for her, his magic lost, no longer the impish demon mediating familiarly between the secret life and the public world. She touched his arm and leaned and kissed his cheek. 'Goodnight, Antoine.'

He stood and watched her go.

She went up the steps and crossed the courtyard. When she looked back, the hallway was empty. She went into her room and closed the door. She sat at the blue-painted table by the window and opened her writing case. By the light of the bell-shaded lamp she began a letter to Georges. She soon tired, however, and pushed the writing case away. She switched off the light and sat in the dark listening to the sounds of the summer night. The bath and the massage at Sonia's hands had left her feeling drowsy and relaxed, almost indeed as if she were drugged, and she found it too great an effort to imagine Georges and the apartment in rue Saint-Dominique. Paris seemed remote. More remote even than Melbourne tonight. Someone was strumming the strings of a lute in the café below the terrace. She got up and climbed into the window recess and rested her back against the wall. She looked out through the bars at the night and the stars. A man sang a melancholy ballad to the accompaniment of the lute. The warm night air through the open shutters was perfumed and sweet.

The group had paused in the centre of the ruined ellipse of the great amphitheatre. The air around them wobbled with the heat radiating off the white blocks of fallen masonry. Antoine and Merrill Miles stood shoulder to shoulder. Emily was between Antoine and the husband-and-wife team of Drs Olive and Kenneth Kallen. They were attending closely to the tall figure of Père Delattre, the scholarly head of the Catholic order of White Fathers. Delattre was elaborating the layout of the excavations, the silver ferrule of his cane describing circles and squares and straight lines in the dust. He was a tall, powerfully built man in his eighties. He had a patriarchal white beard and was dressed in the traditional Arab jibbah, which fell in long white folds from his broad shoulders to his sandals. On his head he wore a scarlet sheshia with a black tassel. Listening to him, Emily decided he could not be merely a showman but must be genuinely passionate in his desire to unveil the antique past of the ruins that lay scattered all around them.

She was eager to continue listening to what he was telling them, but her back was aching and her ankles were beginning to swell in the heat. She looked around for something to rest against and moved a little apart from the group, to where she could ease her lower back against a slab of upended masonry. Antoine looked at her quickly but she waved her hand to him, motioning to him to stay where he was. 'I'm all right,' she mouthed at him and smiled to reassure him.

She raised her hand to the brim of her white straw hat, shading her eyes from the glare and looking over toward the road and the nearby hill of Sidi bou-Saïd beyond. Beside the road Delattre's and Antoine's cars were parked nose to nose in the thin shade of an olive tree. Emily wondered if she might make her way back to the car and rest for a while. Both front doors of Antoine's car were open to catch the faint drift of air. Nabil was lying across the front seats, his cheek resting on his hands, which were clasped under his head in the universal position of supplication or prayer. He appeared to be sleeping. There was no sign of Delattre's driver. Twenty yards or so beyond the cars a young girl was squatting beside the road attending half a dozen freckle-faced sheep that were cropping the desiccated herbage along the verge. Every now and then one of the sheep jerked its head up and stood rigidly staring at the cars. Then it stamped one of its front feet and went back to cropping the bleached grass. The road was empty of traffic except for two workmen in dungarees and cloth caps on bicycles. As the workmen rode past, they looked at the cars and called to each other in Italian. When the workmen were a hundred yards down the road, an open French army truck carrying twenty or thirty soldiers with bayonets fixed and helmets glinting in the sunlight roared past at high speed, scattering the sheep and raising a cloud of dust. As the dust from the truck washed over the car, Nabil raised his head and gazed after it. He turned and looked toward the arena then. His gaze lingered on Emily before he lay down again, settling himself into his former position. The sheep bleated to each other and trotted back to the verge and began nibbling the grass again. The child had not moved. Emily decided not to return to the car.

She noticed now that Antoine was not listening to Père Delattre but was conversing quietly with the young man, Merrill Miles, who looked at him shyly and laughed and touched his arm then looked away. Olive Kallen, who was taller than her husband, was the only one still paying close attention to Delattre. She was pointing to his diagram in the dust and asking him something. Kenneth Kallen was gouging around in the bowl of his pipe with a penknife.

Delattre's voice carried to Emily, 'With God's help, Dr Kallen, we shall raise the necessary funds to expose the entire subterranean workings of the amphitheatre.' He raised his cane and made a sweeping gesture with it, taking in the entire ellipse of the arena. 'And with that, madame, we shall reveal the glorious history of the Christian martyrs who met their deaths in this desolate place.' He reached and peeled off his dark glasses and leaned at Olive Kallen, as if he challenged her to refute him. 'The blood of the martyrs is the foundation of our Holy Mother Church. That is how important our work here is. Come!' he commanded her and pointed ahead with his cane. He led the way, either certain the others followed or uncaring whether they followed or not. He scrambled agilely over the great stones and piles of rubble, the black tassel of his sheshia springing from side to side. Olive Kallen hoisted her long black skirts and scrambled along close beside him. Her husband paused, watched them for a moment, then turned aside and looked for an easier way around. He took off his hat and mopped his face with his handkerchief and peered again into the bowl of his pipe. Antoine and Merrill Miles followed him. They were laughing and deep in conversation.

Emily watched them go. Antoine appeared unaware that she was no longer with them. She envied Olive Kallen her freedom and her unfettered vigour and would have liked to have kept up with her. When they had gone, Emily moved around to the lower side of the block of fallen masonry, where there was a little shade. She lifted her skirt and sat on the ground in the shade, her legs thrust out in front of her. She leaned and massaged her ankles. A few yards in front of her a steep decline led into the underground excavations. Beside the entrance there were piles of loose rubble. She noticed then that the ground where she was sitting was thick with pottery shards and pieces of broken marble. She picked up a piece of pottery and examined it. It was a deep russet, convex, and almost as fine as eggshell. She wet her finger with her tongue and moistened the shard. Where her spittle touched it the colour changed to a subtle orange. She pressed it to her lips. It was cool. She decided it must once have been part of a bowl or a vase and wondered how old it was. She tried to imagine it whole and in a household but was unable to. Despite her years of study, she realized with a feeling of dismay that she possessed no reference to help her determine the age or origin of this beautiful piece of pottery in her hand. Except for her certainty that it had once been part of a fine and delicate vessel, its past was a mystery to her. She sat there for some minutes intently scraping at the shard with her fingernail, cleaning off earth and a thin, cementlike substance that clung to it in small patches across its surface, as if she might eventually get to its secrets by this means. With a sharp exclamation of frustration she suddenly tossed the shard away and stood up. She brushed the dust impatiently from her skirt with her hands.

She was facing the decline into the excavations. 'Damn him!' she said. She bent and picked up a piece of broken masonry and threw it hard into the excavation. The stone tripped and clattered into the darkness. 'Damn him!' she said again, venting her frustration. She picked up another stone and, with one hand to her hat, she spun around and threw the stone with force into the hole. She stood, breathing hard, exultant with a kind of startled satisfaction. Then she saw the man watching her.

He was fifty yards away, over to her left in front of a dark line of cypresses that grew close together beyond the low ruined wall of the amphitheatre. In front of these trees a khaki tarpaulin had been raised over an arrangement of poles, as a temporary shelter or as the focus of some kind of encampment. A workman was standing in the shade of the tarpaulin among a clutter of packing cases and tables. When she looked at him, he did not look away but grew more alert. A companion squatted on the ground beside him. Both men were still and watchful.

Emily looked about for Delattre and the group but could not see them. Apart from herself and the two workmen, the vast ruined ellipse of the amphitheatre was deserted. The place seemed suddenly airless to her, the sun beating down fiercely on the stones, the cluttered space between herself and the cars an impossible barrier. A bead of sweat rolled down her cheek. She raised her hand and brushed at it. As if this was the signal he had been waiting for, the man moved. He came out of the shade of the tarpaulin and vaulted the low remains of the wall and started across the arena toward her. The other man stood up slowly, watching the advance of his companion.

Emily turned abruptly to make for the cars and the protection of Nabil. Her ankle went over on the uneven ground and she tripped and fell heavily to her knees. She gave a cry and scrambled to her feet, reaching to retrieve her bag. The steep decline into the excavations was directly in front of her. She started down the uneven steps. As she stumbled into the cavernlike darkness, she almost lost her footing. 'Oh God!' she groaned, pressing her bag to her stomach and steadying herself with her other hand against the rough wall. At the bottom of the steps the warm stench of carrion rose sweetly from the darkness to meet her. She gagged and gave a sob. She was in a low, bricked vault of cell-like proportions. She looked down. At her feet were the remains of a butchered carcass of a sheep or a goat. The pile of guts glinted in the half-light, attended by a swarm of flies. There was the clink of a stone shifting on the slope behind her. She turned and looked up into the dazzle of sunlight. The man was coming down the steps. She bent to pick up a stone but he was too quick for her. He reached and took hold of her wrist. He was breathing hard.

She cried out, 'No!' and pulled back from him with all her strength.

He released her and she staggered back a pace, stepping squarely into the entrails.

'Hands off the lady, Hakim!' he said mockingly. His English was almost free of an accent. He laughed easily. 'I should have guessed you'd be English.'

'Let me pass!' she demanded breathlessly, dragging herself forward along the wall toward the steps.

'Let you pass!' he said incredulously. 'What the hell do you think you're up to?' He stood aside. 'Go on, then.' He waited for her to go by him in the narrow space. But she stood her ground.

'Frantic to get in here, then frantic to get out again,' he said. 'Well, go on, then. Up you go.' He gestured at the stinking pile at her feet. 'I might have warned you about that if you'd given me half a chance.' He offered her his hand. 'You'd better let me help you.'

'I'm all right!'

His anger flared. 'Just give me your hand and let me help you up the steps before you make a complete mess of yourself.' He took her firmly by the wrist and went ahead of her, looking back to see how she was managing. Out in the sunlight of the arena he released her wrist and gave a mocking bow. 'Hakim el-Ouedi at your service, madame.' He was without a hat and was clean-shaven. 'How's your ankle? Not broken, by any chance?'

'It's all right.'

He stepped back and examined her. 'Your knees aren't all right.'

She looked down and lifted the hem of her dress. Both her knees were grazed and bleeding. She bent and brushed at them. 'It's nothing.' Her stockings were ruined.

He regarded her in silence. There was contempt but also amusement and a guarded curiosity in his eyes. 'If we've quite finished with the little melodrama, you'd better come over into our bit of shade and wait for your friends,' he said. 'They're not likely to get away from Moses for a while yet. And anyway,' he added cheerfully, 'they don't seem to have missed you particularly, do they? Anything might have happened to you for all they seem to care.'

She went with him. At the wall he offered her his hand but she declined to take it and scrambled over without his help.

In the shade of the tarpaulin the air was cool and delicately perfumed by the cypresses. He offered her a canvas chair and said something in Arabic to the other man. She sat in the chair and examined her knees.

The other man went to the table and filled a glass tumbler from a tin kettle. Hakim el-Ouedi turned to her and handed her the drink. The other man stood and watched.

She took a sip of the tepid liquid. It was intensely sweet, a heady infusion of mint, the aftertaste on her palate clean and refreshing. She took a larger drink. 'Thank you.'

He rested his weight against the table, his gaze on her blouse.

She put her hand to her breast, her fingers touching Antoine's brooch.

Hakim nodded, 'So, he's given you Perpetua's medallion?'

'It was a present from Monsieur Carpeaux, if that's what you mean. Why do you call it that?'

'The giver of gifts,' he said and jerked his head toward the excavations. 'My father found it over there beside Perpetua's cell more than twenty years ago. That's what we've always called it.'

'I understand it belonged to Monsieur Carpeaux's father.'

'That's what Antoine understands too,' Hakim said mildly. 'In England they always said finders keepers.' He took a packet of French cigarettes from his shirt pocket and shook it. He leaned forward and offered her one.

She hesitated, then took a cigarette from the packet and waited for him to light it. 'Thank you.' She inhaled the smoke gratefully.

'Everything belonged to Antoine's father.' He was watching her, waiting for something. At last he said, 'I don't suppose you have to introduce yourself if you don't want to. It's not compulsory.'

'I'm sorry. Forgive me, Mr el-Ouedi.' She laughed quickly. 'I took you and your companion for workmen.'

He turned to the other man and said something in Arabic. They laughed and looked at her, amused and disdainful.

She was blushing. 'What did you say to your friend?'

'I told Ahmed the mad, stone-throwing English woman had mistaken us for native labourers. He finds that amusing. If you want to see a native, you should look over there.' He pointed with his cigarette to where the cars were parked under the olive tree by the road. 'That girl looking after the sheep is a native. You can always tell who the natives are. They're the ones with the skinny sheep. My mother was a native.' He watched her, then added, 'A Berber.'

'I'm not English,' Emily corrected him. 'I'm Australian.'

He shrugged.

She held out her hand. 'I'm Madame Georges Elder.'

He reached and shook her hand.

'Emily,' she added. 'My name is Emily.'

'Well, it's very pleasant to meet you, Madame Georges Elder, Emily. And what's the difference between an Australian and an English woman?'

She felt as if she had had this conversation before. 'There isn't any, I don't suppose. Not really. Or if there is, I don't know what it is. My father would be happy to explain it to you. He's been explaining it to me for twenty years.'

'And you still don't know what it is?'

'I know I'm not English, Mr el-Ouedi.' She looked at him. 'What's the difference between a Berber and other Arabs?'

'It depends who you ask. You won't get the same answer twice.' He kicked at the rubble with the toe of his dusty shoe.

'What do *you* think the difference is?' she persisted.

'My answer's under your feet. You have to get down on your knees to find it.' He chuckled. 'Which is what you were doing, I suppose.'

She sipped the mint tea. He watched her.

'Me and Ahmed couldn't figure you out. I said you were a tourist. Ahmed didn't think so. Then when you started throwing stones, we thought you must be mad and were going to fill in our hole for us. So we decided it was time to stop you.'

'Is it your excavation, then?'

'It's Père Delattre's.' He gestured around the arena. 'Everything's Père Delattre's. Ahmed and I dug the hole. Which some people would say ought to make it ours. But it doesn't.' He put his cigarette between his lips and squatted, squinting through the smoke and sorting the rubble with his fingers. He selected several shards, then took his cigarette out of his mouth and wet his thumb with his tongue and wiped one of the pieces. He looked up at her and tossed it into the lap of her skirt. 'Roman red slip. Second century A.D. About the time they were playing their delicate games here.' From his squatting position he drew on his cigarette and stared boldly at her legs. 'There's tons of that stuff mixed in with the earth.'

It was a piece of the orange pottery. His matter-of-fact dismissal of it disappointed her. She felt his gaze on her legs. She looked up and held the shard out to him.

He waved it aside.

'It's pretty,' she said. 'I was wondering about it before.'

He took another piece of pottery and rubbed at the dirt and handed it to her. She took it from him. It was a dark green glaze.

'Part of the handle from an Islamic drinking bowl. Five hundred years later than that piece in your hand.' He stood up and watched her. 'We don't have to move from this spot. It's all here.' He pointed. 'There's the lip of a Punic amphora over there. Second century B.C.' He gazed around. 'It's everywhere. In Tunisia you can ignore history but you can't avoid stepping on it.'

She said, 'I'll keep these.'

He looked at the fragments in the palm of her hand. 'You were only one generation out. It was my father who was the labourer. He worked for Antoine's father all his life. My father ignored our history. When he died, he had nothing.'

They looked at each other in silence.

'That's the lesson of the shards,' he said. 'If you ignore history, you stay in the dust. The soul of the Arab is in the dust today.'

She looked again at the pieces in her hand.

He turned toward the sunlit arena. 'Here's your friend, Monsieur Antoine Carpeaux, the magnanimous giver of gifts from the dust.'

She stood up. Antoine was hurrying across the arena toward them. He waved his hat when he saw her and she raised her hand. Her ankle was throbbing. She turned to Hakim and handed him the glass with its thick wad of green sodden mint leaves. 'Thank you for the tea.'

He took the glass from her. He looked miserable suddenly. 'What *were* you doing?'

Their eyes met.

'I don't know.'

'Why did you throw stones into the excavation, then go in after them? You must have had a reason for doing it.' He waited. 'What did you come here for?' he asked her with sudden bluntness.

'I came to have a rest from Paris.'

He laughed loudly. 'That filthy hole you just went into was the prison they kept Vibia Perpetua in after she'd been condemned to the beasts. If you ask Delattre, he'll tell you she was a martyr of the Holy Roman Church. The Christians claimed her and made a saint of her. But I say she was a misunderstood Berber woman and her life was a mystery. She was a young married woman from a respectable family and she waited for days in there to die in the arena and no one really knows why. It must have stunk then the way it stinks now. Flies and blood and rotting carcasses piled up all over the place. People and animals waiting to die. They let her keep her baby with her, but she chose to give the baby up and die alone. And while she waited to die she quietly composed a journal. A record of her imprisonment. Condemned to the beasts, the Romans called it. *Damnatio ad bestias*. It always makes me think of being condemned to become the beast, rather than to be killed by one.

Condemned to become the beast in yourself.' He looked at her. 'Do you
think that might be our fate?'

'The fate of the Arabs, you mean?'

He examined her appreciatively. 'Some poor devil stole a sheep
and slaughtered it in there a few days ago. Food for his little family. It's
all the same, isn't it? What's changed?'

'What's all the same, Hakim?' Antoine asked in French as he hurried
up to them. He took Emily's arm. 'Are you all right? You gave me a fright.
I thought the heat must have been too much for you and you'd gone back
to the car. Then Nabil told me he hadn't seen you.' He glanced at her
knees. 'You didn't faint, did you?'

'No, of course I didn't,' she said impatiently. 'It isn't too hot
for me, Antoine. I was just doing a bit of exploring on my own. Mr
el-Ouedi was kind enough to tell me about Perpetua's cell. He's been
explaining something of Tunisia's history for me.' She turned to Hakim.
'I am interested, Mr el-Ouedi.'

Hakim smiled, his gaze on Antoine.

Antoine held her arm possessively. 'Well,' he said. 'How are you,
Hakim? Delattre tells me you and Ahmed may be going to Dougga to
look after things there.'

'I'd be less of a nuisance to him out there.' Hakim was amused.
'I'm happy here, Antoine. So I'm resisting Delattre's thoughtful plans
for me.'

Hakim's French was as fluent as his English.

'Dougga's a great opportunity for you, surely?'

'Let a Frenchman have it, then.'

Antoine turned to Emily. 'You've done something to your ankle?'

'I'm fine, Antoine. Stop fussing, please.'

Hakim watched them, amused.

'Well,' Antoine said uncertainly. He seemed a little at a loss with
Hakim. 'Thank you for taking care of Madame Elder.' He shook hands

rather formally with Hakim. Then his manner softened and he said, 'You'll have to come up to the house for some of Mounir's cooking. It's been too long.'

'I'd enjoy that.'

The two men looked at each other in silence.

'Good,' Antoine said. 'That's settled, then. We'll arrange an evening with the Kallens. You should meet them anyway. They may be of some help to you.' He took Emily's arm and helped her over the low wall and they walked out onto the arena together.

At the car she looked back toward the cypresses. Hakim was still standing there watching them from the shade of the tarpaulin.

The Kallens and Merrill Miles had gone with Père Delattre in his car. Antoine was silent as they drove along the road, gazing out the window. He scarcely responded to her remarks about the amphitheatre and Delattre. When Nabil slowed the car at the base of the hill of Sidi bou-Saïd, she asked, 'Something's troubling you, Antoine. What is it? Have I misbehaved? Please tell me.'

He glanced at Nabil and leaned close to her and said in a low, peevish whisper, 'Tunisia's not Paris, Emily. It doesn't do for you to be seen alone in public with Arab men, my dear. How on earth did you manage to do that to your knees?'

She laughed. 'And in Paris it would be proper for me to be seen alone with Arab men?'

'You know what I mean,' he said testily. 'You must promise me not to just go off like that again without saying anything.'

'You were so busy talking to your new friend, I didn't think you'd noticed.'

He looked at her. 'You misunderstand me. You could have gone back and waited for us in the car. That is what I thought you intended to do. Nabil will talk in the café. People will get the wrong impression. It's important what people think of us in the village.'

'I'm not interested in waiting for people in cars,' she said. 'Hakim was a perfect gentleman.' She waited, then added, 'I liked him. He is intelligent. I bet your theatrical priest didn't even notice I wasn't there.'

'So, it's Hakim already, is it?' Antoine said disapprovingly. 'Oh yes, Hakim is interesting. As a matter of fact he's a very fine scholar and linguist. In the ancient languages he has Hebrew, Aramaic, Greek, and Latin, and his Italian is every bit as good as his English and his French. Hakim is interesting. No one will dispute that.'

'You almost sound as if you're jealous of him.'

Antoine put his hand on her arm. 'I'm an amateur, Emily. A dilettante. I admit it. I've said it before. I'm not ashamed of that. My interest in Tunisia's past is driven by nostalgia, a motive that is despised by Hakim. He's contemptuous of my gentle antiquarianism. For Hakim history is a weapon with which he hopes to defeat the French. For Hakim the past is not a nostalgic dream as it is for me. He wishes to shape the future of the Arabs in Tunisia with his knowledge of history. He is a fine professional archaeologist, Emily. He's the only Tunisian to have trained at the Sorbonne and at the British School of Archaeology in Athens. He worked at the British Museum for two years after Athens and has published numerous papers in scholarly journals. His professional credentials are impressive. He is respected abroad. He's very intelligent, hardworking, and ambitions. All those things in abundance. And he burns with the ardent fire of Arab nationalism.'

She laughed. 'Now you sound as if you're proud of him.'

'I love Hakim,' he said simply. He drew breath and was silent. They had reached the piazza. Nabil stopped the car in front of the studded door and he got out and went over and opened the door. He went through the door and bounded up the steps. Antoine didn't move. 'Hakim's father worked for my father. When he died, I paid for Hakim's education in Paris and took care of the family. And, yes, you are quite right, I'm a little jealous and a little proud of Hakim.' He paused. 'He is like a son to me.' He fell silent again. 'Sons don't always do as their fathers wish them to. It's only through me that Hakim has had the opportunity for a decent life. Now all he cares about is to rid Tunisia of the French.' He turned to her. 'A father who expects thanks from his son is a fool, no doubt. When he was young, I promised myself that no matter what path he chose to follow in life I would support him in it.' He was silent for a moment, then he said with feeling, 'Now I fear for him. There are powerful people here who are convinced he is a dangerous man. If it weren't for my influence with Delattre, these people would almost certainly pressure him to get rid of Hakim. And Hakim resents my protection as much as he needs it. But he's mistaken about Tunisia. This country can never belong simply to the Arabs again. When he's an old man, he'll see his mistake and will regret the way he misused his gifts and opportunities. I know all this, but how can I tell him it? Like all young people, Hakim thinks he's immortal and is deaf to advice.' He sat staring out the window of the car.

Nabil came down the steps and stood by the bonnet and looked at them.

'Nabil is waiting for his car,' Antoine said. But still he didn't move. 'Mine is the hostility and disappointment of a father for a son who has grown beyond his influence.' He turned to her and smiled. 'We'd better let Nabil have the car or he'll be late for some important rendezvous.'

They got out of the car and he took her arm and they went through the door and up the steps together. They stood on the terrace looking out over the limes and the oleanders toward the roofs of the village and the blue of the gulf beyond. Nabil closed the door to the piazza. There was the sound of the car door slamming, then the whine of the gears as he reversed out of the piazza.

'French culture has given Hakim everything he prizes most in his life,' Antoine said. 'My father despised the Arabs. He thought them a doomed race. I often heard him say they are lazy and without a future.

But I've always believed that if we gave the Arabs the chance for a decent life, they would be content to live in peace with us. That's all I've ever wanted for Tunisia. I was born here, Emily. Tunisia is my home. We must live together. There's no other way. Please don't take Hakim's side against me. You don't know Tunisia. Things look peaceful and friendly to you, but a lot of blood has been spilled here over the interpretation of our history. There are hatreds and resentments that aren't openly spoken about. Every once in a while our conflicts flare into violent action and someone is hurt or killed. At such times no one who was born here speaks of innocent bystanders. That is a term employed by the French press. There are no innocent bystanders in Tunisia. We are a family. We have inherited our feuds from each other and must deal with them ourselves.' He turned to her and took her hands in his. 'Enjoy my home, Emily. Rest. Get well and strong. But please don't involve yourself in our disputes or our politics.'

'I'm here, Antoine!' she objected. 'How can I help being involved? Don't ask me just to be a tourist. I'll never take anyone's side against you.' She touched the brooch, 'He called it Perpetua's medallion. He said his father found it.'

Antoine looked at the brooch.

She said, 'Now you *are* regretting giving it to me, aren't you?'

'It didn't occur to me then that you would ever meet Hakim.'

'We don't think how things might turn out,' she said thoughtfully. This time she did not offer to return the brooch to him. She was suddenly thinking of Bertrand saying mysteriously, 'In the matter of friendships we can never know how we are to be used.' There was an excitement for her now in her possession of the medallion. 'It *makes* me one of the family,' she said. 'That's what you intended, isn't it? To include me?'

'Not in our disputes,' he said. 'Come!' He was impatient suddenly with the conversation. He took her arm. 'Mounir will have lunch waiting for us. I hope you like fish. He is famous for it.'

They went into the house together and crossed the cool hallway. 'It can be dangerous here to reinterpret our history,' Antoine said.

She looked at him quickly, intrigued, perhaps excited, by such an idea. 'I've never thought of history as dangerous,' she said. 'I abandoned it because it seemed so very dull and safe.'

Mounir waited for them at the end of the dining room by the open doors to the loggia, where he had set a table for them in the shade. He greeted them softly in Arabic and drew out a chair for Emily.

Antoine sat opposite her. He said, 'The only history that satisfies our sense of justice is the history we write ourselves.'

THREE

—◆—

Emily was sitting in the window recess with her legs thrust out in front of her and her green morocco writing case open on her lap. The afternoon was hot and still. If it had been Melbourne, she would have been expecting a storm later. She was wearing only her chemise. The red-and-green cushions from the wooden armchairs were arranged in the window, piled against the stone wall and on the platform. The deep recess between the shutters and the grille had been transformed into a comfortable nest. The effect – of being in the open air while remaining concealed and safe – reminded her of the screened verandah at the back of the house at Richmond Hill, where her father had set up a camp bed for her each summer when the nights became too oppressive to sleep comfortably inside the house.

She looked up from her writing. The bushes in the garden were draped with washing drying in the sun. Beyond the roofs of the village – on which the dark sprawled bodies of the dogs lay asleep as if they had been shot – the gulf and the hills beyond were hidden by a yellow haze. She rested her head against the cushions and closed her eyes. There was a steady throbbing ache in her bowels. She eased her weight. How many women before her, she wondered, had sat concealed in the window recess, to gain some respite from the summer heat, and perhaps to spy on their husband's visitors to the house. The sound of roosters crowing to each other back and forth across the village came through the window, and from the courtyard there was the musical tinkling of the fountain. She put her writing case aside and climbed down from the recess. She paused at the blue-painted table and picked up the fragment of Roman red slip. She touched the shard to her cheek and closed her eyes, pressing the cool of its glassy surface against her skin, a material miraculously crafted for the climate – she imagined it belonging to a lost civilization once precisely attuned to the geography of its place. She set the shard on the table and went over and opened the door of the wardrobe.

On the inside of the wardrobe door was a long dressing mirror. She slipped the silk chemise over her head and tossed it onto the bed beside her dress. Naked, she stood side-on to the mirror and examined her profile. There was a definite rounding of her lower belly. She placed the flat of her hand against the soft bulge. 'You are a pregnant woman, Emily Stanton,' she said, as if her own fate were detached from the fate of the woman in the mirror. She closed the door of the wardrobe and went into the bathroom and stepped into the bath and turned on the lion-headed tap. She cupped her hands and splashed the cool water over herself.

She got out of the bath and went back into the bedroom and put on her chemise and climbed into the window recess. She dried her hands on her chemise and took up the unfinished letter to Georges and read it over. She had not mentioned Hakim or the startled fear of her abrupt descent into Perpetua's cell. She picked up her fountain pen and bent over the paper.

I am forgetting that you spent two years in Tunisia and visited Antoine's house often. Perhaps you know this window where I am sitting writing? Are you familiar with this room? Perhaps not. It feels to me as if this has always been a woman's room. I have hesitated, for a reason I'm not clear about, to ask Antoine to show me your old room. But I shall ask him. I have seen only my own part of the house, and of course the garden and the terrace and

the dining room, and those other places where we all meet. I have
a sense that there are many lives lived here. I don't dare explore
on my own. I don't feel invited to. There is a kind of reticence,
a delicate privacy, that is called for by the silence, by the stillness
here, and if one does not move, time seems to stand still and to
wait for one to move. As if the moment possesses no velocity of
its own, as it does in Paris, and everything depends upon one's
own will. There is surely a secret life of Sidi bou-Saïd that I know
nothing of, except I sense it in this peculiar stillness. Imagine Paris
at a standstill! The eeriness of such a silence. There are moments
when I am sure I forget to breathe.

She wondered if Georges would take her meaning. There was a soft
drift of air through the grille and the sudden intense smell of rosemary.
She looked up. Out in the afternoon sunlight of the garden Sonia was
collecting the washing from the bushes. The little girl was helping her
mother fold a sheet. The girl's arms were held above her head as
high as she could reach and her head was thrown back. Sonia called
encouragement to her and when she reached her she wrapped her in the
sheet and cuddled her. The child struggled and screamed with delight.

There was the roar of a truck approaching up the hill. Sonia left the
washing and went across the garden and down the steps to the gate. Emily
leaned into the belly of the grille to see who had arrived. Sonia opened
the gate. A moment later Hakim came in. He shook hands with Sonia
and offered her something he was carrying in his hand. Sonia turned and
pointed to the house. The three of them mounted the steps to the terrace
and passed out of Emily's line of sight. A couple of minutes later there was
a soft tap-tap at the door. Emily got off the window and picked up her
dress from the bed and slipped it over her head. She buttoned the dress
and went over and opened the door. Sonia's daughter stood there.

'Please, madame,' the girl said, 'There is a visitor to see you.'

He was waiting for her on the terrace. Mounir was with him. They were talking. When they heard her sandals on the flagstones, both men turned and looked at her. She shook hands with Hakim. Mounir said, in French, they should go into the house out of the sun. 'I shall bring you some tea.' They went into the cool of the hallway and sat a little apart on the bench against the wall. Hakim turned to her and offered her the book he was carrying. 'It's in English. You said you were interested.' His manner was abrupt, faintly aggressive, impatient.

She took the book from him. 'Thank you,' she said. 'It is very kind of you.' It was a slim, red clothbound volume with the title in heavy black lettering, *Passio Perpetuae, The Passion of Vibia Perpetua.* 'Is it the journal you told me about? That she wrote in her cell while she was waiting to die?'

He glanced at the book. 'I stole it years ago from the British Museum.' His khaki shirt was stained with sweat. A packet of cigarettes bulged in the breast pocket. She could smell the dust of the arena on him. He seemed ill at ease. She opened the book.

He leaned across and turned the page and stabbed his finger on the beginning of a paragraph. 'She begins here. The introduction's Tertullian's. It's not to be trusted. You may as well read Delattre as that nonsense.'

Emily read, *While I was still with the police authorities my father out of love for me tried to dissuade me from my resolution . . .* She looked up. Hakim was watching her narrowly. 'I'll read it later,' she said.

'Sure.' He sounded as if he did not believe her.

She closed the book and held it on her lap. 'You haven't made a mistake, Mr el-Ouedi. I assure you, I shall read it.'

'Good. I'd better be getting back.' He stood up.

'Mounir's bringing us tea.' She looked up at him and smiled encouragingly. 'You must give me a chance to return your hospitality.'

He looked about uncertainly. 'Is Antoine at home?'

'Merrill Miles called for him after lunch. Nabil drove them somewhere. I don't know where they went.'

Hakim reached into his shirt pocket and took out the packet of cigarettes. He tapped the packet and offered it. She shook her head. 'No thanks.'

He sat on the bench again and lit a cigarette. He put the burned match back into the box and sat leaning on his elbows smoking.

The silence between them dragged on.

To ease the situation she asked, 'Why do you say Tertullian is not to be trusted?'

He nodded at the book. 'She must have given her diary to Tertullian for safekeeping, probably the night before she was killed. It's a murder mystery. The Romans murdered her. No one denies that. But why did she give up her baby and desert her family? What were her real motives? Tertullian says she did it for the nonsense of eternal life. European historians have let Tertullian's explanation that she was a Christian martyr stand without ever questioning it. Her case has remained closed since Tertullian gave us his verdict. No one since then has asked what her real motives might have been in acting as she did. Maybe this is the moment to reopen her case.' He laughed. 'Père Delattre's going to close it for good soon. He's got big plans for her. He's going clean it all up and get rid of the evidence. In the autumn he'll have his fine ceremony down there with the bishop and the French resident general and they'll dedicate her cell as a sacred chapel of the martyrs. Whitewash and a couple of candles and some lilies, that's all that'll be left of it. After that, anyone who asks awkward questions will be committing heresy. They'll be challenging the French. Read it. Let us know what you think when you've read it. That little book isn't the writing of a madwoman. She didn't give up her kid for eternal life. I don't believe that. No one who thinks about it believes that. No mother would do it.'

He reached and took the book out of her hand and opened it and read a few lines. He stopped reading and looked at her. 'It's not the writing of a mystic. It's documentary.' He slapped the book. 'It's the facts. It's what happened. But why? Perpetua's is the mystery at the centre of that arena down there. Question the victim's motives in this story and you question everything. Delattre thinks he's got the answer. But his answer's Tertullian's answer. He's wrong. Perpetua's case was closed for convenience, not because it had been solved.' He leaned and placed the book in her lap. 'People keep quiet about their real motives. Motives are mysterious.'

Mounir came and placed a small round table before them. He left them and returned through the archway at the end of the hall. His grey slippers made no sound on the marble flagstones. He came back a moment later with a tray, on which there was a copper teakettle, two glasses on small saucers with long silver spoons, a small stoneware bowl filled with dark green mint leaves, and another bowl with a neat pyramid of sugar cubes. He set the tray on the table, murmured something in Arabic, and left them.

'I'm not sure what you do,' Emily said. 'Do the leaves go in first?'

Hakim reached and placed several mint leaves in each glass then poured hot water on them from the kettle. They sat watching the water in the glasses turn a clear pale green. He put half a dozen lumps of sugar in one of the glasses and stirred it with the spoon until the sugar dissolved and clouded the tea. He handed the glass to her, balancing it on its tiny saucer.

She thanked him and took it from him. 'Why do you hate the French?'

He stirred his tea. 'I don't hate the French.'

'You are opposed to them.'

'I'm opposed to the oppression of Arabs.'

'Antoine says you will use history as a weapon to get rid of the French.'

He looked for somewhere to put the butt of his cigarette, then he crushed it on the tray. 'Antoine bought me an education with his money. Now he doesn't like what I'm doing with his gift. Shall I give it back to him?' He laughed, sardonic. 'If we don't tell our own story, someone else tells it for us.' He looked at her. 'Then instead of us being the heroes in our story, we're the villains.'

'And the French are the villains for you?'

'I'm sure it's no different in Australia. You don't let other people write your history for you.'

She laughed. 'Oh, no one writes Australian history, Mr el-Ouedi. It's unheard-of. I can't imagine what we'd write about. If we wish to write history in Australia we must write about the ancient Greeks or the kings and queens of England.' Emily saw Sonia and the little girl coming up the steps. Sonia was carrying an enormous basket piled with washing. Hakim turned and looked at her. He stood up. 'Thanks for the tea. Ahmed will be waiting for me.' He held out his hand.

Emily stood up and shook his hand. 'Thank you for coming,' she said. 'I look forward to reading her journal. How shall I return it to you?'

'Antoine has invited me to his important dinner with the Kallens and Père Delattre.' He looked at her. 'You can return it to me then.'

Sonia drew level with them. 'Wait, Hakim! I'll send Houria with some pastries for Ahmed.' She hurried across the hallway and went through the arch at the end. The little girl lingered behind, gazing at Emily. Sonia called to her.

Emily and Hakim stood waiting, the silence between them difficult again suddenly. A moment later the little girl ran out from the archway and held up a small cloth bundle for Hakim. He took it and thanked the girl and she ran off. He looked at the bundle and then at Emily. 'This wasn't my idea,' he said.

She was unable to keep the disappointment from her voice. 'To give me her book, you mean?'

He shrugged. 'We talked about you, Ahmed and me. After you'd gone.' He looked into her eyes. 'Ahmed believes everything has its reason. She came here just at this time, he said. A year ago we hadn't opened the cell. Another year and it will have become a chapel for the Catholic Church. And she was wearing Perpetua's medallion. Give her the book, he told me. She's a young married woman and is to have a child soon.' Hakim smiled, embarrassed. 'Ahmed notices everything. He thought you might see something in her situation that we don't see. That's all.' He laughed, mischievous suddenly as he had been at the arena. 'Ahmed believes in the cosmic plan.'

'And what do you believe in, Mr el-Ouedi?'

'I've offended you now. I'm sorry. I didn't mean to. This is important to us. Ahmed thought your visit might be an opportunity for us. We're always looking for opportunities. For cracks in Delattre's armour. You're not French. We argued about it. I told Ahmed, If you think it's such a good idea, then why don't you take the book to her yourself? But he wouldn't. He would have done it much better than me, however. With more grace and mystery. He wouldn't have embarrassed you. He would have bowed and handed you the book and left without a word. And you would have stood and watched him go and have asked yourself why the stranger had given you the book.'

'I've been asking myself that ever since you arrived, Mr el-Ouedi. Or am I to accept your explanation of your reasons at face value? Where should my questioning of motives end, do you think?'

He laughed and held out his hand. 'I'll tell Ahmed her diary's in good hands. Good-bye, Madame Elder.'

They shook hands and she went onto the terrace with him and stood and watched him go down the steps. He turned at the door and lifted his hand. He went out and she heard the slam of a door and a moment later the truck roared to life. She turned and went back into the house and crossed the hallway and went on across the courtyard. As she passed the fountain, she paused and wet her fingers and touched them to her throat. In her room she took off her dress and climbed into the window recess. She opened the book and began to read: *A few days later we were imprisoned. I was terrified because never before had I experienced such darkness. What a terrible day! Because of the crowded conditions and rough treatment by the soldiers the heat was unbearable. My condition was aggravated by my anxiety for my baby . . .* She sat engrossed in the diary and did not look up until she came to Tertullian's description of Perpetua's gruesome death in the arena in front of the jeering crowds – the way she had stood, just before she died, and looked at them. There were tears in Emily's eyes.

FOUR

— ∼ —

During the following days Emily saw little of Antoine. She heard the car arrive and leave at various times of the day and night, and occasionally she caught a glimpse of Antoine and Merrill Miles as they hurried down the steps together or returned, laughing, to the house from some excursion. There was little to break the monotony of her days. Dr Domela visited her and brought a fresh supply of the iron tonic. She breakfasted alone each morning on the terrace at a table that was always set for two by Mounir in the shade of the lime trees. The empty place at the table beside her made her feel a little sad, as if she waited for a friend who did not come. After breakfast, she returned to her room, or walked for a while in the garden until the heat grew too oppressive. She read Perpetua's journal again, then began one of the volumes of the French history of the Abbasid caliphate that someone had left on the blue-painted table. She was eager to talk to Hakim of her ideas about Perpetua. Perhaps the story should not be taken as literally, she thought, as he seemed to take it. Wasn't it intended, after all, as a fable to illustrate the strength of the young woman's faith? One had to wonder what Tertullian had meant by 'Eternal life'? Her name, Perpetua, was itself a kind of metaphor for eternal life. Emily, however, heard nothing from Hakim. She felt starved of company and conversation and looked forward to the time each evening before dinner when Sonia came to her room to give her a bath and a massage. After the bath, Sonia returned to her own part of the house and Emily did not see her again until the following day. The weather continued extremely hot and the brown haze deepened over the gulf, until a half-light pervaded the hours of daylight, the sun an enormous crimson disk in the gloomy silence of the sky. Emily resented Antoine's neglect. She was bored and restless and began to feel like a prisoner in the isolation of her beautiful room. Gazing out over the village through the bars of the pregnant grille, it seemed to her that a curtain had been lowered over Sidi bou-Saïd, shutting the village off from the rest of the world, from a view of the gulf and from a sight of the modest hills of Djebel bou-Kornein – the view that had reminded her, when she had first arrived, of the You Yangs across Port Phillip Bay. One stifling day followed another without variation. A little after sundown each evening a breeze shifted uneasily among the garden foliage, setting the oleander leaves trembling, then failing before the heavy stillness, which settled on the house for the night as if a great door had closed. The temperature scarcely dropped more than a degree or two before dawn. Emily had begun to experience nausea in the mornings and by the afternoons her ankles were swollen and throbbing. She longed for a cool change. At night she lay naked and sleepless, stretched out on the cushions in the window recess, getting up every hour or so to wet her feverish skin in the bathroom.

She was finishing her breakfast when Mounir came silently to her side and placed a letter on the cloth beside her plate. She gave a start of surprise and looked up and thanked him. He smiled to see her pleasure and returned into the house. She opened the envelope eagerly with her knife, delighted with this unexpected break in the routine of her day. There were two sheets filled to the margins with Georges's small, neat handwriting. She read his letter slowly and with close attention.

Paris, 14 September

My Dearest Wife,

It is past midnight and I am sitting here at the table by the window under the lamp thinking only of you! Léon telephoned a few days ago to tell me that Raymond Domela had cabled him and had seen you soon after you arrived and that all seemed to be well. Pray God your health continues to improve and you and our baby grow strong under the care of Sonia and Mounir! So much has happened since you left that I scarcely know where to begin. I hope you will not be angry, but I sent Sophie back to stay with her aunt in Belleville until your return. She comes every day and takes good care of me. I have the flat to myself at night, however, and can work at all hours without disturbing her or being disturbed by her. I long to see you! The board of Baume Marpent are pressing me to go to Haine Saint-Paul to give them a report on our progress, but I am resisting them. It is all due to Jacques Lenormand, who has unsettled them and made them nervous. He returned recently from a tour of engineering plants in the USA and England and has told them the Cleveland Bridge Company are far ahead of us with the preparation of their tender. He has got some of them into a dreadful funk. He would like to make them believe we cannot possibly win the tender with my design. Jacques Lenormand has never liked me and has always opposed my championing of the Australian bridge. He is doing his best to convince them to withdraw. But I still have staunch allies on the board and a great team here in Paris. Have no fear, I am determined to resist him and his cronies until you return. Then you and I shall go to Haine Saint-Paul together, at a time of my own choosing, and I shall show them the wonderful work we have done, which will astonish them and silence Lenormand, for we are making great progress.

I work day and night since you left. I imagine us with our

dear little baby together next year in our house overlooking Sydney Harbour, with all this nonsense and weakness of Lenormand's behind us and the bridge underway. After I have reassured the directors, we'll show them how truly confident we are. Since you left I am more determined than ever that you and I shall spend a holiday together. Have we been alone even once since the day we met? I cannot think of an entire day when it has been just you and me, with no other person to distract us. I shall hire a car in Haine Saint-Paul and we will take a motor tour around Namur and the forest of the Ardennes. It is a beautiful part of Belgium and you will love it. Léon says it will do you no harm. We shall wander wherever we choose each day and in the evenings we shall find a friendly inn beside the road.

Not all is good news. Otto has written to say that he fears Mother's heart may be failing. She tires more quickly now it seems and is finding it more difficult to get up to the cathedral each day. I telephone her every Sunday, but my calls seem to upset her rather than to give her any joy. It is partly my own fault. When she asked after you, I was afraid she might wish to speak to you and so I foolishly told her you had gone to Sidi bou-Saïd with Antoine for a holiday. I am quite unable to reassure her that Antoine will not corrupt you in some unspeakable way. Aunt Juliette, who has always liked Antoine, scoffs at her. But it seems that Mother lives in a past that is foreign to the rest of us. I can do nothing. When our baby is born in January, I am certain she will change. I have never seen a grandmother who did not love her grandchildren more than she loved her own children. Letters have arrived for you from Australia. I don't send them on in case you return before they reach you.

How I long to see you and to hold you in my arms again! If only Paris were connected directly to Sidi bou-Saïd by telephone, then I should be able to hear your dear voice. How terribly far away you seem to be from me. I think of Antoine's house and try to imagine you. I have asked myself a thousand times since you left whether it was a mistake to let you go. I cannot bear to imagine what accidents might befall you. Léon laughs at me for these anxieties, but I have promised myself that when you have returned safely to me I shall never let you out of my sight again.

She finished reading Georges's letter and put it beside her plate. She caught a movement out of the corner of her eye and looked up. Antoine was coming across the terrace. He wished her good morning and sat down opposite her. He unfolded his napkin and topped an egg, as if it were his regular habit to take breakfast with her.

'The Municipal Theatre and Winter Garden in Tunis are closed for the summer,' he said. 'It's a pity, but there are no carnivals or public fêtes at this time of the year. You mustn't return to Paris, however, without a visit to the souks.' He looked at her and smiled and spooned egg into his mouth. His hand trembled.

She watched him. His cheeks were hollow, his skin shadowed and gray, his wispy hair gleaming and unhealthy in the gloomy light. There were small circular patches of inflamed skin at his temples. 'I'd love to go into Tunis,' she said. 'But isn't it far too hot for that?'

He looked up quickly and laughed. 'Oh, I thought it couldn't be too hot for you.' His small shoulders were hunched, his delicate hands motionless on the cloth, his eyes glittery with spite.

She picked up Georges's letter and pretended to read it.

After breakfast, Nabil brought the car to the gate and drove them along the causeway into Tunis. They entered the dim subterranean alleyways and wandered with the throng among the colonnades of green-and-red pillars where craftsmen worked in small niches in the stone walls, surrounded by their merchandise. Emily bought a silver bangle for Sophie. Antoine established the price for her with the stallholder. 'It belonged to a Berber woman,' he told her, handing her the weighty bracelet.

In the cool twilight of the covered market they forgot for a little while the fierceness of the summer day outside. Antoine took her arm and pressed it to his side. 'I see you've had a letter from Georges. How is he? How does his bridge progress?'

'Georges is well and busy.'

They said no more and walked on arm in arm. 'I suppose there's been no word from your priest?' Antoine suddenly asked.

She looked at him with surprise. Neither of them had mentioned Bertrand since the evening of her confession on the boat and his question came as a shock to her. 'Chartres has seemed a world away,' she said. 'Now you bring it back. How would there have been any word from him?'

'Oh, I don't know,' Antoine said, impatient and miserable. 'Merrill's gone back to New York,' he said, his voice hollow with dismay. He drew her quickly to where a trader sat cross-legged in his niche in the wall, surrounded by hundreds of colored flasks and bottles set in rows on little shelves and lit by the light of an oil lamp. 'Precious distillations and rare fragrances,' Antoine said. 'Please do allow me to make amends for my bad manners. I shall buy you some perfume.' He spent a quarter of an hour trying perfumed sachets. The trader offering them and Antoine rejecting them. The trader remained calm, patient, and attentive, either certain of a sale sooner or later or indifferent to the outcome. Finally tiring of the game, Antoine gave him some notes and took a tiny amber bottle from him. He turned and gave the bottle to Emily. 'They've been here for centuries,' he said. 'They were here when the Spaniards came and they'll still be here when the French leave.' He seemed suddenly exhausted. 'Take care of the bottle. It's hornbill.'

On the drive back to Sidi bou-Saïd through the blazing heat Antoine sat slumped in his seat staring out the window of the car and smoking one cigarette after another. They scarcely exchanged a word until they reached the house. Before he left her among the blue shadows of the hallway he turned to her. 'Forgive me, Emily,' he said. Tears gleamed in his eyes.

She hesitated, then she put her arms around him and hugged him to her. 'My dear Antoine!'

He laughed and liberated himself from her embrace. He held both her hands. 'You shall see. Everything will soon be wonderful for us again. We shall have our grand dinner with Delattre and the Kallens.' His gaze went beyond her, into some infinity of thought. 'The way it is for us with some people,' he said. 'When you are with them, you feel yourself to be confident, intelligent and strong. Then with other people you are weak, unsure of yourself, and unable to make any sense of your life, and you begin to wonder if anything is ever going to work for you.' His gaze focused on her and he smiled. 'It isn't anything they say or do but the way they see you. They might not even know how they make you feel. You have these vague dreams and you are restless and discontented and can do nothing. Then this person is there with you and suddenly everything is precious to you again and you begin to hope that you may accomplish something fine and beautiful. And you don't know why it is like that for you with this person. But it is.' He fell silent. He let go her hands. 'Then you lose them,' he said. 'And you know there is nothing to be done.'

He seemed suddenly a shadowy figure standing before her in the cool blue light of the hallway. Old and unwell. He smiled and squeezed her hand. 'We shall have our dinner party.'

Dr Domela came out from Tunis again the next day to see her. Sonia came into Emily's room with the doctor and stood and watched. He was a small alert man, his manner dignified and faintly disapproving, his movements precise and formal, as if he had thought out everything beforehand. He wore a crumpled white linen suit and a black tie and carried a white solar helmet in one hand and a black bag in the other. He placed the helmet on the covers of the bed and he opened his bag. He asked Emily to lie on the bed and took out a thermometer from his bag. He bent close to her, his gaze intent, tiny beads of sweat glistening on his upper lip, and he slid the glass tube between her lips as if he were a little boy inserting a pencil into a keyhole, curious to see if it would fit. He took out his watch and opened it and sat looking at it, waiting for the minutes to pass. He reached and took the thermometer from between her lips and held it up.

'You've a slight temperature,' he said. He wiped the thermometer and put it away in his bag. 'Nothing to worry about so long as you keep cool.' He turned and fed the end of his stethoscope between the buttons at the front of her dress. As he manoeuvered the stethoscope about under Emily's dress, Dr Domela's gaze took on a faraway look, as if he saw in the scarlet-and-gold brocade of the baldachin above his head a strange, intriguing vision. He nodded and made a small approving sound in his throat several times, then removed the stethoscope and folded it away.

'All seems in order.' He looked at her. 'Have you felt nothing yet, Madame Elder?'

'There's a fluttering sometimes,' she said. 'When I lie down. A tickling kind of movement.' She pressed her fingers to the left side of her belly 'Here.'

He glanced at her fingers. 'That's your baby, Madame Elder. He's becoming active.' He warned her not to exert herself in the heat and advised cold baths every two hours. He told her he would send her more of the iron tonic. He turned to Sonia. 'See that Madame Elder is provided with plenty of fresh drinking water day and night.' He put his stethoscope in his bag and stood up and retrieved his solar helmet. 'I would take it most kindly if you would remember me to Dr Chaussegros when you return to Paris.'

Sonia escorted him to the door. As he was leaving, he paused in the doorway and turned back. 'Take care, madame, you have a dangerous trial before you.'

FIVE

The sound of hammering entered her dream and she woke. The bedsheet and pillowcase beneath her were sodden with her sweat. She remembered then the agonizing cramp during the night, climbing out of the window recess and crawling across the floor to lie on the bed. The shutters banged violently against the wall, as if someone had kicked them with heavy boots. It was the sound that had woken her. She sat up. The shutters sucked closed again with a crash, only to be thrust open again by the following gust, smashing against the stone wall of the window recess. Her writing things had been swept from the blue-painted table and were scattered across the floor. She got off the bed and went over and stood at the window with her arms wide, holding the shutters back and looking out at the iron light that hung over the garden and the village. The wind on her naked body was hot. She expected the smell of bush fires. The cypresses thrashed about, black and helpless. The hibiscus flowers were closed, the leaves withered and gray, their backs flattened to the heaving sky. Through the window's elaborate grille the bronze light cast pearly shadows across Emily's body and as she thrust against the heavy timber shutters two dimples were discretely modelled in the glossy rise above her buttocks.

She forced the shutters closed and drove the bolts home into the worn holes in the stone sill. The wind moaned between the slats and slammed the shutters back and forth on their slack hinges. She turned back into the room and moistened her dry lips with her tongue. There was fine grit between her teeth. She collected her papers from the floor and weighted them with the lamp. She looked at her watch. Delattre and the others would be arriving for dinner at any moment. Sweat crawled over her scalp. Sonia had not come to wake her for her bath.

She went into the bathroom and stood in the marble bath and splashed water over herself, then she went back into the bedroom without bothering to dry herself and opened the wardrobe. She reached and pulled her dresses aside one by one. She chose a simple red silk dress with straps over the shoulders. She held the dress against her, the cool folds of the silk soft against her skin. She stood considering her reflection in the mirror. Her condition would show, but there was nothing to be done about it. She tossed the dress onto the bed and opened a drawer and took out fresh underwear.

While she was dressing she heard a car arrive in the piazza. She went over and opened the shutters and climbed into the window recess and looked. Olive and Kenneth Kallen were struggling up the steps against the roaring wind, their heads bent and their clothes flapping, grasping at each other for support. Antoine was hurrying down the steps to meet them, his hand extended as if they were coming ashore in a storm.

Emily brushed her hair and put on her lipstick and went out. In the courtyard withered leaves from the wisteria vine skittered across the marble flagstones, snatched by violent eddies of air in the corners. She went down the stairs and crossed the hall and went into the dining room. It was a long room, its white walls tall and bare and broken only by heavy blue shutters over the windows. A Spanish chandelier, fashioned from curled and twisted iron, hung from the centre of the ceiling. Orange-and-blue tiles around the skirting and the windows and architraves of the doors glistened with a high glaze. The dining table, oblong and solitary, stood at the centre of the room. Six high-backed chairs upholstered in crimson silk were drawn up to the table. On the table a silver candelabrum with five candles gleamed in the silver and glass on the white linen. Against the wall a marble sideboard with more candles and decanters of red wine. Sonia was setting dishes of food on the table. Houria was helping her. Sonia looked up when she saw Emily come in. There was a nervous, apologetic expectancy in her manner.

'It's the samoom, madame. There's no such wind as this anywhere else in the world.'

At the far end of the room, out on the loggia beyond the shuddering glass of the French doors, silhouetted within the colonnade of slim Moorish columns and arches, Antoine and Olive and Kenneth Kallen stood gesticulating in the violent wind. Their agitated figures against the glowing sky. She went across and pushed open the doors. The glass rattled and the rush of wind almost snatched the door from her hand.

Antoine turned to her, grey trails of hair plastered across his face and the black tails of his coat snapping about his skinny thighs like the broken wings of a crippled bird. He shouted, 'I'm showing the doctors our view over Cape Carthage.' He laughed wildly, pointing for the Kallens' sake. 'Usually you can see the lights of the hotels and European residences down there. Hopeless!' he said. 'Let's get inside and have a drink.'

The Kallens turned and stared at Emily, the dark air surging and struggling about their heads in the arcade. They bumped against each other getting through the door.

Antoine held the door for Emily. 'Delattre's late,' he gasped, his mouth close to her ear. His breath was stale with tobacco and alcohol and his eyes searched her face. He struggled to close the door and she leaned and helped him.

In the sudden stillness of the tall room she linked her arm in his and turned to him. She smiled into his frenzied eyes. 'It will be a success, Antoine. Believe me.'

He plucked at the wisps of faded hair, as if he were weakly attempting to free himself from the clinging skeins of a fine net that had been cast over him. He unlinked his arm from hers and went to the sideboard and took a bottle of champagne from a silver ice bucket. He eased the cork from the bottle and poured the yellow wine into four glasses. He handed each of them a glass and they stood and sipped the crisp cold wine and looked at each other in amazement.

Kenneth Kallen said, 'My God, Antoine, that's some wind!' He emptied his glass and set it down on the marble sideboard with a sharp click. He turned to Emily. 'We get wind in New York, Madame Elder. But nothing like this.' Impressed, he listened to the wind moaning and smashing outside. 'Just listen to that!' He looked at Antoine. 'Are we safe in here?' He examined Emily admiringly. 'How do you manage to look so cool, Madame Elder?'

She sipped her champagne. 'We have a wind just like it in Melbourne, Dr Kallen. It brings the hot air from the desert and covers our city with red dust.'

Kenneth Kallen glanced at his wife. 'Oh, indeed,' he said.

'Our wind is from the north, however, not the south.'

'Well, thank you for the warning, Madame Elder,' Kenneth Kallen said. 'I shan't visit you in the summer in that case.' He laughed. As he lifted his wineglass to his lips, he gazed through it at Emily, his eyes lingering on her shoulders and belly.

Olive Kallen stepped across and slipped her arm through Emily's. 'Emily's not afraid of the samoom, are you, my dear? Not like our poor Merrill. Dear boy, he was quite prostrated by the weather and has had to retreat. I'm afraid he won't do us for Africa after all. We shall have to find a replacement for him.' She turned to Antoine. 'While we're all waiting for your guest of honour to arrive, Antoine, Emily and I are going to admire your splendid house.' She led Emily away from the men toward the high arch of the main door. She reached and stroked the tiles with the flat of her hand. 'Spanish,' she said approvingly. 'Sixteenth century. What a great treasure this house is for Antoine. Has he told you its history? You know it was supposed to have been the home of a pirate chief. I'll bet you there's a treasure chest hidden somewhere behind these walls.' She touched the wall and moved on. 'Everyone has conquered North Africa. The Arabs say Allah made Tunisia to be colonized.' She turned to Emily. 'You must tell me all about yourself, Emily. Your husband must be an extraordinary man to let you come here without him during the height of summer.' She stopped and smiled, friendly and curious. 'Or did you insist on your liberty? If so, then I thoroughly approve. You have intrigued me, my dear. Antoine has refused to tell me anything about you, except that you have a first in history.' She stood looking at Emily, considering her. 'What have you written?'

Emily was taken aback by Olive Kallen's unexpected question. She felt ashamed to have to admit to this robust and independent woman that she had not written anything. 'Why, nothing,' she said softly and looked away. 'I've written nothing.'

'Don't worry, you will, my dear. You will. I can tell.' The older woman reassured her. She took Emily's hand and tucked it possessively under her arm. 'All in good time. There's no hurry. You are young. When is your baby due?'

'In January,' Emily said, and she looked at Olive Kallen.

'It didn't stop me from working. Our son will be twenty-seven this year. I kept working right up to the day before he was born. Then I got him a wet nurse.' She laughed. 'What are you reading?'

'I've just read Perpetua's diary.'

'The *Passio*, you mean?' Olive exclaimed, pleased and surprised.

'Yes. Do you know it?'

'You see! I knew you were up to something. It's a wonderful document. Moving. Beautiful. Utterly authentic.' She was very pleased. 'I knew I was right about you. I said to Kenneth that day at the arena, that girl's not just here for a rest. I was watching you. What brought you to your interest in Perpetua?'

'Hakim el-Ouedi loaned me his copy of her journal. He showed me her cell that day in the arena. He has excavated it. Have you met him?'

'Now, there is an intriguing man. I do believe Delattre's just a little afraid of him. It's extraordinary. He hasn't breathed a word to me about Perpetua's cell being uncovered. This whole thing is so riddled with politics for them. You'll soon see. It's going to be very interesting tonight to see those two at dinner together. Did Antoine tell you I'm working on a biography of Septimius Severus?'

'He's told me very little about you,' Emily said, and she looked at Olive Kallen with admiration.

'I'm afraid Antoine has the annoying habit of keeping his friends in separate compartments. But you and I aren't going to let that stop us, are we? As you know, Septimius Severus was the first African to become a Roman emperor. Probably the most powerful African ruler in history. There are scholars who are convinced he changed the direction of the entire history of the Mediterranean and consequently of Europe. And that is my own view. He's enormously important. Certainly the great Arab conquerors had nothing on him. Nor the Turks. He was Emperor in 203, of course, when your Perpetua was murdered. What is it you propose to do with her?'

'I'm not sure yet,' Emily said. 'Do you think the emperor would have been present in the arena when she was killed?'

'He was certainly travelling in Africa, we do know that much. But it was his son's birthday the day she was killed, so they were probably occupied celebrating that event. But how exciting this is! What an impressive writer she was. Didn't that strike you immediately? I've always said she must have written a great deal more than has survived.'

'Perhaps it didn't suit Tertullian to let all her writing survive.'

'Quite possibly.' Olive Kallen looked at her. 'That's very shrewd of you. Impossible to demonstrate, however. Why do you think she wrote it?'

'To keep herself calm,' Emily said without hesitation.

'Not for the greater glory of God, then?' Olive asked, not entirely serious.

'So she wouldn't panic and let them see how terrified she was,' Emily said. She looked at the older woman. 'So she wouldn't feel so utterly alone with her fate. To *explain* herself. In the hope that someone would read it one day and understand what she'd gone through in that cell and would see why she'd been so stubborn about her beliefs. That's why people write, isn't it?'

'So they won't feel alone?'

'To be understood.'

Olive Kallen said thoughtfully, 'What a pity you and I haven't had a chance to meet like this before today. Antoine does annoy me with his careful protocols about his friendships. We've known him for years and have hardly met anyone through him. He's afraid to let his friends take risks with each other.'

'It's he who's taking a risk tonight, though, isn't it?' Emily said. 'I mean, inviting Hakim and Delattre to dine together at his house.'

Olive Kallen smiled. 'You're right. And you're right to be so loyal to him. Antoine's a thoroughly unique man. Kenneth and I both adore him. What was it that impressed you most in Perpetua's account of her ordeal?'

'The moment she describes when she kissed her child for the last time and passed him between the bars of her cell and gave the little boy into the safekeeping of her father. She says nothing of how she felt. But we know it is the last time she is ever to see her child.'

'Oh yes,' Olive said, and she touched her fingers to her throat. 'That is a terrible moment. You know her account is one of the few indisputably authentic documents of the period. I'm afraid you'll find it a very thin period for reliable documents. But I can help you. Did you cry? You did. I can see you did. For yourself as well as for her.' She leaned and kissed Emily's cheek. 'You and I must be friends, Emily. I shall want to know everything about you. Your hopes for yourself. You must tell me everything. Where do you read in Paris?'

'I really haven't started reading yet in Paris.'

'You must go to the Bibliothèque Sainte-Geneviève. They keep all the journals and have everything of Tertullian's. I'm well known there. I'll give you a letter of introduction. Émile Sant will look after you. You've got Latin, haven't you? Of course you have. You couldn't have got a first without Latin. You must acquire German. It won't be difficult for you. The Germans have done great work in this area.' There was a sudden gust of wind and the loud crash of a door being blown violently shut. They stood gazing toward the archway. 'This will be Père Delattre now, I daresay,' Olive said. She turned to Emily. 'It has occurred to you, I suppose, that Perpetua's journal, as you call it, and I like that very much, is the only literature we have from this period from the point of view of a woman?'

'I didn't know it was the only thing.' Emily saw Hakim stride into the dining room through the archway. He looked across at them and went straight over to where Antoine and Kenneth Kallen were standing by the sideboard.

'Here's your interesting friend, Monsieur Hakim el-Ouedi,' Olive said. 'Let's go and join them. What a confident-looking man he is.' She laughed softly and started across the room, her arm firmly in Emily's. 'Her journal's also the earliest Christian literature in existence *anywhere* by a woman, you know. You really are venturing onto very fruitful ground indeed, Emily. I find your interest in her so exciting. Your being here just now is extraordinary. There are never any other women here.' She spoke with energy and certainty, as if she could not imagine an obstacle to her purpose. 'I must say I've never heard it proposed before that Perpetua wrote in order to keep herself calm. But of course you are absolutely right.' She was silent for a moment, then said with conviction, 'You're going to read with such a fresh eye all those old sources that we've been turning over for decades. I just know you'll do something quite fine.'

Emily laughed, excited, flattered and abashed by Olive Kallen's confidence in her. 'I hardly know what I shall do,' she said. 'I've really not planned anything yet.'

'But you shall. I'm not mistaken about you.'

'You make anything sound possible,' Emily said.

'And so it is.'

They had reached the men by the sideboard.

Antoine introduced Hakim and Olive and they shook hands. Hakim said hello to Emily and she took his hand and said hello back to him.

'We heard at the hotel earlier there'd been some trouble in Tunis today?' Olive said. 'We'd proposed going in but decided against it. Do you know anything about it, Monsieur el-Ouedi?'

Hakim looked at her. 'I was there, Dr Kallen. It's why I'm late. I thought Père Delattre would be here by now. I can give you the real story.'

Kenneth Kallen smiled at Emily, as if he imagined they had an understanding, and said with faint amusement, 'Are we to take it there is also an unreal story, then?'

Olive Kallen said, 'You were there? Well, then, you must tell us everything.'

Hakim turned to Kenneth Kallen. 'You'll read the unreal story in your French newspaper at your hotel over breakfast tomorrow morning, sir.'

Antoine stood with his back to the sideboard. He was frowning at Hakim and looking miserable.

Hakim said, 'I'm sorry I'm so late. No sign of Delattre, then?'

Antoine said unhappily, 'If you'll all excuse me. I shall put through a call to the Grand Séminaire. Père Delattre has obviously been delayed.'

Emily watched him walk across the room and go out through the archway.

Hakim took an olive from a bowl on the sideboard and put it in his mouth. The Kallens watched him chew the olive.

'And the true story is the one we'll hear from you this evening over dinner?' Kenneth Kallen asked. 'Is that so?'

Hakim said, 'I was hoping Père Delattre would be here to hear it too.'

Olive Kallen said, 'I read your paper on the horoscope of Julia Domna last year in the *Journal of Roman Studies*, Monsieur el-Ouedi.' Olive waited for his attention.

Hakim took the olive stone from his mouth and placed it in a small blue-and-green ceramic dish. He turned and looked at her.

She measured him with her look, as if she interviewed him for employment. 'It was very strong,' she said, delivering a judgment.

'Thank you.' He was pleased.

'I agree with almost everything you say there.'

Hakim looked at her. 'But what?'

'I think you give too much credence to Septimius's reliance on the supernatural.' She turned to Emily. 'Julia Domna was Septimius Severus's second wife.'

Hakim turned to Emily. He smiled. 'That's Ahmed's influence, I'm afraid. Did you read the little book?'

'Yes,' she said. 'I should like to visit her cell again. But I'm afraid there isn't going to be time. We're leaving on Saturday.'

'Ahmed tells me you'll come back and see us again.'

Antoine came through the door and they all turned and waited for him expectantly. He stood before them, small and shrunken, like a schoolboy reporting a tragic failure to his assembled masters.

'What is it?' Hakim asked. He reached and put his hand on Antoine's shoulder.

Antoine made a helpless gesture of apology and irritably shrugged off Hakim's hand. 'Père Delattre is indisposed. He's not coming,' he said bleakly. 'I'm sorry.'

'He can't take the samoom,' Hakim said gleefully, and he reached for another olive and put it in his mouth and chewed it.

Kenneth Kallen said, 'Well, now, I don't believe that to be the case, Monsieur el-Ouedi.' His tone was dignified and reproving. 'It is my conviction that Père Delattre has proved himself a man of considerable determination and resourcefulness in this somewhat difficult country of yours.'

'It *is* difficult,' Hakim said playfully. His black eyes gleamed with excitement.

Olive Kallen said, 'Delattre's an extraordinary individual. Quite extraordinary. Enormously resourceful. I'm so disappointed he won't be joining us for dinner, Antoine. It really is too bad.' She looked at Hakim. 'I hardly think Père Delattres's going to be put off by a bit of wind. I think my husband's got you there.' She turned to Emily and took her arm. 'What do you say, Emily? Do we stick together on this?'

Antoine gestured at the table. 'Won't you all please sit down. Père Delattre insists on living as the humble of this country live. He and his White Fathers dress as they dress and eat as they eat. He was to be our guest of honour this evening. So I'm afraid there's no French cooking tonight. But there's plenty of French wine.'

They found places at the table, leaving the chair at the head of the table vacant. Hakim held a chair for Emily then sat next to her. Olive and Kenneth Kallen sat opposite them, and Antoine sat alone at the foot of the table opposite Père Delattre's empty chair.

Sonia came in and went around filling their glasses with wine and urging them to help themselves, explaining the heaped dishes of spiced lamb and baked mullet, and the oily slices of sautéed aubergine and the green and red capsicums, and the aromatic rounds of tajine.

'The humble of this country live mighty well, by all appearances,' Kenneth Kallen said.

Olive Kallen looked across at Hakim. 'You were going to tell us about the trouble in Tunis.'

Hakim seemed keyed up and eager to speak about the morning's events. 'Six thousand striking workers assembled early this morning in the avenue de France. This was before the samoom struck. We went along quietly.'

'You mean you were with these people from the beginning?' Olive asked, surprised. 'You had planned to join them?'

He looked at her, addressing his story to her as if there were just the two of them present. 'We proceeded, madame, in an orderly formation until we reached the place de la Résidence. There were more than a thousand armed French soldiers and police waiting for us there. We stood and looked at them and they stood and looked back at us. After an hour, their colonel told his men to fix their bayonets. They did it in that lazy, well-practised way the French soldier has for doing everything. It's a pleasure to watch, if you know what I mean. As if he's really doing it for himself and would go on being a good soldier doing these things instead of being a farmer or getting a job in a factory or an office, even if his government decided it no longer had a need for soldiers to do these things. That is the French soldier. The German soldier is a Roman compared to the French soldier. The French soldier receives an order, but he carries it out as if he's decided on just that particular course of action for himself, quite independently of the wishes of any superior authority. He smiles and touches his moustache and you wonder whether he's going to obey the order, or has even heard it. This creates a certain suspense and you observe him closely to see what he will decide to do, this free man obeying an order. Then he yields to some deep inner prompting and reaches around in his belt and draws his bayonet from its scabbard and gives it a fond look. He clips the bayonet to the barrel of his rifle, as if he is the only man in the world who has ever thought to do such a thing. As you observe him, you begin to think of him as a man just like yourself. When his bayonet is fixed, however, then he fixes his gaze on you. And you see in the pale eyes of this French boy from the pastures of the Val-de-Loire, with its camellias and roses, that he will kill you in the same lazy, easygoing way that he fixed his bayonet to his rifle. And suddenly you are afraid. You look at him standing there in front of you in his blue uniform with his rifle and his shiny steel bayonet, and he is so relaxed you'd think he might close his eyes and have a little nap before he gets on with the real business of the day, and there's a tingling in your legs urging you to run away from him.'

'Very fanciful indeed. Well done,' Kenneth Kallen said, his mouth full of fish and aubergine, his tone faintly derisive. 'This is the true version of events, ladies and gentlemen.' He laughed. 'The fish is superb, Antoine.'

Hakim stopped speaking and stared at him.

The samoom moaned through the house.

They watched Hakim, waiting to see what he would do. Antoine was slumped in his chair, the stem of his wineglass clutched in his fingers, his gaze going from Hakim to Kenneth Kallen, a smile on his lips. Olive Kallen said peaccably, 'Please do continue, Monsieur el-Ouedi.'

Hakim looked at her intently, as if he was to read his story in her attention. 'We could have been there with our families watching a military parade, madame. It might have been a national holiday. The sun was shining. Everything was peaceful.' His hands described the expansive summer day above the cloth. 'Now the bayonets were fixed, however, an uneasy shifting in the crowd began and you felt the people standing beside you wanted to discover an excuse for going to the back of the crowd. One or two turned round and looked toward the back of the crowd, as if they were hoping to see a friend and might decide to go back there and join the friend. And some did this, frowning and looking concerned so we'd know they weren't just going to the back to get out of the way of the bayonets but were forced to go back to rejoin the friend they'd glimpsed. And others looked at you and waited to see if you were going to do this. And if you did, then maybe they would too. And when they saw that you were not thinking of going to the back but were standing your ground, they made some little gesture to let you know they were with you and would also remain staunch. And, of course, you *had* been considering going back yourself. But once you'd exchanged this acknowledgment with your neighbours you felt that for the sake of your dignity you couldn't go back now. And you began to feel trapped in the open out there at the front of the crowd with nothing between you and the bayonets and to envy those who'd made their move early and gone back while there was still the chance of doing so without looking as if they were deserting the cause or being cowardly.'

He stopped speaking and looked at Kenneth Kallen. 'And that's how it was, sir. When you read your newspaper at breakfast, you'll see how we started throwing stones at the military. But if you go down to the place de la Résidence yourself and have a look, you'll see there are no stones there. There are never any loose stones lying around in the French boulevards. Especially in the business sector of the city. That's something you'll notice straightaway when you go in to Tunis for a visit. The boulevards are clean and well cared for and are even washed down before dawn by the water cart every day. The French are good housekeepers. Well, then, if that is the case, your newspaper will inform you soberly, if there were indeed no stones in the place de la Résidence, then these striking workers must have brought the stones with them to the place de la Résidence from the Arab quarter where, as everyone knows, there are always piles of rubble and stones lying around on every corner and no one ever bothers to clean them up. Which renders their actions premeditated and even more culpable than if they'd thrown the stones out of a passionate outburst in the heat of the moment. Which would be understandable even if it wasn't forgivable with the samoom blowing up and making everyone short-tempered and irritable. But no, they didn't even have that excuse, the reporter will tell you. The action of the striking workers was nothing less than a determined conspiracy to commit insurrection and to challenge the lawful authorities. That's what they'll say. And so the demonstration had to be put down with the full rigour of the law. And so on. Column after column. You'll need a third cup of coffee to get you through it all.'

Hakim speared a piece of lamb and put it on his plate.

'Then what happened?' Olive asked. 'You can't leave us there.'

'They charged us and we ran away.' Hakim said, as if he had lost interest in the story. 'They chased us all the way home to Halfaouine and they beat up anyone they caught and then they went around smashing in doors and searching houses in the usual way, arresting a few notable Arab intellectuals, who they'll describe as the ringleaders of a conspiracy.'

Emily noticed that Antoine was drinking steadily and had not eaten anything. The skin of his cheeks was yellow and his bald head glistened damply in the lamplight.

'And is that to be the end of it, then?' Olive Kallen asked incredulously.

'No, it is the beginning of it, madame,' Hakim said. 'There are two million Arabs in Tunisia and fifty thousand French.' He speared another piece of lamb with his fork and put it in his mouth and chewed and then washed it down with wine. 'Before the end many people will die.'

There was an uncomfortable silence.

Antoine said softly, 'Someone died today.'

They looked at him.

'Who?' Olive Kallen asked with astonishment, almost as if she thought there might be a chance of the victim being known to her.

'A French policeman,' Antoine said. He didn't look at Hakim. 'He wasn't involved in the attack on the marchers. He was on duty in his usual place in the rue d'Italie near the central market. He knew the market people well and was liked by them. He had a wife and five children.' Antoine paused and took another drink. 'They stabbed him and left him to bleed to death in the street. No one went to his aid.'

Hakim scoffed, 'How do you know this?' He turned to Olive Kallen. 'It's the usual rumour of atrocity started by the police to justify their violence.'

'Nabil was there,' Antoine said quietly. 'He saw it.'

Olive Kallen said in a shocked voice, 'Oh my God, how horrible! The poor man.'

Her husband looked at her. 'Is your sympathy for the policeman, my dear, or for Nabil?'

Antoine heaved himself upright in his chair and reached for the decanter. 'Thank God Delattre didn't get here tonight!' he said.

Hakim looked at him.

'How serious is this thing? Playfair's always telling us Tunisia's been as safe as Algeria since the taking of Kairouan.'

Hakim laughed. 'If we're at peace with the French, sir, why is every town and important strategic point in this country garrisoned with French troops?'

Kenneth Kallen said triumphantly, 'Why, Mr el-Ouedi, that is to defend your country for you from the Italians. Which is something you Arabs do not appear to be capable of doing for yourselves.'

Hakim made a disgusted gesture at Kenneth Kallen with his knife. 'You know nothing about us!'

'Do you think perhaps Père Delattre stayed away tonight because he'd heard of the trouble?' Olive Kallen asked.

No one answered her.

Antoine filled his glass and drank. Damp hanks of hair stuck to his cheeks and neck. He looked up at them, his eyelids heavy. 'Hakim's right,' he said. 'Why is he always the only Arab at my dinner table?' He laughed heavily and emptied his glass. 'Do you ladies mind if I smoke a cigarette?'

Hakim set his knife and fork squarely on his plate and he wiped his lips with his napkin. 'It's time I left,' he said. He looked at Emily, 'I'm sorry we didn't get a chance to talk.'

'Oh, don't go taking offence,' Antoine said. 'Kenneth didn't mean anything. Did you, Kenneth? You didn't mean anything. He'll apologize if you like. Say you're sorry, Kenneth. Go on. It won't hurt.'

Kenneth Kallen stared at his wife and said nothing.

'It's true anyway, Hakim. You know perfectly well if it weren't for the French the Italians would be all over you,' Antoine said. 'Stay! We've only just started. Stay and talk to us. Tell us another of your cheerful stories.' He laughed thickly and fumbled in his pocket for his cigarettes.

Hakim stood up. He bowed to Olive and wished her goodnight.

Emily said, 'Wait. I'll get your book.'

'Please keep it,' he said. 'I don't need it.'

'Are you sure?'

'I'd like you to keep it.'

The others watched them – older people watching young people, as if there was something to be understood that they knew they would not understand any longer but had understood once.

Antoine said, 'What book?'

Emily got up and went with Hakim to the terrace. They stood in the wind together.

'It's over,' he said. 'It'll be raining by morning.'

'I can smell the gum tree,' she said. 'It smells like a summer night at home.'

'You miss your home?'

'No,' she said too quickly. Then, 'Sometimes. But I don't want to go back. Not yet. I feel I must do something before I go back.'

They were silent.

'My mother's people used to strike their tents and travel while the samoom was at its fiercest. The samoom was their ally. Their friend. They slipped away under cover of it and deceived their enemies and then attacked them from an unexpected quarter.' He was silent for a while. 'This wind has been the dark clothes of my mother's people through two thousand years of invasions. It's how we know the stranger. The stranger is afraid of our samoom. The stranger always describes the samoom as an evil wind. There's a kind of sacrilege in that for us. That's Kenneth Kallen. Nothing is sacred to a man like that. Desert people believe God's secret dwelling place is in the wind.'

'Do you believe that?' she asked softly.

'There are days when I believe it and there are days when I don't believe it. When I meet my enemy, on those days I believe it.'

'And do you believe it today?'

He turned and looked at her, the lamplight from the hallway falling across his face. 'But most of the time I'm like you and I don't really know what I believe.'

'How do you know I don't know what I believe.'

He shrugged. 'It's obvious.' He smiled. 'Anyway, Ahmed said so.'

'You quote Ahmed to me all the time, but you didn't bother to introduce him that day. Why not?'

'Ahmed is very correct. Every day, whether he sees his enemy or not, is a day of belief for Ahmed. For him to know you in any way without your husband being present would be to insult you. He would not have invited you to share our camp as I did. He thought it most improper.' He held out his hand. 'I'd better get going.'

She took his hand.

His gaze touched her dress. 'You're not wearing her medallion tonight.'

'No,' she said. 'I felt it needed a rest. I think I was right, don't you?'

'I first read her journal in the British Museum,' he said and was thoughtful. 'I miss England. I admire the English. They believe in themselves and are generous with their beliefs. It was from them I learned that true scholarship is to put aside your prejudice and to acknowledge your ignorance. Surely the hardest thing for any man to do. It is a standard they have set for the world of scholarship. But I was sick of London's rain and cold weather and was longing to come home for some warmth. Maybe if I'd read it here it wouldn't have meant so much to me. I carried her book about with me in my pocket as a kind of talisman. I was always meaning to take it back, but I never did.' He looked at her. 'You will soon discover what a treacherous business history is. When you begin to uncover what has been concealed for hundreds of years, you never know what you're going to find. You will unearth things which you will wish had remained hidden. Delattre lacks the detachment of the English scholars. That's why I oppose him. Not because he is French. But because he will put back into the earth the things he doesn't wish to find there.' He relinquished her hand. 'I'll expect a letter about Perpetua. Ahmed will be disappointed if we don't hear from you. Good-bye, Madame Georges Elder, Emily.'

'Good-bye, Hakim. And by the way, it isn't a matter of not believing in anything. I'm just not sure that I know yet what I want from life.' She watched him go down the steps. The studded door closed behind him and he was gone. She stood in the sacred wind breathing the familiar smell of the gum tree and listening to his truck going down the hill. She was suddenly thinking of her childhood and of her father. She would write to him and tell him about Olive Kallen.

When she got back to the dining room, the Kallens had risen from the table and were saying their farewells to Antoine. Antoine was protesting and trying to convince them to stay. Sonia was standing by the door watching Antoine anxiously. Emily went over and took Antoine's arm firmly, steadying him against her side, feeling the slightness of his body, like a child's body almost. She turned to the Kallens and smiled. 'The wind is dying down,' she said. 'The worst of it is over. Antoine and I will see you to the car.' She turned to Sonia. 'Tell Nabil that Monsieur and Madame Kallen are leaving, will you please, Sonia.'

When the Kallens had gone, Emily told Antoine she was tired. They said goodnight and she went to her room. She opened the shutters and took off her dress and lay on the bed. The ghostly canopy of her tent glowed in the night above her. She had been lying there for some time, her mind agitated and excited with thoughts and impressions and half plans for what she would do when she got back to Paris, when she felt the strange, delicate fluttering in her belly. She put her hand on the smooth rise above her mound of Venus. The bewildering other being within her, the stranger growing from her own flesh. She lay there scarcely breathing, as if she might detect a stealthy sound – its voice, its will, its desires and hopes and the force of its destiny. She felt terribly alone and thought of Olive Kallen. She knew then suddenly that if she were ever to be truly mistress of her own life, as Olive surely was, then she would have to have the courage to go back to Chartres and to see Bertrand before the baby was born – to confront him with the consequences of their meeting, and to confront the uncertainty of her own feelings and memories of that day. She knew suddenly that unless she was able to put her moral house in order she would never be free to choose her own way. She wondered what Olive and Hakim would think of her if they knew the uncertainty of her child's paternity. Ahmed, no doubt, would regret his sympathetic intuitions and condemn her to some outer region. The thought of Madame Elder and Georges and her own parents waiting with certainty for the child to be born, almost as if they themselves had brought it into being, seemed to her an obscenity.

Restless, confused, and agitated, she got up and went over to the blue-painted table and switched on the lamp. She found the card with Olive Kallen's New York address on it and stood looking at it, reading it over as if it were a charm with a secret power. She slipped the card between the pages of Perpetua's book and switched off the light and went back to bed. She lay wide awake for hours, unable to sleep, excited and appalled, filled with hopes and plans one moment, despairing the next.

Emily and Antoine stood in the shelter of the hallway while Nabil carried their luggage down the steps to the car. It was raining steadily. Sonia clasped Emily in her arms and kissed her and she looked into her eyes and smiled. 'You will come back to Sidi bou-Saïd, madame.'

'I hope I shall, Sonia.'

Antoine embraced Sonia. Mounir stepped forward and gravely shook hands with Emily.

'We didn't hear your stories, Mounir,' she said.

'This was not the time for my stories, madame,' he said in French.

They went down the steps to the car and Nabil closed the yellow door behind them. He drove down the hill along the narrow streets gleaming with soft rain and out along the road past the turnoff to Carthage. Emily looked back out the car window down the road to the amphitheatre. A Berber child minding sheep was curled up asleep in the rain under an olive tree. The sheep looked up as the car went past. Nabil blew the horn at a donkey loaded with wet bales of hay and shouted cheerfully to the donkey's driver. Antoine was silent, curled into the corner of his seat. His arms were folded across his chest and his eyes were closed. She thought he was asleep. Then he said, 'Why didn't you tell me Hakim had been to see you?'

'I thought you'd be annoyed.'

He opened his eyes and looked at her. 'If you try to please me, Emily, instead of pleasing yourself,' he said, 'it will be an impossible labyrinth for you.'

Neither spoke for some time.

When she looked at him again, his eyes were closed. 'I feel afraid of returning to Paris,' she confessed. 'There is so much to be decided.'

Antoine said nothing.

~ PART THREE ~

The Conditions of Faith

ONE

— ◆ —

There were wild storms in the Mediterranean and the sea was rough on the crossing from Tunis to Marseilles. Emily was seasick and scarcely left her cabin. By the time she and Antoine boarded the train at Marseilles she had kept almost no food down for two days and was pale and exhausted by her ordeal. Before boarding the train she telephoned Georges at his office in Paris. The line was bad and they shouted at each other. She could not recognize his voice. He sounded like a stranger. After she had hung up, and in case he had not understood her, she sent him a telegram with the time of their expected arrival at the Gare de Lyon. She and Antoine spent that night and half the next day on the train. They pulled into Paris just after midday.

Antoine stepped onto the platform and turned and reached up and took her hands. There was a cold wind and she stood close against him. She turned the collar of her overcoat up. While the porter collected their luggage for them they searched the crowded platform for Georges. They saw him just as he saw them. He waved his hat and pushed his way toward them.

Georges came up and he took Emily in his arms and held her against him. 'I shall never let you go away on your own like that again, my darling. It's been only half a life without you.'

'I'm sorry,' she said. She pulled away from his embrace and looked about her in distress. 'I'll have to sit down somewhere for a minute.'

Georges supported her with his arm and led her to a wooden bench. Alarmed, he looked questioningly at Antoine.

Antoine shrugged helplessly, as if he did not expect to be believed. 'I promise you, Georges, Emily was well until we left Sidi bou-Saïd. The journey's been endless. A nightmare. It has exhausted us both.' He turned away and told the porter to wait for them with the luggage. They waited until Emily was recovered then went together out into the forecourt of the station where the taxis were. They climbed into a taxi and drove to Antoine's apartment in the Quai des Célestins. It was raining steadily and the streets were cold and wet and filled with traffic and crowds of people hurrying along sheltering under black umbrellas. Emily shivered and closed her eyes and she squeezed Georges's hand and murmured, 'I'm sorry. I'll be better when I've had a rest.'

They stopped outside the building in the Quai des Célestins where Antoine had his apartment. He leaned and kissed her. She said she would telephone him. She touched his cheek with her fingers. 'We'll talk soon, Antoine.'

The taxi turned around to cross the river at the Pont Sully. As they drove away, Emily looked back. Antoine stood on the footpath in the rain with his suitcase in his hand gazing after the taxi, like a man abandoned.

They drove along the boulevard Saint-Germain until they reached rue Saint-Dominique. 'How familiar it all seems,' she said. 'It is as if I had lived here for years, instead of just a few months.'

Georges held her hand and studied her anxiously as she looked out at the passing street. 'You're home now,' he said. 'I should never have let you go away like that. It was stupid of me.'

'No,' she said firmly. 'I can't tell you how important it has been for me. This is nothing. I'll be myself again in a day or two. Antoine was right, the journey home was a nightmare. I didn't know travelling could be so exhausting.'

He asked carefully, 'Everything is all right with the baby?'

'Yes. Of course. There's nothing to worry about,' she reassured him. She was thoughtful, looking out at the streets. 'Paris is so enormous and grey after Tunisia.' She was silent for a moment. 'I shall go back one day.'

He laughed uncertainly. 'But not right away, I hope.' He patted her hand. 'Everyone says that after they've visited Sidi bou-Saïd for the first time. They return enchanted. After a week in Paris, you'll have forgotten the place.'

'I *was* enchanted,' she said. 'But that isn't what I meant.'

'We'll talk when you're rested.'

The taxi turned in under the covered way beneath the faded sign LINGERIE MERCERIE BONNETERIE. 'Home,' he said. 'Sophie has everything ready for you.'

The robinia tree in the center of the courtyard was bare. The earth beneath it within the circle enclosed by iron railings was thick with its golden leaves. The rain fell straight down, drumming on the roof of the taxi. Madame Barbier hurried across the courtyard. She was followed by the two old men. They wore corn sacks over their heads and shoulders. While Georges paid the driver the old men unloaded Emily's luggage and carried it to the entrance. Georges sheltered Emily with his umbrella and they went across the courtyard and in at the door. Madame Barbier grasped Emily's hand. 'Welcome home, Madame Elder.' The old men in their hooded sacks waited in the shadows at the bottom of the stairs with the luggage. They watched Emily and Georges go ahead of them up the stairs.

Emily had to stop to catch her breath on the way up. Georges held her. Madame Barbier and the old men with the luggage watched silently from below.

Sophie was waiting on the landing, the door to the apartment wide open. 'Welcome home, madame,' she said. She was wearing a freshly laundered green-and-white striped apron over her long black dress. Her hair was pinned in a tight bun at the nape of her neck.

'You look like a real maid, Sophie.' Emily went in. She stopped and looked about her in surprise. 'Why, you've changed everything!'

Sophie and Georges exchanged a look. 'Do you like it?' Georges asked.

The apartment had been freshly painted a pale creamy white. Blue-flowered curtains hung at the windows and the floorboards had been polished. In place of the worn brown rug in the center of the room with the two old leather armchairs, two cane chairs with green-and-red peony-flowered cushions faced each other across a wine-madder Persian rug. The low circular table with the brass reading lamp and the pewter ashtray in the shape of a swan were still in place. A bunch of white chrysanthemums in a yellow jug stood on the table by the window next to the telephone. But it was an entirely new arrangement between the windows that Emily went over and examined.

Sophie and Georges and Madame Barbier and the two old men stood and watched her.

A high-backed wing chair upholstered in heavy green tapestry was the centrepiece of the arrangement. In front of the chair was a low footstool upholstered in the same green material, its four turned legs miniature replicas of the chair legs. To the right of the chair, on the window side, there was a delicate marquetry-inlaid sewing table. It was the object on the other side of the chair, however, that Emily went up to. It was a crib. The basket was suspended at either end from a leather thong attached to the curled ends of two elaborate bentwood uprights. The basket was without bedding and resembled the dark ribcage of some animal. Emily reached and touched it, setting it swinging back and forth on its hangers. It creaked emptily. She stilled it with another touch of her fingers.

After the creaking of the empty crib, there was a silence. Georges and Sophie waited for Emily to say something. The pigeons cooed privately on the guttering below the window. 'A mother's welcome,' Madame Barbier said, and she clapped her hands.

One of the old men murmured, 'The Madonna's throne.' They both cackled and coughed and hawked breathlessly, nodding to each other in their hooded sacks like eastern patriarchs.

Georges went over and put his arm around Emily's waist and he reached and set the crib swinging. 'Mother sent it up from Chartres. It's my old crib. An Elder family heirloom. It belonged to my father's family. What do you think?'

Emily looked across the room to where Madame Barbier and the two old men stood by the door with Sophie.

Georges followed her gaze. He went over to them and gave the old men a couple of francs each and thanked them and saw them out the door. 'My wife's tired after the journey, Madame Barbier,' he explained. 'Perhaps you'd like to come up and have coffee with us in the morning.' He closed the door on the concierge and turned back into the room. He opened his arms. 'Well, what do you think? Sophie did most of it.'

Emily said, 'Thank you, Sophie. It's wonderful.'

'It was Monsieur's idea, madame,' Sophie said modestly. 'I only made the curtains.'

'The curtains are beautiful.' Emily looked around the room. 'Everything is beautiful. You've both done so much.' There were purple half-moons under her eyes and her cheeks were grey and hollow. She appealed to Georges. 'I'm going to have to lie down for a while, if you don't mind. Would you bring the small bag for me.' She turned and went into the bedroom.

Georges picked up the suitcase and he and Sophie exchanged a look. He took the suitcase into the bedroom and set it on the floor beside the bed. He pulled back the covers of the bed and helped Emily off with her overcoat. He dropped the overcoat on the bed and put his hand over her belly. 'My God! How it's grown.' He looked at her. 'It's real!'

'Yes.' She looked down at his hand over her swollen belly.

'My child!' he said, awed. 'Can you . . . What do you feel? Does it move? Do you feel as if there is a little person in there? Or . . . I'm sorry,' he said quickly. You're exhausted. I'm rattling on. It's so good to have you back safely. You can't believe how good it is.'

He helped her get undressed. She put on her nightdress and got into bed and drew the blankets up to her chin.

He stood looking at her. 'I'll call Léon to come and look at you.'

She reached out of the blanket for his hand. 'No. I just need to rest for an hour or two. I'll get up later and have a bath. I don't want to see Léon just now. I'm all right. I promise. The apartment looks lovely. Thank you for everything.'

'You like it, then?' he said eagerly.

'Yes. It's just perfect.' She closed her eyes.

'Isn't the green chair beautiful? And the footstool?'

She opened her eyes. 'Yes. It's all wonderful.'

'There's everything you could possibly need in the sewing table.'

She didn't speak.

He leaned and touched her cheek with the back of his hand. 'Well,' he said. 'You rest, then.' He waited. 'Your mother sent the layette. We didn't unpack it. We thought we'd leave that for you. We've put it in the little room.'

Emily nodded and murmured, 'Thank you, Georges.' She didn't open her eyes.

'I'm afraid I have to go in to the office for an hour or two. I wouldn't but Jean-Pierre rang. It's urgent. Sophie will stay. One of the maids moved out and Madame Barbier has given her the room upstairs in the chambres de bonne.'

Emily opened her eyes. 'Good,' she said. 'That's good.'

'All right, then.' He lingered.

'Go and see to your work,' she urged him. 'I'll have a sleep.'

He kissed her and went out and closed the door softly, as if it were the room of a sick person.

After a few minutes, Emily heard the front door close and then the sound of his footsteps as he crossed the landing and went down the stairs. She turned on her side and stared at the wall. She wept silently.

For two days Emily rested. Léon called and examined her and pronounced her too ill to get up. She obediently ate the soup and the steamed fillets of sole that Sophie cooked for her. Then, on the morning of the third day, after Georges had left for the office, she decided she could wait no longer. She put on her winter clothes and caught the Métro to Cluny–La Sorbonne and she became a student once again. Olive Kallen's letter of introduction to Émile Sant at the Bibliothèque Sainte-Geneviève proved effective and Emily was soon settled in the great reading room at a table close to a heater with a pile of books in front of her.

When she got home that evening, tired but elated from her day's work, the smell of the library still in her nostrils, she was glad to find that Georges was not yet home from the office. The apartment was silent and empty and all her own. She heated a little of the lamb stew that Sophie had left and stood by the kitchen window looking out at the courtyard and the roofs of Paris eating the stew from the saucepan with a spoon. Afterward she made a pot of tea and took it into the sitting room. She sat at the table by the window and sipped her tea and opened her writing case. She took out the notes she had made in the library during the day and set them to one side. The rain tapped against the window and the gas fire murmured. The shard of Roman red slip lay on the table beside her writing case next to the *Passio Perpetuae*.

During the following hour Emily wrote two letters. The first letter she wrote was to her father. The second was to Hakim. She put these letters in envelopes and addressed them then withdrew several fresh sheets of writing paper from the side pocket of her writing case. She was about to begin her third letter when she noticed that when she had removed the fresh sheets of paper, a corner of the English version of her first letter to Bertrand had been drawn out of the writing case with them. Curious, and a little apprehensive, she took the letter out all the way and opened it. She sat reading it. She could not recognize herself, however, in the breathlessly passionate words. She was disturbed to realize that she had written to him with so much emotion. Might he still imagine her to be longing for him? She found this idea intensely repugnant and could not bear to think of it. Impatiently she folded the letter and thrust it deep into the side pocket alongside her second unsent letter in French, which she did not take out and read.

She took up her fountain pen and leaned over the fresh notepaper. She hesitated, then wrote:

Rue Saint-Dominique, Paris

Dear Dr Kallen,

I feel I should address you by your Christian name, but I shan't until I hear from you. I began reading today in the Bibliothèque Sainte-Geneviève. Have I become a student again? Or am I to be an independent scholar? Goodness, how grand that looks when I write it! Monsieur Sant was most helpful and has promised to find me everything I need. He asks to be remembered to you. I told him you were in great spirits when I saw you – can it really be only a week ago? – in Sidi bou-Saïd. I have called my modest history, if that is what it is to be, *The Secular Perpetua*. How do you like my working title? I am certain it will appeal to Hakim el-Ouedi and to his friend Ahmed. But what will Père Delattre think of such a title?

I am still strangely weak from the rigours of traveling. Such a thing has never happened to me before. I was seasick all the way across the Mediterranean and yet I sailed half around the world on a rolling merchant ship without losing my appetite for a single day! So it is my pregnancy that alters me. I confess, there are moments when I feel threatened by this child. But I must say no more of that. I am enthusiastic and bold! It is an astonishing liberation to possess a project of my own at last – and one that has come into my possession through the medium of new friends! How fortunate I am to have met you. I must acknowledge at once that I also owe a special part of this liberation to my chance meeting with Hakim el-Ouedi that day in the arena – his friend Ahmed would call our meeting providential. But I insist it was mere chance, though chance of the very best sort, that led me to her cell and to the discovery of her story – and once we have begun a story can we be at peace until we know how it is to end?

Already I have chanced upon an important discovery and cannot wait to tell you about it and to hear from you what you think of it. When I made this discovery, my last doubts vanished and I knew at once that I must go on with this project at all costs. Before beginning to read the numerous volumes of Tertullian's writings I looked him up in the *Dictionnaire d'archéologie Chretienne et de Liturgie* – to consult the official and contemporary view of him, and to learn something of this man whose writings are to be so important in reaching an understanding of the times in which she lived. I was astonished to find the following – which I transcribe for you here from my notes, 'Tertullian was the creator of Christian Latin literature'. No less! 'Cyprian and Saint Augustine both stand on his shoulders. These three North Africans are the fathers of the Western churches.' So this was Perpetua's friend and confidant, the man (we are asked to believe) to whom she felt able to entrust her precious diary on the last day of her life? This man, none other than the first of the founding fathers of the Western churches!

Before the end of the day, however, I was certain it was not possible that this man could have been the confidant and friend of any woman, let alone have been admitted to the trust of a woman of Perpetua's percipience and courage. The first work of his that I read – it was its title that attracted me – was his essay to women, 'On Female Dress.' I wasn't sure what to expect. It seemed an auspicious title to begin with and I suppose I anticipated something light, friendly, and entirely sympathetic to women. This is what I found. 'The sentence of God on this sex of yours lives in this age: the guilt must of necessity live too. You are the Devil's gateway: you are the breaker of the seal of that forbidden tree: you are the first deserter of the divine law: you are she who persuaded him whom the Devil was not valiant enough to attack. You destroyed so easily God's image, man. On account of your desert – that is, death – even the Son of God had to die . . . Accordingly these things are all the baggage of woman in her condemned and dead state . . .'

And so on. Page after page of it. He has not one kind word for us. While I was reading this vicious diatribe I forgot where I was and thought vividly of her cell in the arena. When I looked up from the book and saw the other readers around me and smelled once again the smell of the library, I knew I had already found a sufficient reason to reopen this case. Hakim was surely right when he cautioned me to distrust everything Tertullian has to say about Perpetua and her motives.

Now there is suddenly so much to do! For the first time in my life I feel the past is a mystery directly affecting me – is something urgent and immediate, in which there are questions that must be answered. It is late now and I shall finish this letter tomorrow. Or, perhaps, I will post to you what I have written and will send you another installment of my adventures very soon. Please reply at once! I am anxious to know your response to my discovery. What have you written? you asked me. I was dismayed to be asked such a question and ashamed to have to answer that I had written nothing. Now that is to change. I am determined to inquire assiduously into this mystery and to write my conclusions when my inquiries are complete. When I finished my degree, I gladly abandoned scholarship in the certainty that the past was dead and was of no use to me. Now I approach it once again, but this time I approach it with a vivid sense that the past is as much in me as it is in the documents I am reading. The dust and the heat and the smell of the arena are as close to me in this as the books are. And she is. I feel I know her. I cannot claim to be cool and detached. I am not that. Indeed, I must be careful not to get into a fever of impatience.

Forgive me, I am suddenly exhausted. I shall post this to you tomorrow. How long does it take a letter to go from Paris to New York? Not nearly so long, thank goodness, as it takes to go from Paris to Australia. Will you return to Carthage in the spring? Oh, there are so many questions. To think I have imagined myself bored with life! My father used to lament what he called my wasted years. Now there seems to be so little time. If my husband's design is successful and his firm wins the tender he is working on, then we shall be returning to Australia in the spring. And by then I shall be a mother.

I know that with you and Hakim and Antoine I have come into possession of true friendship and certain encouragement.

When Georges came in through the covered way, it was after midnight and the lights in Madame Barbier's rooms were out. As he crossed the courtyard, he glanced up at the apartment windows. A light was burning. On the landing at the top of the stairs he put down his heavy briefcase and stood easing his back. He drew his keys from the pocket of his overcoat and opened the door. A gust of warm air rushed out of the apartment.

Emily was lying curled up asleep on the Persian rug in front of the gas fire. Georges closed the door and went cautiously across the room and stood looking down at her. She lay on her side facing the fire. Her knees were drawn up and her blue dressing gown was pulled close around her. Her cheeks were flushed from the heat of the gas fire. Her hands were pressed to her swollen belly, as if she protected the baby. She had placed a peony-flowered cushion from one of the cane chairs under her head. Her mouth was open and a nerve twitched in her cheek. On each exhalation of breath she made a small moaning sound, as if she confronted some torment in her dream.

Georges took off his hat and he stepped across the room and put the hat on the table by the window next to the telephone. It was the light of the reading lamp that he had seen through the window from the courtyard. He set his briefcase on the floor beside the table and picked up her letter to Olive Kallen. As he began to read, he sat slowly in the chair. He read the letter from beginning to end, setting each page aside as he finished it. When he had read the last page, he sat staring at it. 'There are moments when I feel threatened by this child,' he read aloud. He looked across at Emily sleeping by the fire. He put the letter down and began to examine the contents of her writing case. There were other letters, he discovered, folded and tucked away in the side pocket. He pulled out one of these and opened it. The pages crackled.

'What are you doing?' she asked, her voice filled with alarm.

He started guiltily and turned toward her, holding her letter to Bertrand between his fingers as if he'd caught it out of the air. 'You're awake.'

She scrambled to her feet and came over and snatched the letter from him. She folded it and pushed it deep into the pocket of the writing case. 'How dare you search through my correspondence!' She closed the writing case and fastened the buckles. Her hands trembled and she breathed heavily, as if she'd run up the stairs.

He picked up the letter to Olive Kallen. 'I can't let you send this.' He looked at the letter. 'I can't believe you've written these things. You tell this woman you feel threatened by our child?'

She reached and took the letter from him. He relinquished it to her.

'I can't let you send it. You must understand that. You can't possibly go on with this insane idea. How could you have even thought of it?'

She stood, stubborn and silent, holding her letter and not looking at him. 'What else did you read?'

'Isn't this enough?'

She looked at him. 'I wasn't going to keep my plans a secret from you. There hasn't been a chance to talk to you.'

He said incredulously, '*Plans?* Plans, for God's sake? You're having a baby. Isn't that plan enough for you?' He wrenched off his overcoat and tossed it onto the back of the chair, as if he couldn't bear the weight of it another moment. 'It's like a furnace in here.' He went over and turned down the gas fire. 'I can't believe you'd go and do all this without saying anything to me. That letter insults me. I don't understand.' He stood looking at her. 'Aren't you going to say anything? Mother was right about Antoine and Sidi bou-Saïd. Not in the way she meant, but she was right. You've fallen under the influence of these people. It's their lives. It's not your life.' He stepped across to her and took her gently by the shoulders. 'It's not your fault. It's mine. I should never have let you go.'

She withdrew from his embrace. 'It is my life,' she said. She looked at him, her expression closed and stubborn. Her short brown hair was flattened damply against the side of her head where she had been sleeping and her eyes were bright and glassy with fatigue and emotion.

'It's late,' he said, making an effort to keep his tone neutral. 'It's after midnight. Let's not talk about it now. I thought you'd be in bed fast asleep by this time. It's dangerous to overtire yourself.' He looked tired himself. His shoes and the cuffs of his trousers were stained and muddied from the wet streets, his shirt collar rumpled, and his tie crooked. A man harried by the demands of his heroic undertaking, by the urgency to complete seven million calculations in order to suspend fifty thousand tons of steel above the waters of Sydney Harbour. He was a man at the end of a long day in need of a woman's tenderness.

Emily lifted her chin, indicating the green chair with its footstool. 'I suppose you and your mother expect me to sit over there sewing all day and waiting for my time.'

He made a helpless gesture with his hands, as if he cast something at her feet. 'Ah, Emily! Why so bitter? Let us stop this. You've returned so changed,' he accused her sadly. 'What is it? Why are you being so unforgiving? Where's the girl who charmed me on the beach in Melbourne that summer day such a little time ago?'

'I haven't changed. This is me, Georges, as much as the girl on the beach was me.' She looked at him. 'How little we have got to know each other.'

He went over to the bookcase and reached and took the bottle of whisky and a glass from the shelf. He poured an inch of whisky into the glass and turned and looked at her. He lifted the glass to his lips and drank the whisky. He reached for the bottle and poured another inch of whisky. He stoppered the bottle and put it back on the bookshelf.

They stood looking at each other across the room. A door slammed somewhere in the building. The gas fire murmured. She sat on the hard-backed chair.

They were silent for a long moment.

Then he said, 'We had some good news today.' He took hold of the cane chair by its back and turned it to face her and sat in it. 'I was looking forward to telling you.'

'What is it?'

'The Cleveland Bridge Company has withdrawn from the tendering process. They were our main rivals. Jacques Lenormand's scaremongering's been put an end to. I shan't need to go and report to the board at Haine Saint-Paul.' He looked into his glass, then looked up at her. 'Our little motoring holiday in the Ardennes will have to be postponed for a while.'

'I hadn't really expected to go.'

'No. I suppose not.'

A clock somewhere struck the first hour of the new day.

Georges closed his eyes, then opened them and rubbed his hand over his face and through his hair. He drank the rest of the whisky and heaved himself out of the chair. He put the glass on the table beside her. He stood looking down, his fingers playing with the fragment of red slip. 'I feel as if the bridge is taking our lives from us sometimes,' he said, then fell silent, waiting for her to speak. She said nothing. 'I wonder if it can be done . . . You and me and the baby and this bridge.' He waited again. 'Now there's this.' He pushed at the letter with his fingers.

She looked up at him.

'I was afraid of the Cleveland Bridge Company.' He laughed. 'I thought of my counterpart over there as a kind of superhuman incapable of feeling the strain the way I was feeling it. When Jean-Pierre told me this afternoon Cleveland had withdrawn, the first thing I felt was envy, not relief. I envied their designer his freedom. I thought of him putting on his hat and closing the door of his office and going home to his wife. I wanted to send him a telegram congratulating him and telling him how comforted I was to find out that he was just a man like me after all. I imagined us becoming friends.' He looked at her and smiled. 'He's the only other person in the world who knows what I'm going through. It's true. I'm sorry but it's true. The weight of this thing is in my head all the time. I sat at my desk after Jean-Pierre had gone out onto the design floor and I seriously thought of putting a call through to the chief engineer of the Cleveland Bridge Company and telling him how scared I was of what this bridge was doing to me and you.'

She reached up and put her hand over his. 'Don't give up,' she said. 'You mustn't give up.'

'I feel as if it might leave us with nothing before it's done.'

'And so it might,' she said. 'That's the risk you've taken, isn't it? Isn't this what you expected? What you had prepared yourself for? You didn't think you'd pay nothing for your dream, did you? You can't have the biggest bridge in the world for nothing, Georges. My father reminded you that some men pay for big bridges with their lives. That must have seemed to you cruel of him. But, remember, he has never been prepared to take such a risk himself. That's why he envies you. Yes, he does! I know him. His own ambition is compromised. He knows that. He admires men who take extraordinary risks for their dreams, but he can't help hating them at the same time for doing what he has always feared to do. I know my father, Georges. I know how complicated and tortured his attitude to ambition is. There will always be something in him that is not satisfied. That's why he was so disappointed when I refused to go on to Cambridge. He saw his own life repeating itself in mine.'

He looked at her. 'You believe all that?'

'I know it.'

'I have never admitted my fear to anyone before this. Are you ever afraid?'

'Sometimes I can hardly bear to think of the future and what might happen to us.'

He stroked her hair. 'Imagine a room,' he said. 'Fifty times the size of this room. An enormous room. A hundred times the size of this room. Rows of tables, one after the other, as far as the eye can see. Big flat tables covered with enormous drawings. Each drawing representing a section of steel. Hundreds of them. Thousands of them. Some of them yards long. Each section calibrated to within a few microns of accuracy and costed to within a few centimes of its fitted price. You *can't* imagine it. No one can. It's like trying to imagine infinity. My head aches with it all the time. Draughtsmen sitting up on their stools for ten hours a day drawing. Other men come along and check their drawings. Then they check their own checking. Doing nothing else. Day after day after day.' He was silent. Then he said with awe, 'I think of John Bradfield living with this bridge for forty years. And I know I'm not in his class.' He looked down at her, his hands on her hair. 'When you were away, I had a terrible dream.'

She waited.

'It returns to me while I'm working during the day. I am haunted by the image. You were standing at the foot of a flight of steps. It was dark. You had your back to me and didn't know I was there. But I knew it was you. At the top of the steps there was an open door. A figure stood in the doorway looking at you. It was Death. I called to you, but my voice was too feeble and you couldn't hear me. My limbs were paralysed and I couldn't go to you. I watched helplessly while you went up the stairs and through the door. I knew I was never going to see you again. In the dream I'd forgotten the baby. There was no baby in the dream.' He gestured at the room and the new furniture. 'The music teacher moved out of her apartment just before I had the dream. She's gone back to her family in Warsaw. The building felt empty. Everything seemed silent and deserted the night she left. As if I was soon to be the only one in the building. She was selling her things and I bought these pieces from her. She said she was glad they would have a good home. I thought how silly it was of her to speak about furniture, as if it cared what happened to it. But I understood her all the same. That green chair was sitting over there but you weren't here. Every time I saw it I thought to myself, Emily's never going to sit in that chair. After I woke from the dream, I lay awake till dawn. At one point during that night I made up my mind to abandon the bridge and to go to Marseilles and take the boat to Tunis. I imagined us together at Antoine's house, carefree and in love. Just as we were that day on the beach in Melbourne.'

She reached and squeezed his hand. 'I'm here,' she said. 'There's a kind of panic in you now that you're getting close. But you mustn't give up. Let the Cleveland designer and Lenormand and these other people panic. Let them be the ones to give up. If you stay calm while they let their fear get the better of them, you will get the bridge. Then you'll look back and laugh at yourself for having been afraid.'

He helped her to her feet and held her against him and looked into her eyes. He kissed her gently on the lips, then drew away. 'I scarcely know you. You're right. You're a mystery to me. But I love you. I loved you the first moment I saw you in the entrance hall of your parents' home that day. Your hair was long and it glowed in the light of the coloured windows. I can still see the way the sunshine was in your eyes that day and the way you looked at me, as if you expected something from me.'

She swayed on his arm.

'I've exhausted you.' He put his arm around her waist and leaned past her and switched off the reading lamp. Together they went across the room and into the bedroom.

TWO

Emily lay awake watching the sky grow pale above the Dôme. The baby was moving, slowly extending a limb, then withdrawing it. The room was cold and the wind was rattling the window. Careful not to disturb Georges, she slipped out of bed and put on her dressing gown in the chilly grey light and went out into the sitting room and lit the gas fire. Then she went into the kitchen and put the kettle on. While she was waiting for the kettle to boil she opened her dressing gown and lifted her nightdress and examined herself. She reached and touched herself, then looked closely at her finger. Her fingernail glistened moistly with the pale, translucent blood. She filled a bowl with hot water from the gas heater and had a wash. When the kettle boiled, she made the tea. She poured two cups and took one in to Georges. She set the tea on the cupboard beside the bed and reached and touched his shoulder. 'It's nearly seven,' she said.

He opened his eyes and looked at her, startled. 'What's wrong? Why are you up?'

'There's your tea,' she said quietly. 'Nothing's wrong.' She went out and stood with her back to the gas fire warming herself, holding the steaming cup in both hands and looking out the window, watching it getting light and waiting.

While Georges was shaving in the kitchen she got dressed. Black ribbed stockings and a gray woollen skirt. Over her blouse she wore the long green cardigan with the amber buttons. The skirt was too tight and she left the top button undone and pulled the cardigan down to cover the twisted crease in the waistband. The faint cedar smell of her old wardrobe at Richmond Hill lingered in the winter clothes. She stood before the cheval glass and brushed her hair, the oval of her face pale and colourless in the weak electric light, her lips thin. There were dark shadows and a tight web of lines under her eyes. She rubbed at the lines with her finger. The green cardigan looked enormous, outlining the bulge of her stomach. She stood with her hands by her sides staring at her reflection. 'I've become ugly,' she said.

Georges came in. He looked at her and pulled his braces over his shoulders and began to fit a clean collar to his shirt. 'You mean to go to the library, don't you?' he said, as if he were accusing her of planning a crime.

In the doorway she paused and looked at him.

He reached and picked up his front stud from the tray.

She waited for him.

He looked up, his chin held high, his fingers at his throat pinching the stud through the starched collar. 'I can't allow it,' he said.

'You can forbid me, but you can't compel me,' she said sweetly, and she went up to him and reached and straightened his braces where they were twisted over his shoulder. 'If you forbid me to do what I want to do, then we shall both be unhappy.' She leaned and kissed him lightly on the cheek and smiled at him. 'Then the baby will sense our unhappiness and it will be unhappy too.'

He frowned uncertainly. 'You don't really believe that, do you?'

'Oh yes. It's true. My mother told me. Anyway,' she said lightly, 'women work while they're pregnant. Olive Kallen worked right up to the last day. Her son is twenty-seven now. Nothing awful happened to them.'

'Olive Kallen!' he said with disgust. 'I wish to God you'd never met the woman. You're not strong. You've not been well. Léon says you have to be careful or you could miscarry.'

'I shan't miscarry, Georges. I promise you.' She turned to leave the bedroom.

'I'll only agree,' he said, 'if you'll let Léon look at you again and if he says it's all right.'

'I don't need looking at,' she said. 'It *is* all right.' She went out into the sitting room.

He followed her. 'Just go for the morning sessions, then.'

'If I get tired, I'll come home. I promise you.'

He stood looking at her. 'I don't understand you.'

'No. Well, never mind. I'll put your eggs and bacon on.'

Half an hour later she watched him cross the courtyard. When he reached the robinia tree, he turned and looked up at the window and raised his hat and saluted her. Behind the glass she lifted her hand and watched him until he went out through the covered way. She turned from the window and went over and dragged the crib across the floor to the door of the small spare room. She opened the door and pushed the crib inside and closed the door. She heard Sophie coming down the stairs from her room and she went over and opened the door for her. She took Sophie by the hand and led her into the bedroom. She opened her bag and took out the silver bangle and slid it onto Sophie's wrist. It was too loose and she gripped it with both hands and closed the soft metal. 'There!' She held Sophie's hand up for them to admire the effect. 'You have lovely hands, Sophie. I knew silver was your color.'

Sophie stared at the heavy bangle on her wrist.

'It's yours!' Emily laughed, and she leaned and kissed her.

Sophie pulled the bangle off her wrist and put it on the dresser, her eyes bright and appealing. 'No, madame! I can't take it.'

Emily picked up the bangle and took both Sophie's hands and

enclosed the bangle in them. 'It's yours!' she said firmly. 'I was thinking only of you when I bought it in the market in Tunis. I wouldn't have bought it for myself. Who am I to give it to if you won't take it?'

Sophie looked down at the bangle in her hands. A sudden spiritedness gleamed in her eyes. She looked up at Emily. 'On what occasion shall I wear it, madame?'

'Oh, we can't tell when we shall *do* things, Sophie. Your life isn't always going to be cleaning rooms and shopping and carting laundry about the place for people.'

'I like my work, madame.'

'I'm sure you do and you're very good at it. For heaven's sake, put the bangle away if it embarrasses you. One day, when you're older, you'll take it out again and it will give you pleasure.' Emily looked at the bangle in Sophie's hands. 'There are always little mysteries in these things. They're important to us in the end, Sophie, believe me. Gifts are mysterious.'

'Yes, madame.' Sophie said, as if this had been a lesson. She put the bangle in the large pocket of her apron and went out to the kitchen.

Emily sat at the table by the window and opened her writing case. She called to Sophie, 'It isn't just a matter of being obedient, you know.'

'No, madame,' Sophie replied.

Emily took out her letter to Olive Kallen and read it through. When she had finished it, she put the letter in an envelope and sealed it. She wrote the New York address carefully on the envelope. She picked up the other letters and put on her overcoat and hat and took her writing case. She looked in to the kitchen on her way. 'The flat's yours for the day, Sophie. I shan't be back till late.' She hesitated. 'Do you still see your young man from the carnival?'

Sophie set the breakfast dishes in the sink carefully one at a time.

She didn't look up. 'No, madame,' she said softly. 'He wasn't from the carnival.'

'I'm sorry, Sophie. I shouldn't have asked.'

'It's all right, madame. I never think of him.'

Emily looked at her.

She went down the stairs and out into the courtyard, her writing case tucked under her arm. Madame Barbier was standing in the covered way by her door talking with the woman who scrubbed the stairs. Both women watched Emily approach, then the other woman moved off and picked up a bucket and a mop and went across the courtyard.

The concierge stepped into Emily's path. 'Good morning, Madame Elder. I haven't forgotten Monsieur's kind invitation to take coffee with you one of these mornings.'

Emily paused beside her. 'Perhaps tomorrow, then, Madame Barbier?'

'That's very kind, madame, but tomorrow's laundry day and I have to keep an eye on the girls. I hope Madame is well?'

'Yes, thank you.' Emily was about to move off when a watchful expectancy in the concierge's manner made her hesitate.

The concierge cleared her throat. 'There was a . . . young priest came around asking for you when you were away, madame.'

Emily felt the blood drain from her face.

'It obviously wasn't a matter of life and death, so I've waited till you got back.' She smiled. 'I didn't think it was worth troubling Monsieur with it, so I've said nothing in that area.' She watched Emily closely. 'He left something for you, madame. I've not managed to catch you on your own till now or I'd have given it to you sooner.' She reached and took Emily's arm. 'You look a bit on the pale side, madame. You'd better come in and sit down while I fetch it.'

'No!' Emily drew back. 'I'll wait here.'

'I told him you'd gone away for a rest. To a foreign country, I said. I didn't mention Tunisia or Monsieur Carpeaux, even though I knew well enough where you'd gone, as I didn't think that was any of his business.'

Emily murmured, 'Thank you.'

'I'll fetch it, then,' Madame Barbier said, and she went into her doorway.

Emily stood waiting.

The concierge was back in a moment. She handed Emily the lost *Baedecker*. 'He said you left it in the cathedral when you were visiting.'

Emily took the *Baedecker* from her. 'Thank you.' Her voice was small and uncertain.

'You're sure you won't come in and sit for a minute. I've got a little something that'll bring the colour back to your cheeks, madame.'

Emily stood looking at the *Baedecker*.

Madame Barbier nodded at it. 'I lent him a bit of paper and a pen for a note. He slipped it in next to the map of Chartres. He said you'd know where to find him if ever you needed his help.' She nodded to give emphasis to her words. 'Then he was off. Just like that. Gone!' Madame Barbier leaned and looked out through the covered way to the busy street, as if Bertrand had left only just that minute. She examined the palms of her hands, then the backs of them. Then she looked up at Emily. 'I don't have a lot of time for them, Madame Elder, but this one was a useful-looking young fellow for a priest. Are you sure you don't want to come in and sit for a minute?'

Emily thanked her and she left her standing there. She walked to the corner of rue Amelie and stopped outside the florist's. She opened the *Baedecker* and took out the scrap of paper. 'The good Madame Barbier tells me you have gone abroad. She is discreet and will not tell me where. I have visited Madame Elder and her sister Juliette in the rue des Oiseaux a number of times to take them fruit and to speak with Madame Elder of her spiritual concerns. She has told me your news. I think of you often.'

The note was signed 'B.' There was no salutation. Emily put the note and the *Baedecker* in her writing case and walked to the post office in the rue de Grenelle, where she posted the three letters. On her way back to catch the Métro at École Militaire, as she was approaching the corner of rue Saint-Dominique, she saw Antoine ahead of her. She called and hurried after him. He heard her and stopped and turned.

'Bertrand came to see me!' she said breathlessly.

'Good God. Does Georges know?'

'No.'

He took her arm and they walked to a café in the avenue de la Motte Picquet and sat at a table in the window. Antoine ordered a cognac for her. The café was quiet. The waiter stood beside them at the door looking out into the street. Whenever a customer approached he opened the door for the customer and served the customer and then came back and stood looking out the door again.

Emily sipped the strong spirit. 'He knows I'm having a baby.'

Antoine smoked, the air about him pungent with the smell of cloves. He leaned his elbows on the table and watched the pedestrians going past the window, holding the thin hand-rolled cigarette delicately between his thumb and forefinger an inch from his lips, then touching the brownstained end of the paper to his lips and drawing in the smoke, his eyes narrowed.

'He won't come again,' he said. 'You can forget him.'

Emily watched him 'I've made up my mind to go and see him before the baby's born.'

He turned to her. He seemed preoccupied, as if he had not quite focused on her problem. 'Why would you do that?'

'I just know it will haunt me forever if I don't go and see him and finish it.'

'What's unfinished about it?'

She looked into her glass. The cognac was the same colour as the buttons on her cardigan. She and Antoine and the waiter standing by the door were mirrored in the inverted globe of the liquid. She looked up. 'You don't understand.'

He waited.

'I must go while I'm still me. Before I become a mother.'

He lifted his shoulders expressively and smoked his cigarette.

'What are you thinking? Tell me, Antoine. I need to know what you think of me now.'

He signaled to the waiter and ordered coffee. When the waiter had gone, he smiled at her. 'I was thinking of Merrill, my dear. He's in Paris, you know. We're dining together this evening.'

'I thought he'd gone home to New York.'

'He went to London. He's come over for a few days. To see me.'

She looked at him. 'You're happy.'

'Fleetingly, I daresay. You know, happiness.' He laughed. 'I shouldn't worry about your priest. Obviously he's not going to give you any trouble.'

'Don't call him my priest. Please.'

'The priest, then.' He examined her. 'You want everything, Emily.'

'Don't you?'

'Not anymore.'

'But you did once?'

'It's hard to remember what I wanted.' He laughed. 'I don't think I've ever known what I've wanted from life. That's Georges, isn't it? It's not me. Knowing what he wants and going after it and never faltering. I think I've just had this vague apprehension that things might have made more sense if . . . well, if I'd settled to something. But perhaps not. Who knows.'

The waiter brought the coffee. He wiped at the table with his cloth and set the coffee in front of Antoine and returned to his vigil by the door.

She twisted her wedding ring on her finger. There was an indentation in the reddened skin under the ring. She rubbed at it. 'When Madame Barbier told me Bertrand had been to see me . . .' She looked up. Her voice broke and she swallowed and looked down at her hands again. 'You can have no idea what it's like . . .' She brought her hands to her face and bent over the table and burst into tears.

Antoine put his hand on her shoulder and squeezed gently.

The waiter opened the door for a customer and there was the roar of the traffic, then quiet again as he closed the door. He glanced at Emily and went over to the bar and served the customer. The customer and the waiter both looked at Emily.

She dried her eyes and blew her nose and drank the last of the cognac. She pulled on her gloves and looked at Antoine. 'I was on my way to the library. Were you coming to see me?'

'I thought we might have lunch. We haven't really spoken since we got back.'

She picked up her green morocco writing case and her handbag and stood up. She waited while Antoine paid the bill.

He walked with her to the Métro at École Militaire. 'I'll come with you,' he said at the last minute. On the train there was a woman sitting opposite them with a baby. Antoine smiled at the woman and she looked pleased and touched her baby. When the woman got off the train, Emily said to Antoine, 'Do you know why mothers with their babies always wear that look of smug security?'

Antoine said cheerfully, 'It has always been a great mystery to me.'

'They know that so long as their child needs them they have solved the problem of a reason for living.'

Antoine suggested they get off at Odéon. They went up the steps and walked along the boulevard Saint-Germain. It had begun to rain. Two dappled Percherons stood facing the curb, unharnassed from their carts, their backs steaming, their brown eyes half closed. Antoine and Emily passed the medical school and crossed the boulevard Saint-Michel and went on past the Sorbonne and the Faculté de Droit. When they came to the north side of the place du Panthéon, he turned to her. 'I'm meeting Merrill at the Brasserie Équivoque this evening.'

'I shall imagine you there.'

'It's where I gave you her medallion,' he said.

They stood, uncertain with each other suddenly.

'How will you find the priest when you get to Chartres?' he asked.

'I shall find him.'

He considered her. 'There is a strength in you, Emily, that Georges doesn't see.'

She kissed him quickly and stepped off the curb and crossed the road to the library. She didn't turn around, but went in and hurried across the foyer and up the stairs. She stood on the landing looking in. The reading room was divided down the center by a row of slender cast-iron columns. The columns, each rising from a tall pedestal of masonry, supported two lofty barrel roofs on intricate cast-iron arches, so that the roof resembled the roof of a railway station. On either side of the central masonry pedestals there were rows of long wooden tables. She could see no empty place. There was a smell composed of books and of damp clothing and polished wood and the subdued sound of pages turning and pens scribbling and the breathing and sighing and restless shifting of people at work. Every so often the scrape of a chair on the timber floor or the thump of a heavy volume on a table echoed among the lofty spaces and tall arched windows. She stood waiting for a seat.

THREE

In the first week of November Emily suggested to Georges they go down
to Chartres to see his mother. He was pleased to hear the suggestion
from her but said he could not spare the time and that they would
go down as soon as he had submitted the tender documents to the
directors in Haine Saint-Paul. They both worked. He on one side of
the river at the offices of his firm in the rue des Petits Champs and
she on the other side of the river at the Bibliothèque Sainte-Geneviève.
Soon they had established their divergent routines. When she got home
from the library each evening, she eagerly searched the day's post for a
reply from Hakim or Olive Kallen, but she heard nothing from them.
She knew it was too soon for a reply from her father. She continued
to lose a little blood and there was a whitish discharge that persisted
and which worried her. She was afraid that if she told Léon or Georges
about this, however, they would insist she stay in bed, or at least remain
at home. Her time in the library was limited and was precious to her.
So she said nothing. And each day she penetrated a little deeper into
the puzzling enticement of the mystery of Perpetua's life in Roman
Carthage. Lost in that world during the hours of her reading in the
library, it seemed to Emily that Perpetua's journey, begun so long ago,
was not over yet and that she was herself accountable in some way to
that unfinished journey. She saw how poorly Tertullian had represented
Perpetua's case in his eagerness to represent his own and she began to

see herself as the advocate of this troubled young woman's cause. Then a letter came from Hakim.

Sophie had propped it against the lamp on the table by the window – a brown, official envelope, with the address in bold black letters across the top, INSTITUT D'ARCHÉOLOGIE ET D'ARTS, RUE DE L'ÉGLISE, TUNIS. She didn't bother to take off her hat and coat but tore the envelope open and stood by the table reading the letter.

Dougga, November
Dear Madame Georges Elder, Emily,

I received your letter only three days ago when my post was at last sent on from Tunis. Soon after you left, Père Delattre ordered me and Ahmed here to the foot of the Atlas Mountains to organize the excavations of this beautiful and desolate Roman town. In the evenings, after the sun has set, Ahmed and I sit at the entrance to our tent among the haunted ruins and watch the sky turn from pink to gold and then at last to a deep and radiant purple filled with stars. The stars are so bright that even on those nights when there is no moon we can plainly see spread out below us the beautiful Medjerda Valley, the slopes of the pastures fat and glossy and elaborate as the detail of a Persian carpet. After we have had our fill of gazing at the landscape of the night, we light our lamp and Ahmed brews the tea and we withdraw into our tent. We take out your letter and read it again and talk together of what this mysterious story might be that you have glimpsed in her remains – for, like you, we too are certain that such a story exists if only its scattered fragments can be located and pieced together. We recall then how you appeared to us outside her cell in the arena that day, as if you had arrived just in time to give us the answer to her enigma. Perhaps Ahmed and I are a little influenced by the melancholy and romantic setting of our tent among the ruins on this rocky hillside, but we agree without dispute that our first impression of you was the right one. Ahmed reminds me it was he who saw you first that day. He touched my shoulder and said, There she is! As if we expected you.

Sitting in our tent at night, the farmers' fierce dogs howling to each other across the ravines and hillsides, knowing you cannot hear us, we sometimes speak of you as if you are our familiar and we take certain liberties that we would not take if you were present here with us. We speak of you softly and with respect and as if you are our friend. And if we doubt that this is so, for it seems astonishing to us that it can be so, we look again at your letter: *I see now that the things you and Antoine have given me are the fragments of a mysterious story.* Your words reassure us and invite us to consider you our friend and collaborator. I took the liberty of disclosing to Ahmed the details of your social situation. He listened gravely and in silence, and when he had considered what I told him, he said, Madame Georges Elder is fitted in every way to find Perpetua's story and to tell it.

The letter ended there with a formal salutation and began again on a fresh page.

Tunis.

I've left Ahmed at the camp in Dougga and I'm back at the Institute for a few days. I'll post this letter to you today. I hope you're still as enthusiastic as you were when you wrote to me in October. I know what a lonely and tedious business it can be searching through sources in those big libraries – and cold and miserable weather, which I don't envy you! Don't let the grand imperial boulevards of Paris put your Tunisian adventure in the shade! Perpetua's not going to be an easy task. We really need to find more of her writing. But there's little hope of that, I'm afraid. You've touched the nerve of this thing already, however. You've brought together the elements that give her problem a life and have given more meaning to my father's medallion and to her journal than I ever could have. What else do we look for? If we don't respond to that, we condemn ourselves to a pointless existence.

I hope we meet again one day, but I'm not counting on it.

May your gods grant you your story.

Hakim el-Ouedi.

She kissed the letter and said gaily, 'Oh, thank you, letter! Thank you, thank you!'

A few minutes before ten the next morning she hurried across the place du Panthéon and joined the crowd of students and scholars waiting for the library doors to open. She was out of breath. She stood among the students, who were lighting cigarettes and talking and calling to each other, and she leaned against the wall and closed her eyes. She pressed a hand to her diaphragm, an expression of strain on her face. As soon as she was still, the stealthy movement in her belly began again — as if a hand blindly explored within her, feeling its way cautiously against the inner membranes and structures of her body until it touched the nerve. She gasped with pain and opened her eyes. The movement ceased, as if the being within sensed it had been detected, or was satisfied to have claimed her attention.

A bell began to ring the hour. Before it had finished there was the sound of the bolts being drawn. The doors of the library were opened by a uniformed attendant. The students pinched out their half-smoked cigarettes and pocketed the butts and moved forward in a body, crowding together through the doors and hurrying across the foyer and up the stairs to the reading room. Emily claimed a seat between two other readers halfway down the room. She left her writing case in the place and went to the counter and ordered her books. She had taken to keeping her overcoat buttoned to hide her swollen belly, which had drawn disapproving glances from the attendants and from some of the older men and women who were regular readers in the library.

The attendant brought two of the heavy volumes from Clark's series of the Ante-Nicene Theological Library and Emily carried them back to her place. She set the books on the table and squeezed into the narrow space that had been left for her between the two students — they kept their heads down over their books, pretending they saw no reason to move over and make a little more room. She opened the first volume at the beginning of Tertullian's *Apologeticus* and cast her eye over the now familiar legend that appeared before each of his works, 'The African Quintus Septimius Florens Tertullianus was born at Carthage and was active between 190–220. Tertullian was the earliest and, after Augustine, the greatest of the ancient church writers of the West.' She realized she had begun to think of him as the enemy.

Sitting there leaning over the desk reading, the distended globe of her belly was pushed down onto her thighs and upward hard against her diaphragm. She was forced to straighten up every few minutes to take a deep breath. She longed to spread her legs, but there wasn't enough room under the desk for her to sit with her legs apart without pressing against the legs of the students on either side of her. It was a physical effort for her to keep her legs together. After half an hour or so, her bladder was throbbing painfully. The pain grew steadily worse. Eventually she admitted she was not taking in a word of what she was reading but was totally preoccupied with controlling her bladder. As she shifted uncomfortably, once again the student to her left paused in his writing and glared at her. She murmured an apology and kept still. The student, who gave off a rank smell of garlic and stale sweat, muttered something under his breath in a language that was not familiar to her and he hunched his shoulders and went on with his work.

She suffered it for a little longer, then she put her pen down and pushed her chair back and got up and went to the lavatory. The minute she sat down again after she returned from the lavatory her bladder began to throb painfully once again. She endured it until half past eleven, when half an hour of the morning session still remained, then she could bear it no longer and reluctantly she abandoned her studies for the day and left the library.

Almost in tears she walked along the street a little way, but the discomfort in her bowels was so acute she had to find somewhere to sit down. She went into the church of Saint-Étienne-du-Mont and found a dark corner near the base of some stone stairs. She sat on the edge of a chair and leaned on the back of the chair in front of her, as if she were at her devotions. She spread her legs and thrust her hand under her skirt. With relief she sat massaging her belly and her groin.

The church was silent and empty, except for two worshippers or tourists who were standing gazing up at the stone staircase that spiraled around one of the great pillars. Emily had not been inside a church since Chartres.

She had been sitting there for some time, her legs spread and her hand pressed to her belly, when a timber door closed on the other side of the nave, the booming of its closing echoing through the nave and the gallery. She looked up. A priest was striding across the flagstones toward her, his short, heavyset figure in a waisted soutane, the square biretta set crookedly on his head, his spiky hair jutting out untidily, the unmistakable thrust of his powerful shoulders and the confident way he stepped toward her.

Her heart froze. She removed her hand from under her skirt and stood up.

As he walked past, he glanced at her. He nodded, murmuring a greeting or a blessing. Then he was gone.

She stood staring toward the archway where he had disappeared. It had not been him, of course. She knew that. She was not utterly deluded. Yet her mind, her memory, insisted otherwise. The sudden illusion of his presence had been so vivid, in fact, she fancied she had smelled fruit and wheaten straw as he passed her, close enough for her to have reached out and touched his arm and to have murmured his name. 'What am I going to do?' she whispered. She was shocked by the strength of the sudden apparition, the conviction that somewhere in her emotions she still longed to see Bertrand Étinceler – as if he might solve her dilemma, or offer her the comfort of his understanding, their momentary passion linking them in a kind of indissoluble partnership.

Outside the church she walked past the iron railings of the Panthéon. She was preoccupied with her thoughts and did not consider where she was going. A few minutes later she came out onto the boulevard Saint-Michel. When she saw the gates of the Luxembourg gardens across the road, she realized she must have taken a wrong turn. She crossed the road and went in through the gates and walked along the broad, tree-lined path. A moment later she came to the octagonal pond. The gay blue and red of a Tricolour fluttering in the chilly breeze in the grey November scene attracted her attention. A massive stone urn stood emptily on a square pedestal beside the pond beneath the Tricolour. An old woman wrapped in dark clothes sat on a stool out of the wind hard up against the stone pedestal. She was bent over, reading a newspaper with the aid of a magnifying glass. She held the newspaper spread across her broad lap, anchoring it against the cold wind with her forearms, and gripping the magnifying glass an inch or two away from it, moving it slowly down the columns of print. Beside her was a sign, LOUEUR DE BATEAUX 2FR. A dozen model sailboats mounted on three-wheeled carts, their sails set and trembling in the wind, stood in a row next to the sign, ready to be trundled to the water's edge. There were no children in the park, however, and the few pedestrians who were about hurried past without paying any attention to the woman and her sailboats.

Emily went over to the boats and she reached and touched the sails of the nearest. The old woman looked up at her, examined her briefly, then returned to her newspaper.

'Pardon, madame, may I ask you how long you have been coming here?' Emily asked.

The old woman didn't look up but continued to peer closely at the newspaper through the magnifying glass. 'I'm here by ten every morning, rain or shine,' she said flatly.

'I meant, were you here twenty years ago?'

The old woman looked up and examined Emily more closely. She asked suspiciously, 'What are you after, then?' She thumped the stone plinth behind her with a mittened fist. 'Everyone knows I was here.' The wind was blowing Emily's coat against her. 'Never mind about me, I know where *you* should be. Home by the fire with your feet up, instead of gallivanting around the park on your own asking hardworking people silly questions.' She nodded at Emily's bulging belly under the overcoat. 'That little mite's going to catch his death in this wind if you don't watch yourself, my girl.'

'I was here twenty years ago too,' Emily said eagerly. 'With my mother and father. My father hired one of your sailboats for me. We have a photograph at home. I should have brought it. I was five.' She stood looking around at the scene, as if she expected to find its features familiar. 'I have always known I would come back to this spot one day. How extraordinary it is to be standing here! And nothing has changed. Except then it was spring.' She looked at the old woman. 'It must have been you, madame, who my father hired the sailboat from.'

The old woman put down the magnifying glass and pulled her woollen shawl close around her ears and gestured at the grey sky. 'Well, it's not spring now, is it?' She looked up at Emily. 'That's a story that's got to be worth a couple of francs to a poor woman, wouldn't you say?'

Emily opened her purse and gave the woman five francs.

The woman put the money in the pocket of her skirt without looking at it and she picked up her magnifying glass and returned to reading her newspaper, as if they had not exchanged a word.

Emily stood looking at the sailboats regretfully for a moment, as if she might have considered hiring one and sailing it on the pond. Then she turned away and walked back along the path toward the park gates. She turned left along the boulevard Saint-Michel and made her way toward the Métro at Odéon. She felt cold and tired and fragile suddenly and she wondered how much longer she would be able to continue her reading. How had Olive Kallen, she wondered, worked until the last day? It did not seem possible. As she walked along the crowded street, Emily's thoughts were filled with a confusion of impressions and memories, things she thought she had left in her past were suddenly with her again, troubling and unfinished. And beneath it all the interminable haranguing tones of Tertullian's writing, masking the gentle intimate confidences of Perpetua's journal beneath his rhetoric of power and the law. For the first time since she had returned from Tunisia Emily's confidence faltered and she wondered if she had taken on a task that would prove to be beyond her. She tried not to hope too hard that there would be a letter for her today from Olive Kallen.

On the way home to rue Saint-Dominique she went into a store and bought two cheap overall dresses. One was a pale pastel blue and the other was green of a similar insipid hue. The woman took them out of a deep drawer where they lay side by side with a dozen others of exactly the same cut and she placed them on the counter for Emily to look at. 'These are the only colours available, madame,' the woman said, and she smoothed the folded dresses with her hand.

Emily rested on the fourth landing then continued slowly up the stairs. On the sixth floor she paused to catch her breath again. Her heart was pounding against her ribs and there was a whining sound in her ears. She went across to the door and put down her parcel and the writing case and took her key from her handbag and opened the door.

Léon was sitting in the music teacher's green chair in front of the fire. His black bag was on the floor behind the chair. His legs were spread in front of him embracing the footstool, the material of his trousers tight over his fat thighs and the globe of his paunch thrust out as if he sat there warming it before the gas fire. He placed his glass on the floor and stood up. He held a lighted cigar in his other hand. Georges, who was looking agitated and concerned, came across from the window and he kissed her and took the parcel from her. 'You look half frozen,' he said. 'What are you doing to yourself? Sit by the fire! I'll get you a hot drink. Léon and I were discussing whether to go to the library and fetch you by force. This business has to stop right now.'

Léon took her hand and raised it to his lips and kissed it. 'Georges is right, my dear. Your behaviour is endangering your own health and the health of your child.' His deep voice was grave and confiding, as if he revealed an intimate secret, his breath warm in her face, rich with the smell of tobacco and whisky. His small black eyes examining her, as if he searched for a clue to her obscure and mysterious motives.

'Hello, Léon,' she said lightly. 'I've only been reading books, not digging trenches.' She went over to the window and put her writing case on the table and took off her hat and coat and put them on top of the writing case. She turned to Georges, who stood impatiently behind her. 'I'll be out in a minute.' She took the parcel from him and went into the bedroom and closed the door. She took off her skirt and blouse and untied the string of the parcel. She shook out the blue dress and drew it over her head and stood in front of the mirror smoothing it. The shapeless dress made her stomach look vast. The material smelled of the shop and the woman who had served her. She examined her reflection with distaste. Her cheeks were bloodless and there were deep purple-and-gray shadows under her eyes. Her body ached.

She turned from the mirror and went out into the sitting room. The vacant music teacher's green chair and footstool waited for her in front of the gas fire. Georges took her hand and led her to the chair. She did not resist. When she was seated, he kneeled and eased her shoes off and put her feet on the footstool. She closed her eyes. 'Thank you,' she said. 'Is there any post for me?'

The two men stood looking at her.

'No, there's nothing,' Georges said. 'I'll get you a cup of tea.' He went into the kitchen.

Léon stood behind her at the window, smoking his cigar and looking out at the wintry afternoon.

The gas burbled and the pigeons cooed on the guttering. There were voices on the stairs.

A few minutes later Georges came in with a tray and the tea things. He set the tray on the table by the window next to her coat and stood pouring the tea. 'I'll be going up to Haine Saint-Paul with the tender documents the first week in December,' he said, making his news sound like an official announcement. He came over and handed her a cup of tea. He stood looking down at her, his hand resting on her shoulder.

She looked up at him. 'You've nearly finished, then?'

'Another couple of weeks at the outside. It only seems unexpected to you because you've scarcely concerned yourself with it.' He watched her sipping her tea. 'We were discussing what to do with you while I'm away.'

'I shall be working at the library,' she said.

'No, you won't. I've spoken to Sophie. She'll sleep in the little room while I'm away and Léon's going to call in every morning on his way to the hospital.'

Léon said, 'When you've finished your tea, my dear, I'll examine you.'

There's no need, Léon. I'm just a bit tired. That's all.'

'Tell her, Léon,' Georges said, exasperated.

'Tell me what?' she said.

'All in good time,' Léon said calmly. 'Don't alarm yourself, my dear. Drink your tea, then you and I will have a little talk.'

He stepped across to the chair and picked up his bag.

She reached and set her cup on the floor. 'I'll drink it after.' She stood up.

Léon went over and opened the bedroom door and stood waiting for her.

Georges watched them.

Emily went into the bedroom and Léon followed her and closed the door.

She sat on the edge of the bed, watching him fetch something out of his bag.

He straightened up, his stethoscope dangling from his chubby fingers like something he'd dredged out of a rock pool. 'Georges called me from his office this morning.'

'I thought he must have.'

'He's extremely anxious about you and the baby. I believe he has good cause to be. You're behaving very selfishly.'

'I haven't fainted again or anything,' she said, sullen and resentful.

Léon sat heavily on the bed beside her. 'Georges saw spots of blood on the bedsheet. I told him at once it could be a dangerous sign at this stage.' He said sternly. 'I warn you, Emily, you must take your condition seriously.'

'He might have said something to me.'

'Are you listening? You could *lose* this child.'

She looked down at her hands. 'I've only been going to the library. Can't I even do that? Some women work until the last day.'

'You're not some women. Every woman is different. You can't pretend you're still your own person. Your body isn't yours to do with as you please any longer. Your body belongs to your baby. Your child must come first. It is a law of nature, Emily, and you must submit to it or bear the consequences. You will feel differently about all this once your baby's born. Every mother always does. Now undo your top button and let's have a listen to you.'

She undid the top button of her dress. He told her to lie down and he leaned over her and pushed the stethoscope down the front of her dress and listened and moved it about. He asked her to sit up and he moved it around on her back. When he'd finished, he reached and pinched the flesh of her arm above her elbow between his thumb and forefinger. 'You've lost condition. Take off your things and let me have a look at you.' He went over and stood at the window with his back to her while she got herself ready.

'I'm ready,' she said.

He came over and bent and examined her. When he had finished, he covered her with the blanket. 'How long have you been losing blood?'

'For a few weeks.'

He turned to her. 'You've noticed the discharge?'

'Of course.'

'You've got a local infection. It persists only because you are run down and because you insist on dragging yourself out to the library every day in all weather. Intellectual work is depleting. More so even than manual labour. You are exhausted. If you don't stay in bed and rest and put on a bit of condition, you will present this infection with an opportunity to take a hold on your entire system.' He waited for her attention, then said gravely, 'If that happens, Emily, there will be nothing medicine can do you for you. Do you understand me? If you don't do as I say and rest, this infection may kill you. You and the baby with you. You look disbelieving. But I cannot put the case to you more simply or more honestly than that. You're over seven months advanced. You can't have more than six or seven weeks to go, yet you behave as if nothing has changed for you.' His manner softened suddenly and he put his hand over hers on the covers. 'In a few weeks you are going to be a mother. There is no going back now to your former self, my dear. You must wish that carefree girl adieu for good.' He smiled. 'It is an irreversible condition, you know, motherhood. Once a mother you will be a mother until the end of your days. There's nothing else for it.' He shook his head and reached for his bag. 'Ask your own mother. Ask Madame Elder.'

When Léon had gone, Georges came into the bedroom. He stood in the doorway looking at her. 'You put the crib away,' he accused her.

'The model sailboats are still for hire in the Luxembourg Gardens,' she said. 'The same woman's still there. Can you believe it? After all these years. Do you remember the photograph on the mantelpiece in our dining room? I showed it to you the day you arrived at Richmond Hill.'

'Of course I remember it.'

'You said, "She clings to her little ship of liberty."'

'Did I?'

'Why did you say that?' She patted the covers. 'Come and sit on the bed. Don't stand there like that.' She laughed nervously. 'I'm not a criminal, am I?'

He sat on the bed and clasped his hands and looked down at his feet. 'I don't remember saying it. I was in love with you. I probably said the first stupid thing that came into my head. I didn't think I had a chance with you.'

'You couldn't possibly have been in love with me. We'd only met a minute before.'

He turned to her. 'I was in love with you, Emily,' he said. There was a sadness in his voice and in his intelligent grey eyes. 'It only takes a minute to fall in love. So I discovered that day.'

She put her hand over his. 'You're not sorry, are you? I need to do this reading. It is important to me. Please try to understand.'

'I have been trying to understand.'

'I can't talk to you about it,' she said, and she withdrew her hand. 'We sleep in the same bed but we seem to live in different worlds, you and I.'

'Antoine's world!' he said bitterly.

'You see! My work sounds selfish and trivial whenever I say something to you about it. Your bridge is too real for it. It is too big and too worldly.'

'My bridge and my baby,' he said. 'The two of us seem to be getting in your way.'

'Léon says I'm being selfish.'

'Léon admires you.'

'Will you win the tender?'

'There's no saying. The English firm Dorman Long have taken over Cleveland's drawings. Your father warned me that Empire was always going to play a part in Bradfield's final decision. He told me the tender would go to an English firm.'

'But you never thought of not doing it for that reason? You didn't let him convince you to give up. My father doesn't wish you to succeed with the bridge, you must understand that. He can't. He'd like to be more generous about it. But he can't be. He's jealous of you and Bradfield. Whatever he told you it would always be a reason for compromising your ambition.'

'We have a good design,' George said. 'We all believe in it. Bradfield knows the Belgians can build this bridge. Dorman Long hasn't built a long span bridge for more than ten years and they've never built a big bridge outside England. Baume Marpent are the best in Europe. They've built big bridges all over the world. They can move out there and do it. Bradfield knows that. They have the people to do it.'

'They have you,' she said, and she squeezed his hand.

He looked at her. 'I've thought of you and me in Australia. I think of it every day. The three of us. In a little house in Sydney overlooking the harbour. Tell me honestly, is that such a stupid dream?'

'Why should it be stupid?' She examined her hands. Then she looked up at him. 'What will you do if you don't win the tender?'

'I don't know.' He was silent. 'We'll see.' He looked at her. 'Are you going to do as Léon tells you?'

'Of course.' She reached for his hand and placed it on her belly. She whispered, 'Can you feel it? That's its foot. Close your eyes and you'll feel it. How strong it is!' She looked down at her belly. 'I lie awake at night and wonder who it is, this stranger growing inside my body. What life will it have? How will it think of me one day?' She could still see the priest striding toward her across the nave of Saint-Étienne-du-Mont. She gazed at Georges. His eyes were closed, his hands spread on her stomach, his fingers long and pale – he was concentrating, as if he were a shaman at a laying on of hands, striving to exorcize the demon that possessed her.

Her whisper was scarcely audible, 'I am afraid.'

Georges opened his eyes. 'Of what? If you do as Léon says, everything will be all right. Won't it?' He waited for her but she said no more. 'Is there something you haven't told me?'

'No,' she said softly. There were tears in her eyes.

FOUR

— —

Sophie knocked and came in. She was carrying a tray with Emily's breakfast. 'Good morning, madame,' she said brightly. She set the tray on the cupboard next to the bed.

Emily struggled into a sitting position. The watery glow of a pale wintry sun was shining on the wall. 'What time is it?'

'Why, it's after eleven, madame.' Sophie fetched Emily's dressing gown and draped it around her shoulders and plumped the pillows at her back. She took up the breakfast tray and set it on the covers on Emily's legs. 'Can you manage it like that?' She withdrew an envelope from the pocket of her apron and put it on the covers next to the tray. 'There's a letter for you from America, madame.' She stood and looked, then turned and went out and closed the door softly.

Emily saw at once the letter was from Olive Kallen. She slit the envelope and unfolded the sheets of notepaper.

New York, November 1923

My dear Emily,

Your long and very exciting letter was waiting for me when Kenneth and I returned from giving our lectures in Boston several days ago. Believe me, I have been impatient to reply to you, but I've not had a clear moment until now. What a wonderful girl you are to write me such a long letter! I knew I was not wrong about you.

So, let me deal with all you have to say point by point, for there is so much I want to say to you too that I fear our correspondence will become confused if we do not attach some method to it. First, of course you must address me by my first name. We are friends. Let us settle that right now. I am so pleased that Émile Sant was able to help you find what you need in Sainte-Geneviève. You ask me what I think of your working title. I cannot tell you how important I believe this work to be that you have begun – so bravely and alone! I have already spoken to several people here at the Museum of Natural History and they are all very excited by what I have told them about you. But more of that in a minute!

First, a note of caution. It is undoubtedly true that Hakim el-Ouedi and his colleague, Ahmed, will be delighted by your title, *The Secular Perpetua*, as it indeed implies more scope than Delattre's approach for the history of the native peoples of the Mahgrib. But we must not forget, the Arabs did not conquer the Maghrib until five hundred years after Perpetua's time. After our dinner at Antoine's that evening, neither you nor I can doubt Hakim el-Ouedi's passionate partisanship on the question of Arab nationalism. I would caution you to hold yourself aloof, therefore, from an engagement with the fierce politics of these people. You will discover that assiduous diplomacy and the practice of a balanced neutrality are essential skills for all of us who venture to ply our trade in foreign lands. In your enthusiasm do not, I beg you, underestimate Père Delattre. He is a scholar of formidable intelligence and ability. It has been his guardianship alone over the past half century that has preserved the principal remains of Roman and Punic Carthage from being utterly obliterated and built over by new suburbs. Without the work of Delattre and his White Fathers there would be nothing left of Carthage for you and I, nor for Hakim el-Ouedi, to study and to disagree about. But Delattre is an octogenarian and you and Hakim are both young. For you, Delattre is a man from another time. I understand that. It is a ready fault in all young people impatient for the truth to judge the past by the standards of the present – the only standards you possess, after all, and so you mistakenly believe them to be timeless and universal. But experience soon teaches us that no standards are more fickle than those we apply to the writing of history. If we are not vigilant, it is soon our own work that is unread and out of fashion.

You have made such a very important beginning! You have impressed us all with your resolve to make Perpetua's voice audible to us at last above the din of Tertullian's bleak and heartless rhetoric. Now that you have stated it so simply, we all see yours as a project we would like to have conceived ourselves. We long to see you go on and to succeed in it. But I fear for you. You say you are still strangely weak from the rigours of traveling. Of course you are! At this moment you are confronting the most critical challenge you will confront in your entire life. The manner in which you resolve it will determine your future. You must resist this lethargy with all your will! You must not permit your enthusiasm or your boldness to falter now! Motherhood is the greatest test we ambitious women are called upon to meet, and we either meet it boldly and with courage or it defeats us utterly. If you falter now, believe me you will never take up the challenge again. I have seen a dozen promising young scholars fail in just these circumstances. If they ever do summon the will to re-enter the profession, it is only to do so with the most modest and commonplace of ambitions for themselves and for their work. A sad affair indeed when one has witnessed the bold vision they began with. Take courage, Emily! Keep working! At all costs! It is the answer. We are too easy on ourselves. Do not fear a little pain at this moment.

Now let me tell you my news. On my recommendation, and with the eager support of a number of eminent colleagues, the governors of the museum have voted a modest sum to the work of Delattre and the White Fathers in the next stage of their excavations at Carthage. The museum's funding is only for one year at present. It is probationary and by way of a trial. I shall be returning to Carthage in the spring to supervise this (the museum's first) joint project with Delattre and the White Fathers. If all goes well, the museum will increase its involvement over time and may one day hopefully establish a permanent presence at Carthage.

I shall need an assistant. Merrill Miles was to be my assistant. But as you know, poor Merrill has proved not to be up to the job. I must warn you, your stipend would not be large, it would indeed be scarcely sufficient for you to live on. So you will need a private source of funds. I am certain I can convince the committee to agree to your appointment for a year. The barriers, however, in your present circumstances, do appear on the face of it to be insurmountable. I have never yet permitted insurmountable barriers to stop me from making my plans. So I put it to you boldly, Emily: If it is at all possible for you, will you come to Carthage with me in the spring? You can commit yourself initially for three months and see how it works out for you. Together shall you and I not make Tertullian and Septimius Severus feel our presence! What do you say?

If you cannot agree to this, how then do you propose to continue your splendid work on Perpetua if your husband's firm wins the tender for this bridge and you return to Australia? Or have you resigned yourself to giving up your work if you return to Australia? In your letter you imply that you will continue with your work at all costs. I am not sure what I am to think of this. Have you indeed yet settled upon a plan? If I am to put your name forward, I must know your mind soon. For myself, in your position the choice would have been perfectly clear. But I have been fortunate in Kenneth. He has been prepared to walk in my shadow. There are those who accuse me of having given him no alternative. But no one can decide these things for us or know what inner promptings determine our course. What seems heartless and cruel to those who do not know us and our private realities is often merely a solution they envy. I am encouraged in my hopes for you by the fact that your husband permitted you to travel to Tunisia without him. I can only think he must be a man of unusually liberal principles. But I may be wrong. If I'm not wrong, then you are indeed fortunate. We do nothing alone. No matter how strong or how determined we are, we all need the support of those who believe in us. You say at the end of your letter that I and Antoine and Hakim el-Ouedi have each given you our friendship and encouragement. That is true. But we would not have offered you our friendship if we had not each recognized in you a rare quality of spirit that we admire and wish to be close to. What else is friendship but this recognition and a desire to see it succeed?

The letter continued, but Emily had stopped reading. She sat staring at the pale patch of sunlight on the wall, her breakfast tray forgotten. Out the window the sky above the roofs and the Dôme was thick and gray and wintry, swirling with rain and wind and brief glimpses of blue. Her throat was burning. She drank the tepid tea in gulps and set the cup on the tray. She put the tray on the cupboard and swung her legs over the side of the bed. She sat on the edge of the bed with her head down, the letter clutched in her hand, fighting the dizziness and the wave of nausea that gripped her stomach.

Sophie opened the door. 'Oh, madame!' she exclaimed. She hurried across and stood in front of Emily. 'You're not to get up! Let me help you back into bed.'

Emily stood up. She reached and put a hand to Sophie's shoulder, steadying herself. 'I'm going to the library, Sophie. Help me get dressed.'

Sophie started back. 'I won't do it, madame! I promised Monsieur. Dr Chaussegros has forbidden you to go out.'

'They don't understand, Sophie,' Emily appealed to her. 'Just help me. Please! I need your help. Don't refuse me. There's no one else I can ask.'

'I can't do it, madame.'

Emily looked at her. 'Are you content, Sophie?'

'Pardon, madame?'

'What do you dream of for your*self*? What do you hope for?'

'Why, nothing, madame. I . . .'

'Oh, don't lie, Sophie!' Emily said, exasperated. 'Everyone hopes for something.'

'There was a time, I suppose, I thought I might join the order. They wanted me. Not all the girls got asked.'

'That was at Chantilly?'

'Yes madame.'

'You liked the nuns.'

Sophie looked out the window, her gaze distant and thoughtful. 'The convent was my home. They were my family.' She looked at her hands, then looked up at Emily, a sudden smile in her eyes. 'I was taught the piano. That is what I miss.'

'So why don't you join the order, then? Why don't you do it? It's what you miss. It's what you love, isn't it? You must find a way to do what you love, Sophie. It is never easy to do what we love. It is always the hardest thing. I don't know why that should be. But it is. It always is. We make it hard. But we must do it all the same. We have to find a way.'

Sophie looked at her. 'Oh, the order's not for everyone, madame,' she said, as if Emily had not understood.

'Fetch me my dress. It's in the second drawer. The blue one. What a pity the piano teacher left, you could have had lessons. I would have paid for you.'

Sophie said, 'She was not the only piano teacher, madame.'

Emily laughed. 'Well, we shall find you another one.' She slipped off her nightdress. 'I'm freezing! There's a spencer in the bottom drawer. Get it for me. If Monsieur or Dr Chauessgros telephone, just say I'm sleeping.'

Sophie handed her the spencer. 'I'm no good at lying. They'll guess at once I'm not telling the truth.'

'You lied to me easily enough a minute ago. We lie when we want to. *Pretend* it's the truth. Pretend I *am* sleeping. Just do this for me. We can help each other.'

Sophie murmured, 'I'll try, madame.'

'Men don't understand these things, Sophie. Don't think of it as deception. Think of it as our truth.'

Sophie looked doubtful. She reached and turned down the collar of Emily's dress at the back and patted it into place. 'You must wrap up well, madame. And don't stay too long at the library. It's a wonder to me they let you in the place in your condition.'

It was a quarter to two by the time Emily arrived at the Bibliothèque Sainte-Geneviève and joined the crowd of students waiting for the doors to open for the afternoon session. She was trembling and exhausted. It was raining and bitterly cold. There was nowhere to shelter along the plain façade of the building and many of the students were poorly dressed and did not have umbrellas. They stood against the wall with their arms folded across their chests, sheltering their notebooks under their jackets, their coat collars turned up and their hats pulled over their eyes, gazing at the wet pavement and smoking cigarettes. Two young women looked at Emily's belly and spoke to each other and turned away. A few of the noisier young men banged on the doors and demanded to be let in. When the bell nearby began to strike the hour, the doors were opened by the attendant.

Emily managed to get the last seat at the end of a table closest to the book stacks and farthest from the central dividing columns. No one would be seated on her left and she could sit more comfortably with her legs spread apart. She left her writing case and her gloves in her place and went to the desk and ordered the volume of Tertullian and she returned to her place and sat and waited. She kept her overcoat on. The heated reading room soon began to grow stuffy, the warm air reeking with a mixture of the smell of books and the wet clothes and the smells of the students. She closed her eyes. She was trembling all over, as if an electric current were passing through her. The pressure on her diaphragm was making it difficult for her to breathe. She gasped and murmured and opened her eyes. She saw the uniformed attendant at the door watching her. He shook his head and wagged his forefinger at her. She looked away and opened her writing case. She took out her notebook and placed it on the table in front of her. She could feel the attendant watching her.

The man in his long grey smock who delivered the books came over. He leaned and placed the heavy volume in front of her. She turned and thanked him, the smell of old vellum and dust and antique paper swirling around him as he turned and passed on to the next student, his arms filled with books. She opened the old volume and turned the crackling pages filled with black columns of type until she came to the bold italic heading *De Spectaculis* Her vision swam unsteadily and the blood left her head as she leaned over the book and read the opening phrases of Tertullian's condemnation of the Roman games. She laid her finger against the page under the opening words and made an effort to focus,

Qui status fidei, quae ratio veritatis . . . She reached for her fountain pen and unscrewed the cap, the page tilting and slewing away. She gripped the pen and scrawled her translation unsteadily at the head of a clean page in her notebook: *The conditions of faith*, she wrote, *the reason inherent in truth* . . .

She felt the attendant's hand grip her elbow and his urgent whisper close to her ear, 'Come, madame! Can you stand? I've telephoned for a taxi to take you home. You cannot stay here. This is no place for you.'

The students along the table paused in their work and watched, curious, detached. Emily saw in the eyes of the young woman opposite her a mixture of pity and fear. The uniformed attendant gathered her things and put them in her writing case and he closed the case and put it under his arm and helped her to her feet. Emily leaned her weight against him gratefully. He was warm and smelled of cologne. He supported her and went with her down the stairs to the foyer and found a seat for her. He waited with her until the taxi came, then he went out into the rain and helped her into the taxi.

She looked out of the window. The taxi was passing the ornate pilastered entrance to the church of Saint-Étienne-du-Mont, the great carved doors closed against the driving rain. She lay back against the cushions and closed her eyes, anger sweeping through her. She felt bitter and vengeful at the thought of Bertrand going on with his life, untouched and unchanged, while she was transformed, crippled and frustrated. She determined that if she was not to be allowed to do her work, then he would not do his work either. She opened her eyes. Her mind was made up. It would be her opportunity when Georges took his documents to the directors in Haine Saint-Paul. She would take the train down to Chartres and confront Bertrand with her situation. She could be back in Paris the same day. Georges and Léon need never know. She vowed to have her satisfaction before the child was born.

She would let Father Bertrand Étinceler see what had become of the carefree girl he had met that day in the lamplight among his seductive ripening peaches and his soft piles of straw. It was not over yet. She would see to that.

~ PART FOUR ~

THE HOUSEHOLD OF
THE ELDERS

ONE

Georges slipped out of bed and stood in his bare feet on the floor. He stood listening to Emily breathing, then he felt in the darkness and lifted his dressing gown from the back of the chair and put it on. He went out, easing the bedroom door closed behind him. In the sitting room he switched on the brass lamp on the table under the window. His black leather briefcase and rolled umbrella lay ready on the chair beside the table. He stepped across to the gas fire and took the matches from the tray and squatted and lit the gas. When he had lit the gas, he went over and tapped on the door to the small room. He waited, listening. He reached for the knob and opened the door a little way and looked in. The air was close and still and smelled faintly of the chamber pot. The small oblong of the skylight was a graininess against the dark, the empty ribcage of the crib looming by the wall beside him.

He whispered, 'Sophie!' and waited. He stepped into the room and leaned over the narrow iron bed and felt for her, finding the warm roundness of her shoulder under the blankets. 'It's time to get up, Sophie.' She moved and murmured at his touch and he stepped away. At the door he turned. 'It's time to get up!'

The bedsprings creaked and her sleepy voice came softly out of the darkness, 'Is that you, monsieur?'

While he was shaving she came into the kitchen. He wished her good morning and went on with his shaving. Sophie's dark hair was tied loosely with a blue ribbon at the side. Her cheeks were rosy and soft with bedwarmth, as if she were still a child. She was wearing a grey woollen cardigan over her black dress. She finished buttoning the cardigan and took her apron from the hook next to the door. She prepared the coffeepot and carried it into the sitting room and set it to brew on the gas fire. She came back into the kitchen and stood looking at him.

Georges stropped his razor and bent to see his jaw in the small square of the mirror. 'It's winter suddenly,' he said. 'You were all cosily tucked up in there. I didn't like to wake you.'

'Do you want me to cook you something, monsieur?'

He turned to her and held up two fingers. 'Two rashers and two eggs.' He grinned to see the look she gave him. 'Toast would be nice too, if you can manage it.'

She reached and took down a small copper skillet. 'I don't know how you can eat at this time of the morning, monsieur. It still feels like the middle of the night.' She leaned past him and opened the cupboard above the sink and he stepped back to give her room. She took out a small piece of bacon wrapped in greaseproof paper. She cut two slices from the piece and put them in the pan.

He rubbed at his cheeks and neck. 'I'll be on the train by six.'

She stirred at the bacon with a fork. The fat popped and the rashers curled in the hot pan.

The smell of coffee wafted in from the sitting room.

She moved the bacon to one side of the pan and took an egg from a white china bowl on the blue tiles and she broke the egg on the side of the pan. She tilted the pan and watched until the white began to congeal, then took another egg from the bowl and broke it into the pan.

'It smells good, Sophie,' Georges said. He wiped his face with the towel and patted his cheeks and shrugged his shoulders into his dressing gown. 'I'll be two minutes.' He went out and crossed the sitting room. He opened the door and stepped in. He closed the door behind him and stood accustoming his eyes to the dark. There was a sound like moths' wings beating softly at the window. Big, pale snowflakes driven by the wind were slapping against the panes. They slid down the glass, turning to water.

Emily said, 'I'm awake. You can put on the light.' Her voice was husky and unfamiliar. She suppressed a tight cough, turning it into a clearing of her throat.

He felt for the lamp and switched it on. The naked bulb lit the room coldly. He looked down, examining her, his grey eyes bright in the hard light, his chestnut hair a halo of pale fire. He bent and kissed her forehead. 'Your're hot,' he said. 'Be sure to drink plenty of water today, won't you?'

She lay watching him dress. Her hair at the nape of her neck was dark with sweat and the pillow under her head was damp. She reached and turned the pillow over. She shivered and drew the blankets close about her chin. 'What time will you get there?'

He pulled his braces over his shoulders and felt around the waistband of his trousers, tucking his shirt in. 'Some time this evening. If it's not too late, I'll ring you when I get to the hotel. But don't worry if I don't ring tonight. It'll just mean I've been held up. I'll definitely ring in the morning before I go into the meeting.' He reached for his tie. 'That's if Jean-Pierre has arrived safely with the documents.'

'Are you nervous?'

'I'm more nervous about you.'

'I've got Sophie. You'll only be gone a couple of days. I'll be all right.' She coughed and grimaced and pressed her hand to her chest under the bedclothes.

'I meant next month.' he said. 'It's only four weeks now.'

'Yes.'

They looked at each other.

'I try to imagine it,' he said. 'Three of us. But I can't. Can you? Do you see it? Do you think of it as a boy or a girl?'

Sophie tapped at the door and called softly, 'Your breakfast's on the table, monsieur.'

Emily had closed her eyes.

He turned back to the cheval glass and finished tying his tie. He buttoned his waistcoat and put on his jacket and went out into the sitting room. He sat at the table by the window and drank his coffee and ate the eggs and bacon.

Sophie came in. 'Shall I ask Madame if she'd like a cup of tea?'

'Yes. She's awake.'

When Georges had finished his breakfast, he went into the bedroom and put on his scarf and his overcoat. He stood beside the bed, his brown trilby in his hand and his gloves sticking out of his coat pocket. He rested his hat on the mound of her belly and reached into his inside pocket and took out his wallet. He counted out banknotes, murmuring the count to himself. 'There's four hundred francs there,' he said and put the money on the cupboard beside the bed. He buttoned his overcoat and picked up his hat and stood looking at her. 'Time to go.'

She freed a hand from the blankets and reached for his hand. 'Good luck.'

He bent and kissed her, then stood holding her hand, considering her.

'You'd better go,' she said. She withdrew her hand from his. 'You'll miss your train.' She smiled, 'It will be a triumph for you.'

'Things are never as we expect them to be. It's a great design. Everyone's been magnificent. I'm confident they'll go ahead and submit it to Bradfield.' He bent and kissed her again, unwilling to leave. 'I'll be back Thursday.' He stepped to the door and blew her a kiss. He put on his hat and tugged the brim and he stepped across to the table and picked up his umbrella and his briefcase.

Sophie went with him to the door.

He put down his briefcase and hung his umbrella in the crook of his arm and pulled on his gloves. 'Take care of her, Sophie. I know you will. She's not to get up until her temperature goes down.' He leaned and picked up his briefcase. 'You've got Dr Chaussegros's telephone numbers at his home and at the hospital. If you're at all uncertain about anything, ring him at once. And if there's anything else, fetch your aunt up to help you. Madame Barbier knows I'll be away for a couple of days. Leave nothing to chance, Sophie. I'll telephone tonight or in the morning and I'll be back on Thursday.' He looked at her levelly. 'I'm leaving Madame in your good care.'

Sophie did not meet his eyes. 'Yes, monsieur,' she murmured.

He put a hand to her shoulder, then turned and went down the stairs. She stood and watched him until he was out of sight. She closed the door and turned back into the room. Emily was standing in the bedroom door tying the belt of her dressing gown. They went across to the window together and looked down into the courtyard, their shoulders touching. Sleety rain was sheeting across the face of the buildings, the bare branches of the robinia tree trembling and twitching in the swirling gusts. A moment later Georges hurried across the courtyard and went out under the light through the covered way. He did not pause or turn to look up at the window.

'He's gone,' Emily said, and she went across to the gas fire and took up the coffeepot. 'I'll have a bath now, Sophie.'

'Yes, madame.' Sophie went into the kitchen and took down the tin bath.

Emily came and stood in the kitchen door. She sipped her coffee and watched Sophie filling the bath. 'I'll be back by this evening before Monsieur's even reached Haine Saint-Paul. If Dr Chaussegros telephones before I get home, tell him my temperature's gone down and I'm sleeping.'

Sophie helped her off with her things.

'Is it Monsieur's mother you're going to see, then?' Sophie asked.

Emily laughed and coughed. She stepped into the bath and stood looking down at herself, her hands gripping the enormous globe of her stomach. 'It's better you don't know.'

Sophie fetched a towel and stood looking at her.

'You're not going to cry, are you?' Emily said severely. 'There's nothing to cry about.'

'I promised Monsieur solemnly, madame. What if something happens to you?'

'What can happen to me? You'll need another woman's help yourself one day. I hope there's someone there for you then.' She looked at Sophie. 'Have you never shared another woman's secret?'

'No, madame.'

'Look at me!'

Together they gazed in awe at her body.

'You see what happens to us? Does it terrify you?'

Sophie's gaze was fixed on Emily's enormous naked belly, pale and glistening in the electric light.

'How can they know what we go through? How can they know anything about *this*?' Emily stroked herself, then looked up at Sophie. 'If only our lives could be simple and innocent.'

When she'd finished her bath, Emily went into the bedroom and put on her warmest underclothes. She had to sit on the bed twice to catch her breath. Her heart was pounding and she was breathless. A fine sweat covered her body, making her shiver. There was a dullness in her chest, as if a hand pressed on her sternum, and her cough was tight and dry. Over the shapeless blue dress she put on her heavy cardigan and wound a scarf around her neck. She buttoned her long green overcoat across her belly and turned up the collar. She stood in front of the mirror and set the grey velour cloche well down over her forehead and carefully inserted the long hatpin. She put two hundred francs in her handbag and went into the sitting room. She picked up her writing case. The rain rattled against the windowpanes. Outside, the sky had turned acid grey.

Sophie watched her. 'Won't you eat something before you go, madame?' She asked with concern. 'You've only had that cup of tea.'

'I don't feel hungry. I can have something at the railway station if I need it. There's bound to be a wait.'

'Oh, madame, I'm so afraid. Please won't you let me come with you?'

'Don't be silly! I need you here. As long as you're here to keep our secret safe, it will seem only that I've slept through the day.' She picked up her handbag and went back into the bedroom for her umbrella. When she came out again, she stood looking around the sitting room, as if she thought she might have forgotten something. She turned to Sophie. 'I'm ready.' She kissed Sophie on the cheek. 'Stop worrying. I'll be home this evening. Cook me something nice for dinner. I'll tell you all about it then.'

Sophie followed her to the door and out onto the landing. She stood at the head of the stairs and leaned over the bannisters to watch Emily go down. Emily turned at the next landing. 'Go back inside. You'll freeze.'

 ━ ⌐

As she came out of the building into the gray half-light of the wintry December morning, the wind sucked at Emily's overcoat and buffeted her and the freezing rain stung her cheeks like a vicious slap. She gasped and put her hand up to her face. Halfway across the courtyard she turned and looked up. Sophie's silhouette was at the window of the apartment. There was a light on in Madame Barbier's rooms but no sign of the concierge. She went out through the covered way and turned left into rue Saint-Dominique. The baker's shop was busy with early customers. She clutched her writing case and held her umbrella out in front of her against the wind, which threatened to snatch it out of her hand. She turned left opposite Saint-Pierre-du-Gros-Caillou and made her way down through the narrow streets to the avenue de la Motte Picquet and the Métro at École Militaire. The streets were already filled with people hurrying on their way to work. The cafés were busy, their interiors bright and welcoming and their windows steamed up. As she passed their doors, she smelled fresh coffee and heard the lively hubbub of conversation.

On the Métro a man stood for her. He raised his hat and offered her his seat. The women held their bags on their knees and eyed her. She got off at Montparnasse and struggled up the stairs with the crowd to the mainline station. Her bladder was on fire and she looked for a lavatory. When she came out of the lavatory, she went to the ticket office.

'What time is the next train for Chartres?' she asked the ticket seller.

He turned aside and consulted a timetable on the wall beside him. He thrust his lips out and stroked his mustache, considering. 'The 7:42's gone. The 9:15's not running today. So . . . the next Rennes train stopping at Chartres will be the 11:04 from platform nine.' He swung around and looked at her. 'That's the mail, madame. It will be stopping at all stations. It gets in to Chartres at half past one.'

She said, 'There's nothing sooner?'

'No, madame.'

She asked him for a first-class day return. He pushed the ticket and her change under the grille and looked past her shoulder to the man behind her in the queue.

She went into the station buffet and bought a cup of tea and a croissant and found an unoccupied table by the window. She opened her writing case and spread her things in front of her. She reread Olive Kallen's letter through from beginning to end, then carefully folded it away and put it back in its envelope. She took out Hakim's letter and glanced through it. She put it to one side with Olive's letter. From the side pocket of her writing case she removed her unsent second letter to Bertrand and the English original of her first letter to him. She held the letters folded in her hand, considering them. Then she unfolded the sheets and tore them across. She turned the pages and tore them across again. She got up and went out onto the station and dropped the pieces of the letters into a rubbish bin. She went back into the buffet and sat down.

She sipped her tea and opened the *Passio Perpetuae* and sat reading, drinking the tea and nibbling the croissant. After a time, she closed her eyes. She sat very still, her hands resting on the slim red volume. Every now and then she coughed and grimaced, pressing a hand to her chest. When she had been sitting there for an hour, the waitress came over and asked her if she was all right. 'Can I get you something, madame?'

Emily opened her eyes. She smiled at the waitress and thanked her. She said she didn't need anything. 'I missed the early train. I'm going to be later than I thought.'

At ten-thirty by the station clock Emily put her things away in her writing case. She put on her gloves and picked up her bag and her umbrella. She got up, steadied herself with a hand to the table, then went out. She found the sign RENNES, ALL STATIONS. She showed her ticket at the barrier and went onto the platform. The train was already standing there, the wind blowing the steam and smoke along the platform. A long mail-and-goods wagon stood against the buffers, its doors open. Beside the wagon on the platform were piles of parcels and packages and boxes and various crates and packing cases. There were bundles of ploughshares and cultivator tines and wheels and there was a white dog on a leash that followed her with its sorrowful gaze. Porters were reading the destinations off the labels and shouting to each other and loading the things into the wagons.

A guard with a blue cap and gold braid approached Emily and saluted her. He examined her ticket and escorted her to the first-class compartment. She asked him to be certain not to let her miss Chartres but to warn her when they were getting close. He said he would gladly do it. He withdrew and closed the door.

There were no other travellers in the compartment. She sat by the window facing the front. She put her writing case and her handbag and her gloves and umbrella on the seat beside her. She undid her overcoat and loosened her scarf. The compartment was heated but she did not take off her coat. She sat and waited, impatient for the train to start, her back pressed against the cushions, her eyes closed, her hands clasped over her stomach. A sheen of sweat glistened on her forehead and she breathed through her mouth. Her lips were cracked and dry. Every now and then she gasped and gave a moan and tightened her hands across her stomach. Sweat trickled down her cheeks and neck and under her hair . . . At the shriek of the guard's whistle outside the window she jumped and opened her eyes. There was a tight, gripping ache in her lower back and the globe of her stomach under her hands was as hard as wood. The train gave a jolt and moved off, slowly gathering speed and passing in review the people on the platform, their curious eyes catching at her as she went by – as if they saw her story in her face at the window.

When the train left the shelter of the station roof, the rain lashed across the window. Emily gazed out at the blurred expanse of suburbs. She closed her eyes. The carriage rocked from side to side and clattered over the points. Her throat was burning. Her chest felt as if someone was standing on it. A while later the train slowed and came to a halt. She looked out. The rain swept the platform. The engine stood panting for ten minutes while men unloaded parcels, then a whistle blew and the train jolted into motion again. It seemed it had only just got up speed when it slowed again and stopped at another station. She rubbed the glass and looked out. The sign on the platform read TRAPPE.

As the train rocked along slowly through the rainswept countryside, in a sudden moment of lucidity Emily wondered what she would say to him if she found him. Now that she was nearing Chartres she could not imagine actually being in his presence. She could not visualize her reaction to him. Her journey began to seem to her dangerous and irrational, a reaction to a kind of inner panic that she had failed to recognize . . . At Rambouillet the door to the compartment slid open and a woman and a man with two young boys came in. The man bowed to her and wished her good afternoon and the woman nodded and sat at the window seat across from her and told her boys to read their books. The boys sat next to their mother and opened their books in their laps and they stared silently at Emily, then looked at their mother and back again at Emily. The father told them sternly to read their books. The woman kept glancing at Emily and then at her husband. After a while, she caught Emily's eye. She leaned across and said, 'Is everything all right, my dear?'

Emily smiled and said she was just a little fatigued and that everything was all right.

'Is someone meeting you?'

'Yes, of course.'

The woman clicked her tongue disapprovingly. 'Forgive me, but you should not be travelling alone.' She turned to her boys and told them sharply, 'I told you to read your books!'

The family got off at Maintenon. As they went past the window, the woman looked in at Emily and turned and spoke to her husband. He shook his head and they went on.

The train moved off and Emily pressed herself to the seat and clenched her teeth against the gripping pain in her back. Each jolt of the wheels drew a gasp from her . . .

There was a roar of noise and she opened her eyes. The guard stood at the open door, his watch in his hand. He touched his fingers to the peak of his cap. 'Chartres in three minutes, madame.' He snapped the watch closed and turned away and slid the door closed.

Emily buttoned her overcoat. She held her handbag and the writing case and her umbrella ready on her lap. She looked out the window at the rain-swept fields. She could see nothing through the heavy mist and overcast. The train slowed, passing wooded parkland on the left, and a moment later pulled into the station. She gripped the windowsill and stood up. She stepped across the compartment and slid the door open and went out into the corridor.

A dozen or so passengers descended from the train ahead of her. Most of them hurried across the forecourt of the station and got into a waiting steam tram. Others were met by family or friends or hailed a taxi. Emily opened her umbrella and stepped out of the shelter of the station into the rain. She walked across the forecourt and set off up the hill along rue Jean de Beauce. She went past a lighted café and some shops and continued on across the place Châtelet, where the tram tracks diverged to the left and right. She stood holding onto a lamppost steadying herself, catching her breath. The tram from the station went past clanging its bell, passengers pressing their faces to the windows to look at her. When the tram had gone, she crossed the tracks and went on. She was like an old woman, stopping every few yards to rest and gather her remaining strength.

She emerged at last from a narrow street onto the open space before the west front of the cathedral. She stood and rested, her hand against the wall. There were no groups of tourists or pilgrims. The leafless trees and empty benches gleamed wetly in the silvery light of the deserted square. Across the eroded face of the great church sheets of rain swept like seaspray against a grey cliff, the towers and spires lost in the lowering overcast. She crossed the square and went along the north side past the porch until she came to the steps leading down to the crypt. The iron gates were locked. A chain fastened by a bronze padlock secured their endposts.

She stood in the rain looking through the bars of the gates into the darkness of the crypt at the bottom of the steps. The rain dripped steadily from the padlock into a puddle at her feet. She stood for some time before she turned aside and made her way back along the north side. As she was passing the steps to the north porch, a door in the central bay opened and a woman came out. The woman paused in the shelter of the deep porch to open her umbrella, then hurried down the steps.

Emily went up the steps into the cathedral. She stood in the dark transept, the great shadowy spaces before her, the gleam of candles, the glimmer of blue and red from the high windows, like the distant lights of a city, and shadowy figures of priests or worshippers moving among the columns. She turned and went along the north aisle as far as the second window. She could go no farther. She sat on a hard-backed chair in the dark beside a column.

She set the writing case and her handbag on the floor. As she leaned forward, her umbrella slipped from her lap and fell clattering to the flagstones. She sat with her knees spread, her head bent forward on her chest, her hands gripping her thighs. Her heart thudded heavily in her chest and sweat trickled down her scalp. She had been sitting there for some time when she lifted her head and cried out.

At Emily's sob of pain a woman rose from kneeling in prayer in the dark against the wall. The woman turned and looked, her scrutiny intent and curious, the wide brim of her black hat like the silhouette of a great agitated bird against the luminous window behind her. Then she limped away, the bronze ferrule of her cane tapping the flagstones as if she were blind and felt her way in the darkness.

Emily sat slumped forward in the chair. An hour went by and she did not move. The grey light of the December day was already beginning to fail. Emily remained there for another hour, sitting on the chair in the shadows, as if she were a devout who prayed or contemplated some strange and puzzling fact of existence that resisted her and refused to unbind to her understanding. Then her water broke, a sudden release of warm fluid between her thighs, the *liquor amnii* of birth, the water of life. She moaned in distress and raised her head and looked along the dark aisle toward the steps to the north tower. A figure approached, visible for a moment between the clustered columns, then lost again in the shadows.

Emily called, 'Help me!'

The figure paused, casting for her in the darkness, the narrow waist and full skirts of a priest's soutane against the gleam of candlelight.

Emily called again, 'Help me! I must see Father Bertrand Étinceler! Tell the Father I am waiting for him!'

The priest in the shadows shifted uncertainly, as if he would turn and leave.

Emily stood up and called Bertrand Étinceler's name again and she reached to support herself but there was nothing to hold onto and she fell forward. The crack of bone on stone echoed along the aisle like the sound of a hammer blow as her skull struck the flagstones.

The priest hurried forward out of the shadows and went to her. He lifted his soutane and knelt beside her and spoke to her urgently. She did not respond.

TWO

— ∽ —

The river Eure flowed silently around the sagging timbers of the laundry hutch at the back of Aunt Juliette's house in the lower town. The wind had dropped and the rain fell straight down, dimpling the surface of the water in the light that fell from the windows. The daylight was almost gone now, a last slash of silver between a break in the clouds to the west. In the kitchen at the back of the old house in the rue des Oiseaux Aunt Juliette reached and took down her favourite omelette pan from its hook to the side of the stove. The salt-scoured copper flashed a signal across Madame Elder's dreaming features in the lamplight as Juliette turned and set the pan on the stove to heat. The kitchen was warm and smelled of woodsmoke. Juliette spooned a knob of bacon fat from a stone crock and tapped it into the pan. She took two eggs from a saucer and broke them evenly into a china bowl. She put the shells back on the plate and stood beating the eggs with a fork. The bacon fat sizzled in the pan and filled the kitchen with its salty, appetizing smell.

Madame Elder sat at the scrubbed table waiting for her supper. She was half turned away from her sister, facing the window and the river, as if she gazed out into the night. Her left hand rested on the table and her right hand clasped the head of her cane. She murmured to herself, her lips moving, her sallow cheeks twitching. Her lamplit reflection in the window gazed back at her, her gilded features suspended in the dark above the river. Every so often she made an impatient exclamation and tapped the ferrule of her cane against the floor.

Aunt Juliette took the pan by the handle and tilted it. She poured the mixture from the bowl, rotating the pan until the mixture covered the bottom evenly. She set the bowl aside and took up a wooden spatula and eased the edges of the omelette as it began to brown, letting the rest of the mixture run against the hot sides of the pan.

There was a sudden violent hammering on the front door at the end of the passage. A man's voice shouted through the letter box.

Madame Elder's cane clattered to the floor. It rolled and brought up against the base of the stove, its polished ferrule gleaming in the shadows. Aunt Juliette stood with the wooden spatula in her hand, staring at the kitchen door. She looked around at the sound of the cane falling to the floor. She leaned and picked up the cane and held it out to her sister. When Madame Elder did not react, she tapped the cane against her leg and said sharply, 'Answer them, Heloise! It's for you!'

Madame Elder said, 'Who can it be?'

The shouting and hammering at the front door were renewed.

'Answer them!' Aunt Juliette demanded, as if she were accusing her sister of some breach of faith. 'There's nothing in my past to bring on such a commotion as this.'

Madame Elder took the cane from her and set her weight on it. She grimaced and stood up, the pain snatching at her hip. She drew breath and looked at Juliette. 'Something terrible's happened to Georges. I just know it.' Turning to leave she paused and put out her hand and rested it on her sister's shoulder, as if she steadied herself or wished to reassure her sister, or perhaps to reassure herself. She nodded at the stove. 'The omelette's spoiling.' She stepped across to the door and opened it and went out into the passage.

The man's voice shouted through the letter box, 'For the love of God, Madame Elder, are you there?'

'I'm coming!' she called. It had been just such a wintry evening as this in Glasgow twenty-three years ago when there had been another knock at her door. The explosive hammering of a man's fist, then the telegram with the news of her husband's death in Panama. The passage was dark and icy cold after the warmth of the kitchen. Madame Elder drew her shawl close around her shoulders. She crossed herself and murmured, 'Mary Mother of God save us!

She reached and opened the front door. The light from the streetlamp fell on Emily's bloodless face in the arms of Father Étinceler. Beside him another priest, and behind them in the road the black car, its engine throbbing and the chauffeur's face a pale oval at the window. Madame Elder made an exclamation and stepped aside. 'Where did you find her, Father?'

Bertrand carried Emily over the threshold, her features in the dim passage a deathly violet against the sable of his soutane. 'She came to the cathedral to give thanks for the child before coming on to you, Madame Elder. But the child has overtaken her.' Emily seemed no burden to him in his strong arms.

'Bring her quickly!' Madame Elder led him along the passage to the stairs.

Aunt Juliette stood at the kitchen door staring, the wooden spatula in her hand. Madame Elder paused to let Bertrand go past. 'Telephone Otto at once, Juliette! Tell him to bring the midwife. It's Emily! She's having her baby. She came to us, Juliette!' There was a light of excitement in Madame Elder's eyes. She followed Bertrand up the stairs. He stood waiting for her on the landing. She opened the door of the bedroom at the back of the house overlooking the river, where Emily and Georges had spent their first night in Chartres in the spring. She followed Bertrand in. He laid Emily on the bed. The other priest came in behind them and put Emily's writing case and her handbag and umbrella on a chair. He stood looking on.

Madame Elder touched Bertrand's sleeve. 'You've done well, Father. You can tell me everything afterward.' She was busily unbuttoning the cuffs of her black dress. 'Go down and tell Aunt Juliette to put on the big pan to boil. And get her to prepare plenty of clean linen.'

He stood looking at Emily. He seemed like a boxer who stands looking at the opponent he has felled, surprised and as if he looks at himself.

'Hurry, Father! This baby's a month early already and means to be born tonight whether we're ready for it or not.'

He did not move. 'Is she going to be all right?'

'Pray for her, Father. She's going to need all our prayers in the next few days.'

He took a last look at Emily, then turned and went out.

Madame Elder rolled the sleeves of her dress above her elbows, pushing them up until the abundant flesh of her upper arms gripped the bunched sleeves. She turned and bent over Emily and took off her shoes. She dropped the shoes on the floor beside the bed and unbuttoned Emily's overcoat.

Juliette came and stood in the doorway. 'Otto's on a call at Lèves.'

'Who did you speak to?'

'Anna. I told her he was needed here urgently. And to bring the midwife.'

'Have you set the big pan to boil?'

'I've done it.'

'Set the fire in here, then. This room's like the grave.' Madame Elder turned and looked at her sister. 'Go on. The child's about to be born.'

Juliette said, 'You climbed the stairs without your cane, Heloise.'

Madame Elder grunted. She bent over Emily and carefully rolled her first on one side, then on the other, removing first one arm then the other from the sleeves of her overcoat, then drawing the coat out from under her. When she rolled Emily onto her side, Madame Elder saw the dark wad of dried blood in her hair. She did not pause to examine the injury but placed the overcoat over Emily's upper half. She pulled up Emily's dress and petticoat and bunched the surplus of these garments under her back. Emily's gloves, stockings, and suspender belt she placed one by one on the floor beside the shoes. She worked speedily but without panic, murmuring encouragement to Emily all the while. When she removed Emily's bloodied and soaked drawers and saw that labour was well advanced into the second stage, her heartbeat surged and she gasped, 'It's coming!'

Emily opened her eyes and gave a great sob. She reached and gripped Madame Elder's arm as the contraction built powerfully in her uterus and the muscles of her abdomen. At the peak of the contraction the crown of the infant's head appeared at the mouth of the birth canal. Madame Elder's teeth were clenched. 'That's it, Emily! That's it! Keep going!' She leaned over Emily, both Emily's hands gripping her arm, her other arm supporting Emily's shoulders.

The crown of the infant's head seemed like nothing human but a grey stone swelling mysteriously from the elliptical aperture of straining flesh. Blood mixed with whitish mucous and a thin stream of golden excrement oozed from Emily as she bowed under the thrust of the contraction, no longer herself but an instrument of birth. For seconds her gaze held Madame Elder's. As one person, the two women ceased to breathe, each holding at the limit of her strength. Then Emily sank back and groaned and the tight ring of flesh around the infant's head reasserted its grip and her body began to engorge the head again with a series of small convulsions. It was not possible to know if Emily's body strove to expel the child or to retain it.

Aunt Juliette came and stood at the door. In her arms she held freshly laundered towels and sheets. She gazed at the scene of struggle on the bed without speaking. In the pause between contractions Madame Elder took the linen from her sister and set it on a chair beside the bed. 'Go and get the kindling,' she said gently, and she smiled to see her sister's fear and awe at the smell and the sight of Emily's struggle. 'Light the fire, Juliette.' She placed a towel beneath Emily and wiped away the excrement and blood. She paused in her wiping and turned to the door and called after Juliette, 'Tell Father Étinceler to bring the water as soon as it's hot. That pan will be too heavy for you on the stairs.'

She sat on the bed holding Emily's hand, waiting with her for the next contraction. While they waited she dabbed a towel to the sweat streaming from Emily's brow and neck. 'You're burning with the fever,' she said. 'You didn't come to me a minute too soon.' Emily moaned and moved deliriously at her touch. 'Do you know where you are, my dear?' Emily did not respond. Madame Elder spoke softly, speaking more for her own comfort than for Emily's. 'I was alone too in a foreign city without my mother or my husband when I went into labor with Georges, just like you in that apartment of his in Paris. I sent my maid for the midwife that night, but by the time she brought her Georges was in my arms. I lay there alone on my bed in that great cold barn of a house in Glasgow with Georges against my breasts for hours, the cord still joining us. While I waited for them to come and help me I told him where he was in this world. I explained to him it was his father's city, the city of engineers, and that the sound he could hear was the riveters hammering the steel plates of ships together three miles away in the yards. I talked to him as if he could understand me and was already grown up, and I knew this must be what my mother had done with me, and what every mother must do. It came suddenly clear to me that night that all us mothers are one and the same mother when it comes to giving birth, and that we all do the same thing over and over, countless times, again and again, and that nothing changes or is different from one generation to the next, and has never been different and never will be different for us so long as the human race continues on this earth. I was so happy to know this, to know myself to be a part of this great creation, that I promised the Holy Mother that night I would offer her my thanks every day for the rest of my life. And I have kept my promise.'

Emily drifted in and out of consciousness, the murmuring of Madame Elder's voice like the sound of a conversation in another room, one moment her gaze clear and focused and full of understanding, and the next an absence in her eyes.

'The instant I saw you in the arms of Father Étinceler I knew it was your longing to be with another woman that had made you leave the flat this morning and come to me, despite all the risks of the journey.' Madame Elder put her hand to Emily's brow. 'My daughter!' she said tenderly. 'To think you entrusted your life and the life of your little one to my care. When our time comes, we all understand the truth of our condition.' She wiped at the sweat and the trickle of pale blood that ran from above the hairline on Emily's neck. She bent and kissed Emily on the forehead.

A few minutes later the contractions started coming close together, and soon there was no break between them. Emily raised herself from the bed and gripped Madame Elder's shoulders. On the third peak of the contraction she howled and the head of the child was expelled from her body. The two women were like wrestlers, or lovers, their sweating limbs glistening in the yellow lamplight, knotted to each other by their struggle, unyielding and locked until the tiny shoulders followed the head and the child slithered from Emily's body with a sudden rush into Madame Elder's hands.

Madame Elder held the little girl cupped in her palms. She did not move but stared at it. The infant was a greyish blue and as soft as warm marshmallow to her touch. It sucked a tiny breath of air and writhed. Then it screamed. Its cheeks at once turned a delicate rosy pink, like a peach that begins to ripen. Madame Elder's heart raced at the sound of the baby's cry. She laughed with relief and wrapped it carefully in a towel, the purple tendon of the cord like a length of exposed bowel reaching out of the swaddling into Emily's body, the discharge of blood and fluids soaking the bedding and the towels.

Emily lay like a dead woman in her mess, her blue dress pulled up and her bare legs splayed and dirtied, as if she had been abandoned, the broken victim of a vicious attack.

The baby stopped screaming and lay still in the swaddling, its wrinkled features closed, as if it imagined itself returned to the haven of the womb. Its head was covered with a thick mat of black hair smeared with the cheesy vernix of its shield.

Juliette came and stood at the door, the coal scuttle in one hand, twists of paper to kindle the fire in the other. She stared at her sister. Madame Elder's cheeks were flushed and she was kneeling beside the bed, leaning into the mattress, cradling the swaddled infant to her breasts. Tears were running freely down her cheeks.

Juliette stood and looked at her.

Madame Elder turned and looked up at her. She laughed to see Juliette's expression, her grey eyes bright and youthful suddenly in the lamplight. 'Oh, it's a beautiful little girl, Juliette! A beautiful little girl!' she cried, her voice filled with emotion and enthusiasm. 'Look!'

Aunt Juliette stepped forward. She leaned and looked down at the infant. 'How ugly the poor little mite is.'

'That's not ugliness you see there, Juliette.'

'It'll do me for ugliness.'

There was a hammering on the front door downstairs. Juliette set the scuttle by the hearth and went out onto the landing. She shouted over the bannisters, 'Answer the door, will you, Father?' She came back into the bedroom and glanced at her sister. She shook her head and said, 'I don't know. You're a real sight, Heloise. You should see yourself.' She picked up her scuttle and knelt in front of the hearth and set the fire.

There was a sound of voices and the thumping of boots on the stairs. Otto Hopman came into the bedroom. He adjusted his spectacles with his middle finger and bent over Madame Elder. He put a hand to her shoulder. 'Well done, Heloise!' He put his bag on the bed and took off his coat and laid it over the back of a chair and rolled up his sleeves. His arms were thin and white, the flesh almost translucent. He looked at the baby, then at Emily. 'It was to be January, wasn't it?'

'So we thought.'

'It's the early ones that always take us by surprise. So she had a fall? Has she roused at all? She's got a fever. D'you see that? Where's Georges?'

A stout woman of middle age came into the room, her shoulders twice the breadth of Otto Hopman's. She stood and breathed heavily, her gaze on the baby. 'Good evening, Madame Elder. So you're a grandmother at last?'

Madame Elder looked up and nodded. 'Good evening, Madame Brébeuf. A beautiful little girl. I wondered if I'd ever see the day.'

The midwife went round to the other side of the bed and rolled up her sleeves. 'We'd better have this out before she decides to keep it.' She raised her skirt and put one plump knee on the bed, then placed a large reddened hand on Emily's stomach and reached between Emily's legs. She took hold of the cord and slowly withdrew from Emily's body the livid sac of bloodrich membrane. When she had freed it, she stood holding the afterbirth for Otto to look at. They leaned together, gazing curiously at the weighty sac, touching it and turning it in Madame Brébeuf's hands, as if it were not the child but life itself in the form of this mysterious organism that they had come to harvest from Emily's body.

Otto turned away. He reached and gently took the baby from Madame Elder. 'You couldn't wait to join us, eh?' He unwrapped the swaddling while the midwife stood by with the dripping afterbirth in her hands. The baby began to scream. 'Fresh as a new bun.' Otto examined the baby with rough familiarity. 'A delicious little girl.' He reached for his bag and opened it. He took out a steel clip and snapped the clip over the cord and he slipped a pair of scissors from a case and sliced the cord through.

'Georges went to Belgium this morning,' Madame Elder said, watching. 'The poor girl must have felt her time coming on soon after he left her.'

'She's brought nothing with her,' Aunt Juliette said, looking around the bedroom. 'Just her handbag and this writing case here.'

Otto handed the liberated infant to Madame Elder.

The midwife slid the afterbirth into the washbasin on the stand under the window.

Bertrand stood in the doorway holding a pan of steaming water in one hand and a jug of cold water in the other. He stared at Emily, then looked at the baby. His face was white as bone.

Otto Hopman glanced up at the young priest from Artois, his spectacles flashing in the lamplight. He laughed. 'Birth's more upsetting than the sight of death, eh, Father? Is this the first time you've witnessed the Lord's work while it's still hot?'

Madame Elder said, 'Will you bless my granddaughter in the first hour of her life, Father?'

Otto Hopman was leaning over Emily. 'This young woman's going to need all the help she can get. You'd better give her your blessing too, while you're at it. The mother's blessing? What do you call it?'

The fire began to take, the light of the blue-and-yellow flames dancing against the ceiling. The midwife wiped the blood from her hands and reached and took the heavy iron pan of steaming water from Bertrand. 'Put the jug on the washstand, Father. There's enough of us here to do the work now.'

He stood unmoving, staring at Emily, the white jug gripped in his large workman's hand, the calluses along his thumb polished and ingrained with dirt, the firelight playing across his broad features, his expression a mask of uncertainty.

Aunt Juliette took the jug from him and passed it to the midwife. 'Come on, then, Father.' She took him by the arm. 'If you're not going to be doing any blessing, you'd just as well come with me and leave these good folk to get on with it. Let's make ourselves useful and put the kettle on and make us all a cup of tea, shall we?'

The midwife took the infant from Madame Elder and set about bathing it in a basin of tepid water on the rug in front of the fire. The baby screamed, its face purple with rage, its scream held to the point of choking, then sucking another breath to scream again.

Madame Elder looked over Otto's shoulder at Emily. 'She hasn't heard her baby's first cry.'

'It's hard to know what she'll remember of this.' Otto put his arm under Emily and took hold of her shoulders. He looked at Madame Elder. 'When I lift her, put those towels under her.' He lifted Emily. 'There's nothing to her.' When they had arranged Emily on the clean towels, he took a swab and he bent close and cleaned away the discharge of blood and debris from her gaping vagina. He covered her and turned his attention to the wound on her scalp. 'Bring me some warm water, Heloise. This is going to need stitches. Where did she do this?'

Madame Elder held the enamel bowl for him. He rinsed the cloth and the water turned pink. 'The Father's got the answers for us. She must have fallen in the cathedral. This the second time he's rescued our Emily. We have much to thank him for.'

'She's got a severe concussion.' He handed her the cloth. 'What was she doing up there in this condition? Pass me my bag.' Madame Elder handed him his bag. He threaded a needle and began to stitch the wound in Emily's head. When he had finished, he stood up and eased his shoulders and looked about the room. 'How long since a child was born in this house, Heloise?'

Madame Elder was at a loss for an answer for a moment. 'I suppose it must have been me, Otto,' she said with surprise. 'There's been no one since.'

They looked at each other.

He took his stethoscope from his bag and unbuttoned the top of Emily's dress. 'Help me lift her while I have a listen to her lungs.' Madame Elder held Emily against her abundant breasts and watched him. They laid Emily down again. 'This is pneumonia. It's not good, Heloise. We're going to have to get her temperature down right away and keep it down if she's to have a chance.' He looked at her, his small bright eyes behind his spectacles filled with concern. 'Can you reach Georges tonight? He must be with her.'

Emily moaned and shifted restlessly and they turned and looked at her. Her mouth was open and her breathing unsteady. Her face and neck were wet with sweat, her skin blotchy with livid patches. Otto put his instruments back in his bag and rolled down his sleeves and put on his jacket. Madame Elder began to remove Emily's dress and underwear. Otto went over to the fireside, where the midwife was drying the baby. He stood watching her. 'Can you strip a little colostrum for her tonight, do you think? We'll need a wet nurse before morning.'

The midwife said she would see what she could do. 'There'll be a wet nurse in the house before I'm done tonight.'

Madame Elder sponged the sweat from Emily's skin with a wet cloth. She covered her and went downstairs and fetched one of her own nightdresses. She came back and put the nightdress on Emily. The midwife gave the baby to Otto to hold and she lifted Emily while Madame Elder put fresh linen on the bed. When they had finished their work, the three of them stood considering Emily.

'She's young,' Otto said. He handed the baby back to the midwife. He smoothed his moustache with one finger. 'When she rouses, be sure to give her plenty to drink. And keep cooling her with a sponge.'

Madame Elder looked at him, anxious for his instructions.

Otto took off his spectacles and pulled his handkerchief from his trouser pocket and polished the lenses. He held the spectacles up to the light and squinted through them, then gave them another polish before he put them on again. He turned to Madame Elder. 'You have to get hold of Georges as soon as possible.'

'I'll send him a telegram.'

'Tell him . . .' Otto hesitated. 'There's no point in alarming him. Tell him he's got a beautiful healthy daughter and he'd better get home as soon as he can.'

'They're to decide on his bridge design tomorrow,' Madame Elder said.

The midwife held the sleeping baby in her arms. The room was warm now. The fire had settled, the coals glowing red on the underside with blue-and-yellow flames misting across their surface like some mysterious subterranean fire.

'We'll move her to the hospital in the morning,' Otto said.

'No,' Madame Elder said firmly. They looked at her. 'I'll take care of her myself.'

'It'll be too much for you, Heloise. She's going to need someone by her night and day until this fever breaks. You've done your bit for her.'

'I shall take care of her, Otto,' Madame Elder said calmly. 'She'll not be leaving the house now.'

Otto looked at her. He reached and put his hand on her shoulder. She put her hand up and took his hand in hers. Her eyes were bright. 'She came to me, Otto. She is my daughter.'

He patted her hand, then released it and reached for his bag.

They left the midwife in the bedroom with Emily and the sleeping child and went downstairs to the kitchen. Juliette was alone. She looked up as they came in. The two cold halves of the omelette lay untouched on the plates in their customary places, Madame Elder's at the window end of the table and Juliette's on the stove side.

Otto sat at the table and Aunt Juliette poured his tea. 'Where's the Father?' he asked her.

'I'll go and send the telegram,' Madame Elder said. She left them at the table drinking their tea and she went out into the passage. She closed the kitchen door behind her. Her cane was lying against the skirting board. She bent to pick it up and the priest rose toward her from a chair in the shadows. She started back in alarm, 'For the love of God, Father! You'll be the death of me! Why aren't you sitting in the warm with the others?'

He stood before her in the half-light, a short, muscular man with close-shaved black hair, the faintly disconcerting smell of earth about him, which she had not grown used to but had come to expect. 'I shall go up and sit with her,' he said, his voice low, his diction careful, as if he considered each word.

'We have much to thank you for.'

In the semidarkness of the passage the grey oval of the priest's face above the impenetrable black of his soutane was as opaque and unreadable as a frosted window.

'Give them your blessing, Father. It is a precious night for all of us.' She watched him lift his skirts and climb the stairs, his darkness and his silence that she had come to know a little and which drew her to him, as if he were a mysterious child who followed some compelling adventure of the mind. When he had gone, she reached and took the telephone from its cradle on the wall and rang the exchange.

As she dictated the telegram, she felt a strange reluctance to include Georges in this moment, a detachment from him that surprised and puzzled her and made her feel guilty. A desire to hold this night as her own and to keep it. She directed the telegram to the offices of Baume Marpent in Haine Saint-Paul. Georges would receive it in the morning when he arrived for his meeting with the directors: *My Dearest Son, Emily gave birth to a beautiful little girl this evening. You are a father. I delivered the child myself. Emily is a woman of courage and determination. Make all haste. Telephone me as soon as you receive this. If you can manage it, see that the layette, the crib, and nightclothes for Emily are sent on. All my love, Mother.* The girl on the exchange read the telegram back to her and Madame Elder thanked her and hung up. She didn't go back to the kitchen but went down the hall to the sitting room. The room was bitterly cold. There was a smell of mice. She lit the gas and sat at the English cabinet and composed a cable to Professor and Mrs Richard Stanton. At the end of her brief message she added, *It was an easy birth, with doctor and midwife in attendance. Emily and the baby are both doing well.* She blotted the sheet and folded it and put it into the pocket of her dress. She closed the front of the bookcase and went over and turned out the gas and left the room.

Emily opened her eyes. The priest stood before the fire, his head bowed. He was reading by the light of a faltering candleflame. The pain gathered slowly in her groin, grew along her bones, entered her viscera, its grip tightening. She closed her eyes, holding the pain at bay. It rose into her chest and pressed down on her, an enormous weight that she could not resist . . . It was Georges's dream of a figure at the top of a dark staircase that she saw. When she woke again, the priest was gone, The candle no longer burned on the mantelshelf. An even grey light filled the cold room and a strange lucidity filled her mind. She felt she had known another life long ago, had embarked boldly upon a journey in a broken wilderness where she had met the best of friends and where her purpose had been to search for the precious lost things she had once possessed.

THREE

—— ——

Georges stepped out of the taxi. He turned with his hand on the door and leaned in, instructing the driver to bring the things into the house. A horse and van waited in the narrow street to pass the taxi, the horse pawing the cobbles and tossing its mane. The street was crowded with pedestrians and traffic. The bleating of penned sheep, thin and penetrating in the air like the cries of gulls. The crib and Emily's cabin trunk were strapped to the roof of the taxi. A misty rain drifted down between the houses. Georges knocked and waited, one foot on the doorstep. Aunt Juliette opened the door and he stepped up and embraced her. 'How is she?'

Juliette held his gloved hands in hers. 'Your mother's with her. Go on up. I'll see to these things.'

Georges didn't pause to take off his hat and overcoat. He hurried down the passage and took the stairs two at a time. He pushed open the bedroom door and stepped in. The curtains were drawn and the room was in semidarkness. Emily and his mother were both asleep. Emily still and pale, the sheet at her chin. Madame Elder in the chair by the fire, her head thrown back and her mouth open. In the grey light she looked like a dead woman. Her bony fingers were curled around her spectacles in her lap and wisps of hair had come loose from her pins and clung to her sunken cheeks. The antimacassar had fallen from the back of the chair and lay across her shoulder like a waiter's cloth. The air was heavy with a smell of coalsmoke and carbolic and of women and sickness.

Georges stepped across to the bed and looked closely at Emily. She resembled a sick child, her cheeks flushed and her lips as vivid as the flesh of cherries. A large blue medicine bottle, a glass measure, and a teaspoon lay on the cupboard beside her. There was a bitter smell and a sourness on her breath. He touched his lips to her forehead and whispered, 'I love you.' He straightened and stood looking at her, his hat in his hand. 'Please, God, let her be all right!'

Madame Elder opened her eyes and sat up. 'You're here!' She struggled to get up. In her agitation her spectacles fell from her lap. 'I must have gone to sleep.'

He put his hat on the bed and went over and picked up his mother's spectacles. With a smile he took the antimacassar from her shoulder and embraced her. 'Dearest Mother,' he said. 'You are exhausted.'

Madame Elder pulled away and looked at Emily. 'No, I'm all right, Georges.'

'Where's the baby?'

She pointed at the ceiling and whispered, 'The wet nurse is with her. We've made a little nursery in the attic. Did you bring the crib?'

'I brought everything.' He looked at Emily. 'Is she going to be all right? Is Otto coming this morning?'

'Come,' Madame Elder said, and she took his arm. 'We can talk about all that in a minute. Come and see your daughter.' They went out onto the landing. They had to go in single file up the narrow flight of stairs. At the top of the stairs there was a bare landing lit by a skylight, a plain, unpainted timber door on either side of the landing. Madame Elder tapped on the left-hand door. She lifted the iron hasp and opened the door. Georges followed her into the tiny room.

Inside the air was warm and there was the sour smell of babies and milk. Under the low sloping ceiling a narrow iron bed stood hard up against the far wall. A young girl of about eighteen sat on the bed. Her blouse was open and she had a baby at her breast. She looked up at them as they came in. The baby gulped and choked on the abundant flow and the girl eased her dark nipple from its lips. A glassy trail of milk drooled from the baby's mouth and dribbled across the pink flesh of the young girl's naked breast.

Madame Elder stepped across and put her hand on the girl's shoulder. 'This is Monsieur, Marthe. He's come to see his daughter.' She turned to Georges and indicated a drawer under the narrow window. The drawer overflowed with bedding.

'She's asleep, madame,' Marthe said. 'She had her feed not long ago.'

Georges and Madame Elder went over to the drawer and looked down. The baby's tiny features beneath a cap of spiky black hair were all that was visible of her among the bedclothes, her eyes tightly closed behind swollen lids, her flat nose turned up, her red lips pouting with a look of aggrieved discontent.

Georges knelt on the boards beside the drawer and gazed in at the baby. His fingers gripped the edge of the drawer. 'My God, she's so beautiful!' he whispered. He looked up at his mother. His eyes were glassy with emotion.

Madame Elder rested a hand on his shoulder. 'Yes, darling. She is quite perfect.'

Marthe said in a normal voice, 'You can pick her up if you like, Monsieur Elder. You wouldn't wake her with a gunshot at this minute.'

Georges looked at his mother uncertainly.

'Let me.' She made to bend down to take the baby from its makeshift crib but was seized by the stiffness in her hip. She stumbled and clutched Georges's shoulder, grimacing with the pain. He reached and held her. They looked at each other.

'I'll do it, Mother.' He put his hands under the baby and scooped her out of the drawer and stood up, cradling her against the lapels of his overcoat. He looked down at her sleeping features. 'Has Emily seen her?'

'No.'

'What shall we call you, little one? You're so new we don't even know your name. We'll get Father Étinceler to baptize you at once. I'll pay him a visit this afternoon. I should take him a gift. You've come to know him a little, Mother. What do you think he'd like? What does one give a man who has bound himself to poverty and chastity?' He laughed. 'There's not a lot left really, is there.'

'He's not a mystic, dear. He likes to read. He borrows your father's books and teaches himself English,' Madame Elder said. 'I've tried to give him lessons, but I'm afraid I'm not very good at it. Did you bring the layette?'

'I brought everything. All Emily's things. The crib. Everything. Juliette's seeing to it now.'

They stood gazing at the baby in his arms. Marthe's baby was making sucking noises again and Marthe was talking to it.

The floorboards creaked under Georges's heels. 'You delivered her . . . It astonishes me to think of it. How I wish I'd been here.' He fell silent, studying intently the features of his tiny daughter. 'It seems incredible that the two things I've longed for should both have happened on the same day. The porter came into the meeting to give me your telegram. He interrupted us. They were all there. The directors and Jean-Pierre. There was a deathly silence while they watched me open the telegram. I read it and then I looked at them and told them, My wife has given birth to our first child in Chartres. For a moment I forgot the bridge. I'm a father, I said. The bridge didn't exist. You would have thought I'd given them a prize. They cheered and gathered around me and they laughed and patted me on the back and congratulated me. Suddenly these anxious, suspicious old men were all laughing and talking at once like a roomful of schoolboys. We carried on as if we'd just won the tender. It was so unexpected. I'll never forget that moment. Jacques Lenormand – you know, he's always been my enemy, though God knows why – he came over and took my hand and wished me well . . . And I *liked* him! I actually liked that man.' Georges laughed. 'Everything's changed,' he said. 'Nothing will ever be the same for us again.'

Madame Elder looked startled. 'What do you mean, everything? You're a father, Georges. Emily will soon be well.' She sounded a little impatient with the grand sweep of his claim. 'You have your own family . . . And not before time. Have they sent your design to Sydney?'

'It's on its way, Mother. There will be a mention of it in the Paris papers, either today or tomorrow.'

'Now it's up to the Australians. Everything is happening at last as it should. Your bridge will be all your father believed in and hoped for.'

'It's not mine yet.'

'It will be,' she assured him. She glanced at Marthe and said in English, 'I won't deny it, I was very upset when I received your telegram from Melbourne. But, really, I think I always knew, once you'd left, that there was going to be a kind of fate in you marrying an Australian girl. When you consider it, you were bound to meet someone while you were out there. Don't you think? It preyed on my mind the whole time you were gone.' She reached for the baby. 'Let me hold her.' She leaned and made a cradle of her arms and he passed the sleeping baby to her. 'Your grandparents thought it a great disaster when I told them I was to marry your father and was to go and live with him in Glasgow. But they eventually grew to like him. He was charming to them whenever we visited Chartres and treated my father with great respect. In the end my father used to take his side against me.' She laughed. 'Aunt Juliette envied me in those days. She used to blush whenever Andrew spoke to her.' She looked at Georges quickly. 'Don't tell her I told you that. She would be utterly mortified. But it's true. She was terrified of being left on the shelf, and of course I was so much younger. She was jealous of me for years. And yet, you know, I believe she's been the most content of us, living here and taking care of this old house. Now here we all are! Who would have thought we would all be here like this together one day? This place always seemed so temporary to me. At first, after your father died, I thought I'd only stay for a month or two, and then I'd work out some arrangement for us. It's twenty-three years. Sometimes it all just seems like yesterday.'

The baby sneezed and gave a start.

'We're unsettling her,' Madame Elder said, reverting to French. 'You'd better put her down.'

He took the baby from her and leaned and kissed its head. 'Just look at her hair. It's astonishing. Where does she get that hair from?' He kneeled and gently put the baby in the drawer.

'Wrap her tightly or she'll wake!' Madame Elder watched him anxiously. 'Marthe will fetch you an Australian bonnet in a minute or two, you poor little thing. And your father will bring your crib upstairs.' She turned to Marthe. 'Monsieur has brought baby's layette with him from Paris. It's downstairs. You can unpack everything as soon as you've finished with your little one.'

'Yes, madame.'

They went back to Emily's bedroom. Georges left his mother with Emily and went downstairs. He put through a call to the apartment in rue Saint-Dominique.

'My mother's exhausted,' he told Sophie. 'We need you here to look after Madame. Everything's all right. You needn't start crying again.' He instructed her to take the Métro to Montparnasse in the morning and to be sure to catch the ten-thirty train to Chartres. 'Use the housekeeping for the fare. I'll be at the station to meet you.'

After he had spoken to Sophie, Georges went into the sitting room and stood by the cold hearth and smoked a cigarette. He reached and took down the photograph of his father with Ferdinand de Lesseps and his son Charles in the excavations of the Panama Canal. He stood smoking and staring at the photograph. There was little resemblance between himself now and his father then. It was his mother he took after. He put the photograph back on the mantelpiece and tossed the stub of his cigarette into the grate. He went out into the passage and telephoned the Episcopal Palace.

He introduced himself and asked if he might speak with Father Bertrand Étinceler. The person on the other end of the phone asked him to wait and went away. A minute passed. Then another. Georges stood for five minutes with the handpiece pressed to his ear before a man's voice apologized softly for keeping him waiting and introduced himself as the bishop's private secretary. The secretary asked Georges if he could come to the palace at four that afternoon. 'His lordship wishes to meet you, Monsieur Elder. He is eager to speak with you.'

Georges was surprised and puzzled by the bishop's pressing invitation. After lunch, he bathed and changed his collar and walked up the hill. He crossed the square and walked along the north side of the cathedral. He passed the deep porch and the entrance to the crypt without glancing at them. He went on across the cobbles and through the iron gates of the palace. The guard saluted him. In the foyer he announced himself to the liveried porter. The bishop's secretary met him and escorted him up a broad flight of stairs to the bishop's private sitting room on the first floor. The room was modestly furnished. The windows overlooked an extensive garden and the rain-swept plains beyond the town.

The elderly ecclesiastic, a tall, stooped man of extreme thinness, his skull visible through his skin, rose from his chair by the fire and greeted Georges. When Georges would have kissed his ring, the bishop withdrew his hand and made an impatient gesture.

'There's no need for that, Monsieur Elder,' he said shortly. He invited Georges to sit opposite him by the fire.

The bishop listened to Georges's account of the birth with an abstracted and preoccupied air, as if he was eager to get on to other, more important business. He agreed that the infant must be baptized at once and, on account of the mother being *in pericolo*, said he would permit a dispensation for the sacrament to be administered in the home. He apologized to Georges for the absence of Father Étinceler at this meeting but said that the young priest had had other urgent duties to attend to. He instructed his secretary to inform Father Étinceler of his decision and to make the necessary arrangements for the baptism in the Elder home. Then he dismissed his secretary.

When they were alone, the bishop leaned forward and looked searchingly at Georges. 'Let you and I speak together as men of the world, Monsieur Elder.' He touched Georges lightly on the knee with his long, bony index finger.

'Why, of course,' Georges said.

The bishop rose from his chair, his movements stiff, precise, and considered, and he went to a small table that stood beside the bookshelves. He picked up a copy of *L'Echo de Paris* and flourished it. 'It's all here! You can't pretend.' He put the newspaper down on the table. 'When I heard you were in Chartres, I determined at once to meet you. I'm eager to hear the details from you, Monsieur Elder. Can you spare me a little of your time?'

'I'm at your disposal, Monseigneur.'

The bishop lifted the stopper of a decanter. 'A glass of cognac?'

They settled themselves with their cognac in the high-backed chairs before the fire and raised their glasses and toasted each other's health. The bishop looked at Georges, his bony fingers clutching his glass, his long, fine head sunk into the hollow between his shoulders, his shrewd, intelligent eyes eager and impatient. 'So a Frenchman from Chartres has designed the biggest bridge in the world? Fifty thousand tons of steel! Tell me, is it really so? Can our journalist be trusted?' He laughed with anticipation and sipped the cognac. '*Show* it to me, Monsieur Elder! Let me see your great bridge in my mind as clearly as I see the Sphinx of Gizeh and the Coliseum at Rome. For this is surely to be as great a monument as those.'

Georges looked into his glass. 'Not quite a Frenchman, Monseigneur,' he said modestly, and he looked up and smiled. 'It sometimes seems an unholy arrogance in the face of God's works to attempt these things. I have dreamed . . .'

The bishop interrupted impatiently. 'Please! Monsieur Elder,' he begged him. 'Not your confession. Let us be men together today, not priest and supplicant. Give me your bridge as boldly as you have designed it! Show it to me. For I shall never see it by any other means. How I should love to be a young man like you and go to Australia and see this marvel take shape. That would be something. Imagine if you and I had watched while Pericles rebuilt the Parthenon!' He sat back against the burgundy plush upholstery of his chair and crossed his legs and sipped his cognac and waited for Georges. There was a mischievous gleam in his eyes. 'When you've built your bridge, no doubt we shall be required to address you as the chief bridge builder, our *Pontifex Maximus*. What do you say to that, Monsieur Elder?' He chuckled. 'Show it to me! Astonish me, monsieur!'

In the old house on the rue des Oiseaux there was the smell of fresh-baked pastries and coffee, and in the dining room branches of nightgreen ilex were arranged in a heavy cut glass vase in the center of the table. A decanter of red wine on the lace cloth encircled by glasses gleamed in the gaslight. The fire was piled with coal and the room was warm and cosy. Outside a wind blew from the northeast. It had been raining steadily all day, a fine steel grey sleet was mixed with the rain.

Georges and Otto were talking in low voices together by the door to the passage. Madame Elder was seated beside the fire, the baby on her lap. The baby wore a lace bonnet tied under its chin with a broad cream silk ribbon. It was dressed in the long white christening gown that Catherine Stanton had sent from Melbourne. Madame Elder wore an old-fashioned, high-collared black taffeta dress. Her hair was combed back into a severe chignon and held in place by a large tortoiseshell comb. Marthe sat across the hearth from her, her own baby held to her shoulder, her reddish hair bound up in a brown scarf. At the window Aunt Juliette stood holding the curtain aside, looking up the road through the sleety rain. 'It will turn to snow by tonight,' she said to no one in particular. And a moment later, 'Here they come!'

Everyone turned and looked at her. Georges and Otto crossed to the window. They stood beside her looking out. The two priests were coming down the hill. They were sheltering under a large umbrella held by the taller of them. The other was Bertrand Étinceler. He cradled a black satchel against his chest to keep it from the rain.

Georges drew away from the window. Juliette let the curtain fall into place. Georges and Otto went and stood beside Madame Elder at the fireside. They faced the door, upright and formal on either side of her in their black suits and stiff collars, an expectant family group with the baby at its centre, as if they posed for a photograph that the infant would examine one day – this sign to their posterity of substance and propriety. A moment later there was a knock on the street door. Aunt Juliette went out into the passage. There was the murmur of voices. She came to the dining room and held the door for the priests. Bertrand came in. He put his satchel on the boards by the door.

Georges stepped forward to greet him, offering his hand. 'What a filthy day, Father. I should have sent a taxi for you.'

Bertrand looked into Georges's eyes. He took his hand and shook it once, then relinquished it. 'Good afternoon, Monsieur Elder.'

Georges reached and would have put his hand on Bertrand's shoulder then but a watchfulness in Bertrand's manner made him hesitate. He withdrew his hand. 'Dr Hopman tells me you saved my wife's life, Father. This family will always be greatly in your debt.'

Otto came forward and shook Bertrand's hand and greeted him.

There was a silence. The coals shifted and creaked. The rain tapped at the window. The tall priest watched from beside the door next to Aunt Juliette. They all observed the three men in the centre of the room – the engineer, the doctor, and the priest.

Bertrand asked, 'Who is to sponsor the infant?'

Otto said eagerly, 'I am, Father. What do you want me to do? You'll have to instruct me. This is my first godchild.'

Bertrand looked at him. 'Will you respond in Latin to my interrogations?'

'Why, yes, I shall.'

When Bertrand offered no more, Georges said, 'Perhaps we should go upstairs?' He turned to his mother.

Bertrand said, 'I'll call you when we're ready.' His gaze swept the room, then he turned, the skirts of his soutane flowing around him, and picked up the black satchel. He left the room, the tall priest following.

Juliette said, 'I'll go and make up the fire.' She went out behind them and closed the door.

Georges stood looking at the door. He turned to his mother and Otto. 'Well, well,' he said. 'He doesn't exactly put one at one's ease, does he? I'm afraid our hero's not half the man his bishop is.'

'He's modest,' Otto said in mitigation of their discomfort, believing himself to be bestowing praise, his way of dealing, perhaps, with the oddly unsettling wash of Bertrand Étinceler's presence in the room among them.

Madame Elder said, 'You must give Father Étinceler a chance, my dear. He is young and serious. An independent thinker. And anyway,' she added lightly, 'he keeps your aunt and me in fruit.'

'I had the impression he resented me,' Georges said.

'You're being sensitive, dear. It doesn't suit you. Just be your normal, generous self. Help me up. Take her, will you, Otto?'

Otto said, 'Nerves, Georges.' He leaned and took the baby from Madame Elder.

Georges offered his mother his arm. She took her cane from beside the fire and stood up. 'I should like a glass of wine before we go up, Georges.'

Georges went to the table and filled a glass with wine from the decanter. He turned and handed it to her. 'Otto? For you?'

Otto held out his free hand, palm toward Georges. 'Let me do this first, Georges. I'll need to be steady.'

Madame Elder lifted the glass to her lips and drained it. She closed her eyes for a moment, then handed the empty glass to Georges. 'Thank you, dear.' She took a deep breath and turned to Otto, 'So you see, we have become a real family at last, dear friend.' She slipped her arm in his and together they looked at the baby. 'I am so pleased you are here with us today. This moment would not have been complete without you.'

Otto's spectacles glinted.

Georges stood with his back to the fire beside Marthe, watching his mother with Otto.

Sophie came and stood in the doorway. Over her black dress she wore a white apron with a pale blue cross-stitched border. Her dark hair was tied back in a glossy ponytail with a blue ribbon. 'The Father asked me to tell you he's ready to begin,' she announced. She stepped to one side and waited while they filed past her out the door.

Georges paused at the door. 'You're looking very pretty, Sophie.'

'Thank you, monsieur.'

'You're coming up, of course?'

'Oh yes, monsieur.'

Marthe came last. She smiled at Sophie and urged her to go ahead.

Upstairs they crowded into Emily's bedroom.

The priests in their white surplices waited for them by the dressing table. Bertrand wore a green stole round his shoulders. His hands were clasped before him. He looked at each of them as they came into the room and watched while they took up their places. A silver-topped bottle and a small silver container stood on the dressing table between two lighted candles. Bertrand's tall companion held the order of the ritual, the text raised toward Bertrand.

Emily was lying on her back, her hands on the covers. She gripped the sheet and breathed noisily, moving her head about restlessly. She was wearing one of her own nightdresses. It was white with a frilly collar and cuffs. Otto cradled the baby in his arms. He went over to the bed and leaned over Emily and looked at her. Sophie stood at his side. Marthe stood beside the fire next to Juliette, facing the priests. Madame Elder, on Georges's arm, took up her place at the foot of the bed.

Bertrand beckoned to Otto to come and stand by him. 'Hold the infant in your right arm, Dr Hopman.'

Emily stirred at the sound of Bertrand's voice. They turned and watched her. It seemed for a moment that she would rouse, then she lapsed once again into an uneasy state of semiconsciousness.

Bertrand turned to them. His clerk stood on his left, holding the order of the ritual. Otto waited on his right, the infant held in his right arm, the white train of the christening gown trailing over the sleeve of his coat and hanging almost to the floor. Bertrand's gaze was focused on a point in space above their heads. 'We are gathered here in this sickroom to administer the holy sacrament of baptism to this infant.' He turned and looked at the child. 'This is the sacrament of faith and illumination through which, born in wrath, this infant is to be regenerated and born again a child of mercy free of sin.' He paused.

In the silence the murmur of the women's voices rose from the shelter of the laundry hutches beside the river.

'*Per aquam in verbo.* Not to be drowned, but to be born again from the water of life. Baptism's defect to be supplied only by martyrdom. The terrible *baptismus sanquinis.*'

Madame Elder drew in her breath sharply and tightened her arm on Georges's.

Bertrand leaned and breathed three times into the infant's face, mouth open, according to Baruffaldi's direction – expelling the power of the old serpent and catching the breath of life. 'Marie Heloise Emily *quid petis ab Ecclesia Dei?*' he interrogated the sleeping infant.

Otto responded firmly, '*Fidem.*' As if faith were a tangible substance of the world, familiar to each of them. He looked up at Madame Elder, his gaze bright with his enthusiasm for what he did.

The baby opened its eyes.

Bertrand leaned over it, '*Fides quid tibi praestat?*' he asked, his inquiry soft, intimate, coaxing, as if in this theater of reality he believed the infant would know his question.

'*Vitam aeternam,*' Otto replied. And there it was. The promise to reveal everything. The gift of apocalypse – to unfold and disclose that which has remained hidden. Eternal life.

Madame Elder felt for the crucifix at her throat . . .

'Marie, *Ego te baptizo in Nomine Patris* . . .' As the water touched her, the baby began to scream and struggle in Otto's arms, her strong cry drowning out the voice of the priest.

Emily opened her eyes and stared at them.

In the kitchen Marthe sat on a low bench with her back to the warm stove, her skirt pulled up and her legs thrust out in front of her, an infant suckling at each breast. Otto said from the door, 'You're a double Madonna, Marthe.' He laughed and turned to Georges. He put his hand on Georges's arm. 'There's no need to be nervous. Emily may be a little upset at first when she sees Marie, that's all. She has only the haziest

recollection of the birth. Try and see things from her point of view.'
He had his overcoat and hat on and his bag in his hand.

Georges watched Marthe.

Aunt Juliette stood at the table peeling apples. She sliced the peeled apples, arranging the slices in a china bowl. Half a dozen large green apples lay on the tabletop in front of her. Beside the apples a plucked chicken lay in a pool of watery blood on a plate.

Otto said, 'She'll need a few days to get used to the idea. She's just a bit confused about things at the moment. Don't rush her. Give her time. She'll soon come around.'

Marthe said, 'I'm done here if you want her, monsieur?' She slipped her breasts into her blouse and began buttoning up.

'I'll call in again in the morning,' Otto said. He grinned at Georges. 'Go on, then, man! I'll have a word to your mother on the way out. See you tomorrow, Juliette.' He turned and went out.

Marie began to cry, a plaintive, grizzling sound, a trickle of milk dribbling from her lips.

Aunt Juliette looked at Georges. 'Are you taking her or not?'

'All right, Juliette. Don't get impatient.' He stepped across to Marthe and leaned and took the fretting baby from her.

'Not like that, monsieur! Hold her against your shoulder or she'll ruin your coat. She's full of milk.' Marthe handed up a cloth to him. 'Here, put this on yourself.'

Georges reached and took the cloth from her. He thanked her and twisted and put the cloth against his shoulder. He stood looking sideways at the crying baby.

'Walk her up and down. She'll settle in a minute. You can talk to her if you like, monsieur. They like to hear a bit of gossip.' Marthe giggled and pressed her nose against her own baby, murmuring to it.

Georges paced across the kitchen with the crying baby held to his shoulder, one hand to its back and the other under its warm bottom. He turned and came back and went and stood at the window. 'Look!' He pointed. 'There's the river. See, isn't it beautiful?' The baby struggled and cried.

Marthe held her own contented infant casually in the crook of one arm while she buttoned her blouse with her other hand.

Georges looked down at her. 'You understand babies, Marthe,' he said, admiringly.

'Babies are babies, monsieur. There's nothing to understand.'

Aunt Juliette set the bowl of apples to one side and took the chicken from the plate. She sliced firmly through the leg joints and laid the legs aside. Then she sliced off the wings and put them with the legs. She slid the knife into the carcass and slit the breast open and pressed her palms to it, cracking the backbone against the tabletop with a sharp report of sundering bone and sinews.

'I'll take her up, then,' Georges said, resolved.

Juliette and Marthe did not look away from their tasks.

The air in the passage was cold after the warmth of the kitchen. The baby sucked its breath and screamed in his ear. 'Hush, there! Hush!' He jiggled her up and down. A stream of warm curdled milk erupted from the baby's mouth onto his neck and the collar of his jacket. 'Oh Christ!' he said softly. He went along the passage and climbed the stairs. He stood on the landing outside Emily's bedroom trying to quieten the baby. It screamed with fury, flecks of milk breaching from its lips. He reached and opened the door and went in.

Emily was sitting up, pillows piled behind her. Sophie stood beside her. They both looked at him and at Marie.

'Here we are, my dearest,' Georges said.

Emily covered her face with her hands.

He went over to the side of the bed. 'Look at her! Your baby is beautiful.'

Sophie said, 'Give her to me, monsieur.'

He hesitated.

She reached and took the baby from him. She held Marie in the crook of one arm. 'Hold still,' she gently admonished the baby. She reached and took the cloth from Georges's shoulder and wiped the milk from his neck and the collar of his jacket. The baby lay sobbing and trembling in the crook of her arm. 'There, monsieur,' Sophie said, calm and assured. 'That's better.'

He sat on the side of the bed and took Emily's hands in his. He kissed her palms. 'You're back with us, my dearest!' The skin of her cheeks was slack and had lost its bloom. She gazed at Marie, her eyes wary, exhausted and afraid.

'I'm so sorry,' she said. Her voice trembled.

He turned to Sophie. 'Let Madame see her.'

Emily said hopelessly, 'I've got nothing for her.'

'That's not true,' he said gently. 'Bring Marie here, Sophie.'

Sophie stood offering the baby.

He reached and took Marie from her. He pulled back the peak of the bonnet and leaned and showed her to Emily. 'Just look at her. Your mother's bonnet,' he said. 'All the way from Melbourne. Isn't she beautiful.'

Emily looked at the baby. 'The poor little thing,' she said, as if she spoke of some chanced-upon creature. She began to cry, helpless against the surge of emotion that filled her chest and throat.

Georges turned to Sophie, who stood waiting beside the bed.

Sophie took the baby from him. He motioned to her and she went over and opened the door. She glanced back at them, then went out and closed the door.

Georges put his arms around Emily and drew her against him. He sat rocking her back and forth. 'It's all right, my dearest. Everything is all right now.'

She was unresisting, sobbing and trembling against him. He said nothing but held her.

When she at last grew calm, she reached into the sleeve of her nightdress. She pulled a handkerchief and blew her nose. 'You don't know anything,' she said. She rested back against the pillows, the handkerchief balled in her fist, her eyes reddened, her lips tight, a fearful stubbornness in her.

He sat looking at her, perplexed, anxious, wanting to release her. She reached for his hand and held it.

'We're all proud of you,' he said, 'Your courage has been an inspiration to Mother.'

She sat holding his hand, staring at the far wall. 'How did I get here?'

'Father Étinceler brought you.'

'It's true, then. I thought I had dreamed it.'

'It must have been a nightmare for you. It's over now. You're safe. We have our little daughter.'

She looked at him, as if she might pity him. She dabbed at her nose with the sodden handkerchief.

'You'll soon get strong again now,' he said. 'I should never have left you alone in Paris with Sophie.'

There was suddenly the smell of the chicken boiling downstairs in the kitchen.

He stroked her fingers, turning her hand in his, examining her dry skin.

She watched him. 'I'm not beautiful anymore.'

He looked up at her and smiled. 'Of course you are, my dearest. You will always be beautiful.'

She said nothing. The house was quiet.

'What is it?'

She looked away out the window at the grey sky, the bare poplars bending in the wind beyond the gabled roofs across the river. 'I'm just tired, Georges. Terribly tired. That's all.'

'I'll let you sleep.' He leaned and kissed her.

She held his hand and looked into his eyes. 'I shall never be me again.'

'Yes, you will,' he reassured her. 'Go to sleep, now. Everything has been for the best.' He stood and helped rearrange her pillows. He pulled the blankets up to her chin and tucked them in around her. He kissed her forehead. 'Go to sleep, now.'

She closed her eyes.

He went across and opened the door. He looked back at her, then went out onto the landing. He stood on the landing listening. Marthe and Sophie were talking together up in the nursery room, the boards creaking as they moved back and forth tending the babies. He turned and went downstairs.

FOUR

———

Days went by. With rest and Juliette's nourishing broths Emily grew stronger. Each morning after her bath she sat in the armchair by the fire and Georges brought Marie for her to hold for a little while. Now she lay awake, thinking of the day ahead, watching the ribs of light appear through the slats of the shutters, and wondering what she would say to him. For she had decided she would meet him today. It had been arranged that he would call after lunch. In the silvery dawnlight she studied the room, evoking her anxieties. The heavy wardrobe leaning in the corner – the shadowed room in its mirrored doors canting away, an illusion, like the deck of a fantastic ship imagined long ago in childhood. The dressing table beside the chest of drawers. The pair of pewter candlesticks. The candles he had burned for the baptism. The black crucifix on the wall above. The washstand by the window. The swelling shapes of the porcelain jug and basin like cold, pale flesh in the grainy light. The vacant armchair beside the dead fireplace. The sewing table next to the armchair, a glass vase on a doily with three dusty stems of bulrush gathered at the riverbank years ago, the glass of the vase glinting with a thin reflection of the light between the shutter slats. The striped wallpaper without colour at this hour, bulging as if it sagged under the weight of damp from the river. She knew she would remember this room forever and would never know what had been dream and what reality of her days spent in it.

One of the babies was crying in the nursery above. She listened.

The boards creaked and a moment later the child fell silent. She could not tell the cry of her own child. She knew now there was no instinct for such knowledge. She slept again . . . A metallic clatter woke her. She opened her eyes and lifted her head from the pillow. Aunt Juliette was kneeling on the hearthrug setting the fire, murmuring to herself. Emily turned on her side and pulled the blankets over her head . . . She woke to Sophie's knock. The shutters stood open and a broad band of wintry sunlight fell across the quilt. The coal fire creaked and murmured. The night chill was gone. The room was warm.

She screwed up her eyes against the brightness of the day and raised her head. 'What time is it, Sophie?'

'It is after lunch, madame. Monsieur came in with Marie twice to see you. We thought it best to let you sleep.' Sophie stood just inside the door, the baby in her arms. She was dressed in her street clothes, a long grey overcoat and green woollen scarf, a black beret set at an angle on her head, her dark hair swept to one side and pinned behind her ear.

Emily sat up.

'We're off for a walk in the town with Marthe and her little Victor, madame.' Sophie looked down at the infant in her arms. 'I thought you might like to say hello before we went out?'

Emily rubbed her face with her hands. She looked at the tray with her untouched breakfast on the cupboard beside the bed. She reached for the glass of cloudy apple juice that Juliette had prepared for her and drank it. She replaced the empty glass on the tray and turned and looked at Sophie. 'How is it you come to know so much about babies, Sophie?'

Sophie came and stood beside the bed. 'There was never a shortage of babies at the convent, madame. I used to beg to take care of them. All the girls did.' Sophie bit her lip and looked down at the infant.

'So you've adopted her? What does Marthe say to that?'

'I love her, madame.' Sophie looked up, self-conscious with her feelings for the baby. Her eyes were shining.

'So you are in love?'

Sophie said quickly, 'Only with Marie, madame.'

'Oh yes, of course . . . Only with Marie. But in love all the same, Sophie. Love has its look.' She reached behind her for her shawl and took it from the bedend. She put the shawl round her shoulders. 'Give her to me.' She took Marie from Sophie and held her on her lap. 'You won't be jealous if I hold her for a minute, will you?'

'Please, madame, don't tease me.'

Emily looked down at the child lying against her. The child gazed back at her. 'Hello, Marie. Do you recognize your mother yet from the outside?'

The baby was watchful and still. Sophie leaned and looked at her. 'Of course she recognizes you, madame. There's no one like our mothers.'

'You remember your mother, then?'

Sophie colored. 'No, madame.'

Together they gazed at the baby in silence.

'Who does she take after?' Emily asked. 'Who do the Elders say she looks like? What does Monsieur say? What does Madame Elder say?'

'Everyone says she's like you, madame.'

'But she's not. And you? What do you say? . . . Who do you say she looks like?'

Sophie smiled, as if she knew a secret. She reached and touched the baby's cheek with her finger. Marie turned her head and quested with her lips at the touch of Sophie's finger. 'Marie is like herself, madame. That is who she is.'

They looked at the baby again.

'Do you believe I came to Chartres for Madame Elder's help?'

Sophie said nothing.

'I'm asking you. Everyone says that is why I came. What do you think?''

Sophie looked at her, the sudden spiritedness in her gaze that Emily had seen once before, as if she were provoked and would retreat no further from the truth. 'No, madame. I don't think that. I don't know why you came to Chartres.'

'Have you talked about it with Marthe?'

Sophie held her gaze and said nothing.

'You have, haven't you?'

Sophie looked down at the baby.

Emily put her hand on Sophie's arm. 'It's all right,' she said gently. 'Marthe's your new friend. What does she say about me? Tell me. I want to know. People love to gossip. She must say something. What does Chartres say? Does she tell you?' Emily laughed.

'There's nothing to tell. Truthfully, madame.' She looked up, assessing, her manner cooler, taking care of her own thoughts. 'She'll be waiting for me now.'

Emily breathed. 'Well, anyway, what does it matter what people say. We'll soon be leaving Chartres.' She lifted Marie. Sophie leaned and took her. 'Is Monsieur at home?'

'He went out.'

'Where did he go?'

'He reads his newspaper, madame, in a café in the place des Epars.'

'You speak as if you know Chartres already.'

'Monsieur goes to the café after lunch at the same time every day, madame. Sometimes he joins Marthe and me on our walk with the infants. He has shown us the sculptures at the cathedral.'

Emily turned to the tray. She took a cold croissant and tore it in half. She ate it hungrily. 'On your way out ask Juliette to heat some water for me, will you. I'm getting up.'

—◦—

While she was having her bath in front of the fire Emily heard the street door slam, then the sound of his voice in the passage. A couple of minutes later Juliette came in. 'You'd better get a move on, young lady. Father Étinceler's here.' She stood looking at Emily, who was hugging herself in the tin bath, steam rising around her. 'He's waiting in the front room. I told him you'd be down in a minute.'

'Thanks, Juliette.' Emily didn't move.

Juliette said, 'Suit yourself, then.' She went out and closed the door.

After her bath, she dressed with care. She put on a pair of the black ribbed stockings her mother had packed to see her through the European winter. She chose a grey wool dress. It had a wide, loose belt with a broad, floppy collar and white cuffs. When she had the dress on, she stood in front of the canting wardrobe mirror looking at her reflection. She turned sideways, holding the dress against the low rounding of her belly. She put on a black velvet jacket over the dress. The jacket was big and loose and comfortable with deep side pockets. She pulled the white collar of the dress out and folded it over the collar of the jacket. She didn't put on any lipstick.

When she had finished dressing, she opened the top drawer in the dressing table and took out her green morocco writing case. She removed the medallion from its blue velvet bed in Antoine's silver box and pinned it to the V of her collar. She examined her reflection. 'Perpetua's medallion,' she said, touching the brooch with her fingers. 'Now she is ready to face the world again.'

She went downstairs and along the passage. She paused at the door to the sitting room, gathering her resolve. She opened the door and went in. He was standing by the window reading. When she came in, he closed the book and placed it on the open desktop of the English cabinet.

They stared at each other in the silence. The fire was banked in the grate and the curtains and shutters were open. The room was filled with light and warmth. A smell of coalsmoke and of Madame Elder's liniment. A white china bowl at the centre of the circular table was piled with rosy apples. Withered leaves were attached to the stalks of some of the apples.

'The things I said in my letter are no longer true,' Emily said.

He did not react.

'Am I to thank you for saving my life?' She waited. 'Aren't you going to say anything?' She went across and stood in front of the fire. The photographs of Georges in his school uniform and his father with de Lesseps on the mantelpiece in front of her. She turned and faced Bertrand. 'Is it my thanks you expect? How can you bear to be a priest? You stand there with your certainties of God saying nothing! As if that is enough.'

'I have no certainty of God,' he said modestly.

'Well, whatever it is you do have. It must seem such a sham!' With sudden anger she said, 'This has changed nothing for you! You are just the same. It has nearly cost me my life.'

'You're wrong. I'm not unchanged by it. I don't see anything the way I saw it before that day.'

'You're still a priest.'

'It changed my life. Our meeting changed my life.'

'Meeting! Is that what you call it? Have you rescued any more lost girls?'

He said nothing to this.

'I've asked myself how I can hurt you,' she said. 'Do you understand that? When I came to Chartres, I was prepared to expose you. To risk everything. I wanted you to see me the way I was. Now that I see you, I realize I no longer care.'

'Do you want me to leave?'

'You can leave if you like. It's up to you.'

He didn't move.

'You think it's been nothing,' she said. 'A mere matter of attitude. A bit of remorse and guilt for a few days. A confession of your astonishing sin. What category does such a sin fall into? How does a priest do penance for it? Are you forgiven? Does the forgiveness extend to me?' She turned to the fire and took the photograph of Georges down and held it, remembering suddenly that terrible afternoon in April after the cathedral, alone in this room while Madame Elder told her the story of her family – the feeling of him and his smell still with her. She put the photograph back in its place on the mantelpiece.

He said, 'I'm glad to see you recovered.'

She turned and looked at him. 'How truly strange it is to be with you in this room.' She waited but he offered nothing. 'Yes. I am recovered. I am more recovered than you or anyone else can imagine.'

'The baby is strong too,' he said. 'She grows quickly.'

'That's because she has three mothers and two fathers.' She examined him. She asked bluntly, 'Is she your child?'

He put out a hand and touched the book, adjusting his weight, his silhouette moving against the bright day, his black eyes glinting with twin miniatures of the fire.

'Do you care for her? What do you feel for her? Is it lawful for a priest to baptize his own daughter? What would your bishop do if he knew about us?' Emily stood with her feet apart, her hands thrust into the sidepockets of her jacket. The clock on the mantelpiece behind her went tock-tock-tock. A horse walked by along the street, the carter raising his whip and letting it fall across the horse's withers, his voice urging it.

Bertrand cleared his throat. 'You said in your letter the truth makes outcasts of us. We've both changed but that's still true. The things you wrote to me were true when you wrote them.' He was silent. A van door slammed out in the street and there was the voice of the delivery man calling a greeting to a housewife. 'Your letter was strong and beautiful. I have kept it. There has been nothing else like it in my life.'

She made an impatient noise and turned aside. She sat in the chair opposite Madame Elder's chair and held her hands out to the warmth of the fire.

'I'm sorry you're so angry,' he said.

She looked up at him. 'Yes,' she said, raising her voice. 'I am angry. I have reason to be angry, don't you think?'

The door opened and Aunt Juliette came in with a tray and tea things. She stood looking at Emily, as if she waited for her to say more.

Bertrand came forward and took the tray from Juliette. He set it on the low table between the armchairs in front of the fire.

Juliette said, 'I thought you two would like a cup of tea.'

When Juliette had gone, Emily lay back against the hard horsehair stuffing of the chair and laughed. 'Why don't you sit down.' She looked at him. 'Please.' Her anger was suddenly spent. 'You and I must have a truce, don't you think? Or this subterfuge will prove too difficult for us.'

Bertrand stepped forward. With an almost dainty gesture he lifted his skirts and sat in Madame Elder's chair.

'Sophie's right,' Emily said. 'Marie is herself. She has her life. She mustn't inherit our remorse. Our regrets. Our confusions. That's what you said when you baptized her. I heard you. Or did I dream it? You said she was to be reborn free of sin. I liked that. I thought of it as being free of the awful mistakes we make. I thought it meant me. If that is what it is to be baptized, then we should all do it once a year. On our birthday.' She sat up and reached for the teapot.

He watched her pour the tea.

She handed him a cup. 'Help yourself to sugar and milk. Not everything about your religion is pointless.' She sat sipping the hot black tea, looking at him. 'You don't defend yourself,' she said.

He gazed into the fire.

'You came to Paris to see me. I was in Tunisia.'

He sipped his tea. 'I told the bishop my mother was ill and I had to go home to see her. It was obvious I was lying. He didn't challenge me.'

'That's because you're useful to him.'

'No. It's not that. He knows we're men too.' He looked at her. 'Why didn't you tell me you were having a baby?'

There were sounds at the front door of Sophie and Georges returning with Marthe and the babies. They were laughing and talking. Emily and Bertrand fell silent, listening to them go by along the passage. Emily's fingers at her throat touched the medallion, the firelight bright in her eyes. A moment later the sitting-room door opened and Georges came in. He carried a rolled newspaper. He put the paper on the table in the middle of the room and came over to the fire and greeted Bertrand. 'Don't get up, Father.'

'I was just leaving,' Bertrand said. He set his cup on the low table and stood up.

They shook hands. 'It's a pity you have to go,' Georges said. 'You must come and have lunch with us before Christmas. You and I never seem to get a chance to talk.' Georges turned to Emily and leaned and kissed her cheek.

After Bertrand had gone, Georges sat in his chair. 'He hardly touched his tea. I don't know what it is about that priest, I seem to make him uneasy.' He looked at her and smiled. 'Sophie and Marie are getting on wonderfully. I thought I might take Sophie up to Paris with me next week to help with the Christmas shopping. It's going to be quite a chore otherwise. What do you think? Hasn't our convent girl blossomed since Marie arrived.' He leaned and put his hand on her knee. 'What do you want for Christmas, my dearest?'

'His life is a contradiction,' Emily said.

'Whose life?'

She stood up and took a waxed spill from the blue glass vase on the mantelpiece. She leaned and held the point of the spill to the coals until it ignited. She stood holding the tiny flame in front of her, looking at it. 'How strange that he has become your mother's friend.'

Georges watched her.

She blew out the flame and replaced the smoking spill in the vase. 'We touch things and they are moved,' she said. 'But we can never tell how it will end. Either for good or ill. If we are not destroyed by what we do, we watch our actions slide away from us and become something else, no longer us. No longer a part of us.' She looked down at Georges. 'Sometimes we feel we've lived the life of another person who is not us. And there is a kind of love and a sadness in us for that person. But still they are not us. Still they are a stranger.'

Georges reached up and took her hand. 'Remember what Otto said, dearest. You mustn't overtire yourself. Pneumonia never leaves us.'

She read her father's letter over and set it aside on the English cabinet next to her writing things and sat looking out of the window. The house was quiet. Georges and Sophie had gone up to Paris on the early train and Madame Elder was out, making her slow and painful daily excursion to the cathedral to give thanks to the Mother of God.

Emily picked up her father's letter again.

I can understand your attraction, indeed your admiration, for this older woman, Dr Olive Kallen. Clearly, as you say, she has established her authority in her field and possesses an independent intellectual life that is well grounded in the robust and civilized complexities of New York and the American Museum of Natural History. Hers is an enviable position, but such a position has not been won without considerable personal cost. Of this I am certain and, perhaps, with the advantage of years, see it more clearly than you do. It thrills me to hear you speak once again in this way, with enthusiasm for the life of the mind, my dearest girl, but I do caution you to proceed with infinite care and circumspection. You do not possess the elaborate support women such as Olive Kallen rely upon. I know such women. There are several here at the university in Melbourne. You are a wife and a mother now. I beg you to take one careful step at a time and to do nothing that is not revocable. For I know how rash you can be once your enthusiasm is aroused.

It was her father. It was how he had lived his own life.

She put the letter down and got up. She went out into the passage and stood listening. Marthe and Juliette were talking in the kitchen. She reached and took the telephone from the wall. She asked the exchange to connect her to Antoine's number and stood waiting, looking along the dark passage toward the stairs and the kitchen door. The passage was cold and smelled of cooking. The line crackled and hissed in her ear. The girl said, 'I am connecting you now, madame.' There was a silence, then a voice she did not recognize said, 'Hello?'

'Is that you, Antoine?'

'Yes. Who's that?'

'It's me. Emily.'

'Where are you?'

'I'm here. We're still in Chartres. It doesn't sound like you?'

'Did you get my note?'

'Ages ago. You said you were coming to see me.'

There was a pause. 'I've been busy.'

'Don't lie, Antoine. Just come and see me. I need to talk to you. I need to see you. I've tried writing to you, but I can't. I have discovered that letters just won't do for you.'

'I'll come soon. I promise.'

'Come tomorrow.'

'There are things I have to do tomorrow.'

'Is Merrill still in Paris?'

'No. He went home. But everything's fine between us. He's coming back in the spring.' There was a pause. 'He may decide to live in Paris.'

'Are you pleased?'

He laughed. 'Of course.'

'Then I'm pleased too.' There was a silence. 'Olive Kallen wrote and asked me to be her assistant in Carthage.'

'Yes. She wrote to me too.'

'I must hear you sounding more impressed with this news, Antoine! You must know how important it is to me. I haven't replied yet. I've torn up half a dozen attempts to write to her. I need to see you. I need to talk, Antoine. This telephone is awful. We shall misunderstand each other. I need to see you sitting across from me in a little café, smoking one of your wonderful smelly cigarettes and reminding me of Sidi bou-Saïd. You've no idea how hard it is to believe in things down here. I don't think I ever realized before the way some places rob us of our reality. If I were to send Olive a letter from Chartres, she'd change her mind about me. I should seem like another person to her. I know I should. She would think she had made a mistake and would wonder why she had asked me.'

'You can't be thinking of accepting her offer, though? Can you?'

'Why not? Why shouldn't I? Of course I'm thinking of accepting it. I think of it all the time. I shall never have another offer like it. You must know that? The trouble is, I can give her no certainty. I don't know what's going to happen when Georges hears from Bradfield. What if we have to go back to Australia? What should I do then?'

The kitchen door opened and Juliette looked out into the passage. Marthe stood behind her, leaning around her to see, a baby held against each shoulder. 'I wondered who you were talking to,' Juliette said. She looked at Emily, then went back into the kitchen.

Antoine asked, 'Are you still there?'

'I can't talk here. I can't *think* here, Antoine. There is an atmosphere that closes one's mind and stops one's thoughts. Promise you'll come and see me!'

'All right.'

'When?'

'In a day or two.'

'You don't *want* to come,' she said. 'I can hear it in your voice.'

'Georges has invited me to lunch. A celebration, I imagine. Isn't it? I said I'd come down for that. You and I can go for a walk afterward. Madame Elder's bound to want to go to Mass. She dislikes me. She will be glad if I don't join them. You can say you're tired or something and we can go off on our own.'

'You must promise faithfully to be fearlessly my friend,' she said. 'Just as you were my first day in Paris, when you brought me snapdragons and looked at me as if you wondered if I were real. How different my life would be now without that day and our friendship.'

'You make me sound like Rasputin.'

'No. But you are one of those mythical demons who are familiars of the gods and of mortals and who mediate for us between the world of our dreams and the daily world of our realities. That is how I see you.' She smiled to hear his laughter. 'Now you sound like you again.'

'You make it impossible for me to be anyone but me for long, Emily.'

'I'm glad. I need to have some power over you.' They were silent. 'This past month has been a journey in a kind of broken wilderness. I've never experienced such fearful loneliness. Talking to you now, I feel I've come out into the open again.'

'You arrived, do you remember, in the old Republican month of Germinal? April.'

'And you teased me. But I'm no longer the woman I was that

day. You mustn't expect her. I am a more determined woman than she was.'

'What do you mean?'

'You'll see. There is a moment in our lives when we must decide which world we belong to. The world of our dreams or the other one. Unlike you, we can't all drift back and forth between them without risking losing our place in both.'

'Is that the risk I take, then?' He sounded pleased and intrigued by her suggestion.

'Well, you seem to have a key the rest of us don't possess.'

'Oh, I do like to hear that,' he said.

'It's true! But if we don't have the key, then it's no good pretending we have it.' She said suddenly, 'How I *love* talking to you, Antoine! At once I feel as if everything is possible again.'

'And so it is!'

It was two days before Christmas. The dining room was noisy with their chatter and sudden cries of laughter, the air warm with the coal fire and rich with the smells of the heavy lunch of roast goose they had just eaten – the debris of leftovers and half-empty wineglasses before them on the stained linen. Around them on the floor the coloured wrappings of the presents they had exchanged. They were all there, squeezed against each other around the narrow dining table – Georges and Madame Elder, Bertrand Étinceler, Antoine, Emily, Aunt Juliette and Otto Hopman, and Marthe and Sophie with the infants in their laps. The gaslight glinted on the silver cutlery and reflected in the wineglasses. The heavy velvet curtains were closed against the wintry day outside.

Otto nudged Bertrand's arm, 'Three generations of the Elders at this table. We'll not see it again, Father.' He turned to Georges. 'What do you say? Not since your grandfather's day.'

Madame Elder reached and touched Marie's cheek. 'She's got Uncle

Jules's black hair.' She looked up at Georges at the other end of the table. She had to raise her voice, 'Do you remember your Great-Uncle Jules?'

'You know I never met him, Mother.' He leaned aside to listen to Otto.

Madame Elder said to Emily and Sophie, 'He doesn't remember. He was too young. Of course he met his Uncle Jules. She's the image of him.' She touched Sophie's sleeve. 'You and Marthe had better give them their feed and get them ready. We'll be late for Mass otherwise.'

When Marthe and Sophie had left the room, Otto said with enthusiasm, 'Babies! What a lovely sight.'

Bertrand stood. He said he had duties to perform and must leave them. They fell silent and looked at him. His gaze swept over them, as if he would address them or divulge some portent. But he said nothing. Emily got up and went with him to the front door.

He paused on the step. 'When we met that day in the crypt, you were searching for something . . .' His dark eyes examined her. 'You've found what you were looking for, haven't you?'

'Yes.'

He smiled, gratified. 'I knew.' He stepped into the street and put his biretta on. 'You're not coming to Mass, are you? You will not make an exception.'

'No.' She said. 'Will you always be a priest?'

'Write to me.' His eyes were smiling. 'Tell me what you have found. It will be easier that way. I shall always want to know where you are and what you are doing.'

'Will you write back?'

He laughed. 'I promise.' He lifted his hand in farewell and walked away.

The dining room was silent when she returned. They looked at her expectantly, as if she might have a message for them.

Aunt Juliette said, 'I can still hear him hammering on the front door that night.' Her eyes were alight with the reflection of the gaslight and the startling memory. 'I was in the middle of cooking us an omelette, as usual. Heloise was sitting there in her own world staring out the window. Weren't you, Heloise? Then bang-bang-bang on the door and him yelling down the letter box.' She looked at them. 'Now here we are!'

Otto said, 'Well done, Juliette. A great lunch. Memorable.'

Emily reached and took Juliette's hand. Juliette's hand was cold and dry, the veins standing up under the thin tracing of skin.

Emily said, 'I'll tidy up in here while you're all at Mass.'

Juliette turned to her. 'No, you won't. I'll have this done before you get back.'

Georges looked at Emily, 'You're not coming, then?'

'Antoine has to catch his train,' she said, as if this gave her a sufficient reason.

Georges did not persist.

When the others had gone to the cathedral, Antoine suggested they go for a walk by the riverbank. They had an hour before his train was due. They put on their overcoats and scarves and went out into the frosty air. A gilded mist rose from the water, drifting between the tall houses and the black lattice of bare willow branches. Crystals of frost glistened among the yellowed blades of grass and rotting leaves at their feet. They stopped where the willows grew out over the water, a private sheltered place of gnarled and mossy tree roots. Farther along the riverbank, beyond a tall, ivy-covered stone wall, Emily pointed out to him the back of Aunt Juliette's house, the sagging timbers of the laundry hutch jutting into the river below the window of her bedroom. Downstream a man leaned on the parapet of the bridge, watching them.

Antoine took off his gloves and thrust them into his pocket. He stepped out onto a horizontal willow trunk. He grasped a handful of drooping withies to steady himself and kneeled and reached into the water, letting it flow over his hand. He stood and turned, wobbling precariously on the mossy willow trunk, the low sun dazzling in his eyes. She saw him lose his certainty, saw him teetering in that moment on the brink of something akin to infirmity, unable to play his boyish game with conviction. She reached for him and he took her hand and stepped onto the bank beside her, his glance questioning her, afraid to see her understanding.

'I fell into the Medjerda when I was three. Mounir had taken me to see the flood. I've always been frightened of water.'

Their breath steamed in the cold air. 'Let's find a café,' she suggested. She took his arm and held him to her side and they walked up the hill to the place des Epars and went into a small café. It was warm inside and there was a smell of coffee and a haze of tobacco smoke. Men at the tables stopped talking and turned to look at them.

When they were settled at a table and had been served with coffee, Antoine lit a cigarette. He was himself again. 'What have you told Olive?'

'I haven't written. I can't. I told you why. It's Chartres.'

'I liked your priest,' he said. 'He is mysterious and aloof. I can see him wrestling with the Devil. I almost felt I'd met him before.' He looked at her. 'Now I've seen him I understand.'

'Please, Antoine, I don't want to talk about him.'

'Perhaps not. But if it hadn't been for your chance encounter with him that day, I doubt very much if you'd have come to Sidi bou-Saïd with me when you did.'

She was silent, sipping her coffee. 'Give me a cigarette,' she said. 'I haven't smoked since I had Marie.'

He handed her a cigarette and lit it for her. 'There's always a moment when we register the foolishness of our past ideas about someone. Then they seem foolish too and we want to be done with them. But it's not them, it's us. There will always be something between you and Bertrand Étinceler. He has set a mark on a period of your life. You will acknowledge it one day, when you are older.'

She let the cigarette smoke trail from between her lips. 'You'll be in Paris by tonight. I envy you.'

'You must come back to Paris soon. You're right. One can't think in that damp old house by the river. It has known too many years of silence.'

She walked with him to the railway station and waited until his train arrived. They kissed each other on the cheeks. 'Your visit has made it easier for me here,' she said.

'We'll meet in Paris soon. When will Georges know about his bridge?'

'Next month sometime. Soon. A few weeks. It's not long now.'

They said good-bye. She stood on the platform and waved to him. When the train was out of sight, she walked back alone through the town.

~ PART FIVE ~

DEATH OF THE MOTHER

O N E

◆━━◆

After Christmas, the cold weeks of January 1924 slid by without incident
at the old house in the rue des Oiseaux. While Georges and Emily waited
to hear news of the tender from John Bradfield in Australia the household
enjoyed a calm period of domestic routine – as if a truce had been called
in the affairs of the Elders. Then on the first Monday in February, when
Marie was two months old, Marthe returned to the village of Lèves, where
she was to marry the father of her own child the following week. Emily
and Sophie walked with her to the other side of the place Drouaise, where
she was to catch the steam tram. Low cloud hung over Chartres that
morning, a cold white fog blanketing the houses and the narrow streets.
As the three women walked along the roads side by side, the air was
chill and damp in their faces, setting tiny beads of moisture in their hair
and on their scarves and on the nap of their overcoats. Sophie pushed the
new pram that Georges had brought back with him from Paris. The pram
had a hood and was a deep royal blue with white curlicues painted on the
sides. Marthe carried Victor against her shoulder, her canvas valise in her
other hand. Emily offered to carry the valise, which was not heavy, but
Marthe refused. 'Thank you, madame, but in my book when you can't
carry your own bits and pieces it's time to shut up shop.'

They heard the clanking of the tram and the mournful hoot of
its steam whistle as it approached along the rue de la Couronne
long before they saw it. Sophie and Marthe embraced and kissed

each other. 'I'll never forget you,' Sophie said. There were tears in her eyes.

Emily kissed Marthe on the cheeks. She took from the pocket of her overcoat a small tapestry purse and presented it to her. 'There's a little something extra inside from Monsieur and me. It's just for yourself, Marthe.' She put her hand over Marthe's. 'Don't open it now, my dear.'

Marthe smiled with pleasure and set her valise on the cobbles. She tucked the purse deep in her coat pocket. 'Thank you, madame. You and Monsieur have been very kind to me.'

'Good luck with your marriage, Marthe.'

'Oh, we all need our share of luck with marriage, madame.' Marthe bent and looked into the hood of the pram and she touched Marie's cheeks with her finger. 'God bless you, Marie,' she said. 'You behave yourself for Sophie.'

Sophie said, 'She'll miss you.'

'Only for a day or two. There's no memory as short as a baby's.'

The tram drew up and they waited while the passengers got off. Marthe lifted her skirt and stepped into the tram and Emily handed her valise up to her. They stood and waved as the vehicle coasted away along the shiny rails, adding its plume of white steam to the cold fog, its bogies clanking in the heavy winter silence.

When the tram had disappeared into the fog, Emily and Sophie turned away and crossed the open space of the place Drouaise. They walked on parallel to the river along the rue de la Brèche. They were both silent, thinking their own thoughts, the departure of Marthe putting them in mind of change and perhaps signifying the beginning of the end of their own time in Chartres.

When they turned at the corner of the rue des Oiseaux, Sophie blurted out suddenly, 'If Monsieur's firm wins the tender, madame, you'll soon be returning to Australia.'

Emily smiled and looked at her. 'And seeing Marthe leave us, you're thinking of when you must say good-bye to Marie yourself? Is that what's troubling you, Sophie?'

Sophie stopped abruptly, both her gloved hands gripping the black Bakelite handle of the pram. She turned to Emily. 'I'm not like Marthe, madame. I've no one else now. Marthe has her own child and will soon have a husband. She has her family, madame.'

Emily put her arm round Sophie's shoulders. 'If we go back to Australia, you shall come with us.'

Sophie drew back. 'Madame? Truly?'

'Truly, Sophie. It was Monsieur's idea. We have talked about it and we are firmly agreed. You'll never have to think of saying good-bye to Marie.'

Sophie let go the handle of the pram and put her hands over her face and burst into tears. 'Oh, madame, how can I ever thank you?' She groped for the pram, which had begun to roll forward.

Emily laughed and hugged her. 'There's no need to thank us. It's we who are grateful to you.'

Sophie sniffed and blew her nose and dried her eyes.

When they had gone on some way, Emily said, 'But, of course, Monsieur's firm may not win the tender and we may not return to Australia.'

Sophie looked at her anxiously. 'What will you do then?'

Emily was silent, staring ahead of her along the narrow road, glimpses through the coiling fog of the cold river down the narrow side streets. She turned and considered Sophie. 'I don't know yet what we shall do. It has not been settled. You are lucky,' she said.

'I'm thankful for my good fortune, madame.'

'I meant, you enjoy what you do. You're fulfilled by it. You look for nothing else. Everyone sees that in you and remarks on it. Madame Elder says you have the vocation of service. It's true. You don't long for something that's forbidden to you. You're not restless for some other condition. You already possess the world you love and you just want to be left alone to enjoy it.'

Sophie glanced at her. 'The nuns taught us gratitude, madame.'

'Oh, what nonsense!' Emily scoffed impatiently. 'It's in your nature to be content, Sophie. No one can teach us to be what we're not. Were all the girls at the convent as content as you? Of course they weren't. I'll bet there were troubled souls there who longed for their freedom and who look back on your beloved convent as a purgatory where they knew themselves to be cruelly misunderstood.'

'I did know an unhappy girl,' Sophie acknowledged, gazing into the hood of the pram where Marie slept, soothed by the movement of the springs, her round face peeping from her bonnet. Sophie said, 'You are a mystery yourself, madame.'

Emily laughed. 'Is that what Marthe says about me?'

'No, madame . . . I shouldn't have said it.'

'Yes, you should. I'm glad you said it. It's what you think. You have your reasons for thinking it.'

'You're not angry, then?'

'What if I am angry? What does it matter? You must say what you think. Our freedom is to say what we think. People get angry and then they forgive each other and are firmer friends for it.'

'I wouldn't wish to offend you.'

'I asked for your help in Paris and you gave me your help. You didn't betray me even though I didn't explain myself or trust you with my secret.'

Sophie said softly. 'I don't need to know your secret, madame.'

'It takes strength to do things like that for others. You're unusual. I wouldn't have asked most girls your age to help me.'

'It was a difficult time for you.'

They went on in silence for a while. 'I know I can trust you, Sophie.'

'I don't need to know your secret, madame,' Sophie said again.

'Oh, don't worry,' Emily laughed. 'I don't mean to tell you it. I would need to begin with the day of my birth. I just want you to know that whatever Monsieur and I do, whatever arrangements are made, you won't be parted from Marie, I promise you.'

'Thank you, madame. I believe you.'

They had arrived at the front door of Juliette's house. Emily reached and knocked. It was Georges who opened the door. 'Mother's had a fall,' he said. He leaned and took hold of the extensions at the sides of the hood and lifted the pram in over the step.

'Is she all right?' Emily asked anxiously.

'Otto and Father Étinceler are with her now.'

They went in and Georges closed the door behind them. Otto was at the far end of the passage by the kitchen door. He had his bag and was coming out of Madame Elder's room. Sophie wheeled the pram to where the passage opened out into a narrow hall at the foot of the stairs. She lowered the hood and reached in and lifted Marie out. Marie began to whimper. Sophie held her to her shoulder and shushed her and carried her past Otto and into the kitchen.

Georges and Emily started down the passage toward Otto. The telephone rang. Georges stopped and turned back. He reached and took the receiver from the wall. Aunt Juliette came and stood in the kitchen door, wiping her hands on her apron and looking. They all watched Georges.

'Hello. Georges Elder.' He held the receiver pressed to his ear. He nodded and said a few words then replaced the instrument on its cradle. 'Jacques Lenormand,' he said. 'He's come down to Paris. He's in the office. He wants to see me first thing in the morning.' He turned to Otto. 'How is she?'

Emily said, 'It's the bridge, then? What did he say? Has Baume Marpent won the tender? What did he say?'

Otto said, 'She's had a fright. She's broken nothing, which is a blessing. She's comfortable now. I've given her something to settle her.' He put his hand on Georges's arm. 'It would probably be a good idea to leave her to have a talk with Father Étinceler for the moment. You look as though you could use a brandy, Georges.'

'What did Lenormand say about the tender?' Emily persisted.

'He didn't say anything about the tender. He asked me to meet him in the office at nine. That's all. I'll go up this afternoon.'

'You didn't ask him about the tender?' Emily exclaimed incredulously.

'No,' Georges said. He was reserved. He looked at her, as if he disapproved of her intensity at this moment.

'Well, what do you think? How did he sound? Ring him back and ask him!'

Georges said, 'I have a feeling we shall all know tomorrow.'

'How can you stand there being calm and knowing he knows and you don't know? How can you bear it? Ring him at once! Ring Jean-Pierre. He'll tell you.'

Georges smiled. 'If Jean-Pierre knew anything, he'd tell me. I wouldn't need to ring and ask him to tell me. We can safely assume Jean-Pierre knows nothing.'

Emily almost stamped her foot. 'You're exasperating!'

Georges looked past her at Otto and Juliette. 'Come in by the fire. We'll have a drink before I get ready. You too, Juliette. Come and have a drink with us, for once.'

Juliette sniffed. 'And who do you think's going to do the washing while I'm sitting around drinking?' She turned and went back into the kitchen.

Georges stood aside to let Emily go ahead of him into the sitting room. 'It's not fair,' she said. 'If they know, then I want to know too. Now. This minute. You can't just leave it like this. I won't let you.'

Georges went over and stood at the hearth. He relit his cigar from a waxed spill. He puffed the cigar into life then ran his thumb and forefinger along the spill and killed the flame. He reached and replaced the smoking spill in the blue glass vase. The circular table in the middle of the room was covered with his papers and notebooks, where he had been working.

Otto set his bag on the floor and closed the door.

Georges went over to the English cabinet and unstoppered the whisky decanter. He poured a measure and looked at Emily. She shook her head. He handed the glass of whisky to Otto and poured one for himself.

Otto said, 'I feel it in my bones, Georges, you've got your bridge, believe me. I've never been wrong about this sort of thing. It's a moment of certainty.'

Georges looked at him and drew on his cigar. He blew the smoke from his lips and examined the doctor. 'How is Mother, Otto. You can tell me.'

Otto drank from his glass. 'Her heart is tired, Georges. We can't look for a youthful recovery at her age.'

They were silent. Emily stared into the fire.

Otto emptied his glass and stepped forward and set it on the table beside Georges's papers. 'A call like that when you're not expecting anything is a sure sign,' he said. 'You've got your bridge, Georges. I'll let myself out.'

Emily turned from the fire. She took Otto's arm and went with him into the passage. She stood waiting while he put on his hat and coat. 'How is Madame Elder?'

He smiled and opened the front door. 'My generation is disappearing, Emily.' He looked up the street then back at her. 'The years have gone.' He spoke with a kind of astonishment. 'Suddenly it seems to have been only a moment.'

She put her hand on his arm. 'She's been your friend for a long time.'

'There was a moment . . . when I first came to Chartres and Heloise was newly widowed.' He looked at her, his eyes bright with the memory. 'She was young then. We were both young. I still see that young woman in her, Emily.' He went down the step into the street and waved. 'Till tomorrow, my dear.'

She closed the door and went back into the sitting room.

Georges was gathering his papers. He screwed the top on his fountain pen and put the pen in the inside pocket of his jacket. He stood with his papers under his arm. 'I'll look in on Mother on the way up.' He waited. 'I'll ring you from Paris as soon as I know something definite.'

She stood by the window looking out at the street. 'I may go back to Tunisia for a month or two in the spring.'

'I've no time for this now. I have to get ready or I'll miss my train.'

She turned from the window. 'What will you do if you haven't got the bridge?'

He considered her. 'It has never been real for you, has it? The bridge? My work? They've not affected you. Not really. Don't pretend. They've never entered your life.'

'And my work has entered your life?' She laughed. 'Twenty years with my father, Georges, inured me against a sense of wonder for the great works of ambitious men. I heard of nothing else. Especially the biggest bridge in the world. I've lived with its claims on my attention all my life.' She said seriously, 'I've no wish to see you fail. Don't imagine that. I want you to succeed.'

'But what?'

'But not at my expense. We'll have this conversation another time. Go on. Get ready. I'll walk with you to the station.'

'Why don't you come with me?'

'Do you want me to?'

'Yes. We can go out to dinner. We can be alone. Come up to Paris with me!'

She hesitated. 'You'll think me stupidly superstitious. But I don't want to go back to Paris for a visit. I feel as if I might never go back there to live if I do that. It's irrational, I know. But there.' There was a stubbornness to the set of her mouth. 'Your mother came to this house intending to stay only a month or two. She told me so. Now she will never leave. When I go up to Paris, I want it to be my return from Chartres.'

He shrugged. 'If that's what you feel . . . I have to go.' He turned and went out.

When he reached his mother's bedroom door, he stood listening. The murmur of her voice, the deeper voice of the priest. He bent closer. He could just make out what they were saying . . .

Madame Elder turned her head on the pillow. Her eyes gleamed in the candlelight. 'I was dreaming I was a little girl again,' she said. 'In this house with my father. It seemed so real. He used to carry me up the street on his shoulders. Then I realized I was lying on the floor in the passage.' She looked past Bertrand to the bowl of fruit on the bedside table.

'If you'd like me to, Madame Elder, I'll light a candle for you before the Black Madonna.'

'You don't despise her, then?'

'How should I?'

She gazed up at him. He waited for her. She was not wearing her spectacles. The skin around her eyes was pale and moist in the candlelight, the pupils of her eyes large and black – the eyes of a nocturnal creature startled by the light.

'What is the purpose for which God offers us the gift of eternal life, Father?' she asked, as if she were a child. Her fingers tugged at a loose thread in the eiderdown.

Bertrand examined the callused palms of his hands, perhaps searching for the answer to her question in the grid of lines there. He looked at her. 'I don't know.'

She smiled. 'How I like the simple way you tell me the truth.' She reached and took his hand.

'Who can know his purpose?' he said.

'I have always been determined to face my death calmly and with dignity. Now I understand that is not to be my choice. Lying on the floor in the passage, my body was a stranger and would not obey me. Lying there, I realized that our body does not belong to us,' she said. 'It is true, isn't it?'

'You will face your death calmly, Madame Elder. Have no fear. I know it.'

'I didn't think I'd live to see a grandchild. Light the candle for me.'

He stood up.

'Will you come and see me tomorrow?'

'I will. Until tomorrow, then.' He opened the door and went out.

Georges drew back. They stared at each other.

'How is she?' Georges asked.

They went along the dark passage together to the front door.

'What did she have to say? Is she in good spirits?'

Bertrand paused at the door. 'She asked me for what purpose God offers us eternal life.'

'She thinks she's dying, then. What did you tell her?'

Bertrand squared his biretta and looked at Georges. 'I told her I didn't know.'

Georges frowned. 'Couldn't you have reassured her? Couldn't you have told her that after a lifetime of being a faithful Catholic she can look forward to eternal bliss in Heaven?' Georges laughed incredulously. 'Couldn't you have said something like that? What's been the point of it for her otherwise?'

Bertrand opened the front door and stepped down into the street. 'She asked me the purpose, Monsieur Elder. I don't know it.' He turned and walked away up the hill toward the cathedral.

Georges stood looking after him. He was angry. The solitary figure of the priest going along in his waisted soutane. He wanted to shout after him, What's the point of it, then?

T W O

Madame Elder did not leave her room that evening. Emily ate in the kitchen with Juliette and Sophie. Juliette reached down her omelette pan from the hook beside the stove and the scoured copper flashed a reflection of the gaslight across the yellow, smoke-stained wall, and across Emily's face. Emily was sitting at the scrubbed table in Madame Elder's customary place by the window. She was holding Marie on her lap giving her a bottle. Marie's eyes were closed. The baby sucked then stopped then sucked again and was still again, the milk drooling from the side of her mouth and dribbling onto her smock. Her fist clenched and unclenched on Emily's finger. Emily was half asleep in the warmth of the stove. She was gazing out the window at the night, the moon sliding through the black river, the row of streetlights on the far bank with halos around them.

At the other end of the table Sophie sat darning the collar of a blouse. She bent and bit her cotton and glanced across at Emily and the baby. 'You could put her down, madame,' she said quietly. 'She's asleep.'

Emily looked down at Marie. She eased the teat from her lips and the baby gave a small shudder and settled against her arm. Emily put the bottle on the table.

Sophie set her sewing aside. 'I'll take her up.'

'No. It's all right, Sophie. I'll take her up myself.' Emily got up, cradling the sleeping baby in her arms.

348

Sophie stood and opened the kitchen door for her. 'I'll come up with you.'

'There's no need for you to come, Sophie. I'd like to put her down on my own.'

Sophie looked at Marie. 'Very well, madame.'

Juliette turned the edges of the omelette in the pan. 'Don't be long. This will be ready in another minute.'

Emily went along the passage and up the stairs to the landing. She went on past her room to where the linoleum ended. Carefully she carried Marie up the narrow wooden back stairs to the nursery, the bare treads faintly luminous at her feet. There was no gaslight on the upper floor. A violet stillness of moonlight shone through the skylight onto the bare boards of the landing. There was the smell of the coarse sandsoap that Juliette used to scrub the stairs with. Emily transferred Marie to her right arm and held her against her shoulder. She reached for the iron latch on the door and lifted it and opened the door. The small room was cold and bright with moonlight. Frost had made ovals of the windowpanes. Georges's antique crib stood against the wall under the window, its black ribs softened by the overflow of bedding. The boards creaked as she leaned over the crib and gently laid Marie in the soft nest of bedding. She turned Marie on her side and tucked the blankets firmly around her. Marie slept peacefully, her little features empty of expression, as if she dreamed she floated safely in her mother's womb again. Emily stood looking in at her.

'I wish I could remember giving birth to you. It will always be as if I was not there.' She pushed the crib, setting it swinging back and forth, the leather hangers creaking. 'What will you think of your mother when you grow up?'

She turned aside and examined the narrow room. The low sloping ceiling, a small chest of drawers against the wall opposite the bed. On the neatly made-up covers of the bed the white form of the Pierrot Antoine had brought for Marie, its pale head against the pillow, its arms akimbo, its black eyes staring out in the moonlight. A crucifix hung from the iron bedstead above it – the charmed effigy of a mysterious ritual. A tin trunk stood beside the head of the narrow bed. On the trunk was a crocheted doily, a bible, a half candle in a white enamel candlestick with a box of matches in the drip tray, and beside the candlestick the Berber bangle Emily had given Sophie. Emily sat on the bed, feeling herself surrounded by Sophie's privacy. The cold crept around her feet and against her back. She heard someone coming up the stairs. She stood and went over and looked in at Marie. She bent and touched her lips to the baby's cheek and withdrew, a sad, powerful nostalgia for something she could not name making her hesitate, her hand on the crib. In that moment the world seemed empty and each of them alone in it, encompassed by silence. She longed to be reassured.

Sophie met her on the landing. 'Is everything all right, madame? Your omelette's getting cold.' Sophie looked past her into the nursery. 'I'll just close the door. It'll bang if a wind gets up.'

'We shan't hear her if she wakes,' Emily said.

Sophie laughed. 'Oh, she won't wake now, madame. She's a good sleeper.' She stepped past Emily and looked in at the door then withdrew and closed it. 'She'll sleep like that for hours now. I'll be up before she wakes.'

— ~

Emily was sitting at the round table in the front room. She was reading one of Georges's father's books. A paperknife lay beside the volume. It was Walter Pater's *Studies in the History of the Renaissance*. The pages were uncut. Light snow was falling outside, the wet flakes sliding down the windowpanes and melting against the sill. The telephone rang. She put down the book and got up and went out into the passage. She took the receiver from the wall.

Georges said, 'It's me . . . We didn't get it.'

Emily drew in her breath, a sharp thrill of relief touching something vital in her chest. 'Oh, Georges, I'm so sorry. Are you all right? Where are you?' The kitchen door opened. Juliette came out and stood in the passage looking at her. 'Is it him? Did he get it?'

Emily shook her head from side to side. Juliette blew out her cheeks and made a throwing gesture with her hands. She turned and went back into the kitchen. 'Monsieur didn't get his bridge,' she said to Sophie.

'I've resigned,' Georges said.

'Why?'

'They wanted me to. Lenormand didn't say as much. He was delighted we didn't get it. I could see it the moment I walked in. He was sitting at my desk. He didn't get up. When I offered to resign, that's when he stood up. He looked solemn and shook my hand. He said it was gracious of me to take it upon myself and that perhaps it was for the best. He's got what he wanted all along. Anyway, I've done it and that's that.'

'What will you do?'

'Antoine and Léon are here. They send you their regards. I'll read you the cable. Lenormand was kind enough to give me a copy.'

'Where are you?'

'We're at the apartment. Antoine's taking us to the Brasserie Équivoque. We're going to celebrate my liberation.' He laughed. 'You should have come up with me after all.'

She heard him put the telephone down. There were men's voices and laughter in the background. She waited. She heard papers rustling and the sound of him picking up the phone again.

'My design was disqualified,' he said. 'It wasn't considered. There were twenty tenders in all. Three were disqualified. Ours was one of them. We didn't make the short list. Listen . . .' There was the sound of paper rustling close to the phone again. 'It's from Bradfield. He describes himself as the chief engineer of the New South Wales

Government Construction Authority. Nothing about the bridge. It's addressed to Sully, Baume Marpent's chairman. This is what he says.' Georges cleared his throat. 'Are you listening?'

'Read it.'

'As with the tenders of the Canadian Bridge Company and of the McLintic Marshall Products Company, we are sorry to inform you that the tender submitted by your firm is not considered by us to be in accordance with the specifications and plans issued by the Minister as the basis of tendering, and does not therefore come within the scope of the Sydney Harbour Bridge Act.' Georges paused. 'Disqualified, in other words.'

Emily said, 'But why?'

'Too original for them. They say we exceeded the design brief.'

'You don't sound too horribly disappointed.'

'I don't know what I feel. Liberated. That's what I feel. That's not all he said.' His voice assumed a reading tone, 'We congratulate you, however, on the extreme care that has been devoted to your tender for an arch bridge. The stress analyses, design, and layout of truss members and details have been excellently performed, as would be expected from a firm with the high reputation of Baume Marpent . . .' So he's not charging me with incompetence, thank God. He saves the best till last. He's invited me to visit the construction site. He says I'm welcome whenever I care to come over. What do you think of that? He's not a bureaucrat.' He continued reading, 'Monsieur Elder is an engineer for whose experience, energies, and abilities in the field of advanced steel fabrication and design we retain the very highest respect here in Sydney . . .' He hasn't forgotten me. He doesn't want to give them the chance of blaming me for their catastrophe. But that's what they'll do all the same. It'll be all over France and Belgium within a week. Our national pride will have been hurt. They'll make the point that I'm not really a Frenchman . . . Well, it's done for and that's that. It was always going to be all or nothing . . . Are you still there?'

'I'm listening.'

'Lenormand said France's reliability in tendering for international projects will suffer from this. That's when I offered him my resignation. That did it for me. Well, in that case, I said, you'd better have my resignation. I thought he'd resist. But that was good enough for him . . . It's cost them a lot of money. They have to blame someone or the shareholders will want their necks. He asked me how Marie was doing. Wasn't that thoughtful of him?'

'Do you know who's won the tender?'

'It won't have been decided yet. There's a short list.'

She could hear the pigeons cooing on the guttering outside the window of the apartment in rue Saint-Dominique. She imagined Georges standing by the table looking down into the courtyard, the bare branches of the robinia tree and the black cobbles glistening in the rain. 'Is it snowing in Paris?'

'No.'

'Are you coming back to Chartres this evening?'

'I'll sleep here tonight and go into the office in the morning and sort a few things out. I'll be home after lunch tomorrow.' There was a silence, then he said, 'I feel as if I've been spared.'

'What do you mean?'

'I've wondered how I'd manage if we won the tender.'

'You mean . . .' She didn't finish. It seemed too cruel a question to ask him at this moment if he doubted himself.

'It's Bradfield's bridge,' he said. 'He's spent forty years on it. It's never been my bridge. I'm relieved in a way.' He laughed self-consciously. 'What are you doing?'

'I was reading when you rang.'

'Where's Marie?'

'She's with Sophie in the kitchen.'

'How's Mother?'

'She was up this morning for an hour. Father Étinceler's with her now.'

There was a silence. 'I miss you all.'

'We'll be here when you get back.'

A moment later they said good-bye, an awkwardness unresolved between them, of the distance perhaps and their inability to deal at once with his news. She hung up the telephone and stood in the passage looking in through the open door to the sitting room, Madame Elder's worn mahogany armchair by the fire, a flap of tapestry hanging loose at the side, the lumpy velvet divan, the photographs of Georges and his father on the mantelpiece . . . As she had first seen the room that day in April, Madame Elder rising from her chair to embrace Georges . . . She knew suddenly that the bridge had always been a mirage. Georges was right. It had never entered her life. She went into the sitting room and closed the door. She sat at the table and took up her book. The snow had turned to heavy rain. The drops were rattling against the windows, drips coming down the chimney and spitting in the fire.

She closed the book, unable to concentrate, and sat staring out the window.

THREE

— ⚬ —

Emily was dreaming Marthe had taken Marie by mistake instead of her own little boy, Victor. Emily was calm and even amused by the wet nurse's confusion of the identities of the two babies. The mistake seemed easily remedied. When she lifted Victor from his cot, she was reassured to realize that the nursery resembled her own childhood bedroom in her parents' home at Richmond Hill. She carried Victor along the street and caught the steam tram and followed Marthe into the fog. But when she looked out of the window of the tram, she saw with dismay that she was in Melbourne. Panic tightened her chest. She was suddenly terrified that she would never find her way to Lèves and to Marie. She looked down then and saw that her arms were empty. It shocked her to realize that she must have abandoned Victor somewhere along the way. She was no longer on the tram. She knew suddenly there was no way out of the dream . . . The cry woke her. Or perhaps it had precipitated the dream. She lay in the dark listening, puzzling with her understanding of the dream, wondering if the cry that had woken her were real or an echo of her own cry in the dream.

The greenish rectangle of the window loomed out of the wall. The air was cold on her face . . . She lay listening, waiting, hearing the cry in her mind. Not the cry of a child but a howl of despair emptied into the night. She was drifting uneasily into sleep again when a board creaked on the landing. There was a knock at the door. Someone opened the door and looked in. Emily raised her head from the pillow. Sophie's shape was silhouetted against a thin light from the stairs.

'Are you awake, madame?' Sophie's whisper was urgent.

Emily sat up. 'What is it, Sophie?' Her chest was tight with anxiety. 'Where's Marie?'

'It's the mistress, madame. Juliette says you're to come at once.' She turned and left, leaving the door open, her bare feet soundless on the linoleum.

Emily got out of bed and put on her dressing gown and searched under the bed for her slippers. Sophie's smell, a mixture of babies and something of her own delicate girlish innocence, lingered in the room. Emily went downstairs and along the passage to Madame Elder's bedroom. The door was open.

Aunt Juliette was standing beside Madame Elder's bed. Juliette's grey hair escaped in long straggles from a white linen cap that was held in place with a draw-ribbon under her chin. She wore an old grey robe that reached to her ankles. The robe was fastened close around her thin neck with a large black button. Neat patches of a paler material were sewn into the front and at the elbows. Her wrinkled face and hands were chalky white. Her stove lamp stood on the mantelpiece above the cold hearth, the broad flame in its smoky chimney casting a bronze light against the walls. There was a smell of camphor and liniment. Emily touched her arm and looked down at Madame Elder.

Madame Elder's face was waxen in the lamplight, her eyes two black sightless holes, her mouth open, her lips drawn back, a frown wrinkling her brow, as if her imploring cry were caught on her parted lips.

'She called for our father,' Juliette said, astonished, her voice small, hollow, emptied of certainty.

Emily held her arm.

'Papa, help me! she cried. As if she thought she was a little girl again and was running after him up the street the way she used to.' Juliette stood over the bed staring at her crippled sister, as if she proposed some powerful action to remedy the situation but could not decide what the action she proposed might be – as if she might even lean and shake her sister and call on Heloise to come to her senses and wake. 'Our father has been dead for more than forty years!' Juliette said. 'When she cried out for him, I could see him stop and turn back and wait for her. The way he used to pick her up by the waist with both his hands and hoist her to his shoulder and carry her off up the street to the premises with him, the pair of them as happy as they could be together.'

Sophie came in and stood beside Juliette.

Emily turned to her. 'Is Marie all right?'

'She's sleeping, madame. I went in and had a look at her.'

Sophie looked down at Madame Elder and then at Aunt Juliette. She reached and took Juliette's hands. She put her arm around the old woman's shoulders and held her.

The three women stood in silence looking at Madame Elder.

Emily said, 'Go and telephone Dr Hopman, Sophie. Tell him he's needed here urgently.'

Sophie leaned and kissed Aunt Juliette. She gently withdrew her embrace and went out.

Emily bent down to Madame Elder and reached under the bed-clothes for her hand. She felt for her pulse. Madame Elder's cold fingers closed on Emily's hand, a surprising strength in her grip. Her lips moved and she murmured. Emily bent closer, her ear to Madame Elder's lips. She caught a faint whisper, a sibilation of air empty of any message.

Aunt Juliette said, 'She called for him, as if she was a little girl again.'

'Why don't you get the fire going?' Emily suggested. 'It's very cold in here.'

Aunt Juliette looked at her and then at the white ashes in the grate.

She went out. A moment later there was the sound of her chopping kindling on the laundry stoop behind the kitchen.

Alone with Madame Elder, Emily sat on the side of the bed massaging the old lady's cold fingers. Madame Elder's lips were greyish blue and the skin of her cheeks was slack and coarsened. Her mouth was open, the light of the lamp gleaming on the black-and-purple stains on her teeth, the greenish membrane of her palate quivering delicately with each small draught of air. A noise came from her throat, a clicking repeated at intervals, as if at a distance someone tapped a dry stick against another, waiting for an answering signal. When Emily leaned close, she caught the smell of nutmeg on Madame Elder's breath.

Sophie came back. 'The doctor's on his way.'

'What time is it?' Emily asked her.

'I don't know, madame. Shall I go and look?'

They spoke in hushed voices.

Emily put her hand on Sophie's arm. 'No. It doesn't matter.'

They waited.

Madame Elder's breathing was shallow and uncertain. For minutes at a time she seemed to cease to breathe. Emily rubbed her cold fingers and leaned down and whispered encouragement to her.

Aunt Juliette returned with a handful of dry sticks and the black scuttle filled with coal. She put these down inside the fender and knelt at the hearth and rattled the ashes through the grate and began to set the fire.

They heard the car. Sophie went out and let the doctor in.

A moment later Otto came into the bedroom. He greeted Emily and Aunt Juliette and took off his hat and put it on the bed with his bag. He did not take his overcoat off but leaned and looked closely at Madame Elder. With his thumb he delicately held back her eyelid. The fire began to crackle and the light of the flames danced on the ceiling and over their faces. The three women watched the doctor examine Madame

Elder. When Otto had completed his examination, he placed Madame Elder's hands under the blankets and pulled the blankets close around her neck. He straightened, his hand resting lightly at her shoulder.

'I'll go up to the palace and see if I can raise Father Étinceler. She'd want to have him by her.' He turned to Emily. 'Telephone Georges and tell him he's needed at his mother's bedside. I don't suppose there's a train till morning?'

Emily looked at him. 'Will she survive the night?'

He thought about her question. 'My experience of death is that people die when they're ready to die, my dear.'

They stood looking at Madame Elder.

'But I don't think Heloise will rally from this,' he said. 'The powers of nature are exhausted in her. The Father's more use to her now than I am.'

The room was growing warm.

Emily followed Otto out into the passage. She opened the door for him. When he had gone, she went back along the passage and lifted the receiver. She asked the Paris exchange to connect her to the apartment in rue Saint-Dominique. While she waited she imagined Georges asleep in bed, the apartment dark and silent, the sloping ceiling above his head, through the window the black silhouette of the Dôme of the Invalides above the rooftops, the night sky glowing with the apricot fire of the city. From Madame Elder's bedroom she could hear the murmur of Sophie's voice comforting Juliette.

The man at the exchange came on the line again. 'There's no answer from that number, madame.'

She asked him to try the Brasserie Équivoque. 'I don't have the number,' she told him. He said he would find the number of the brasserie and would ring her back when he had raised them. She put up the phone and went back to Madame Elder's bedroom.

Aunt Juliette and Sophie were standing at the foot of the bed with their backs to the fire, their arms around each other, looking at Madame Elder. Madame Elder stared emptily at the ceiling, her head back and her mouth open, her breath clicking in her throat. The three women waited, watching her. The telephone rang. Emily went out into the passage and lifted it from its cradle. The exchange had raised the Brasserie Équivoque. There was a din of voices in the background. She asked if Antoine Carpeaux were there. The man told her Monsieur Carpeaux had left with his party some hours ago. She asked the exchange to connect her to Antoine's number. While she was waiting she heard Otto's car pull up outside. She put the phone down and went along the passage and opened the door for him.

Otto stood in the road under the gaslight. Bertrand waited a pace behind him. She stepped aside and they came in. Bertrand carried a small black leather case with brass fittings.

Bertrand stood in the passage and looked at her, his broad features pale and serious in the shadows. He greeted her and reached and held her hand. 'Madame Elder received the *viaticum* yesterday.'

Emily returned the pressure of his fingers. 'Now you are her priest.'

Otto said, 'You'd better hurry, Father.'

Bertrand released her hand and followed Otto to Madame Elder's room.

Emily took up the telephone. The line hissed emptily. She tried again. But the exchange could raise no one at Antoine's apartment. She went along the passage and stood in the doorway of Madame Elder's room.

Otto and Sophie and Aunt Juliette were kneeling at the foot of the bed. Their eyes were closed and their hands held before them in the position of supplication and prayer. The firelight played across their hair and shoulders. Bertrand was bending over Madame Elder, his violet stole, the color of sorrow and affliction, drifting out as he bent and touched the crucifix to Madame Elder's lips.

Emily kneeled in the doorway. She closed her eyes and held her hands before her face, her thumbs touching her chin, as she had kneeled to pray when she was a little girl.

Bertrand anointed Madame Elder's ivory forehead with the blessed oil, intoning the words of the *Sacramentum Exeuntiam*, the last farewell to the traveler in eternity. '*Per istam sanctam unctionem et suam piissimam misericordiam indulgeat tibi Dominus quicquid deliquisti . . .*' In turn he touched his thumb to Madame Elder's eyes, to each of her ears, to her lips, and to her nose, '*Per sensus visum, auditum, gustum, odoratum et tactum.*' He removed Madame Elder's hands from under the blankets and smeared her palms with the last vestiges of the oil.

He completed the sacrament. They opened their eyes and stood up and looked at him. He stood with two fingers on Madame Elder's jugular, his eyes closed, listening for her pulse. After a moment, he opened his eyes and turned to them, his fingers still resting lightly on Madame Elder's neck, as if his gesture were a caress. 'Our sister is at peace,' he said.

Aunt Juliette sobbed and leaned against Sophie. Sophie held her, as if she were a stricken child.

Otto said, 'It's over, then.' There were tears in his eyes.

Bertrand removed his violet stole. With care he folded it, then he collected the artifacts of his ritual and placed them in the black case. He fastened the bronze hasps of the case and took it by the handle, his business done.

'I'll stay for a while,' Otto said. 'Juliette may need me.'

Emily went with Bertrand along the passage. They stood at the open door together. It was grey dawn. There was the sound of the milkman's cans a street away and his call to his horse to come on.

She could smell the river in the cold air. She turned to Bertrand. 'I can think of nothing to say.'

He looked at her. 'You kneeled.'

'Yes. I kneeled for her. For . . . I don't know. For Madame Elder. It was . . .' She put her hand on his arm. 'You are a good priest, Bertrand.'

He shrugged. 'What is a good priest?'

'Georges will be bereft.'

They were silent. Then he said, 'The bishop is to travel to Rouen for the Eucharistic Congress.' He turned and waited until she looked at him. 'I'm to travel with him. We're leaving the day after tomorrow. You'll probably have left Chartres by the time I come back. Don't forget to write and tell me your news.' He stepped out into the street. 'Good-bye, Emily.' He turned and walked briskly away through the grey dawnlight.

She stood in the doorway watching him. At the corner he turned and lifted his hand in salute to her. She raised her hand and kept it raised until he had gone out of sight. She closed the door and went into the sitting room. She stood by the round table staring into the shadows of Madame Elder's old room. The moment was filled with contradiction for her . . . The clock on the mantelpiece ticked steadily . . . She did not know what she felt. She turned and went out into the passage and lifted the receiver. She asked the exchange to try the rue Saint-Dominique number again.

Georges answered at once. He coughed thickly and cleared his throat and excused himself. 'Who's that?'

'It's me, Georges.'

'I think I'm still drunk,' he said. Then his voice filled with alarm, 'Is Marie all right?'

'I'm afraid there's no other way for me to tell you this . . . Your mother died less than an hour ago. I've been trying to reach you. I'm terribly sorry.'

There was a long silence. She heard him sucking his breath. He said tightly, 'She believed in the bridge. It was her dream for me.'

'She died peacefully, Georges. Otto was there and Aunt Juliette.'

'Did she have a priest?'

'Yes. Everything was done as she would have wished . . .'

'Étinceler, I suppose?'

'Yes.'

She heard the gust of grief sweep into his throat. 'I wasn't with her!'

'I'm so sorry, Georges.'

'I'll catch the first train . . .' He fell silent abruptly.

She felt him fighting his grief.

'Are you all right?'

'Yes. I'll be all right.'

'I'll come down to the station and meet you.'

'There's no need. I'll be all right in a minute. I'm all right *now*. It's over . . . We'll make a new beginning. You and me and Marie. The three of us together. I've been thinking about it. I talked to Léon and Antoine about it tonight.'

'Yes,' she said. 'Of course we shall.'

'This has settled it. I'll cable Bradfield in the morning before I leave. I'll ask him for a position on his team.'

'*Bradfield?*' Her subdued question was an exclamation of dismay.

'It's finished for us here now. Marie will be an Australian. I'll work on the approaches with Bradfield.'

'You're not just running away?'

'Australia,' he said. 'You'll be going home. It will be our new beginning. I'll always be known here for the disqualification of my design. It's never going to leave me. It will follow me around. We have to get away and start again.'

FOUR

——◆——

Two days after Madame Elder's funeral, when the smell of incense and of the mourners' damp clothes and the sweet perfumes of the hothouse flowers had all but faded from the rooms of the old house in the rue des Oiseaux and been replaced by the fishy smell of Aunt Juliette's court bouillon simmering on the woodstove, the telegram boy came to the front door. He propped his bicycle against the wall and knocked. Aunt Juliette opened the door to him. She brought the telegram into the sitting room and handed it to Georges. She stood and watched, waiting while Georges opened it.

Emily's fingers played nervously over the brailled surfaces of Perpetua's medallion at the throat of her blouse.

Georges read the cable to himself. 'It's from Bradfield.' He looked up. 'He wants me.' He read, *'Site supervisor northern bridge approaches yours. Confirm your acceptance at your earliest. We are delighted you wish to join us. I look forward with great pleasure to welcoming you and your family to Sydney.'* Georges reached and handed the cable across to Emily.

Juliette said, 'You'll soon be off, then, leaving your old aunt to herself.'

Georges stood and put his arms around her. He kissed her cheek and drew her against his shoulder. He wore a black armband on the right sleeve of his jacket. 'Come with us, Aunt Juliette. Come and see Australia! Why not?' He looked at Emily. 'What do you say, dearest?'

Aunt Juliette freed herself from his embrace and said impatiently, 'You do say the silliest things sometimes, Georges.' She stepped across and stood holding the door to the passage, looking back at him. 'I was born in this house. I've never left Chartres. I've done my duty by Heloise as our father would have wished. She was always his favourite. Now I'm due for a rest.' She said emphatically, 'A little something for Juliette, for a change.' She went out and closed the door firmly behind her.

Georges stood looking after her. 'Her duty? Was it only her duty, then?'

Emily said, 'She's tired and upset. She doesn't mean it.'

He went over and stood with his back to the hearth. 'Mother told Étinceler things she would never have dreamed of telling me. We were so careful with each other, Mother and I. We hid everything. We made a secret of our lives. I never once sat down with her and asked her to tell me about her childhood. I took her existence for granted.' He looked at the cable in her hand. 'We can be in Sydney by April. It won't be spring over there, will it? What will it be?'

'Autumn.'

'You'd better cable your parents. They're going to be delighted with the news. I've always known I'd finish up in Australia.'

Emily sat at the round table holding Bradfield's cable in her hand. She said carefully, 'I understood your ambition to go to Australia to build the biggest bridge in the world. In some ways, I know, I didn't approve of it, but I did understand it.' She looked up at him. 'But approaches? To supervise the construction of approaches? Is that a sufficient reason to go to the other side of the world? You could do approaches in France. You could make a new beginning here as a supervisor of approaches.'

He lit a cigar with a spill and blew the smoke into the room. He stood with the lighted spill in his hand. 'I don't know that you did understand. I don't know that I understood myself.' He looked at her. 'It might sound heartless but Mother's death has made me feel free.

When my father died out there in Panama when I was a boy of eleven, I felt responsible for Mother and for the life I knew she expected to lead. I never questioned my responsibility to her. I accepted that I'd provide for her, now my father had gone.' He slid his thumb and forefinger along the spill, extinguishing the flame. He replaced the spill in the blue glass vase. 'We were poor. He left her debts and these bits and pieces. It must have been humiliating for her to have to come back to Chartres and rely on the spinster sister she'd left behind twelve years earlier.' He turned and ashed his cigar in the coals and stood looking down at the fire. 'I never really knew my father. He was always away in some foreign place supervising the construction of a road or a bridge or a canal. He wrote to me regularly. I kept all his letters. They're upstairs here somewhere with my old school notebooks. It's probably time to throw them out . . . I imagined him as he described himself, but I didn't know him and he didn't know me. We imagined each other. He was the ideal engineer to me, out there building the civilized world, and I was the perfect son for him, believing everything he told me and dreaming of being him one day. But if you ask me to remember his smell or his laugh or the way he ate or . . . I don't remember ever being alone with him. I used to think I was like him. It was a coincidence that the year of his death was also the year of John Bradfield's Sydney Harbour Bridge competition. At the Academy in Glasgow we were all going to be engineers. It was all we ever talked about. Our heroes weren't Scott and Amundsen. Our heroes were Isambard Kingdom Brunel and John Augustus Roebling. Engineers who'd constructed enormous objects that had changed forever the way cities looked and people lived. We all thought we could do it.' He paused and drew deeply on his cigar. 'But that's Bradfield, not me. He's one of them. He's like that. John Bradfield is Australia's Brunel or Roebling. It will be a privilege to work alongside him. He's still there after all these years, the war and everything, struggling to build his bridge. Believing in it with a kind of mad tenacity. The one idea ruling his life . . . To join the two halves of Sydney together and change his city forever. There's never been anything else for him. Whoever wins the tender now, the Sydney Harbour Bridge will always be Bradfield's. Without him it wouldn't exist. It takes a kind of madness like his to bring these enormous objects into being.'

She sat looking at him. 'Australia is just another country,' she said. 'It isn't going to work a kind of magic for you. I know. I know Australia.'

'I'm not talking about magic,' he said impatiently. 'It's a realistic plan. It's a modest reality. It's *me*. I know it is. These past few days have been a strange mixture of grief and elation for me. You can't know what I mean. The mad dream has gone.' He looked at her. 'Now that Mother's gone I don't have to dream of being my father any more.'

She looked at him. 'You talk about your failure as if it were success. What would you have done if Bradfield had awarded the contract to your design?'

'Maybe your father's prediction would have come true and the bridge would have killed me. It will kill a lot of men before it's built. I've got my freedom now,' he said. 'That's what I want you to understand. It's the last thing I expected. It's like an unexpected gift.'

She put Bradfield's cable on the table. She pushed it away with her fingers. 'I intend to go to Tunisia to work with Olive Kallen in the spring.'

'There won't be time to arrange excursions now,' he said. 'I'll have to settle my affairs here and in Paris and we'll be on the boat by the middle of March. Sooner, if possible.'

'It's the first of March on Monday. That's only two weeks away.'

'I'm determined we'll be in Sydney by the end of April.' He turned and tossed the substantial stub of his cigar into the fire. He stepped across to her and leaned down and kissed her cheek. 'I'll go up to the post office and cable my acceptance to Bradfield.' He buttoned his jacket and went out into the passage. A moment later she heard the front door slam. She had the wild thought that while he was out she would pack a few things and take Marie and disappear from his life forever . . . She sat at the table staring across the room.

FIVE

— ~

The mantelpiece had a plundered look. The framed photographs of Georges and his father, the clock and the blue glass vase with the waxed spills, were gone. Beside the window Georges reached into the English cabinet and took the last book. The doors of the cabinet stood open, the bevelled panes of glass reflecting disjointed aspects of street, sky, and room. The shelves were empty. There was a line of dust on each shelf. Furry bodies of desiccated moths lay where his father's books had rested undisturbed for a quarter of a century.

'The carter will take these pieces and our trunks on ahead to the station,' he said. 'We can ship the cabinet and the books to Australia in the hold. Juliette will never have a use for any of this. It will be a comfort to us to see a few of Mother's things in our house in Sydney.' He fingered the buckram of the gilt-embossed volume in his hands and opened it. 'I may decide to read these.' He stood looking down at the printed page, as if the idea of reading his father's books had been in his mind for years. He riffled the pages and paused randomly and read aloud to her – his manner, as he read, posed and self-conscious, as if it were not the meaning of what he read that engaged his mind but an image of himself at his leisure, established in their house on the shores of Sydney Harbour, a man middle-aged and liberated from his past and from the onerous delusions of youth and ambition. Georges's retracted pronunciation of the letter *r* was more noticeable in English and he seemed suddenly more the Scotsman that he really was, *'Experience, already reduced to a swarm of impressions, is ringed round for each of us by that thick wall of personality through which no real voice has ever pierced on its way to us, or from us to that which we can only conjecture to be without . . . each mind keeping as a solitary prisoner its own dream of a world.'* He stopped reading.

Emily was about to speak, then changed her mind. She went back to feeding Marie.

Georges closed the book and considered it. He brushed at its covers with the flat of his hand, then turned and set it squarely on one of the piles of books already on the round table in the middle of the room. He stood watching Emily feeding Marie. 'She doesn't seem to miss Marthe,' he said. 'I wonder if she thought Marthe was her mother?'

'So long as she gets fed, she probably doesn't care who feeds her.'

Emily was sitting up to the table on a hard-backed chair with Marie in her lap. She was spooning puréed carrot into Marie's mouth from a shallow stoneware bowl. Marie was gazing at her own fingers, which she held close to her eyes. She was working the sugared carrot out of her mouth with her tongue and dribbling it onto her chin and her bib.

'She's not swallowing it,' Georges said. 'Make her swallow it.'

'She's practising,' Emily said easily. With her finger she scooped the carrot from Marie's chin and wiped it on the edge of the bowl. She reached and held Marie's tiny hands, enclosing them in her own. She put her face close to Marie's and murmured to her. The baby gazed at her, an excited curiosity in the deep pools of her eyes, as if her mind charted a familiar feature of her own future. She smiled and made a gurgling sound. 'Look!' Emily whispered. 'She is really smiling at me.'

Georges squatted beside them. He rested his hand on Emily's knee and leaned close, gazing keenly at Marie. 'I wonder what her first word will be? I wonder what she's thinking? Do babies think? . . . You can

almost see your own first memories in her. Like feelings you dreamed.'
He reached and touched Marie's lip with the side of his forefinger.
She sneezed, spraying puréed carrot and looking startled, as if it were
someone else who had sneezed.

Georges wiped his face. They laughed together.

Emily lifted Marie and held her against her shoulder and patted
her back, the cloying baby smell strong in her nostrils. Marie's eyelids
drooped sleepily, then closed.

'I'd better get on,' he said, 'if I'm to get everything done in time.'
He made no move to get up. His hand shifted on Emily's knee and he
looked at her.

'What is it?'

His fingers caressed her thigh through the soft wool of her skirt.
'You've no idea how much I've missed you.'

She smiled and put her hand over his and whispered, 'I think she's
gone to sleep. I'd better put her down.'

'It's time I came back to our bed,' Georges said.

They looked at each other. The baby slept against Emily's shoulder.

Two days later the taxi waited for them on the cobbles in the middle
of the road outside Aunt Juliette's front door, white vapour rising from
its exhaust, its engine knocking steadily. The car's dark-green-and-black
paintwork glistened in the soft rain that was falling from the cold March
sky. The driver stood holding the back door of the taxi open for Emily.
She leaned and placed her green morocco writing case on the backseat.
She stepped onto the running board and climbed in and turned and took
Marie from Sophie.

A neighbour across the street lifted her curtain and watched.

Aunt Juliette stood with Georges in the shelter of the narrow
doorway. He held his brown trilby in one hand and clasped Aunt
Juliette's hand with the other.

'Now you're out of the house, I'll give the place a good going over and get everything back to normal,' she said.

'Back to normal, Aunt Juliette!' Georges exclaimed with disbelief. 'You mean as it was thirty years ago?' He laughed, as if they were not, after all, saying good-bye for the last time.

Sophie climbed into the taxi and settled herself beside Emily on the backseat. They waited, leaning forward to see out the rain-streaked windows of the taxi, watching Georges and Aunt Juliette in the doorway of the house. The driver stood holding the car door, the rain dripping from the shiny peak of his cap, an expression of sleepy resignation on his face.

Georges and Juliette clasped each other in a tight embrace. Neither spoke.

At length Juliette disengaged herself. She held him away from her, her hands on his shoulders. Then she leaned and kissed him. 'Go on, now, or you'll miss your train. I've got plenty to do here. I'll be too busy to think.'

He couldn't speak. He let go of her hands and stepped into the street. He put his hat on and climbed into the taxi beside Sophie. The driver shut the door and went around and got into the cab. He closed his own door and tugged his cap down and settled himself. He engaged the gears and the taxi gave a lurch and moved off.

Juliette stood at the door waving, a thin stooped old woman in an old-fashioned, grey-striped dress and black apron reaching to her ankles, her straggly grey hair caught up untidily in a headscarf. A young housewife filling her bucket at the hydrant on the corner at the end of the arcades lifted her head and watched the taxi until it turned at the bridge and went out of sight.

Aunt Juliette went back inside and closed her door. She went along the cold passage to the kitchen. She lifted the lid on the vegetable stock she had set to simmer on the stove earlier and took a wooden spoon and stirred it, leaning and sniffing the steam. She replaced the lid and opened the fire door of the stove. She selected pieces of split wood from the alcove and shoved them into the grate one at a time, poking them about until each piece sat in the fire to her satisfaction. She closed the fire door and wiped her hands on her apron. She stood looking out of the window at the river. The stone bridge, the women kneeling under the shelters at their laundry, their hands white with cold, their shouts and laughter and the drumming of their heavy wooden buckets on the timber slats.

She stood at the window for a long time, listening to the small disturbances of the house subsiding around her. Eventually she turned from the window and reached and took down her omelette pan from its hook beside the stove. She set the pan on the hotplate and scooped a quantity of lard from the stoneware bowl with a wooden spatula. She watched the pale fat slide across the scoured bottom of the pan. Behind her the brass ferrule of Madame Elder's cane caught the light where it hung on the back of the empty chair by the window. 'That's that, then,' Aunt Juliette said. She reached and took a brown-shelled egg from the saucer and cracked it against the rim of a china bowl.

~ PART SIX ~

HER PAINTED TABLE

O N E

—◠—

Emily was alone in the apartment. She was sitting at the table by the window overlooking the courtyard. The sun was shining through the window, the pigeons circling restlessly — around and around they went, settling, then rising again, as if they sensed the approach of spring. Emily's green morocco writing case was open on the table in front of her, beside her the unfolded pages of Olive Kallen's November letter from New York.

Emily leaned over the fresh sheet of writing paper and began:

Rue Saint-Dominique, Paris
3 March 1924
Dear Olive,

At last I am home and have come out of the silence. But where have I been all winter and why have I been silent? I do not imagine you are still waiting for a reply from me, but have surely settled the question of your assistant long ago. I have been in Chartres since early December. I know you will be disappointed to learn that I have done no more on *The Secular Perpetua*. Unlike you, for me there was no question of working until the last day. I became ill and my baby was born a month premature. Now I am back in Paris, as you see — the wonderful, vast grey anonymity of Paris — where I have begun to think again! I have a beautiful little girl. We have called her Marie. So I have become a mother. Am I still the woman you met in Sidi bou-Saïd? The woman I was before I became a mother, with the same hopes and enthusiasms for my own life? This is a question that only time will answer. And perhaps there will never be a satisfactory answer to it. When my mother gave birth to me, did she feel then as I feel now? In the presence of our child's needs we are women divided against ourselves. Is this, indeed, a secret all mothers share but dare not disclose to their children? For women such as I — for I cannot stand so unequivocally, so firmly and heroically, aside from the conventional course of life as you do — must the birth of a child signify the end of our own future? I know it will require more courage than I have ever needed to answer this question for myself. And whichever way I answer it, there will be no escaping a sacrifice I scarcely dare think of. Either I must abandon myself or I must abandon my husband. If we would live well for ourselves as also for our families, then the state of motherhood makes of our lives a terrible contradiction. But enough of that.

I have just read again your wonderful letter. Your faith in me, your enthusiasm for *The Secular Perpetua*, the excitement you express for my ideas, these are more sustaining to me than I can possibly tell you. One important thing I have understood about Perpetua without doing any more reading. Tertullian, and the commentators since, were mistaken — whether willfully or not I cannot say, but mistaken all the same — in dealing with her hideous end in the arena as if it were her courage in the face of death that signified the climax of her sacrifice. The truth is surely rather different. For she herself records the true moment of her sacrifice when she tells us how she passed her infant through the bars of her cell to her father, knowing then that she was never to see the child again. Any mother might have told Tertullian this, if he had cared to listen. Plainly, to understand some truths of history, scholarship is not needed, and may even be a hindrance. The mystery of Perpetua's story is preserved for us in the moment when she hands over her child, and not, as Tertullian would have us believe, in her eager embrace of death for the sake of eternal life. To describe her as a martyr, as he does, is to silence her. To understand why she sacrificed her motherhood – a far more elusive enterprise – will be to hear her story at last, as she surely hoped we would hear it when, condemned to the beasts, she wrote her desperate journal in that cell beneath the arena. Who did she write it for except for us? I am convinced we have not heard her story yet . . . But you see! Writing to you inspires me! Shall I ever be free of this until I find the end of her story? This strange, elusive, puzzling enticement that I am presented with? This half-imagined story of hers? A thing that cannot exist until it exists complete in my own thoughts!

My difficulties seem no less now than they did when I first wrote to you. Indeed, without the fever of impatience that possessed me after my return from Sidi bou-Saïd in October (when I was blinded to the realities of my situation) my difficulties are even greater now than they were then. I have only a short time left in Paris before we sail for Sydney.

It is when we need courage that we fear we have none. At other times we believe we have courage in abundance and that nothing has the power to subdue our spirit.

Emily ended the letter. She walked around to the post office in the rue de Grenelle and posted it. On the way back she bought a packet of cigarettes. She didn't return at once to the apartment but walked for an hour on the Invalides, then went into a café and ordered a coffee. She sat in the window of the café smoking and looking out at the busy street.

When she got back to the apartment later, Sophie was cooking in the kitchen. Emily looked in. 'Where's Marie?'

Sophie sliced a chicken leg through at the knuckle and drew out the white tendon. She looked up. 'She's sleeping, madame.'

Emily went into the small room. Georges's crib had been crated and sent from Chartres with the other pieces direct to the warehouse at Le Havre in readiness for shipping to Australia. Sophie had corralled Marie safely on the bed between a pillow and the folded eiderdown. Marie lay on her side, one chubby arm across her chest, the other held out, her fingers clutching a corner of the pillowcase. Careful not to disturb her, Emily sat on the bed. The light in the room was dim, filled with shadows, an uncertain illumination admitted through the dirty skylight. Emily sat unmoving, gazing at her daughter for more than an hour.

When she heard Georges come in, she got up off the bed and eased her shoulders. She went out into the sitting room.

He dropped his hat on the table by the window. He was breathing hard from the climb up the six flights of stairs. He looked at her. 'Your father was right. The imperial connection held. The English firm, Dorman Long . . . They got the bridge.'

It was after midnight by the time Georges finished the last of his correspondence. He put down his pen and reached and switched off the lamp by his elbow. He rubbed his eyes with his fingers and sat in the dark gazing out at the night sky. One or two lights still burned in the windows of the apartments across the way. He got up and listened at Sophie's door, then he went in to their bedroom. He closed the door behind him. He removed his watch from his waistcoat pocket and placed it on the dressing table. He slipped his braces off his shoulders and pulled his shirt over his head. He finished undressing and eased himself into the bed beside her.

Emily whispered. 'Did you get everything done?'

'I thought you'd be asleep by now.'

'I couldn't sleep.'

They lay there beside each other in the dark, still and wary. When his foot touched hers, she did not move her foot away but left it there, the small curl of her toes resting against the bony contour of his ankle.

He felt for her hand.

She lay with her eyes open, looking at the rectangle of glowing sky through the window. She moved her toes against his ankle. He reached across and laid his hand on her hip, his cold fingers playing over the sensitive skin of her groin. She turned to him, his shoulder and the rounding of his chest against her breasts. They kissed, careful, tentative, uncertain – like strangers who have yet to know each other, their feet touching, this their only certainty . . .

When they had made love and lay recovering their breath, he asked, 'I didn't hurt you, did I?'

'No. Of course not. Please don't talk about it. You'll spoil it.'

The warm smell of their intimacy rose between them from the sheets.

When she was certain he slept, she slipped her legs over the side of the bed and stood up. She went out into the dark kitchen and took a glass from the shelf above the sink and filled it at the tap. She stood drinking the cold water, looking out through the narrow window at the night. There was a smell, comforting and familiar, of gas mingled with Sophie's stockpot and her own bedwarmth. She set the empty glass on the tiles and filled an enamel bowl with water. She lifted her nightdress and squatted over the bowl beside the cupboard. She douched herself thoroughly, the dread of another pregnancy vivid in her mind. She dried herself with a towel and emptied the bowl into the sink. She went back into the bedroom and closed the door and got into bed. Georges was snoring.

She lay beside him, wakeful, gazing into the darkness of the room, the deeper shadows of the bed and their shapes within the cheval glass. She heard a bell somewhere strike the first hour of the day. Later Marie began to cry. There was the sound of Sophie's door opening. Light shone around the cracks of the bedroom door. Marie's cry grew louder, touched with rage. Georges stirred beside her. Marie's crying ceased abruptly, and Emily imagined her eagerly taking the warm milk. The light went out and she heard Sophie's door close. Emily's mind refused to still. Her thoughts whirled around and around, the same thoughts, the same dilemma, around and around like the restless pigeons circling the courtyard, longing to settle but unable to.

TWO

—◆—

Georges reached around her and placed on the dressing table in front of her a jewelry box. The box was in the shape of a three-quarters moon and was covered in faded purple velvet. He leaned and opened the box. A double string of pearls lay circled in a bed of violet silk. 'They were Mother's,' he said. 'My father gave them to her when they were first married.' He took hold of the gold clips between each thumb and forefinger and lifted the pearls out, holding them to the light for her, suspended in a loop from his fingers. Then he placed them around her neck.

The mock-bamboo lamp stood on the dressing table, the light of its bare bulb hard and direct in her face and on the creamy lace of her chemise at the rise of her breasts. The pearls were cold against her skin. She touched them. 'They're lovely.' Her gaze met his in the mirror, his grey eyes uncertain, his mother's eyes. She smiled, resisting him. 'I'd rather not wear them, if you don't mind.'

'Wear them for me.'

Her hand against the pearls, the plain band of her wedding ring. She was remembering Madame Elder dying in her bed, the click-click of her last breaths, as if ivory counters were being set with deliberation upon a glass table, until the last of them. 'I don't know why,' she said, no longer meeting his gaze. 'But I've never really liked wearing jewelry.'

He lifted the pearls from her neck and set them in the box. 'You wear that brooch of Antoine's all the time.' He contradicted her without rancour, an observation. He went over to the chest of drawers and took the freshly starched stand-up collar from its tissue and put it around his neck. He reached behind him and inserted the back stud.

She sat looking at the pearls in the open box. She closed the lid of the box and put it to one side and picked up her hairbrush and began to brush her hair. When she had finished brushing her hair, she put on her makeup.

Georges sat on the edge of the bed tying his shoelaces.

She got up from the dressing table and went over to the wardrobe. She unhooked the hanger from the bar and lifted out the dress in its cotton cover. She laid it on the bed and undid the studs on the cover and slipped the cover off, lifting the dress away. As the dress slid out of its cover, she caught the faint smell of the perfume she had worn the night of the dance at Richmond Hill. She stood holding the dress up, turning it around and looking at it.

Georges watched her.

The dark blue silk shone in the light of the bamboo lamp, soft and heavy and falling against itself, a river of blue light. She closed the wardrobe door and held the dress against herself, examining her reflection in the cheval glass. Georges stood behind her watching.

'I may not fit into it now.'

She rucked the long skirt up, bunching the material against her arms, and she reached in and took hold of the bodice and she lifted the dress over her head and eased it down over her tummy and her hips. She reached behind her and held the eyehook closed at her waist, turning to look at her reflection. The dark blue silk hung against her body, glossy and smooth, reminding her of Melbourne and the night of the dance. She made a face at her reflection, secretly pleased with the effect. 'I could wear my red one.'

Georges stood up. 'Don't take it off!' He stepped across and took her in his arms. He held her and kissed her on the mouth. He searched in her eyes, remembering. 'There was a storm. Then it rained. The lanterns danced in your eyes on the lawn. There was the smell of the peppermint gum.'

She touched his chest and eased herself from his embrace. 'I'll have to do my makeup again.'

He stepped away from her and stood looking at her. He watched her put on her makeup. 'You always seem to be just out of my reach,' he said. He turned and took up his waistcoat and put his arms through the holes and shrugged it into place on his shoulders. He took his watch from the dresser and threaded the T end of the chain through the middle buttonhole and slipped the watch into the pocket of his waistcoat. He looked at himself in the mirror, tugging the flyaway points of the waistcoat, then he turned and took his coat from the back of the chair and put it on.

They emerged at last from the bedroom dressed in their finery, Emily in her dark blue mantle and Georges beside her with his white silk scarf and his high collar – an almost theatrical elegance in the formal pairing of their uncertainties, as if they were to undergo a mysterious initiation.

Sophie was sitting in the green tapestry chair in front of the gas fire, her feet resting on the footstool. She was darning the heel of a black stocking. The marquetry sewing box was open beside her. She looked up at them and smiled, her eyes shining in the gaslight.

'What do you think of us, Sophie?' Emily said, her arm through Georges's arm, standing before Sophie to receive her approval.

'Why, madame, you look as solemn as English royalty,' Sophie said. She laughed and bent forward and covered her mouth with her hand.

Georges pulled his watch from his waistcoat pocket and he opened it and looked at it. 'It's time to go,' he said.

The taxi pulled up in the rue de Clichy a few yards from the entrance to the Casino de Paris. It was a fine mild night. Lines of motor taxis and horse cabs were drawn up along the curb. A crowd of fashionably dressed revellers milled about in front of the casino and the brightly illuminated entrance to Le Perroquet next door. A man in a green cap and white gloves came forward and opened the door of the taxi. Emily gathered her skirt and wrapped her mantel around her. She ducked her head and put one foot on the running board and stepped out onto the cobbles. Georges got out of the taxi behind her. He took her arm and they crossed the forecourt together. Above the glazed doors a green-and-red electric parrot opened and closed its beak. The doorman in his green-and-gold tailcoat held the door and saluted them gravely. They went into the wide foyer. They left their coats and scarves at the cloakroom and went on in to the restaurant.

The orchestra was playing a softly syncopated Paul Whiteman arrangement, the snare drums holding the rhythm against the wandering melancholy of a saxophone. Couples revolved under the chandeliers on the dance floor, the pastel colors of the women's dresses mingling with the black and white of the men's evening clothes. There was a hubbub of talk and laughter, the clink of glasses and cutlery from the crowded tables that surrounded the dance floor on three sides, a blue haze of cigarette smoke drifting under the chandeliers. Georges turned to her and pointed to a table against the mirrored wall. Léon and Antoine were sitting there. Léon saw them. He waved his cigar at them. They made their way across.

Antoine and Léon stood up and stepped away from the small circular table. Léon bowed and came forward and took Emily's hand. He bent and kissed her fingers, looking into her eyes and smiling. He was wearing a monocle in his left eye and a violet orchid in his buttonhole. In his white tie and tailcoat he was large and elegant. He held her fingers delicately, 'You are more beautiful than ever, my dear. Motherhood suits you.' He looked about the restaurant. 'Soft lights and sweet music for your farewell to Paris.'

'This is very generous of you, Léon,' Georges said.

Léon shrugged. 'I practically live here.'

Emily turned to Antoine. He took her hands in his and leaned and kissed her cheek. He pulled out a chair for her and held it until she sat. He sat to her left. He was not wearing evening clothes but a dark lounge suit. His shirt had a green-and-white striped-collar and his tie was a matching green, silk and crumpled. There was a gold-and-diamond pin in the centre of his tie. When he sat, his jacket collar stood away from his neck and shoulders as if his coat were several sizes too large for him. The long wispy hanks of his faded hair drifted against his cheeks. He was pale and there were grainy shadows in the lines under his eyes. He sat with his chair pushed back from the table, his small shoulders rounded, one leg crossed over the other, his foot beating time to the dance music. He took out his cigarette case from the inside breast pocket of his jacket and selected one of his thin hand-rolled cigarettes and lit it. He leaned back and blew the smoke toward the high, distant ceiling. Emily thought he was probably a little drunk. Georges and Léon were talking. Antoine signalled the waiter and when the waiter came over he asked him to bring a bottle of champagne to their table.

Emily looked across at Georges. He was telling Léon about his plans for their life in Sydney. She heard him say, 'A new beginning.' She looked away and opened her bag and took out her cigarettes. She held the cigarette to her lips. Antoine struck a match and held it for her and she drew in the smoke.

Antoine put his hand on hers. 'You're trembling.'

She looked into his eyes. 'I've made my decision.'

'Have you told Georges?'

'Not yet.'

'I see.' He looked across at Georges, his eyes narrowed against the smoke of his cigarette.

The waiter leaned between them and filled their glasses with the sparkling yellow wine. He moved around the table and filled Georges's glass, then Léon's. Léon lifted his glass, waiting for their attention. 'God bless you, dear friends all!'

They touched their glasses and looked at each other and drank the cold wine. Georges put down his glass and stood up. He pushed his chair back and came around the table and offered his arm to Emily. She stood and took his arm and they went together on to the dance floor. He held her at the waist, his hand on the curve of her back, the heaviness of the blue silk of her gown under his fingers.

A beautiful young woman with dark hair sauntered onto the rostrum. She took the microphone in both her hands and she smiled and looked around the room and began to sing, her voice lazy, slow, weighted with desire, with the yearning of the music. 'When day is done and shadows fall,' she sang, her gaze roaming the room, touching a man here and there, a melancholy smile on her carmine lips, as if she really thought she would find her lover, 'I dream of you . . .'

Georges held Emily close. They danced until the song ended. Then they danced to the next song. They did not talk. At the edge of the dance floor she stopped and stood away from him, his hand still on her hip, her hand holding his hand, and she looked at him. When she spoke, her voice was shaky and filled with strain. 'You were surprised when I said I'd marry you that night in the garden at Richmond Hill.'

He stared at her. 'Surprised? . . . I was astonished. I didn't think I had a chance with you.'

'I was surprised too,' she said. 'I surprised myself.' Over Georges's shoulder she could see Antoine watching them. Léon was standing beside the table talking animatedly to a man and a woman. He was gesticulating. The man and the woman were looking at him and laughing.

A woman dancing on the arm of a man bumped Georges lightly. She turned to him and smiled, apologizing, and danced away.

Emily said, 'I'm not coming back to Australia with you.'

He looked at her. 'I know.'

'How can you know? What do you mean, you know?'

'I've always known.' He shrugged. 'Since that night really. Neither of us believed it.'

'I believed it,' she said.

'No you didn't. We were both surprised. It was a . . . We were distracted . . . I don't know.' He looked into her eyes, the fact of her statement becoming real. 'So you're not coming back then?'

'No.'

He said, 'Jesus!'

'I'm sorry.'

He gazed down at her. 'I could compel you.'

'You won't do that.'

'No,' he said. 'I won't. But why not? Why shouldn't I? Most men would.'

'You're not like most men.'

'I love you,' he said.

'And I love you.'

'Why then?' He stared at her, his shoulders hunched, his hands in hers, his eyes filled with pain and puzzlement. 'It's ridiculous. Can't we just go on? Things don't have to be perfect.'

'It needn't be forever.'

'If you don't come with me on Thursday, you know it will be forever.'

'This is horrible. I knew it would be horrible.'

'Why?' he said. 'Why do this? Why torture ourselves?'

'It's me. It's not your fault. I don't know why. I just know I shall never be content if I don't do this.'

'Content? For Christ's sake, no one's content!'

'Sophie's content. Aunt Juliette is content. They are content with who they are. You are too. I can't pretend to be who I'm not.'

'How do you know they're content? You don't know that.'

The band was playing an old-fashioned ragtime. Another couple bumped them.

'We're in the way here.' He took her hand and led her off the dance floor toward the table. She saw their reflection in the mirrored wall – elegant, even distinguished, arm in arm, a married couple, an image of propriety and substance. A black man in a white tuxedo had taken the microphone from the young woman. He sang a song her father had played on the gramophone. 'Ole man Johnson's jazzin' aroun'. Don't push him, Don't touch him, or he'll fall to de groun' . . .' The dancers jumped around, the women's skirts flying up, laughing and dragging at each other, miming the song with the singer.

Georges stopped abruptly. 'Would you have come back with me if I'd got the bridge?'

'No.'

They waited to pass while some people were seated. 'You've already organized everything with Antoine and this woman Kallen, then.' He sounded angry, bitter, suspicious.

'No. Antoine's done nothing. He doesn't know. Nothing's been arranged. I've told no one but you.'

'Your mother knew,' he said.

'Knew what? What do you mean?'

'That day at the beach when I didn't swim after you. She said it wouldn't do for me not to follow you. I've often thought about that. She wanted us to be married, but she was afraid it wasn't going to work for us. I think she was trying to warn me that you wouldn't follow me.' They made their way between the crowded tables. 'And what if Antoine and this American woman won't help you? How will you manage?'

'Father will help me. He'll give me an allowance. Or perhaps I'll apply for a scholarship to Cambridge.' She turned and appealed to him, 'I'd be miserable in Sydney being a housewife and having lots of children. So long as we're a family, it is never going to be convenient for me to do this work. I see that now. My misery would eventually destroy all of us.'

He looked at her. 'We all make some sort of compromise. We make a sacrifice so we can have what we want. That is what we do. It is not a matter of being content.'

A thin blue taper of smoke rose from Antoine's cigarette. He stood up and greeted them. The taper of smoke broke into a frenzy about his head. He waited until Emily was seated, then sat, the cigarette between his nicotine-stained fingers thin and mangled and brown. 'Léon's gone off with some friends for a while,' he said. He reached and lifted his glass and drank, avoiding looking at them. There was an open bottle of Batard Montrachet on the table by his elbow and there were plates of oysters on ice and purple anchovies and blood-coloured slices of chitterling sausage. He reached and lifted an oyster in its shell and slipped it into his mouth and swallowed. Georges watched him.

When Antoine looked up, Georges said, 'Emily's not coming back to Australia with me.'

Antoine leaned and coughed into his hand. He said nothing. His eyes were tired, the skin of his cheeks oily with fatigue. His clothes looked disordered and rumpled, as if he had slept in them. He reached for the wine bottle and refilled his glass and held it up and looked at Georges. Georges shook his head. He looked at Emily. She nodded. He leaned and filled her glass. 'It's the wine we drank at the Brasserie Équivoque that day,' he said, and he leaned back in his chair and drank from his glass, his eyes half-closed, his gaze touching them lightly, examining their pain, their reality, their sorrow.

'You're not surprised,' Georges said. 'So don't pretend to be. I'll provide Emily with an allowance.' He waited. 'Will you take care of her for me?'

Antoine pushed the faded strands of hair from his eyes. 'If that's what you want.'

Emily looked at Antoine and then at Georges, sensing the initiative withdrawn from her. Seeing in the manner of their exchange, in their agreement, something of a men's transaction excluding her, their friendship encountering a test they were resolved to meet with honour, with manly reticence. It was their friendship. That was what she felt, the subterranean silence of this peculiar diplomacy, and she felt herself blushing with anger. She turned to Antoine, 'You don't have to help me if you don't want to. I can look after myself.'

Antoine gazed sorrowfully into his wine.

Georges frowned, pained, uneasy, waiting for time to pass. Waiting for it to end.

Antoine looked up slowly and gazed at her. A smile played about his lips, as if he were tempted to voice a private amusement. His forefinger beat time to the music on the rim of his glass.

She was reminded of his distress that night on the deck of the *Gibel Sarsar* when she insisted on sharing her secret with him – the power to destroy Georges and to destroy friendship. A power he did not desire. 'I've no idea how you live,' she said, her voice tight, emotional, unfriendly. She lifted her glass and drank the wine. 'You keep yourself so private, Antoine. We are all in compartments for you. Even at Sidi bou-Saïd.' She saw him flinch and shift on his chair and she felt Georges's questioning gaze on her, his disapproval. 'I've never seen your apartment here in Paris except from the outside, once. I can't picture how you live from day to day. Yet you know everything about us.'

Antoine's finger had ceased to beat time. He was still, one small rounded shoulder higher than the other, as if to shield himself from a blow. He gave a small amused laugh, leaning and coughing into his hand.

'You want everything to be clear. But everything isn't clear. Some things are murky.' He looked at her. 'Aren't they? Some things are not as clear as they might be, are they? You're a mother and here you are about to abandon your child. This is a mystery. This is not something that is clear.'

'I'm not abandoning Marie,' she said and laughed. 'Sophie will take care of her while I work.'

Antoine looked at Georges.

Georges put his hand over Emily's hand. 'No,' he said. 'This is your decision. Not Sophie's. Not Marie's.' He was calm, certain of his ground now. 'If you stay behind, you stay on your own.' He withdrew his hand and reached for the bottle of wine. He filled his glass and drank and put his glass down. 'Sophie and my daughter sail with me for Sydney on the *Ochambeau* on Thursday.' He took out his gold cigarette case and withdrew a cigarette and lit it. 'These are conditions I *shall* compel you to accept.' He looked at her, more distant now – challenged, he had become at once master of his situation. 'You will change your mind, of course, and come with us.' He drew on his cigarette, a bitterness in his eyes.

Emily looked at Antoine.

Antoine lifted his shoulders. 'He can do it.'

She turned to Georges. 'Your daughter?' She let the question hang in the air.

Antoine reached and put his hand on her arm. He gripped her. 'Don't!' he pleaded.

She pulled her arm free. 'Why not? Why shouldn't I? Yes, I do want things to be clear. You're right. And as I'm to be compelled, why don't we have everything clear between us?' She saw the dismay in his eyes.

He looked away and leaned and stubbed his cigarette in the ashtray.

She turned and looked at Georges. He sat smoking his cigarette, watching her, the green chandeliers spinning slowly in his eyes . . . With one word she could bring it all undone for him. His illusion of certainty. She was seeing Bertrand and the crypt that day, the rich smell of ripening fruit, the wheaten straw, the woman she had been then . . . If she were to tell him, where would his certainties be? 'Your daughter?' she repeated. She was suddenly tired. She reached for her glass and lifted it to her lips and drank. She closed her eyes, the taste of peaches blossoming in her mouth . . . She set the glass on the table. 'So, I am to be compelled.' She did not look at either of them. 'I want to go home.'

Georges and Antoine exchanged a look. Georges stood and put his arm around Emily's shoulders and took her hand. 'Come, I'll take you home.'

She stood up. 'Goodnight, Antoine.'

He murmured miserably, 'Goodnight.' He sat alone at the table watching them leave. As they went out the door, the young woman came back and took the microphone in her hands. There was a scattering of applause and she looked around the room and smiled her melancholy smile. Antoine smoked his cigarette and the beautiful singer sang, 'Chicago, Chicago, you toddlin' town . . .,' as if the words of her song contained all the meaning in the world.

THREE

~ ~

The two old men grasped a handle each and they grunted and lifted the heavy trunk and carried it out the door. Madame Barbier followed them across the landing. She leaned on the bannisters and called to them to be careful. She turned and came back into the apartment. She stood with her hands on her hips looking around the sitting room. 'You've got everything, then, have you? The fire's turned off, is it?'

Georges, Sophie, and Emily were dressed in their street clothes. Emily was holding Marie against her shoulder. Marie was wearing the lambswool bonnet Catherine Stanton had knitted for her and was wrapped in the heavy crocheted shawl. She slept against Emily's shoulder.

They followed Madame Barbier out the door. She stood aside and let them pass and they trooped down the stairs behind the old men. Georges carried his black briefcase. He held his free hand to Emily's elbow, steadying her. Sophie followed them. She was carrying the bag packed with Marie's things for the journey. Madame Barbier closed the door of the apartment and followed them. Her keys rattled as she dropped them into her apron pocket.

They came out into the courtyard. The old men were helping the taxi driver lift the trunk onto the roof. Two suitcases were already strapped to the rack. It was just breaking day, the air still and cold. The square patch of sky above the rooftops was a silvery grey. Except for their subdued voices the courtyard was silent, the shutters closed against the tiers of windows, the sleeping occupants of the apartments. Georges set his briefcase on the cobbles and took Marie from Emily. He waited while she got into the taxi, then handed Marie in to her. A black-and-white cat watched them from the iron bench under the robinia tree. Georges paid the old men and they looked at the coins in their hands and pocketed the money and stood and watched. Madame Barbier and Georges went off a few paces from the taxi and spoke together. Georges handed her something and they shook hands and she leaned and put her hand to his cheek and kissed him. He came back to the taxi and climbed in and closed the door. As the taxi went out through the covered way, Georges turned in his seat and looked back.

The taxi turned right along rue Saint-Dominique. Across the street the baker stood at his lighted door in his apron smoking a cigarette. He watched them go by, then flicked the butt of his cigarette into the gutter and turned and went back inside his shop. A street cleaner with his covered cart was the only person on the street. They came out onto the open space of the Invalides and turned left and went down to the purple river and along the Quai d'Orsay. They crossed the river at the Pont de la Concorde and went on past the deserted arcades and the obelisk. There was no one about. Sophie looked out the window of the taxi. Georges watched Emily. She was gazing at the sleeping baby. No one spoke.

In the echoing cavern of the Gare Saint-Lazare they saw Antoine waiting at the barrier. He waved and hurried forward to meet them. They embraced and exchanged a greeting. The porter waited behind them with the trolley piled with their luggage. Georges showed their tickets to the official at the barrier and they went on to the platform. The Le Havre express stood waiting. There was a long sigh of escaping steam and a white cloud rolled along the platform toward them, dissipating among the legs of the officials and the passengers and their friends who had come to see them off. Porters shouted for way, trundling iron-wheeled trolleys piled with suitcases, trunks, and hatboxes. Among the vivid labels on the luggage Emily saw the large yellow lettering on a crimson ground, OCHAMBEAU/SYDNEY. Excited children ran along the platform shouting to each other, their anxious parents calling to them. A disembodied echoing of voices, shouts, instructions, and sudden laughter mingled with the rumbling of machinery in the lofty spaces above them. And over all a smell of steam and coalsmoke, the smell of travelling.

Georges went ahead along the platform with the guard. Emily and Sophie and Antoine followed. They stopped at the open door of a first-class compartment and Georges stood aside and waited for Emily. He took her arm and helped her up the step. He reached for the rail and swung up behind her. Antoine gestured to Sophie, inviting her to go ahead of him. 'Thank you, Monsieur Carpeaux.' They followed Georges and Emily into the compartment. Emily sat by the far window with Marie in her arms. Georges and Antoine went out again and Georges instructed the porter which bags were to travel with them in the compartment and which were to be taken to the baggage car. They returned with two small suitcases and Georges's briefcase. They reached these up onto the luggage rack above the seats. Georges took off his hat and put it on his briefcase. He ran his fingers through his hair and turned and sat in the window seat opposite Emily.

They waited. Antoine and Sophie looked out the windows at the busy platform. Emily gazed at Marie's slumbering features. Georges watched her. Once it seemed Antoine would speak. They all looked at him expectantly, but he said nothing. The guard came out of his wooden office on the platform and stood with his watch in his hand, solemnly considering the time.

Georges leaned across and put his hand on Emily's knee. She looked up at him. 'You're sure you've got all the addresses in a safe place?'

Antoine and Sophie avoided looking at them.

'Yes,' Emily reassured him. She put her hand on his. 'I put everything you gave me in my writing case.'

'Aunt Juliette expects you to go down to Chartres to stay with her for a few days before you leave. She reminded me again on the telephone last night. She'll be very disappointed if you don't go.'

'I shall go. Of course I shall,' Emily said firmly, quite as if she shared his faith that the old house in the rue des Oiseaux was the one immovable structure they could rely upon, for now and forever — as if the household of the Elders were something indisputable and moral, a reality beyond their questions and their doubts and uncertainties.

Antoine stood up.

They turned and looked at him. His image was reflected for them in the glass of the compartment door and in the window of the corridor, as if his ghosts had come to attend him. The guard came along the corridor behind Antoine. He stood in the door and saluted them. 'Two minutes to departure, ladies and gentlemen. Only passengers traveling to Le Havre may remain on the train.' He saluted again and turned on his heel and went on to the next compartment. They heard him repeating his message along the carriage.

Antoine stepped forward. Georges stood and they looked at each other and embraced, clasping each other tightly at the shoulders. Neither spoke. They stepped apart. There were tears in Georges's eyes. 'Good-bye, Georges,' Antoine said, and he turned to Sophie and held out his hand. 'Good-bye, Sophie.'

She reached and took his hand. 'Goodbye, Monsieur Carpeaux,' she said gravely. She was wearing the silver bangle Emily had given her.

'You'll be an Australian next time we meet,' he said.

'Yes.'

Georges said, 'Will you leave us for a moment, Sophie?'

She looked at him and followed Antoine into the corridor.

Georges sat in the seat beside Emily. He leaned over Marie and Emily turned to him and they kissed. Marie murmured and shifted restlessly between them. She opened her eyes and began to cry.

'You can still change your mind,' Georges said. 'Antoine can have your things sent on to Sydney. It can be managed.'

Emily held Marie close and rocked her. 'Hush, little one,' she said. She saw Sophie watching through the corridor window. She lifted her chin and Sophie nodded and stepped into the compartment. Sophie came over to the window and leaned down.

Emily held Marie, folding her in her embrace, pressing her cheek to the silky warmth of the infant's cheek.

Marie wailed and struggled.

Sophie reached and put her hands under Marie and she lifted her away and held her. 'Don't worry, madame, I've got a warm bottle in the bag.'

The guard's whistle shrilled.

Emily stood up. Georges took her hand and she stepped across to the door. Antoine went ahead of her onto the platform. He turned and reached up and she took his hand and went down the two steps. On the platform she turned to Antoine. 'She's stopped crying,' she said.

He put his arm around her shoulders and held her.

The guard slammed the door and turned the handle. Georges let down the window and leaned out. The train lurched and began to move. Emily and Georges looked at each other. 'Good-bye,' she said.

The train gathered speed and rolled away along the platform. Georges leaned from the window, his hand raised, 'You can still change your mind,' he called.

They watched him until the curve of the tracks took him from their sight.

Emily leaned against Antoine. They turned and walked away toward the barrier.

'What have I done? I am a monster.' Her voice was stricken with disbelief, regret, bewilderment, sorrow.

Antoine tightened his arm around her shoulders. 'No. You spared him,' he said.

Outside on the forecourt of the station they climbed into a taxi. Antoine gave the driver the address of his apartment in the Quai des Célestins.

F O U R

❦

Sidi bou-Saïd, 17 June 1924

My Dearest,

It is the hour of siesta once again and I am sitting at my blue-painted table in this enchanted room surrounded by my books and my notes. The house and the village are silent. In the distance out my window the dark cypresses are still and the waters of the gulf are a calm pastel blue. There is one small white cloud in the sky. It is all that is left of yesterday's storm. Now I no longer wake each morning with the feeling that I must apologize secretly for the way I will live the day that lies ahead of me. We go on, wounded and changed, and we do not expect to ever again be whole and without wounds as we once were. And we are astonished that our grief and our dismay and our loss permit us to go on and even to be happy. Yet that is how we live. Today for the first time my journal begins 'My Dearest' because I have understood that I am not writing to myself. Can one ever really write only to oneself? When I sat down a moment ago to begin my journal entry for today, I acknowledged truthfully for the first time that it is to you that I am always speaking in this record of my thoughts and emotions, and that this is the reason I have been able to keep this daily account so assiduously. Your dear grandfather once urged me to keep a journal, a record of my travels. But I was not able to do it and I threw its pages into the sea. It unnerved me to find myself writing something that was to have no end except the end of my own life. As I wrote, I felt myself then to be already the old woman who would one day look back upon those pages with nostalgia and regret for the loss of her youth. Now as I write I imagine you when you will at last come to read this letter-without-an-end, almost a young woman and already at the age of unbelief – those precious treacherous years when we at last challenge our unquestioning childhood beliefs. Those years when to believe ceases to be the easiest thing for us and becomes the hardest thing. Then we spend the rest of our lives searching for the conditions of faith we once possessed so effortlessly and have lost. Those years when I see now that you will want to know me, your mother, and will discover that I am not lost to you. For you and I there will be another way to be a mother, another way to be a daughter. When you are ready, your father will let you come and stay with me at my little apartment in rue Saint-Dominique. Then I shall give you this letter-without-an-end. And when you have read it, we shall be friends.

How does a mother reach a point of such estrangement that she abandons her child? How can I expect you to understand this? Believe me when I tell you that there is no sudden leap to such a place but a daily increment over time. One goes by small degrees, one step at a time, until one stands at last on the place from which one refuses to be moved. And one is more astonished than anyone to see it is oneself who does this. This was Perpetua's gift to me. It is my gift to you. It is why Tertullian, and those who followed him, required her silence. What she did could never be acknowledged. For she broke the chain by which mothers are compelled. When you have read this journal, you will know then that my terrible decision was not the end of our love but was its difficult, painful beginning.

You are never forgotten, my darling, but are with me every day
of my life.

Emily saw the movement from the corner of her eye. She stopped writing
and turned and looked out the window. Antoine was walking along the
gravel path beside the oleanders. He was smoking a cigarette and was in
his shirtsleeves. Emily watched him. He reached the wall at the end of
the garden and stood leaning on the parapet looking down at the village
street below. She put down her pen and got up from the table. She went
out and crossed the courtyard with the copper fountain and went down
the stone steps to the hall. Antoine heard her footsteps on the gravel
and he turned and watched her approach.

She stood beside him and they looked down into the street together.
A group of village boys were gathered outside the doorway of the café.
They were watching a donkey and cart toiling slowly up the hill toward
them, their heads turned at the same angle, like a flock of grounded gulls
in their faded clothes, their bodies alert and expectant. Antoine offered
her a cigarette and she shook her head. He lit a fresh cigarette from the
butt of his old one and he dropped the butt into the gravel at his feet
and ground it with the heel of his shoe. She put her arm through his
and pressed his arm to her side. They leaned on the parapet together
watching the boys and the dog and the donkey and cart approaching up
the hill. They did not speak. The sun was warm on her back through her
blouse and there was the familiar fragrance of cloves in the smoke of his
cigarette. The siesta was coming to an end. Behind them the members
of the household were waking from their sleep.

ACKNOWLEDGMENTS

I am grateful to the Australia Council for their support of a four-year Senior Fellowship.

The idea for this book had its origins in a brief journal my mother left to me, in which were fragmentary references to her life as a girl in a teaching convent in Chantilly and later as a maid and governess in Paris. In these few pages my mother appeared to me as a young woman ardently in search of a reason for living. My chief debt is to her.

I would like to thank a number of people for their generous assistance during my visit to Tunisia. Firstly Mr Bernie Robertson, Australian Consul for Tunisia, and Moncef Jaafar and his colleagues at the Ministre des Affaires Étrangères. Nejib Ben Lasreq, from the Institut National d'Archéologie et Arts, acted as my generous guide and friend, and Mounir Moulay drove me to places in his beautiful country that I would not otherwise have been able to see.

I am particularly grateful to Tim Mathiessen and Laurent de Gaulle for bringing to my attention Jean Gremillon's hauntingly brief 1923 black-and-white documentary film, *Chartres*, which provided me with a precious keyhole view of the people, their town and the cathedral in the year of the novel's setting. Jocelyn Dunphy Blomfield generously shared with me her memories of the religious life in France; and Professor Jean Gassin provided me with glasses of sweet mint tea while recounting stories of his childhood on a farm in North Africa.

My thanks are due to Morag Fraser, Andrew Hamilton S.J., and Dr David Rankin for their reading suggestions during the early days of my research.

Lastly I wish to express my special thanks to Carole Welch.

City Of Light
LAUREN BELFER

At the turn of the last century the thriving city of Buffalo, New York, is poised for glory as the power station at nearby Niagara Falls prepares to deliver electricity to the nation. Within its patriarchal society, Louisa Barrett, the progressive, unattached headmistress of a girls' school, enjoys an unusually influential position. Only she knows how it is constantly threatened by a secret from her past, and now, drawn unexpectedly into a warm alliance with Tom Sinclair – a pre-eminent figure in the violent battle between industrialists and conservationists over Niagara's waters – she finds herself locked in a power struggle both public and personal.

'A superbly crafted debut novel. Belfer has produced a historical blockbuster that not only cleverly overturns tradition but also eerily echoes our own era in its intermingling of private lives and public issues such as race, female freedom and the environment' DAILY TELEGRAPH

'Belfer deftly weaves together fact and fiction in a narrative that is tightly plotted, gripping and packed full of fascinating detail . . . A hugely enjoyable historical thriller' OBSERVER

'An extraordinarily accomplished novel in the great American tradition of Edith Wharton and Thomas Wolfe' IRISH TIMES

'A wonderful debut that defies categorisation. It's a thriller, literary but never difficult, but also a remarkable piece of historical research. From its opening sentence to its last, *City of Light* engages the imagination. It is, quite simply, electrifying' HEAT

'An impressive debut . . . In her powerfully atmospheric book Ms Belfer makes [those times] seem real and very far away, and at the same time eerily familiar and relevant in the present' NEW YORK TIMES

∫
SCEPTRE